3/10

Praise for *New York Times* and *USA TODAY*
bestselling author

ROBYN CARR

"An intensely satisfying read.
By turns humorous and gut-wrenchingly emotional,
it won't soon be forgotten."
—*RT Book Reviews* on *Paradise Valley*

"Carr has hit her stride with this captivating series."
—*Library Journal*

"The Virgin River books are so compelling—
I connected instantly with the characters
and just wanted more and more and more."
—#1 *New York Times* bestselling author
Debbie Macomber

"Robyn Carr creates strong men,
fascinating women and a community you'll want to
visit again and again. Who could ask for more?"
—*New York Times* bestselling author Sherryl Woods

"A thrilling debut of a series
that promises much to come."
—*New York Times* bestselling author Clive Cussler

"A warm wonderful book about women's
friendships, love and family. I adored it!"
—Susan Elizabeth Phillips
on *The House on Olive Street*

ROBYN CARR

MOONLIGHT ROAD

MIRA®

ISBN-13: 978-0-7783-2768-4

Recycling programs
for this product may
not exist in your area.

MOONLIGHT ROAD

For questions and comments about the quality of this book please contact us at Customer_eCare@Harlequin.ca.

www.MIRABooks.com

Printed in U.S.A.

For Tonie Crandall, because the world would be a dimmer place without all the love you have in your heart. Thank you for being even more than a friend—thank you for being a sister.

One

In the two weeks Aiden Riordan had been in Virgin River, he'd hiked over a hundred miles and grown himself a pretty hefty dark red beard. With his jet-black hair and brows and his bright green eyes, this legacy of his ancestors gave him a wild look. His four-year-old niece, Rosie, who sported a full head of red curls to go with her green eyes, had said, "Unca Aid! You're a Wide Iwish Rose, too!"

For a man without a mission for the first time since he could remember, this lay-back time was working out to his liking. Since undergrad in premed, he hadn't been without incredibly stiff goals. Now, at age thirty-six, after fourteen years in the navy, he was between jobs, completely unsure where he'd land next, and he felt *good* about it. *Motivation interruptus* had turned out to be a delightful state of being. The only thing he was certain of, he wasn't leaving Virgin River before the middle of summer. His older brother Luke and sister-in-law Shelby were expecting their first child, and he damn sure wasn't going to miss that. His brother Sean would soon be home from Iraq and planned a short leave before heading with his wife, Franci, and daughter, Rosie, to his next assignment, and Aiden looked forward to a little time with him, as well.

The June sun beat down on him. He wore fatigue pants, hiking boots and a tan T-shirt with salty perspiration rings under the arms. He was wet down his chest and back and smelled pretty ripe. He carried a camouflage backpack for protein bars and water, and strapped to his belt, a machete for clearing any brush that got in his way. He had a ball cap on his head and his black hair had already started to curl out from under the edges. A four-foot-tall walking staff had become his constant companion, and since a chance encounter with a too-confident mountain lion, he now carried a bow and a quiver of arrows. Of course, if he ran into a real cranky bear, he could be toast.

He wandered up a winding dirt road. It looked like it could be someone's driveway or an abandoned logging road, he was never sure which. He was aiming for a ridge he'd seen from below. At the end of the drive, he came face-to-face with what appeared to be an abandoned cabin. Experience had taught him the difference—if the path to the outhouse facilities was overgrown and it was especially run-down, it was probably vacant. There were no guarantees on that, however. He'd made that assumption once and an old woman had leveled a shotgun at him and ordered him to scram. Now, he gave the place a wide berth and walked through the woods toward the ridge.

Of course, there was no path; he used the machete to chop away some of the overgrowth. He came out of the other side to the most amazing, intoxicating sight. A woman wearing very short khaki shorts was bent over at the edge of her deck, backside pointed right at him. Even given his expertise in that department, he couldn't tell her exact age, but that was one beautiful booty on top of a couple of magnificent, long, tan legs. By the collection of ceramic pots and a watering can on the deck, he assumed she was potting plants. One flowerpot was balanced on the deck railing above her. She appeared to be digging in the earth, scooping dirt into a big pot.

He did know a couple of things. That butt and those legs belonged to someone under the age of fifty and there didn't appear to be a shotgun in sight. So, he chopped his way through the trees intending to say a friendly hello.

Still bent over, she looked at him through her legs. A beautiful strawberry blonde, which made him smile. She let out a huge, bloodcurdling scream, straightened abruptly and hit her head on the deck railing, knocking off a ceramic pot, which hit her on the noggin. And down she went. *Splat!*

"Damn," he muttered, running toward her as fast as he could. He dropped the machete and staff about halfway there.

She was sprawled facedown, out cold, so he gently rolled her over. She was *stunning*. Her face was as gorgeous as the rest of her. Her pulse was beating nice and strong in her carotid artery, but her forehead was bleeding. He'd seen the pot hit her in the back of the head, but she must have struck her forehead on the sharp edge of the deck going down, because in the center of that lovely brow, right at her hairline, there was a gash. And it was gushing, as head wounds like to do.

Aiden pulled out his handkerchief, which was, thankfully, clean, and pressed his hand over her cut to stanch the bleeding. She moaned a bit, but didn't open her eyes. With his thumb, he peeled back her lids one at a time; her pupils were equal and reactive to light, a good sign so far.

While applying pressure to the wound, Aiden shrugged off his backpack, quiver and bow. Then he scooped her up in his arms and carried her across the deck and through the French doors that were standing open, into the cabin. "Anybody home?" he called as he walked inside. Since there was no answer, he assumed the woman lived here alone and that the big Lincoln SUV was hers.

The leather sofa looked like a good bet—better than a bed or even what appeared to be a very new and expensive designer area rug and not something she'd want to bleed on. He placed her carefully on the couch, her head slightly elevated.

He looked around. From the outside, the place looked like an ordinary old cabin with new siding and a freshly painted, covered, railed deck with chairs. Inside, it was a richly furnished, very classy showplace.

He gingerly lifted the handkerchief; the bleeding had slowed to a trickle. There was blood on her white T-shirt, however. The first matter at hand was ice, then a bandage of some kind. He was in a large combination living/dining/kitchen area. A table sat in front of the opened French doors out of which he now saw the view he'd been in search of. He'd been so taken with that fine butt, he hadn't noticed the cabin was built right on the ridge.

Aiden looked around for a phone, but didn't see one. Then he washed his hands and rummaged through the freezer for ice, which he wrapped in a couple of dish towels—one for the front of her head, one for the back. The dish towels still had price tags on them. He propped her head against one ice pack and laid the other on her forehead. Even the application of cold didn't rouse her, so off he went in search of a bandage.

The kitchen was on the west end of the cabin, but on the opposite side were two doors. The one on the left led to a good-size bedroom, and on the right, a large bathroom. From the bathroom, the most obvious place to find first-aid supplies, another door connected to the bedroom.

Sure enough, under the sink, he found a blue canvas zipper bag with *First Aid* emblazoned in white on the canvas. He grabbed it and hurried back to the woman. In his experienced hands, it took only seconds to apply a little antibacterial cream and a butterfly to close the wound, covered by a Band-Aid. He reapplied the ice pack.

The next immediate order of business was getting her to an emergency room for a head CT; the loss of consciousness after a blow to the head could mean trouble. The longer she stayed unconscious, the more it concerned him, but he had moved fast—she hadn't been out more than a couple of minutes so far. He saw a purse on the kitchen counter and went to rifle through it for a phone, car keys, ID, anything. He unceremoniously dumped the contents and was bent over the counter, sifting through the loose items, when a shriek rent the air. His head came up sharply and he whacked it on the cupboards that hung over the counter. "Ah!" he yelled, grabbing the back of his head. He pinched his eyes closed hard, trying to get a grip through blinding pain.

But she continued to scream.

He turned toward her. She was scooting away from him on the leather couch, screaming her head off, her ice packs spilled to the floor.

"Shut *up!*" he ordered. She stopped abruptly, her hand covering her mouth. "We're both going to have brain damage if you don't stop doing that!"

"Get out of here!" she commanded. "I'll call the police!"

He rolled his eyes and shook his head. "Great idea. Where's the phone?" He lifted a cell phone from the things on the counter. "This one has no signal."

"What are you doing here? Why are you in my house? In my purse?"

He walked toward her, her purse hanging in his hand. "I saw you hit your head. I brought you inside and put ice and a bandage on the wound, but now we have to—"

"You hit me in the *head?*" she screeched, digging at the sofa with her heels to scoot away again.

"I didn't hit you—apparently I startled you when I came out of the forest and you jumped. You hit the back of your head on the deck railing and one of your pots fell on your head. I think you got the cut on your forehead when you hit the deck on the way down. Now where's the phone?"

"Oh God," she said, her fingers going to the bandage, touching it carefully. "The phone's going to be installed tomorrow. Along with my satellite dish. So I can have Internet and watch movies."

"That isn't going to help much. Listen, it's a small cut. Head wounds bleed a lot. I doubt it'll even leave a scar. But losing consciousness is—"

"I'll give you money if you just won't hurt me."

"I bandaged your head, for God's sake! I'm not going to hurt you and I don't want money!" He lifted the purse in his hand. "I was looking for your car keys—you need a CAT scan. Maybe a couple of stitches."

"Why?" she asked, her voice quivering.

He sighed. "Because you lost consciousness—not a good sign. Now, where are your keys?"

"Why?" she asked again.

"I'm going to drive you to the emergency room so you can get your head examined!"

"I'll do it," she said. "I'll drive myself. You can just go now. Right now."

He took a couple of steps toward her. He crouched so he wouldn't be looking down at her, but didn't get too close because he wasn't sure of her. She appeared to be a bit unstable. Or maybe scared of him. He tried to put himself in her position—she woke up with blood on her shirt, a wild man plowing through her purse. "What's your name?" he asked softly.

She looked at him doubtfully. "Erin," she finally said.

"Well, Erin, it isn't a good idea for you to drive yourself. If you have a serious or even semiserious head injury, you could lose consciousness again, get dizzy or disoriented, get sick, suffer blurred vision, any number of things. Now, try not to be nervous—I'll take you to the E.R. Once I get you there, you can call a friend or family member. I'll have someone pick me up."

"And you think it *is* a good idea for me to get in a car with some homeless guy?"

He stood up. "I'm not homeless! I was hiking through the woods!"

"Well, then, you've been hiking a long time. Because you look like you've been *living* in the woods!"

He crouched again, to get on her level. "Number one—you have to hold the ice packs I made on the front *and* back of your head. I don't see how you can do that while you drive. Number two, it's too risky for you to drive yourself, as I have very patiently explained. And number three, stop being so goddamn prissy and get in the car with a smelly hiker, because your brain could be swelling as we speak and you could be hopelessly disabled for the rest of your pig-headed life! Now, where are the fucking keys?"

She looked over her shoulder. There was a hook by the door; her keys dangled from it. "How do you know that stuff? About brain swelling?"

"I was an EMT in college—a long time ago," he said, which was the truth. He wasn't sure why he didn't just tell her he was a physician. Maybe because he didn't look like one at the moment. As she had pointed out, he looked like a homeless guy. But there was also the fact that his area of expertise was a long way from the head—and he didn't feel like getting into that. She was already spooked. Being spooked didn't stop her from being bossy and bitchy, however. His head hurt, too. And he was fast losing patience with this patient. "Now, let's gather up your ice and little towels and hit the road."

"If you turn out to be some kind of homicidal maniac, you're going to have one pissed-off ghost on your hands," she threatened as he stooped to gather her ice off the floor. When she stood up, she wobbled slightly. "Whoa."

He was beside her instantly, arm around her waist, steadying her. "You took a mean knock on the head, kid. This is why you're not driving."

He walked her outside, grabbing the keys and slamming the door on the way out. That was the first time he realized that the front of the house faced the road. He had to lift her into the front seat and help her arrange the ice in the dish towels so she could put them against her lumps. He noticed that she wrinkled her nose; okay, so it was obvious—he might've generated a little body odor.

"I need my purse," she said. "My insurance cards and ID."

"I'll get it," he said. "I have to close the doors to the deck anyway." But he took the car keys with him, for safety reasons. He scraped things off the counter and back into her purse, returned to the car and put the purse in her lap. Then he got in and started driving. "You might have to give me some directions.... I'm not from around here."

She groaned and dropped her head back. "I'm not from around here, either."

"Never mind, I can fake it," he said. "I can find Highway 36 from Virgin River. What are you doing here, if you're not from around here?"

"Taking a break from work and trying to enjoy solitude," she answered, exasperation in her voice. "Then Charles Manson came through the trees, carrying a three-foot-long knife, and startled me. So much for peace and quiet."

"Come on—I let my beard grow, that's all. I'm on vacation and didn't feel like shaving, so sue me."

"As it happens, I could. I've been known to sue people on occasion."

He laughed. "I should've known. A lawyer. And by the way, I was carrying the machete for cutting away the brush so I could get through the woods when there's no path."

"Why are *you* here?" she asked him.

"Visiting family. I have a brother who lives around

here. He and his wife are getting ready to be parents for the first time and I'm...I'm..." He cleared his throat. "Let's just say I'm between jobs."

She laughed. "Unemployed. Big surprise. Let me guess—you've been between jobs for a while now."

She was pissing him off. He could've leveled with her, that he was a doctor planning his next move. But she was snooty and superior and he just didn't *feel* like it. "At least long enough to grow a beard," he said evasively.

"You know, if you cleaned up a little, you might be able to land a job," she advised very sagely.

"I'll certainly take that into consideration."

"The beard is a little crazy," she said. "It'll put off potential employers." Then under her breath she added, "Not to mention the smell..."

"I'll bear that in mind. Although my niece likes it." He turned to peer at her. "The beard, that is."

"I thought you said your brother was having his *first* child."

"She's a different brother's child."

"Ah, so you have more than one brother. Just out of curiosity, what do your brothers think of this, um, between-jobs lifestyle?"

"I think you should be quiet now," he said. "Save whatever brain cells you have left. We have a forty-minute drive to Valley Hospital, west of Grace Valley. Rest. *Silently.*"

"Sure," she said. *"Fine."*

What did his brothers think of his decision? They thought he was nuts. He'd been totally committed to the navy; he loved the navy. But the military gave with one hand and took away with the other.

When Aiden had been a brand-new M.D., compliments of a navy scholarship, his first assignment was as a GMO—general medical officer—aboard ship. It was a two-year assignment that dry-docked every six months for a few months. They put into port regularly, during which time he could see the world and feel earth beneath his feet, but his life was spent aboard ship. The medical officer was under a great deal of pressure 24/7—being the only doctor in charge of a complete medical staff and the only officer aboard who could relieve the ship's captain of duty. He knew the pressure was extreme when he found himself taking his duty phone into the shower with him—that was over-the-top. They had also spent their share of time in the Persian Gulf, which meant giving emergency medical treatment to civilians in trouble— mostly fishermen or ship's crewmen who didn't speak English.

His reward for that duty was his residency in OB-GYN, which obligated him to more commitment to the navy. But it had been worth it—he took care of the female military personnel and wives of active-duty and retired sailors and marines. It was a good life. He had stayed in one place for a long time—San Diego.

Then he was due a promotion, and the navy felt it was time for him to go to sea again. It would have meant general medical officer once more—not in his specialty. There wasn't a lot of call for an OB-GYN aboard an aircraft carrier. Aiden didn't mind being out to sea so much, but he was thirty-six. It wasn't something he talked about, but he felt there were things missing from his life. A wife and family for one thing, and he wasn't likely to meet a woman who could fill that bill on a big gray boat. He needed to be on land.

Sometimes he asked himself why that even mattered—it wasn't as though being on dry land had worked so far. Right after his stint as a GMO, at the age of twenty-eight, he'd met and quickly married Annalee, who had turned out to be a total nutcase. They were married for three whole months, during which she demolished every breakable object they owned. She had been volatile, jealous and crazed—her moods shifted faster than the sands of time.

That experience left him gun-shy and slowed him down a little, but a couple of years later he was ready to get back in the game, feeling older and wiser. Still, he couldn't seem to meet any women who were contenders for the exalted position as his wife and the mother of his children.

But one thing was for certain—it wasn't going to happen at sea.

Truth was, he just plain wasn't ready to commit any more time to the navy. His brothers thought fourteen years, only six from his twenty and retirement benefits, made him nuts to get out. But in his mind, these were his *best* years. He was still young enough to be an involved husband and father if he ever met the right woman. At the retirement age of forty-two, starting a family would be pushing it.

He glanced at Erin. Her eyes were closed and she

held his ice packs on her forehead and the back of her head. He'd like a woman who looked like that—but she'd have to be sweet and far less arrogant. He was looking for someone soft and nurturing. You don't go looking for a hard-ass to be the mother of your children, and this one was a hard-ass. Of course, what was he to expect? She was a lawyer.

He chuckled to himself. She was probably a medical-malpractice attorney.

Feeling at least partially responsible for Erin's bump on the head, Aiden hung out at the hospital for a while. Not anywhere near her, of course. He got her checked in to the E.R., made sure she had what she needed, explained her injury and loss of consciousness to the E.R. doctor and left her car keys with him so Erin could get herself home once she was cleared to drive. Then he went outside so his less-than-pristine musk would not offend anyone. And there he sat for close to an hour.

He was just about to swing by the E.R. before calling his brother for a ride home when who should happen to walk out of the hospital but Pastor Noah Kincaid.

"Hey, Aiden," Noah said, sticking out his hand. "What are you doing here? You didn't have an accident, did you?"

Aiden shook his hand. "No—I think I caused one. Are you heading back to Virgin River?"

"That's my plan. What's going on?"

Aiden quickly explained that he'd brought Erin to the

E.R. in her car and was going to call for a ride home. "But before I leave, I want to check and see what the doctor has to say. I'm hoping he'll tell me if there's a clean CT. Then I'm clearing out of here before she sees me."

"Fortuitous for the lady that if she had to have an accident, it was while there was a doctor around."

"Well," Aiden said, rubbing the back of his neck, "she doesn't exactly know I'm a doctor."

"Why didn't you just tell her?"

"Truthfully? Because she has *attitude*. She called me a homeless, homicidal maniac who looked like Charles Manson—and she inferred that I didn't smell great."

Noah broke into a wide grin. "Flirting with you, was she?"

"If I had the slightest inclination to do harm, she'd be in a lot of little pieces right now. Very irritating woman. But I'd like to know she isn't brain damaged before I leave the hospital. Can you wait ten minutes? Then give me a lift?"

"Sure," Noah said. "I'll walk in with you. Did you explain to the E.R. staff who you are?"

"More or less. I described the accident, her symptoms and response to the injury, and the nurse asked me if I had medical training. And then I told her the lady had decided I was a bum, without asking me who I was, and as far as I was concerned, she didn't need to be enlightened."

"Ah," Noah said. "So she can feel really stupid when she finds out."

"Noah, I swear, you really don't understand…"

The two of them sauntered into the emergency

room and up to the nurses' station. "How's the woman with the head injury?" Aiden asked. "I'm getting a ride home with the pastor, but before I leave, I wanted to check on her."

"She's going to be just fine," the nurse said. "The doctor wants to admit her for the night for observation, however. Better safe than sorry."

"Probably a good idea," Aiden agreed. "Did her CT come back?"

"All clear," the nurse said. "But she might have a slight concussion."

"Did I hear you tell that *vagrant* my house will be empty tonight?" came a loud, demanding voice from behind a curtain.

Noah immediately started to laugh. Aiden just looked at the nurse. "A good bop on the head didn't hurt her hearing, did it?" he said as loudly as he dared. "I'm getting out of here, but when she settles down a little, tell her I'm going to use her tub and roll around in her satin sheets."

The nurse laughed at him. "I'm not getting into that, Dr. Riordan," she whispered. "This is between you and the lady."

He shushed her with a finger to his lips. "Believe me, there isn't anything between us. And there isn't going to be. Let's go, Noah."

When they were under way in Noah's old blue truck, Aiden asked, "Are you in a big hurry?"

"I don't have all day, but there's no rush. Need to make a stop?"

"If I can find that cabin, can we swing by? I left all my stuff there. The stuff I hike with."

"My pleasure," Noah said. "How's the hiking going?"

"Pure indulgence," he said. "I've logged a lot of miles, seen a lot of the area, but I've never had time like this before. Sometimes I just hike around the mountains, the general Virgin River area. Sometimes I drive over to the coast or down Grace Valley way for a change of scenery. I've never felt better."

"Good for you! Sounds perfect. You'll have to go back to work eventually, I assume."

"I spend a lot of time e-mailing friends and contacts, looking around at the possibilities, trying to avoid any offer that hinges on me starting right away. But I won't hang out here any longer than midsummer."

Aiden didn't have any trouble directing Noah back to the cabin, and it wasn't hard to locate the things he'd dropped when he'd played rescue squad to the dish with the attitude. The machete and staff were lying in the yard between the house and trees. When he picked them up he noticed someone had outlined a good-size square by digging a border, but the inside of the square was still grass, dirt and rocks. Hopes of a garden?

He grabbed the backpack, and in doing so, he noticed it looked as if she'd been attempting to plant a strip of garden along the back edge of the deck. Maybe the square in the yard was just too ambitious for her and she'd opted for a smaller, more manageable plot. The dirt was pretty packed and tough up on this mountain. It looked as though she had some semi-comatose tomato-plant starters, a few marigolds that had dried into confetti and a couple of other plants with very uncertain futures.

Still balanced on the railing was a plastic watering can and on the ground, a couple of garden tools that looked to be about the right size for tending houseplants. Also, for no reason he could fathom, there was a big iron skillet on the deck.

Aiden took his things to Noah's truck and tossed them in the back. "Gimme a second, Noah."

"What's doing?" Noah asked.

"I think she was in the process of trying to revive the poorest attempt at a garden I've ever seen. I'm going to give her dying plants a drink. It'll only take a minute. Do you mind?"

"I'm good," Noah said. "I don't see a garden."

"Yeah, I know. That's the problem. Be right back."

Aiden grabbed the watering can off the deck railing. He put the tools on the deck and sprinkled some water on the plants. Then he took the watering can around to the back of the house to refill it from the faucet and saw a nearly empty box of Miracle-Gro sitting there. It *was* going to take a miracle, he thought wryly. He filled the can and watered again, drenching her little garden. Then he left the empty can on the deck and jumped into the truck with Noah.

This was all very mysterious.

"How did this happen again?" Noah asked with a slight frown.

"I was hiking through the forest when I saw her. I

was just going to say hello, but when I came through the trees, she screamed and jumped up and whacked her head. I dropped all my stuff to take care of her— my machete, bow and arrows, backpack, staff."

Noah glanced at him, wide-eyed. "You came through the trees with a machete? And you're insulted that she had some *attitude?*"

"I see your point...."

Noah laughed. "You might want to cut her some slack there, Aiden." And then he laughed some more.

Two

While Aiden was staying in Virgin River, he rented one of Luke's cabins. He actually paid the going rate, though Luke had a real hard time taking his money. But Aiden not only wanted his own space, he also didn't want to impose too much on Shelby and Luke because he intended to stay all summer. And though the little vacation rental was about as lean as he'd lived since he'd been aboard ship, he liked it. Luke had graduated to satellite hookup for TV and Internet, but the cabins didn't have phones yet. That didn't bother Aiden; he'd e-mailed Luke's home phone number to his contacts, revised the message including Luke's phone number on his cell phone and could still pick up messages and texts in certain parts of the area out of the mountains. Besides, most of the people he was in touch with preferred the Internet. Every morning and evening he checked his e-mail.

When Noah dropped him off, he found a note taped to his cabin door. *Come to the house right away. L.*

Right away, Aiden decided, could afford him the time to take a shower. If Shelby had a problem with her pregnancy, they wouldn't be waiting around for Aiden to finish what could be an endless hike.

When he got down to Luke's house a mere fifteen minutes later, he gave a couple of short taps and walked in.

Shelby was sitting on the sectional with her feet up on the ottoman, a book balanced on her big belly. Luke was kneeling on the opposite side of that ottoman beside a large open box. He seemed to be looking through a few items spread out in front of him. He looked up at Aiden and said, "We got trouble."

"Trouble? What's up?"

Luke stood and handed Aiden a small stack of pictures, pages and envelopes. Aiden leafed through—second- and third-grade pictures, report cards, hand-made Mother's Day cards, memorabilia from his childhood. "So?" Aiden asked. "The problem?"

"Mom sent this—a whole box of it. Even that book I wrote in fourth grade—the one about the meaning of life for me? Which at the time was finding a way to kill all my brothers and make it look like an accident."

Aiden chuckled. He remembered that. They still joked about it when they were all together. Ten-year-old Luke felt he had more than his share of respon-sibility and aggravation with four younger brothers, the youngest of whom was in diapers and followed him around relentlessly. "I guess we should all thank the Virgin you didn't find a way. What's the matter?"

"You got one, too. Colin got his box yesterday, but Colin just figured he'd been written out of the will because he doesn't call or visit enough and that was Mom's way of letting him know. I haven't checked with Patrick. Or with Franci to see if a box was sent to her for Sean. Mom's unloading her house."

Before commenting further, Aiden ripped open his box. He pulled out an almost identical batch of pictures, papers, folders, and underneath it all was a shoe box. He opened it to find Christmas ornaments—the ones that he had made for the family tree when he was a child, as well as the purchased ones that were his favorites. He held up an old Rudolph ornament. "I loved this one," Aiden said. "How does she remember the exact ones I loved?"

Shelby sighed and ran a hand over her belly. "I hope I'm that good a mother," she said.

"Something bad is going on," Luke said. "Either she's dying or selling her condo and moving into a nursing home."

Aiden chuckled. "Or moving into an RV with a retired Presbyterian minister. She's been kicking that idea around since last Christmas."

"She didn't mean it, Aiden," Luke said. "Not her. She was pulling my chain—revenge for all the years I wouldn't get serious. This is Saint Maureen! If she's doing that, she's getting married, and she doesn't know George well enough to marry him. Since they started talking last Christmas, he's lived in Seattle and she's been in Phoenix. She can't marry him. Call her."

"Why do *I* have to call her?"

"Because, Aiden—you're the only one who can really talk to her." Luke took a step toward his brother. "If she ends up marrying George, she might just get stuck with some old guy to nurse through Alzheimer's or something. Call her."

Shelby put down her book with an irritated moan. "Luke thought his mother was sitting up on lonely Saturday nights, looking through his grade-school pictures and report cards. Maybe she's just sick of being a storage shed for your stuff—ever think of that?"

Something caught Aiden's eye and he bent to pull out a small gold object: a little trophy with a swimmer on it. When he was in school, swimming was the geek sport. And he was a geek. "Aw, my only first place ever."

Luke reached into his box and pulled out all his ribbons and tilted his head toward the box; the bottom was filled with trophies and plaques. Luke had been an athlete and won at everything he tried. "If I remember right, you got all the honor-roll stuff. I got sports."

"Luke, Mom said she was going to do this," Aiden reminded him. "She asked everyone if anyone wanted the dining room set, the old quilts, the china…"

"I'm getting dishes," Shelby said with a smile. "I'm scared to death of them—they're very old. I told her I would probably pack them away and guard them with my life because they're so precious. She's also sending some crystal—I'm not sure what it is. Franci is taking on Great-grandma Riordan's silver. No one else wanted anything, I guess," she said with a shrug.

"I thought this was just a test," Luke said. "I didn't think she was really serious about giving away all her stuff."

Aiden tapped the box. "Not her stuff, Luke. *Our* stuff. And stuff that belonged to the great-grandmothers. Stuff she doesn't feel like taking care of anymore. Come on, lighten up here."

"Call her," he insisted. "Maybe she's losing her mind or something."

Aiden gave a sigh and went to Luke's phone. Picking up the cordless, he punched in the numbers to his mother's condo and while it rang, helped himself to a beer from Luke's refrigerator. Before he had popped the top, however, he got the recording. "This line has been disconnected…" He tried not to let the surprise show on his face while he listened to the whole recording. Then he clicked off and said, "No answer. I'll try the cell.…" And he punched in some new numbers. It didn't take long for Maureen to say hello. "Well, hello yourself," he said with amusement ringing in his voice. "You running from the law or something?"

"Oh, Aiden," she said. "I was going to call you, but I've been so busy."

"Yes, packing up and shipping all our childhood treasures back to us. Luke thinks you're dying.…"

"Luke probably *wishes* I was dying," she said wryly. "Hardly. No one wants my old-lady furniture, so I packed up all the heirlooms spoken for, along with all the stuff I've saved since you boys were little, and put the rest in storage. Since I have that cell phone you got me, I thought it was okay to shut down the computer and disconnect the landline. One of my friends has a recently widowed sister who needs a place to rent while she looks around for something to buy. I'm going to let her move in here. We have a six-month agreement."

Aiden reached into the refrigerator and got his brother a beer. He handed it to him, and into the phone he said, "And after six months?"

"Obviously I wouldn't do this if I didn't expect to fall in love with this lifestyle, traveling around, seeing the sights and the family. George will be here tomorrow with a brand-new motor coach. I've seen pictures of it and I can't wait to see it in person. He'll help me oversee the packing and moving of my household, which is all arranged. Then we'll be off. Of course, we'll head straight to Virgin River, but it might take us a while to get there—we're going through Sedona, Oak Creek Canyon, Flagstaff, the Grand Canyon, Hoover Dam and maybe a stop off in Las Vegas. Can you believe I've never seen Sedona or the Grand Canyon, though I've lived in the same state for years?"

"You must be looking forward to it," Aiden said. "Luke wants to know if you're getting married."

Luke choked on his beer and began to violently shake his head.

"Actually, not that I know of. George is very considerate—he said if it was important to me to do that, he would certainly understand. But I think we'll just wing it."

Aiden laughed sentimentally. "Have you ever *winged* anything in your life?" he asked his mother.

"I don't think so," she said. "And if you'd asked me a year ago if I ever would, I would have said no. Emphatically no. But here we are. Aiden, how is Shelby doing?"

"Big as a house," he said, winking at his sister-in-law. "She says she's feeling good and is very excited about the dishes. Oh—and Luke says that if things don't work out with George, he just wouldn't be able to sleep at night if you didn't agree to come and live with him."

Luke shot to his feet, his eyes as big as dinner plates. His cheeks actually reddened and he shook his head again.

"Tell him I'll go to a nursing home first—he's a pain in the butt even to visit, much less live with!"

"This is very unlike you, you know," Aiden said with a kind of tenderness he reserved only for his mother.

"I know. Isn't it perfect?"

"As long as you've thought it through," he said.

"Of course I have, Aiden. Now, don't hesitate to call if you want to discuss it further."

"I won't. And would you like Luke to call if he has concerns to discuss?" he asked, lifting one dark brow toward his brother.

"Actually, no. But thank him for the offer. Luke is not exactly the man I'd take relationship advice from, although he has certainly landed on his feet. Hasn't he?"

"Absolutely. And yet you're willing to discuss it with me?" Aiden asked her. "I haven't hit any home runs lately."

"I suspect you just haven't been up to bat enough, sweetheart," she said with a laugh. "Now, I have to run. Give everyone my best and I'll see you in a week or ten days, something like that."

"Please be careful, Mom."

"Have you ever known me to be careless? Now, enjoy yourself until I get there and turn the whole family upside down with my wild ways."

He laughed as he said goodbye. Then he looked at Luke, who seemed to be fuming.

"I can't believe you told her I wanted her to live with us," Luke said.

"Listen, if you're going to tell her how to live, you have to be prepared to be responsible for her living conditions. Big step, Luke. Lucky for you, she's not interested."

"I can't believe this," Luke said. "Our mother, who was almost a nun, living in sin with a retired Protestant minister?"

Aiden cocked his head to one side and shrugged. "She's sixty-three and he's seventy. There's probably not nearly as much sin involved as they'd like."

There were a number of things in addition to a terrible headache that put Erin in a cranky mood. Like the fact that they had shaved a little bit of her hairline in the middle of her forehead to put in three tiny stitches. She wasn't planning on going anywhere except her hideaway in the woods, but still! She was very particular about her hair. Now she had the opposite of a widow's peak—very ugly.

And she didn't feel like spending the night in a hospital, wearing a hospital gown. Gown? They should not insult high fashion by calling this rag a gown. Her absolute worst painting clothes were nicer.

And she had a roommate. The roommate, who had had a hysterectomy and was staying two nights, had visitors. She was staying two nights, lived ten miles away and her entire freaking family had to come to the hospital to visit her? And there was apparently no rule about how *many* visitors one could have.

If she ever saw that vagrant again, she was going to bean *him* with a flowerpot.

By now she had been informed by a very testy emergency-room nurse that he wasn't exactly a vagrant, but rather a man who had just left the navy and was visiting a relative in Virgin River. So he was a perfectly respectable bad-smelling, horrible-looking, out-of-work man with nothing better to do than impersonate a serial killer, sneak up on her and scare her to death.

It was possible that she was crabby in general. The whole escape-to-the-mountains-alone-for-the-summer idea was probably not the best one she'd ever come up with. At the time she'd thought of it, it had seemed the most logical thing to do. Erin was a woman who had never learned how to achieve that serene, Zen-like acceptance of what the universe tossed at her, and she had reason to believe she'd better figure that out. A summer on a beautiful isolated mountaintop, out of the Chico, California, heat, away from all the pressures of her professional life, should show her how to slow down, learn to relax and enjoy doing nothing. It was time to develop a strong sense of autonomy and remind herself that hers was the life she *chose*. And she was in a big hurry to get all that nailed down. Besides, it was cheaper than going to Tibet.

There were very logical reasons Erin was wound a little tight; the habit of overachieving could take its toll. When Erin was eleven, her mother died. That left her the woman of the house, with a grieving father, a four-year-old sister, Marcie, and a two-year-old brother, Drew. She wasn't solely responsible for them; her dad was still the parent, albeit a little less conscious right after his wife's death. And there had to be a babysitter during the day while Erin went to school.

But Erin rushed home from school to take over and had a ton of chores in addition to child care. She felt it was up to her to be the mother figure in their lives whether they liked it or not. As a matter of fact, as her siblings got older, she concentrated harder on their needs and activities than her own, from soccer to piano lessons to making sure they got good grades and didn't live on junk food. She rarely went out, never seemed to have a boyfriend, skipped all the high-school events from football and basketball to the dances. She did, however, *always* make the honor roll. She had decided at an early age that if she couldn't be *f-u-n*, she would be *s-m-a-r-t*.

She was twenty-two, a new law-school freshman, and still living at home so she could keep an eye on the kids who were then thirteen and fifteen, when their father died during a routine knee-replacement surgery. Erin was again in charge. Not that much had changed, besides missing her dad dreadfully. But technically, she was even more in charge than before, because being over twenty-one, she actually had custody.

Friends and colleagues were in awe of all she'd been able to accomplish. After her younger sibs had survived their teen years, she'd helped her sister, who was married to a marine who had been wounded in Iraq and had lingered in a vegetative state for years in a nursing home before he died. She'd gotten her younger brother through college *and* medical school. And during this time she'd built herself a sterling reputation as an attorney in a very successful firm. The local paper wrote some sappy article on how she was one of the most amazing and desirable single women in the city—the head of a household that depended on her, brilliant in tax and estate law, gorgeous, clearly the woman to catch.

It had made her laugh. She could count on one hand the number of dates she'd had in a year—all of them horribly dull.

Erin had accomplished what she'd set out to do. Her little sister was remarried to her late husband's best friend, had moved into her own home in Chico and was pregnant with her first child. Her younger brother had completed medical school with honors and was an orthopedic resident in Southern California, a tough five-year residency that rarely let him loose. Drew was twenty-seven and lived with his fiancée; he would be a family man in another year.

Erin had fulfilled a great deal by the age of thirty-six; for herself and her brother and sister, this was exactly what she had worked so hard toward. Why, then, did she still feel like something was missing in her life?

Was this how it was *supposed* to feel when your life was really just beginning? Uncertain and as wobbly as a newborn fawn? Or was this, as she sometimes feared, the end of the road? Nothing much to strive for now? She felt more like a grandmother to Marcie's expected baby than an auntie. She was a bit panicked and didn't know where to turn. But of course, Erin had the best poker face in the profession of law and never let it show.

Marcie's new husband, Ian Buchanan, had left behind a dump of a cabin that he held on to when he'd moved off the mountain and back to Chico with Marcie. Erin had seen it. It was a disgusting little shack with no central heat, no indoor plumbing, a small gas generator for a little lighting, and it was only one room. But it was on its own mountaintop and had hundreds of acres with a magnificent view. Marcie and Ian loved it. Though they admitted they'd love it a little better with indoor plumbing and electricity, which they could never afford, but that mountaintop was priceless.

Erin had a little money; she'd been working hard, plus she'd guarded and invested what her father had left in retirement, insurance and savings. She'd gotten bonuses from the firm and an impressive salary—all that had helped her get the kids through hard times and school. She thought it might be worth the investment to raze the old cabin and rebuild something nice—a summer place that could be in the family for decades. But Ian said, "Believe it or not, Erin, the cabin is solid. It could probably use a new roof, bathroom and electricity, but it's in pretty good shape otherwise."

So she asked him if she could have an engineer look it over and maybe fix it up. She didn't say, *Because I can't stay even a weekend in that hovel.* The way Ian had smiled at her when he replied, "Knock yourself out," indicated she didn't have to say it.

It turned out that Ian was right—the cabin was ugly, but well built. She got some remodel designs off the Internet and put the job out for bid to four local builders. A man by the name of Paul Haggerty gave her a competitive price, was able to work via e-mail and phone, and was willing to sign a contract promising the remodel ready on June 1 when Erin wanted to move in. And he had finished early!

She never even drove up once to look at the progress. That alone should have told her she was doing this for all the wrong reasons and it wasn't going to work. But she had told Mr. Haggerty, "I'm a busy attorney with a full schedule until the first of June. Then I'm taking the summer off, my first vacation in over ten years. That's why it has to be right and on time."

It had been a crazy idea. Erin couldn't seem to function *without* a full schedule and she didn't know *how* to take time off. Every time she tried to take a day off, she was twitching by noon.

But she was determined. She was going to learn to unwind, damn it. She was going to learn to embrace solitude and kick this feeling that if she didn't have far too much to do, she wasn't worthy.

"Knock, knock," she heard a small voice say. Erin had the curtains drawn around her bed to block out the hysterectomy patient and her extended family. The curtains parted and her redheaded sister's smiling face popped in. "Are you decent?"

Erin sat up in the hospital bed. "What are *you* doing here?"

"The E.R. nurse called me—you named me as your next of kin. Y'know?" Marcie let herself into the tiny space. She bent close and narrowed her eyes at the bandage on Erin's forehead. "Hmm. Not so bad," she said. "How do you feel?"

"Ugly," she said, plucking at the gown. "And I have a headache."

Marcie laughed at her. "Not such chichi hospital attire, huh? I meant the head wound doesn't look too bad. Small bandage."

"Shaved head!"

"Less than a half inch, Erin. Take it easy, it'll grow right back." Marcie sat on the end of the bed and ran her little hands over her big, pregnant tummy. "Your doctor said if we spend the night with you tonight, we can check you out and take you home. I thought that was reason enough to drive up. I knew you wouldn't want to be in the hospital. Have you ever been in a hospital? Like, in your life?"

"There was Bobby," Erin said, speaking of Marcie's late husband. "Lots of hospital time there."

"I meant, as a patient, Erin!"

She rolled her eyes upward, thinking. "No," she said, shaking her head. "No, I don't think so. Good thing, too. It's *very* boring and like being an inmate." She plucked at the gown again. "The nurses don't like me, I can tell. And can you believe this? They haven't graduated to anything better than this for patients? For God's sake!"

Marcie just chuckled.

"Are you feeling all right?" Erin asked her little sister.

"Great. I'm sorry you got hurt, but I can't wait to see the cabin. I hope it's not too froufrou. I liked the old place."

"Guaranteed you're going to think it's too frou-frou," Erin said. "It's completely livable, unlike before. There are lights and everything. Where are my clothes?"

"I'll find them. Don't get up."

"Where's Ian?"

"He's at the nurses' station, getting your release instructions. I think we mainly have to check to be sure you're still breathing about every seven minutes throughout the night. You'll be a completely cooperative patient, won't you?"

"Just get me out of here," she said. "They were

going to have to hit me in the head again just to keep me here another hour."

"I think Ian was right." Marcie found Erin's folded clothes and shoes stuffed in her bedside chest of drawers along with her purse. "We're not so much rescuing you as the nurses. I bet you're no fun, as patients go."

Marcie drove Erin home to the cabin in her big SUV and Ian followed in his truck. He was impressed with the way the cabin looked, amazed by the impossible transformation. Very classy; very Erin. "God above," he said in a whisper. "When I was thinking of fixing it up, I was thinking in terms of adding a septic tank for a toilet. Look at this place!"

"But do you like it? Do you *really* like it? The rug is an Aubusson, the leather furniture is Robb & Stucky, there's a whirlpool tub and what do you think of the fireplace?"

Ian didn't know from Aubusson or any Robb whomever. He stared out the newly installed French doors in the kitchen. Right outside the west end of the cabin was a deck that stretched the length of the house, taking advantage of the awesome view. "Incredible, Erin. Can we use it sometime?"

She looked shocked. She blinked. They didn't want to be there the same time as she was? "I thought…we'd all use it, now and then," she said cautiously. "I mean, I didn't want to wait to fix it up a little because I was taking vacation this summer, but, Ian, it's your cabin. I think I have to ask *your* permission, not the other way around."

"Okay," he said, smiling. "When I married Marcie, I married the family, Erin, and what's ours is yours. You don't have to ask permission." He turned full circle, looking around. "I can't believe you completely remodeled the whole place by e-mail! It's amazing!"

"I'll be sure and ask if you're already using it before I make any plans," she said.

"He was kidding," Marcie said. "Ian, you're such a dork. We'll all come together. And when Drew visits, he can sleep in the shed." She grinned.

"But you like it?" Erin asked again.

"I think it's great," he said. "You made it beautiful."

Marcie did a lot of oohing and aahing, and Erin seemed to puff up from that. "I don't know how I made it without a real kitchen for so long," Ian said, opening the refrigerator door. When he'd lived here, there was a sink with a pump handle and he'd cooked on a Coleman stove. His mind-set and the emotional landscape of his life back then had been all about deprivation. It hadn't been so much a form of self-punishment as a paring down of baggage. The less he could make it on, the more competent he felt. It had been like an endurance test. And he had passed with flying colors; he had endured like crazy.

Erin had been here almost a week. In the refrigerator he found yogurt, cottage cheese, egg substitute, skim milk, a loaf of thinly sliced low-cal bread, salad fixings, celery and carrot sticks, apples, cheese singles, tofu and hummus. His stomach growled; he wondered if it made her feel more competent to starve to death.

For the hundredth time he asked himself what was

really up with Erin, this isolation on the mountaintop, because this whole "well-deserved vacation" story just didn't add up. Not with Erin.

"Let me cook tonight, okay?" he said. Both women agreed that would be wonderful. So he continued, "Tonight I'm cooking something Preacher whipped up. I'm going to run into town and grab dinner."

"Um, I'm watching my calories," Erin said unnec essarily. "Does he make anything kind of, you know, low cal?"

Preacher was the cook at Jack's bar, and he made one thing every day. Well, one breakfast item, one lunch item, one dinner item. Preacher did what he pleased, and it was always fantastic but none of it was low cal. "He's very conscientious that way," Ian fibbed, and his wife tilted her head toward him, making a face that said shame on you.

Ian was dying for food. Real food, not rabbit food. But then, he could hardly blame Erin; she hadn't been expecting company.

"You girls enjoy your visit," he said. "I won't be gone long." And he headed for town.

When he walked into the bar, Jack greeted him enthusiastically. "Hey, stranger! Long time. You and Marcie up for a little visit?"

"You could say that," Ian said. "We weren't plan-ning to come up so soon after Erin got here, but she had a little accident."

"You don't say? What happened?"

"Freak accident, I guess. She stood up too fast,

whacked her head on the deck railing, knocked herself out. Cold."

Jack whistled. "And called you to come up?"

"Nah, the hospital called us. They said she was fine, they didn't expect any problems, but since she was living alone out at the cabin with no phone, they wanted to keep her overnight for observation. You know—just in case. They said they'd release her if there was someone to pick her up, drive her home and spend the night with her."

"So you rescued her. Nice brother-in-law."

Ian grinned largely. "No, Jack. We rescued the hospital. Erin can be a little high maintenance sometimes. Can I have a cold beer?"

"Absolutely." He drew a draft and put it on the bar. "You know, Ian, when something like that happens, you can always call me or Preacher. We'd have found someone to take care of her for you."

"Thanks, Jack. I kind of figured that, but Marcie would've been jumpy all night, having no contact with her sister. Her hormones are a little wonky right now. You know?"

Jack grinned. "Oh, I've been there. How's she doing?"

"Great, she's doing great. We're having a boy in August. She's gorgeous, kind of in the way a toothpick that swallowed a pea is gorgeous. A toothpick with wild red hair."

"And you?" Jack asked. "How do you like the cabin?"

"I think Paul outdid himself. I can hardly believe it's the same place. Any chance you've seen it?"

Jack smirked. He gave the bar a wipe. "Pal, this is Virgin River. It's what we do on Sundays after church—drive around and walk through new construction and remodels in progress. 'Course, we needed a guide with a key for your place.... Paul took us through a couple of times, hope you don't mind. He's real proud of that fireplace and the deck." Jack whistled. "You gotta be asking yourself how you lived without that deck."

Ian laughed. "If I'd even thought of some of those improvements, it would've been years before I could've made 'em. It took someone with Erin's resources to pull off a job like that."

"How you getting on with the grand dame?" Jack asked.

"Erin? Aw, I love Erin. I mean, I know she comes off as kind of demanding, but that's Erin the lawyer and businesswoman. She's devoted her whole life to protecting Marcie and Drew and there were a lot of times they needed someone as hardheaded as Erin." He laughed. "She'll be fine—nothing could crack that skull. She didn't have to fix up that old cabin—she could've taken a long cruise or a three-month vacation at a Caribbean resort. I won't even pretend to know what she's got socked away, but she's got a reputation as one of the best estate lawyers in five states. I bet she could've bought a small house on a beach. But Marcie loves that old place because it's where we fell in love. I think Erin did it as much for us as herself. And Erin doesn't want to be too far away in case the baby comes early."

"Funny," Jack said. "I thought she was kind of hard edged. Maybe I misjudged her."

Ian just grinned. "I think you probably got her right, just not all sides of her. It takes a tough woman to bury both her parents, take care of a younger brother and sister when she was a kid herself, get them through the kind of difficult shit those two went through and become a successful lawyer on top of it. Plus, we have a common goal—we'd do anything to make sure Marcie is safe and happy."

"So what's she going to do up here for three months?" Jack wanted to know. "Isn't this a little backwoods for your sister-in-law?"

Ian shook his head. "I don't get it. She says it's about time she had a vacation. She hasn't taken more than a day off at a time in ten years. Probably more than ten years. No question, she deserves a vacation more than anyone, but this is really out of character." He'd been turning a lot of ideas over in his mind without mentioning any of his concerns to Marcie; he didn't want his pregnant wife all stirred up and worried. But he couldn't help but wonder why Erin had behaved so radically—remodeling his cabin, committing to a three-month vacation and leave from her law practice, isolating herself like that. Was she sick? Depressed? Was her job in some sort of jeopardy? Was she dealing with something she didn't feel she could share?

"Maybe she won't last a week up here alone. But listen, if there's ever anything you think I should know about Erin, will you give me a call?"

"You're worried," Jack said. When Ian looked shocked, Jack just shrugged and said, "I'm a bartender. We learn this stuff."

"I don't know if I'm worried," Ian said. "It's the kind of thing I'd do…something me and Marcie would do in a second if we could, and love it. But it just isn't like Erin. She's not used to downtime. Even on a Saturday in the park or by the pool, her cell phone rings all day long. This is pretty cold turkey."

"I'll keep an eye on her, buddy," Jack said. "Maybe it'll be good for her."

Ian took home oven-roasted chicken, small red potatoes sprinkled with parsley, green bean casserole covered in baby onion rings—homemade—and frosted brownies. He also stopped by Connie and Ron's Corner Store for whole milk, eggs, butter, bread, bacon, coffee and a six-pack. Marcie and Ian were only staying overnight, but he was going to have real food for breakfast before getting back on the road.

After dinner they sat on the deck and watched the sun set over the mountains on the far side of the ridge. Ian reclined on the chaise lounge and Marcie sat between his spread legs. He threaded his arms under hers so he could rub her belly while she leaned back against his chest. Erin sat on the opposite lounge, alone, of course. As the sun lowered, the June night at five thousand feet got chilly and the crickets came out.

Erin went inside and returned with two throws from the couch, one for her little sister and one to wrap around her own shoulders. She sat back on her chaise and said, "When you were here before, you two, and there was no computer or phone or TV, how did you pass the time? What kinds of things did you do? Besides practice for making junior there."

"We were pretty much snowed in," Marcie said. "And it was a lot of work to cook the bathwater. Ian worked early in the morning, before the sun was up, so he went to bed really early. But he went to the library almost every week and brought home books. When I was here, I went with him and got some books of my own. I read during the day and he read for a while every night." She turned her head to look up at Ian. "I like to read sexy romances, and after Ian and I became friends, he read me the love scenes out loud. It was hot!"

"I brought along some books I've been trying to find time to read," Erin said. "They're not like that, though."

"I can imagine. Try picking up a book with a woman kind of slung over a man's arm on the cover. Or maybe a ball gown with a décolletage. Or some shapely legs with stiletto heels. You might not get smarter, but you'll definitely want to get to the end!"

"Maybe I will…"

"Are you bored yet?" Marcie asked. "I was bored while Ian worked—except for my dangerous trips to the loo out back and the hard work of cooking bathwater. Until I got my library books."

"Not at all," Erin lied. "There are so many things I've never had time to do that now I can finally do. I'm going to spend some time on the coast, for one thing. I can't wait to hit some of the antique stores around here. I'm going to do some writing—nothing entertaining to you, just law stuff, but I might actually come up with a book. I've been thinking about that for years with no time to even outline." She shivered and pulled her throw more tightly around her. "I have to hand it to you, Ian—I don't know when I've seen a more beautiful place." And a little while later she said, "I'm going in. Can I get anyone anything?"

"Not for me."

"I'm fine," Ian said.

When Erin had gone inside, Marcie snuggled against Ian and whispered, "She's already bored."

And Ian said, "Maybe this will all be over in another week. Maybe she'll just come home."

Inside the cabin, curled up in the corner of the leather sofa with her throw around her shoulders, Erin listened to Marcie and Ian murmuring just outside on the deck. Two and a half years ago, Marcie came up to this mountain in search of Ian. It was supposed to be about closure, but it turned into a new beginning for both of them, and Marcie brought him home.

A year and a half ago, right at Christmastime, they married, but they stayed on with Erin and Drew in the house Marcie, Drew and Erin were raised in. Ian had gone back to college, studying music education. They had been a crowded, happy family—Drew finishing up medical school, Erin busy as ever with her practice, Marcie working as a secretary and Ian going to school full-time and working part-time. It felt so natural, so mutually nurturing. Because of all the studying and such going on, it was common to come home to a quiet house, but it was almost never an empty house. The four adults shared space, chores, cooking, and when they were all together their home was full of life.

Then summer a year ago, everything changed. Drew moved out to go to his orthopedic residency program, Ian and Marcie bought a little house of their own because they wanted a family and Erin found herself alone for the first time in her life. *In her life.* And she thought, *I am completely on my own. The staggering responsibility is finally behind me. I have reached that pinnacle we've been struggling toward.*

And then she thought, *Uh-oh. I am no good at being alone, but I damn sure better learn it, because it is what it is.* That was when she asked Ian if she could make some improvements in his old cabin on the mountain so she could use it now and then.

He had grinned and said, "Little rugged for you, sister?"

"It's on the rugged side, yes. But I won't touch it if it has sentimental value as the dump where you found yourself. I can look around for something else for vacations and long weekends."

"Erin, you do anything you want to that dump," he had said. "I'm all done doing things the hardest way I can."

Tonight, sitting on her sofa, listening to them murmur on the deck, the image of Ian running his big hands over Marcie's round belly emblazoned on her mind, she thought, *I will never have that. What I'm going to have from now on is what I have right now— myself. Just myself. Oh, there will be family—Marcie and Drew won't forget me. We'll talk and there will be visits. But I will never have what they have. I had better learn to find value and appreciation in this, because this is what I have....*

I am alone. And I'd better learn how to be that.

Ian was washing up breakfast dishes the next morning when he said to Erin, "You get your phone and satellite feed today, right? So you'll have TV, Internet, et cetera?"

"Hopefully. It was supposed to be done before I moved up here, but they rescheduled a couple of times."

"The minute you get hooked up, give us a call. All right?"

Erin smiled at him. "Sure, Dad."

"How's the head?"

She touched the Band-Aid at her hairline. "Funny looking."

"That's nothing to when Marcie burned off her eyebrows. Now, *that* was funny looking. Doesn't hurt anymore? Any headache?"

"I'm fine. You can go. It's all right."

"When you get the laptop online, are you going to e-mail your office and tell them so they can send you work?"

"No. I brought the computer so I can research if I feel like exploring that book idea, but mainly I want to try my hand at total relaxation. I've never had the luxury before. This is my time and I'm going to—"

"If you get bored or lonesome," he said, cutting her off, "just come back to Chico. We'll all take some long weekends up here, together. All your hard work on making this place nice won't go to waste."

"I won't get bored or lonesome," she said emphatically. "I've been looking forward to this all year. But if I do, you'll be the first person I call."

"You do that, Erin," he said.

Three

After a long day of hiking along the ocean, Aiden went home, showered and walked down the path to Luke and Shelby's house at around dinnertime. He found Shelby in the kitchen, getting some dinner ready. He ponied right up. "Can I help?"

"You can set the table," she said. "But first, there is a call for you on the machine from a guy named Jeff. I wrote the number down, but go ahead and listen to the message if you want."

"Nah, I'll just call him." He went to the cupboard to pull out the dishes.

"Ah, Aiden, you might want to call him now. Set the table after."

"Why?" he asked. He'd kept in touch with Jeff since undergrad days; they'd both been in ROTC and on navy scholarships for med school. Jeff was one of the few people besides his brothers he was in constant touch with.

"It's something urgent," she said, her back to him, stirring a pan on the stove. "Something to do with an Annalee Riordan." She turned toward him. "I know you don't have any sisters."

He was stunned speechless for a second. Then he recovered and smiled. "The ex," he said. "You're right, I'll call."

When he got Jeff on the phone, he was informed that Annalee had been looking for him unsuccessfully. His mother's Phoenix phone was disconnected, all the brothers had moved, Aiden had separated from the navy and was now a civilian. The only one she could round up was Aiden's former frat brother/best friend/best man and currently lieutenant commander in the navy. "She says it's urgent that she speak to you," Jeff said.

"We've been divorced for eight years after a three-month marriage," Aiden said. "We don't have urgent issues."

"Maybe you should respond," Jeff said. "You can hang up on her after you decide she's making excuses."

Aiden looked over his shoulder at Shelby. "I'm telling you, we don't have business. We don't have mutual friends or family, we don't have property, support payments or children. It was a quick, clean break after a short, nasty marriage. But give me the number. If she calls you again, you tell her you gave me the number and you're out of it. How's that?"

Aiden scribbled down a phone number, "Sorry for the trouble, man. You doing okay? Carol and the kids okay? Good, good. Yeah, I'm great—I'm kicking back, looking for the next opportunity, and you know what? This was a good idea, taking a little time off. Hey, Jeff, I'm sorry you had to put up with this. Annalee should be long gone. I haven't heard a word from her since the day the divorce was final, and there is no reason to be hearing from her now unless she's up to no good. You have my blessing to blow her off."

Aiden hung up the phone, crumpled the paper with the phone number on it, pitched it in the trash and continued to set the table.

Maureen Riordan had several big boxes sitting in the middle of her small living room. They were packed with precious family heirlooms—her mother's antique china for Shelby and a box of Great-grandma Riordan's silver flatware that would go to Franci. She had also packed some crystal and silver pieces in Bubble Wrap and a couple of boxes of antique quilts and linens that she'd take as far as Virgin River, hoping to leave those boxes with Luke; the contents were too valuable to put in a storage facility and she intended to save them for future new daughters-in-law. A couple of years ago she wouldn't have been so optimistic, but Luke had finally settled down at the age of thirty-eight, Sean right behind him, so it was still possible for Colin, Aiden and Patrick.

Life was so funny, she found herself thinking. She'd spent a lifetime protecting some of these material things—china and crystal, old quilts lovingly fashioned by her ancestors' hands, linens brought all the way from Ireland—and now the pleasure it gave her to be passing them on to the next generation was immeasurable.

Another bunch of boxes held everyday items she planned to add to what George already had in the RV. They'd gone over the inventory on the phone and in e-mails so many times, she knew almost everything on the list by heart. Clothing, linens, kitchen items and bric-a-brac that she could live without she had already given away.

She and George had seen each other exactly four times since Christmas. Once she flew to Seattle to visit him over a long weekend and three times he flew to Phoenix, also for long weekends, visits that went spectacularly well. Maureen wasn't naive. She knew that when people lived in close quarters for more than a few days or weeks, adjustments were necessary. She might even realize she'd made a mistake, but she didn't expect to. As inflexible as she could be, George was three times as flexible as any man she'd ever known. His good nature had taken an entire layer off her previous narrow-mindedness.

George was now en route and she had talked to him several times a day since he left Seattle. He flew to Nevada, where he picked up the RV; it was only a year old, but had cost more than her condo. At long last her cell phone rang and he was an hour away; finally he was minutes away. "And promise me you're not going to be standing in the parking lot!" he said emphatically. "I want to set her up for your first real viewing." That meant he wanted to pop out the sides, extend the patio cover, turn on the lights and music. He wanted her to see her new home at its absolute finest.

Finally she received a text message; George was fond of texting. Rather than answering, she bolted across her patio, the pool area and to the parking lot in front of the complex. There he stood in front of the most beautiful masterpiece of an RV she had ever seen.

She stopped short and just forced herself to breathe deeply. This would be her home for at least six months and if the experiment was successful, for a few years. Her hand covered her mouth as she slowly stepped toward the luxury motor coach.

George laughed, drawing her attention to him. He leaned against the front of the vehicle, one leg crossed lazily in front of the other, arms crossed over his chest. He had the most engaging, lovely smile. His blue eyes twinkled mischievously; he had such pretty silver hair. A fine figure of a gentleman.

"You should give me a kiss before the tour so I at least get the impression I'm as important as the coach," he teased.

"Of course," she said, going to him. She put her hands on his cheeks, gave him a good enthusiastic peck and said, "Now can I see it inside? I'm dying to see it!"

"I sent you plenty of pictures," he said. "And I invited you to come up to Nevada to see it in person, but I remind you, you wanted me to make the decision on my own and you did approve the pictures."

It had seemed only fair. George was going to own it and she didn't want him buying it for her. Nice of him to ask her opinion if she was to live in it for months, possibly years, but still… Of course, she'd offered to pay for half, but George was adamant—he'd be glad to put her name on the title, but he wouldn't take her money. "Call me old-fashioned," he had said, "but a man still likes to think he can take care of his woman." In the end it was probably less complicated this way, since they'd both been married previously and had grown children.

They had it all planned out—he bought the RV in his name from the proceeds of his house sale. They both put their furniture in separate storage facilities— just till they were absolutely sure they were together for the long haul. It was a struggle, but George finally agreed to take five hundred dollars a month in rent from her; her savings and eventually the money from her condo sale was to stay in her possession. If they married—or *when,* as George preferred to think of it—they would work out some sort of prenuptial thing so that George could leave his RV and savings to his stepgrandchildren and to Noah Kincaid and she could leave hers to her sons. For right now both had pensions that would allow them to pay for gas, insurance, incidentals, hookup space, food, et cetera.

She stepped inside, up the steps. She ran a hand over the smooth white leather of the copilot's seat— lush and rich. And then she stood looking into the interior. On either side were matching white leather couches and between them, what looked like dark, hardwood floors but was actually scuff-free laminate. Just beyond, a spacious kitchen on the left with all the necessary appliances and even an oak cupboard at a right angle to the kitchen that had decorative leaded glass on each side—the china cabinet. Opposite the kitchen, a dark marblish table stood with matching white leather sofa seats that could accommodate four for dinner. There were plenty of kitchen cabinets and storage above the sofas. Mounted above the driver's seat, facing into the living room, was a fifty-eight-inch flat-screen TV.

"My God," she whispered. "It's larger than my condo and more beautiful than any house I've ever lived in."

"You like it?" George asked from right behind her.

"It's amazing." She turned around to face him. "Is it hard to drive?"

"It's easy. Those classes I took really paid off, even though I'd driven Noah's RV in the past. I think you should take them, too. We'll stop somewhere they have the classes and sign you up."

"Can we? That would be so much fun."

"You'd like that?"

"Oh, I'd love that! But of course, it's your—"

He put a finger on her lips. "Let's not do a lot of that, Maureen—all that yours-and-mine stuff. I understand we have an agreement, but we're in this together." He smiled. "And I love you."

She leaned toward him. "That's so nice to hear, George."

"I suppose it is," he said with a smile. "I imagine one of these days I might hear it, too."

She grinned at him. "I was saving it for a special moment—like when we drink champagne tonight at dinner in the RV, but—"

"Perfect!" he said, interrupting her. "I'll be ready!"

"Can we sleep in it tonight?" she asked.

"Wouldn't you like to see the rest of it first?"

"I'd like to see it, but can we?"

"Of course, if you feel like it."

"My house is upside down with boxes. I tore the sheets off the bed and washed them. I put them in the charity box since the bed in here is a king and I've only had a double all these years. I think we'd probably be more comfortable in here, actually."

"Then here's what we do—load it up with the boxes for Virgin River and the household items you plan to add to our inventory. I made a reservation at a park so we can have a hookup. You'll have to learn the difference quick—when we're hooked up, the water, sewage and electricity belong to someone else and we don't drain our supply or have the task of taking care of the lavatory. There will be times we dry-camp, when there's no hookup, but when possible we'll find a park with facilities. So—we have chores, don't we?"

"There isn't that much. Tomorrow when the movers come to crate the furnishings for storage, we'll finish and you can help me tidy up. I hired a cleaning service—the condo management will let them in once we're on the road. I used packing boxes by the measurements you gave me for the storage under the coach—I hope the boxes fit."

"Very well organized," he said. "I'm not surprised at all." He touched her nose. "Did you tell them?"

"More or less. I told Aiden on the phone while Luke was sitting across the room from him. That should catch them all up. I mean, I had told them I was thinking about it, but no one took me seriously."

"How'd Aiden take it?"

"Very well, as a matter of fact. But then Aiden was the one to lecture me when he heard I'd brushed you off last fall. He said I shouldn't assume my life couldn't ever again include a man. In a romantic way."

"Ah," George said, rolling his eyes skyward. "God bless him. I'll leave him my entire fortune."

"There are five of them, George, and they're as different from each other as day is from night. I know you've met them, but you haven't spent any real time with them. There's no way I can adequately prepare you."

"I understand completely. Let's start carting boxes and pack up. The sooner we can get to that champagne dinner, the better I like it."

"I'd like to see the bedroom now," she said. "Have you chosen your drawers and closet space? Your side of the bed?"

"No, sweetheart. I'm waiting for you to decide."

She put her arms around his waist. "I'm so lucky to have found you."

Mel, local nurse-practitioner and midwife, had an appointment with a friend of hers she didn't often see professionally. Darla Prentiss had been in the care of a fertility specialist in Santa Rosa for the past several years, so her women's health needs were handled by him. But Phil Prentiss had called Mel and said that he was bringing his wife in because she complained of a cold and sore throat. "That's not what it is, though," Phil had said. "She waits for me to leave the house or fall asleep, then cries her heart out for hours. She needs someone to talk to. We just suffered our seventh miscarriage."

"Oh, good heavens, bring her. But wait—isn't her doctor supporting you through this?"

"Aw, he's all about the big score," Phil said. "He might have the best track record for getting people pregnant in three counties, but his bedside manner sucks. Darla's crushed."

"Bring her to me," Mel said. "But don't lie to her— tell her you know she doesn't have a cold. I'll do what I can. Phil—I'm so sorry for your loss."

"This one," he said, "was eighteen weeks. We named him and buried him."

"I'm so sorry."

"Thanks," he said.

Mel's heart was in tatters. Instead of seven miscarriages, this wonderful couple should have had seven children. Phil owned and operated the family farm, a vast acreage committed to dairy, pork and silage. It was a wonderful, fun, healthy place and the Prentisses were a positive, beautiful, loving couple. They'd been married quite a while—ten or twelve years—trying most of that time to grow a family. It was so wrong, when the people who could do the best by children had such trouble getting them. It was a miracle the pain of their loss time after time hadn't ripped their marriage apart, yet Phil and Darla were devoted to each other, as in love as the day they met.

When Darla arrived with her husband, Mel just hugged her long and hard. "I'm sorry," she said. "God, I'm so sorry. You've been through so much."

That's all it took for Darla to let the tears loose. Mel took her by the hand and they went into the office to talk for a while. Mel had told Darla a long time ago that in her first marriage, she and her husband had struggled with infertility issues, but for some unknown reason when she got together with Jack—instant pregnancy. Could be coincidence, could be some medical reason she didn't quite understand.

"I can't do it anymore, Mel," Darla said tearfully. "I'm sorry to be such a crybaby, but I think that last one did me in. A little boy…"

"Seven miscarriages is too much for anyone, Darla. Remember when we talked about a surrogate? Someone with a sturdier, proven uterus?"

"I know it's a good option for people like me and Phil, since I have trouble conceiving *and* carrying. My younger sister, who's a mother of three, even offered. But, Mel—oh, God, I know this makes me sound so shallow and self-absorbed—but I don't think I can watch her carry our baby and stay out of her business. I'd be examining everything she puts in her mouth. I'd burn with jealousy that I couldn't carry the baby and feel it move inside me. We talked about hiring a stranger. I know it works a lot, but I don't think we can…."

"Keep an open mind. It's a good solution for couples who have everything they need but a womb," Mel said.

Darla was shaking her head. "There's a message in here somewhere. I'm not sure what it is, but one thing I know for sure—I'm not meant to have a baby of my own. That was the first one we actually buried. Mel," she said, tears streaming down her face. "I really can't do that again."

"I understand," Mel said softly. "Tell me how I can help you now. Do you think a good antidepressant might help?"

"With losing your child? No," she said, shaking her head. "I need to cry about it awhile, feel my husband's arms around me and ask God what his plan is for me. It's not like I'm the first woman who couldn't have her own children. After all, how many women have as much as I have? The most handsome, wonderful, loving man in the world? Poor Phil, his heart must be breaking, too, and I'm only thinking of myself."

"Just reach out for him while he reaches out for you, sweetheart. Then call your doctor's office and tell them you could probably use a little counseling to get you through this last miscarriage."

"But I don't think I want to keep going with this… this crazy desperation to get pregnant and carry a child to term…"

"That's not the point," Mel said, shaking her head. "Whether you keep trying or not, you need a little help getting through the loss. This was a big, hard one for you two. You've paid that doctor tens of thousands of dollars not covered by insurance—he must have counseling staff or at least people he can recommend. You don't have to promise to risk more heartache to get yourself a good counselor. Get some help."

"Maybe we'll see our pastor…"

"See someone, Darla. Please? I just don't want you to hurt. I never had a miscarriage—but I failed to get pregnant every time and I remember the pain and disappointment of that alone. I just can't imagine how hard this must be for you."

Darla was quiet a moment. Then she wiped off her cheeks and said, "I think seven is enough."

"I don't blame you," Mel said.

Every couple of weeks Luke had to drive over to Eureka to shop at the Costco warehouse for stock for his house and cabins. He bought large amounts of toilet paper, bar soap, paper towels, cleaning supplies and sometimes had to replace things like bath towels, washcloths, bath mats, and so on. While he was there, he shopped for some groceries for his own home; there was plenty of frozen fish in the freezer out in the shed next to the house, but they could always use chicken and red meat. Shelby kept a running list of items she was willing to keep in bulk, from ketchup to canned tuna. Now that her nursing-school program was on hiatus for the summer and she was hugely pregnant, her stop-offs at the grocery store on the way home were few. That made Luke's trips to town more frequent.

He didn't have to tell Art when they were going. Art

started asking at least a couple days ahead of time. "We going to Costco yet, Luke?"

"Two days," Luke would answer. Art, an adult with Down syndrome, whom Luke had taken on as a helper around the cabins, was Luke's fairly constant shadow and had his own little cabin next to Luke and Shelby's house.

"What time, Luke?" he asked.

"Let's say two o'clock."

Then: "Tomorrow we're going to Costco, Luke." And then: "Today we're going to Costco, Luke." And then: "Is it time to go to Costco, Luke?"

Going to Costco was Art's absolute favorite chore in the entire world. He didn't mind the hardware store but he *loved* Costco. Luke never made him stick close or help with the shopping and he took his sweet old time because Art wanted to look at *everything,* especially things he would never buy. Art loved the jewelry counter, and he was fascinated by the computers. When Luke had the satellite dish installed, he bought Art an inexpensive laptop and a couple of learning programs to help Art with his spelling and addition and subtraction. Once Art learned something, he was very capable, though it didn't seem he was getting better at spelling or math. It was as though he'd reached his limit—but he loved the computer. Art was also extremely literal, not creative. Art did not think outside the box. If you said, "Take out the trash," he might ask, "Out where?" Instead, you said, "Collect the trash in this bag and then tie the bag closed and put it in the Dumpster."

It took Luke about fifteen minutes to gather up his paper products and cleaning supplies. Then he dawdled around the meat, cheese and vegetables, mentally choosing what perishables he'd select after Art had had plenty of time to enjoy his shopping trip. He bought a few more nonperishables on Shelby's list—olive oil, crackers, rice, pasta, cereal. He grabbed some beer and whiskey. He looked through books, DVDs and music—grabbed a couple of each. Then he went looking for Art.

When he didn't find Art by the jewelry, computer games or computers, he widened his search. He looked in the tools, cosmetics, frozen foods. It baffled him that Art wasn't in any of his usual haunts.

Finally, he found him in a far corner of the store by the dog food, standing very close to and towering above a short, round woman with curly brown hair. They were holding hands and gazing at each other intently. What an odd-looking pair, Luke found himself thinking with a smile. Yet how strangely perfect—great big lumbering Art and this little, chunky woman. "Art?" he asked.

Art turned sharply as if startled. He was smiling and his small eyes were so large it made Luke chuckle. He'd never seen a smile that big on Art. "Luke! It's Netta! From my group home! She was my girlfriend."

"No kidding?" Luke put out a hand. "How do you do, Netta. Hey," he said. "I think I met you once before. Did you work at that grocery store with Art?"

"They took her out of that store, Luke!" Art said excitedly. "They took everybody out of that store!

Stan who owns the store? He got a big punishment for doing things wrong! Netta said he had to pay money and he was *mad!*"

"Very…mmm…mad," Netta said quietly.

"How sad for old Stan," Luke said with a wide smile. "I wish I could feel sorry for him. So, Netta, where are you living now?"

"In a…mmm…house," she said. "With Ellen and Bo. In Fortuna. I help in the bakery."

"And why are you at Costco today?" Luke asked.

"We get our…mmm…stuff at Costco. And Ellen lets me…mmm…shop."

"Art," Luke said, "why don't you buy Netta a hot dog or pizza slice and a cola or something. Sit down. Catch up on the news. I'll get the rest of my stuff very slowly. Take your time."

Art just stared at him.

Netta took his hand. "Let's get…mmm…hot dog, Art."

"Go on, Art. Get a hot dog. Talk with Netta awhile."

Art seemed a little frozen, so Luke turned his laden cart away and walked off quickly, getting out of his space.

Of course, Art had money, and he managed it very well. Luke would never reach into his pocket and give the man money, especially in front of a woman. Art got a disability check from Social Security, some state aid, and Luke paid him for his work. Art paid Luke a bit for the cabin he used as his home, but no money ever changed hands for things like groceries. Sometimes when Art had a little money left over, he wanted to buy something for Luke or Shelby, and that was all right, but Luke kept it within limits. Art was building a savings account, and when he showed Luke the growing balance, he beamed with pride.

Luke wasn't sure about what Netta's issues were. She didn't have Down's; she had a slight hesitation in her speech, not quite a stutter but more an "mmm" while looking for the right word. He thought maybe she was a little slow, but wasn't entirely sure about how disabled. Yet she must have some disability if she'd been in a group home with Art.

But how unexpected—Art had had a girlfriend. Luke thought he might've mentioned someone named Netta, but surely no more than once. He hadn't been pining or anything.

There was a fast-food area in the front of the store, on the other side of the checkout lanes, so Luke steered clear of it. He wasted a good half hour looking at cameras. What the hell—the baby was coming soon and he needed a better camera. By the time he was done, he had a video camera, a digital still camera, a large-screen laptop and a color printer to go with it. He probably should have talked to Shelby about that first, but he was still being trained as a husband. Fortunately, Shelby was very patient with him.

He went to the back of the store and quickly grabbed the meat, produce and veggies he had mentally planned to buy. Time to check out.

Once again, he didn't see Art anywhere.

Lord, this was getting ridiculous. He'd never had this problem with Art before. Luke looked all around the fast-food area and Art was definitely not there. He'd have to look around the whole warehouse again. First, he decided, he'd put his groceries in the truck, then go back inside in search of Art.

But when he got outside, Art was standing there, staring into the massive parking lot. "Well, hey, I was wondering where you were. Did you have a nice visit with Netta?"

Art turned abruptly. He looked a little shell-shocked. "She was my girlfriend."

"So you said," Luke observed. "Come on, let's put this stuff in the truck. Did you have a nice visit?"

"She left. She had to go with that person, Ellen. Where she lives now."

"But did you have a nice visit?"

"She was my girlfriend," Art said again. "I didn't see her in a long time."

"Right," Luke said. Apparently he wasn't going to get an answer to the question about whether they'd had a nice visit. "Help load up, will you, buddy?"

Art did as he'd been asked, but the whole while he mumbled and fidgeted. He was extremely upset, that much was obvious, and Luke quickly learned why. They had barely left the parking lot when Art said, "I have to go to Costco. Back to Costco."

"In a couple of weeks, Art."

"*Now!* I have to go *now!*"

"Forget something?" Luke asked.

"She could come to Costco. Netta could come and I could be there, too—I didn't see her in a long time! I can be there if she comes back. She shops there!"

Since they hadn't driven far, Luke turned into a parking lot and stopped the truck. "She left, Art. Did you get her phone number or address or anything?"

"No," he said, his voice thick. "All of a sudden the woman Ellen came and said time to go. And all of a sudden Netta said goodbye. I have to go back."

"No going back today, buddy. Just like us, she's not going to be shopping for a couple of weeks, I bet. You know her last name at least?"

"Blue," he said. "Netta Blue." Then, with watery eyes, he stared at Luke and in a plaintive voice he just said, *"Luke!"*

Luke felt his heart drop. The poor guy. Art might not know much, but he sure knew when his heart hurt. Netta Blue, his onetime girlfriend, gone. He'd barely seen her after a separation and *whoosh,* she was gone again. He was desperate to see more of her, but did she want to see more of him? And how would her caretaker, Ellen, feel about a Down syndrome man hanging around Netta? This was going to instantly get bigger than Luke was. Lately he felt like everything was bigger than he was.

"Now, calm down, Art," he said. "I'll help you find her. We have to go home first. Netta has gone home, too. We'll go home, and then we'll see if we can find her later."

"Okay, Luke," Art said thickly.

Luke stroked his arm. "Don't worry, okay? It's going to be all right. How many bakeries can there be in Fortuna?"

"I don't know that answer," Art said miserably.

"I didn't need an answer, buddy. I just meant, we'll find her, so don't worry."

He sniffed. "Okay, Luke."

By the time Luke and Art got home, Art seemed much calmer. He had stopped mumbling and talking to himself and he was back to responding in his easygoing, good-natured way. But Luke was a little shook up, maybe a little afraid Art would take off for Costco. After all, that's how Art came to be living with Luke— his caretaker had hit him and Art had run away, preferring homelessness to abuse. For someone who couldn't always think for himself, Art had certainly made a decision there.

Luke said, "I'm going to put the groceries away, Art. Go fish for one hour, then come to the house."

"Okay," Art agreed.

"Look at your watch and remember, one hour. Shelby will be looking for you."

"One hour," he agreed.

Luke stored all the extra paper and cleaning products for the cabins in the shed, then took the groceries into the house very quietly. Just as he expected, the bedroom door was pulled almost closed. Shelby could be lying down with her feet up for a little while or she could be asleep. When she didn't emerge from their bedroom after all the groceries had been stored, he crept out of the house. It was in his mind to make sure Art was fishing, but the door to Aiden's room stood open to catch the June breeze and he saw Aiden sitting inside, his laptop open on the table in front of him.

He gave a couple of taps. "Hey. You back from today's trek?"

"I just went over to the coast to walk along the beach for a few hours," Aiden answered without looking up.

"Got a minute?" Luke asked. "Because I have a situation…"

Aiden sat back with an impatient sigh. "Look, Mom's going to be just fine—"

"Not Mom," he said, walking into the cabin. He sat down at the table opposite Aiden, and his brother slowly closed the laptop between them. "It's Art. I have something going on with Art. And I need someone smarter than I am to talk this out with me."

One corner of Aiden's mouth lifted. "Wanna run this by me?"

Luke leaned forward and told Aiden about what had happened at the store in hushed tones lest Art walk past the open cabin door and overhear. When he was done, Aiden said, "Whoo. Sounds like our man Art met up with an old flame and had a rush of testosterone or something."

"Tes*tost*erone?" Luke repeated in a panic.

Aiden smiled lazily. "That's not the chromosome he's missing, Luke. He's a man. What is he—thirty-one? He's going to have a lot of typical male responses. Then again, some responses that are just pure Art…"

"Oh, Jesus, Mary and Joseph," Luke said, running a hand over his short-cropped hair.

Aiden laughed at him. "Relax—he's completely

calm.… He's not going to go berserk or anything. But for God's sake, he has feelings! Have you talked to him about this stuff?"

"*What* stuff?"

"Girlfriends. Sex. Desire. Caution."

"Well, of course not! Why would I even *think* of that? And what would I say?"

"I'm not entirely sure what you should say—I don't deal with male patients, and certainly not those with Down syndrome. Does he have a caseworker or a social worker? Because if he has a girlfriend, especially a girlfriend with a similar disability, someone should address it before they're both in over their heads."

"Oh God," Luke moaned.

"You need to find an expert—maybe someone with a degree in special ed. Call social services and explain what you're up against, your lack of experience in this area. Get some help."

"What about the girl? I promised him I'd try to find the girl!"

"Then try to find the girl! They lived in the same house together, Luke, they mean something to each other. Well…" He hesitated. "She means something to Art. You probably should try to find out if the feeling is mutual before you turn him loose." Aiden grinned. "I know what you're thinking—there's a little piece of you that's afraid Art will go nuts. No, Luke," he said, shaking his head. "He's mentally challenged but his personality is characterized by extremely cooperative behavior. He's sweet and gentle. He just needs some guidance. Get someone with experience to tell you the best way to handle that."

"You're just faking it," Luke accused. "Are you just faking it to look smart? Because we all get that you're smart—don't show off."

Aiden laughed. "It'll be all right. You're great with Art. Talk to Shelby about it—you two work well together."

Luke grumbled a little bit, then got up and ambled off in the direction of the river.

Aiden shook his head. Luke reminded him a lot of their father—a real tough exterior, but plenty of that old Irish angst inside. Complete vulnerability. All soft and gooey. No one had forced Art on Luke—it was all Luke's idea to take him on. Just like the situation with their mother—Luke was probably the one who was the most concerned about it, and the least likely to talk it over with her.

Luke needed to handle this thing with Art, Aiden thought. It would give him confidence, make him more sure of himself in an emotional situation where he didn't have a lot of experience. It would be good for all of them and good training for being a parent.

Four

Aiden had a few commitments scheduled for the next couple of weeks. First of all, his sister-in-law Franci had sold the house she and Rosie had lived in while Sean was in Iraq. All their household goods would be shipped to Alabama, Sean's next assignment. Franci and Rosie were going to take up residence in one of Luke's cabins, where Sean would join them shortly, before they headed east. But there was a great deal to do around Franci's house before the move—minor repairs, a garage sale, a little painting and yard work, and once the movers had departed, some serious cleaning before the new owners took possession. Aiden had signed on for all of it. He wanted to spend time with Franci and Rosie and they needed the help.

His mother and George would also be showing up sometime in the next week and he wanted to be close by when they arrived.

And of course he wanted to be available if Shelby

needed him for anything; Luke didn't like leaving her side unless Aiden was going to be nearby. And Luke was itching to figure out the situation with Art before his son was born.

Aiden's mission for the summer was simple—be a helpful visitor; enjoy the family. His current plans didn't leave a lot of extra time and there was still one other thing he wanted to do. He wanted to check on the woman with the head injury. Erin.

He dressed for hiking one morning, loaded his backpack and took off in his SUV. He drove toward her cabin, parked on a wide space in the road below the ridge and walked up that dirt road again. When he got to the top, he saw that her car was missing. He walked around the house, checking it out. Nothing much had changed, except it was all closed up. He checked out the garden, or the poor excuse for a garden. Dry, and no improvement. He assumed she'd gone home, but he watered the plants just in case. Maybe it was on her mind to spend the occasional weekend at the cabin.

Then, completely unplanned and for no good reason, he did a little digging in that big square plot behind the house that had proved to be too much for her. He cleared the weeds and sod, dug out the big rocks and heaved them into the woods. The he tilled the dirt until it was loose, soft and ready for planting. He drove into Fortuna and bought a few bags of topsoil, a couple bags of fertilizer, some man-size gardening tools and a hose. Then he went back, hoed in the soil and fertilizer and wet the ground.

Before he left he sat on the deck and looked out at the view while he drank some water. He didn't sit on her nice clean chaise lounges, but on the step of the deck. He happened to glance through the French doors—neat as a pin in there. No sign of life. No books or papers strewn around, no dishes on the table or pans on the stove, no sweater draped over a chair.

So, she was gone.

When he left he took the empty plastic bags that had held the dirt and fertilizer with him and leaned the tools against the back of the house.

The next day he took plants, vegetable-garden starters, flower borders, stakes and a slow sprinkler to hook up to the hose. Again he sat on the deck while he drank his water and again he glanced through the French doors. All tidy.

He wondered if she'd ever come back. Then wondered why he wondered. He didn't like her—she was a pain in the butt.

The next day at around noon he swung by to water, telling himself that there was no place for a garden at Luke's and he was enjoying this. It also crossed his mind that she would eventually come back to her cabin and she might just check on her dead plants against the house. It was fun to think of her spying a new garden back there and wondering who would do such a thing. And why.

He gave the garden a little extra water because the following day he was committed to go to Franci's with Luke, Shelby and Art to help with a garage sale, some minor home repairs and yard work.

* * *

Art, who was absolutely never annoying, had become annoying. Filled with anxious impatience, he was continually asking questions about Netta. "Do you know where she lives now? Do you know where her house is?"

Luke kept saying, "Not yet, bud. I'm making phone calls to bakeries, asking if anyone with her name works there, and so far I haven't found her. Try to relax."

Telling a man with the scent of a woman up his nose to relax was turning out to be about as useful as throwing kerosine on a fire. Nothing could distract him for long. For once, even Rosie couldn't seem to occupy Art. And the garage sale, which really should get his attention, didn't. He kept questioning if there were any updates and Luke kept patiently saying, "Not since the last time you asked me ten minutes ago, Art."

Shelby sat in a lawn chair right in the garage door, fanning herself, haggling with customers while Franci and her mother, Vivian, did any lifting or moving around of merchandise. Aiden did some recaulking in the bathrooms, repaired a gutter along the eave, pulled out and cleaned behind and under the refrigerator, washer and dryer. Rosie stuck to him like glue because he had promised her that when his chores were done she could dress up his beard with clips and bows. All this time Luke and Art were working together on the yard.

"Did you call her yet, Luke?"

"Have you seen me near a phone, Art?"

"Did you?"

"I'm cutting the damn grass, Art!"

"Then will you?"

Aiden didn't mean to laugh at the two of them but he did anyway. He had his own shadow.

"After this job can I brush it? Your beard?"

"Yes, Rose. After this job."

"And put a bwaid in it?"

"Yes, Rose. When I'm done here."

When Aiden was finally finished he settled down in a lawn chair on the back patio with Rosie and her dog, Harry, and while Art and Luke were edging, trimming and raking up clippings, Rosie combed his beard and filled it full of ribbons and barrettes. He closed his eyes lazily, enjoying the fiddling and remembering to stay conscious. Sean had once fallen asleep in Rosie's care and she had put makeup on him with Magic Markers.

"I know what to get you for Christmas," Aiden said. "A doll with hair you can fix. Are you going to be a beautician when you grow up?"

"What's a boo-tician?"

"Someone who fixes hair."

"No, I'm gonna be a jet pilot. It's bery important. What are you gonna be?" she asked him.

Aiden opened one eye and peered at her. "A farmer," he said. "It's bery important, too."

"That's bery good," she said.

Mel Sheridan walked up the porch steps to Jack's bar at two in the afternoon on a weekday. It instantly brought to mind the vast number of times she'd done exactly this in the past. The bar was typically very quiet, often deserted, between lunch and dinner and if her husband wasn't running errands or busy elsewhere, he'd be there. He was usually behind the bar, taking inventory, organizing, setting up for the dinner crowd. Preacher would be in the kitchen cooking, his wife, Paige, and their kids would be in their attached home, and while the kids napped, Paige would often be running receipts on the computer, paying the bills, keeping the books, assisting in the management of the bar.

When Mel came to town four years ago, the bar was where she first got to know her husband. At the time, it was a far-fetched notion that they would even be friends, but it hadn't taken her long to fall in love with him. This was the place they'd had their most private conversations over the years, and when there was something she wanted to discuss with him, this time of day was usually the perfect opportunity.

She walked in and a single glance told her they were alone—Jack behind the bar, no customers. "Hey, baby," he said, smiling.

Ah, four years and so many times she'd walked into his bar and still, every time, he acted as if he hadn't seen her for days. His smile was warm and sexy, his brown eyes sparkling. Maybe four years wasn't such a long time, she thought. Still, she felt completely confident that he would look at her that way in forty more. There was this thing about Jack— he didn't take commitment lightly. He said to her once,

"I'm all in." Three little words that expressed a lifetime commitment. Jack didn't say something like that unless he meant it, and he was a man with the strength to uphold that oath.

She jumped up on a stool and leaned over to kiss him. "Hi, sweetheart. Red-letter day today. Emma is doing it in the potty, full-time."

He grinned. "But is David doing it full-time?" he asked.

"The biggest problem we have with number-one son is peeing in the yard, taught to him by number-one dad."

Jack grabbed both her hands across the bar. "I don't expect you to understand this, being a girl, but it's a very important rite of passage, learning that the world is your urinal." He shrugged. "My son took to the news."

"I know that. He'd rather pee on a bush than in the toilet. There should be a balance—the bush when there *is* no toilet, and so on."

"He'll come around...."

"There's something I've been wanting to talk to you about. I wanted to make sure both kids were potty trained before bringing it up—but one and three-quarters is good enough, I think."

"What's on your mind?"

"I think I'd like to have one more baby. Before I get much older."

The stunned look that came over his face was priceless and made her smile. She gave him a couple of seconds, and noted that he was struggling with the possibility that she'd completely lost her mind. Finally, slowly, he said, "You feel like trying to adopt?"

"Actually, no. I thought we'd have one of our own."

"Mel," he said gently, giving her hands a comforting squeeze. "Mel, between us we might be missing some parts for having our own...."

She laughed a little bit. "I know my uterus is gone, Jack. But I still have ovaries and you still have sperm. We could get a surrogate."

"Huh?" he said, frowning.

"You know what that is, I know you do."

"I do," he said. "But..."

"In vitro—our baby in a surrogate." Then she smiled brightly. "You do make such wonderful babies. And I think we can squeak in one more before we really run out of time. We were sort of thinking about that right before Emma was born anyway. And she's two."

"No, we weren't. I'm forty-four. And you're thirty-six."

"Hardly Grandma Moses and the old man of the sea, Jack," she said.

"Is this something you just started kicking around? This surrogate idea?" he wanted to know.

"I've been giving it some pretty serious thought for a while now. We're not the youngest parents, but lots of couples nowadays start their families in their thirties and forties. We're healthy and strong.... There's no reason to think we won't be around to see them well into adulthood. Of course, one or both of us could fall off a mountain, but that's not an age-sensitive calamity.

When you think about it, with my history of infertility, had we decided to have a family it might well have taken us this long to get started anyway."

He was quiet again. Then he said, "Mel, your history of infertility did not follow you to Virgin River. And we have two kids. Two smart, healthy, beautiful kids."

"Will you at least think about it? Because it's really a logical solution for us. We have everything but a uterus...."

He was shaking his head. "Baby, we don't need a solution! We don't have a problem!"

"Well, if we want one more child, we have a little problem. Jack, it's just surrogacy—it's not brain surgery. There are a number of women who, for whatever reason, are willing to carry a baby for a couple who can't carry their own. They're most often married women who already have children, don't really need or want more, but deal with pregnancy and childbirth very well. Of course, they're paid and their medical expenses covered, but it's rarely a moneymaking proposition for them. It's usually a service they're willing to provide for couples who can't carry and deliver their own baby."

"You really believe that?" he asked. "That it's not about the money?"

She shrugged. "I suppose sometimes money is a major factor, but there are always many screened surrogates to choose from and I wouldn't be interested in one who desperately needs money. Her motivation might not be what we're looking for."

"Listen, I've seen news stories where the woman doesn't want to give up the baby...."

"That usually happens when the woman provides half the biology," Mel said. "When it's her egg involved, sometimes her feelings change while she's pregnant. Then it's *her* baby she doesn't want to part with. Our case wouldn't be like that. In our case, all we need is a womb. A living, breathing petri dish. Problems and complications with screened surrogate applicants are rare." And then she smiled broadly, as if the matter had all just been settled.

Jack picked up his towel and a glass from beneath the bar and began wiping out nonexistent water spots. Mel had learned long ago that that was a move Jack used when he didn't know what to say or how to act. Sometimes he did that to look busy when his mind was spinning out of control, or to keep from throttling someone. "How does it work, exactly?" he asked.

"Well, you determine whether you're good candidates—and I can tell you we are. You look over screened surrogates and interview some. You harvest some eggs from me, collect some sperm from you, have a qualified lab create embryos from our egg and sperm, freeze them, implant a couple in the surrogate and—"

"And get six or eight babies?" he asked, lifting a brow.

"No, Jack. Just one. Outside chance of two, but if you choose a surrogate with a proven uterus who conceives easily, the doctor will only implant one, or a maximum of two embryos. If it doesn't take after a few tries, the doctor might chance three at the outside. Having all the embryos take on the third or fourth try? A miracle. No, Jack. It will be one baby. The chance of two would be the same odds as us having our own set of twins if I still had a uterus and we decided to have one more pregnancy."

His towel-covered hand continued to rotate inside the glass and he was quiet. His face was a stone, void of expression.

"Jack?" she asked. "Not such a crazy idea, is it?"

He let out his breath. "Sometimes it's hard to remember that this sort of thing is your business—your area of expertise. I try, though."

"And?"

"And it might help if you'd try to remember that it is *not* mine."

"And that means?"

He put down the glass and towel. He leaned his elbows on the bar so his face was even with hers. He grabbed her hands again. His eyes and his voice were soft. "Mel, if we hadn't had a baby and you wanted one really badly, I'd do almost anything I could to help that happen for you. If you asked me to think about opening our home up to one more kid, maybe a kid who otherwise might not have parents, I could give that some serious consideration. You know—room in the heart, room in the home. But this thing you're asking…" He shook his head almost sadly. "I don't know if I can watch our baby make another woman fat. I don't know if I can watch our baby come out of another woman's body."

"You don't have to watch," she suggested.

"Getting you pregnant was about the biggest trip I ever had in my life," he said. "Knowing you were knocked up, battling through your mood swings, watching your belly grow and move, then giving birth…it was sacred to me. A miracle. Mel, our two kids and all that went into getting them, hardly anything measures up to that. Something about my swimmers meeting up with your eggs in a dish in a lab, growing inside some woman I don't know…"

"But it's a last resort!"

"No, baby. A last resort is being thankful for the blessings we have. If things had been different and a third one came along, I could live with that. I could be happy about that. But we don't have to have one more." He made a face. "At least not that way."

She chewed her lower lip for a moment. "It's just very strange and alien to you."

"You got that right," he agreed.

"But it's done all the time."

"I don't do it all the time," he said.

"Before you make a final decision, will you at least talk to John Stone about it? The clinic he worked in before coming to Grace Valley had a very active fertility practice. I think Susan said she and John needed a little jump start to get their first child. Would you do that, please? Would you talk to John? Ask him some questions from the man's point of view?"

He pursed his lips for a moment. "For you," he said. "I'll talk to John about it. I'll ask some questions. But the way I feel right now, Mel? This isn't something I want to do."

"Talk to John," she said. "Please?"

He leaned toward her and kissed her. "Okay."

"Thank you, Jack. It would mean a lot to me if you could try to just keep an open mind."

"I'll try, babe. I'll really try."

Erin was bored out of her skull. When Ian and Marcie left her after spending one night, she just sat around for a couple of days. The longest days of her life. But, determined to get a handle on her life and forge a new direction, she pulled out some of the books she'd brought along—self-help books about relaxing, serenity, meditation, the psychology of inner joy, the power of positive thinking, the energy of intention, taking control of your emotional life, and her personal favorite—*Don't Sweat the Small Stuff*.

She'd read many self-help books, but her usual fodder was about focus and effectiveness, organization and efficiency. She *liked* those books; it fed her work habit. In the quiet internal books—she couldn't even find anything to highlight. And Erin *liked* to highlight. It made her feel enterprising.

When she had satellite hookup, she tried TV. Out of three hundred channels, she couldn't find anything to engage her brain. She put on a movie and realized that even her favorite chick flicks weren't as much fun without Marcie giggling or sighing and Ian whining that he was being tortured.

So she e-mailed her office and told everyone even remotely related to her cases and clients that she was computer functional again and already feeling very rested and relaxed, so she had the time to consult if they needed her input. Since they were all at work, the responses came instantly. We're doing fine—just enjoy yourself. Everything under control, boss, have a good time. No problems here, Erin—just make the most of your vacation!

She decided it was probably best to leave the cabin, so the next morning she jumped in her car and headed over to Eureka to do a bookstore prowl. Erin loved to read, but she read for a couple of hours in the evening and had no interest in wiling away an entire day with a book, even a great book. She was much better at staying busy. So, on this trip through the bookstore she bought books on crafts, from gardening to quilting. Before buying any actual craft supplies, she decided she'd graze through the books to see what caught her interest. Lord knew she had never had time for crafts before.

When she got home late in the day, she poured herself a glass of wine and paged through the books. Everything had the same effect on her—it was like watching paint dry. Then she got to the book on gourmet cooking that had slipped in there and her throat tightened up. Her eyes blurred and burned. Gourmet cooking? For one?

The next morning she headed out again—this time to Costco and Target. She bought a hammock to string between two trees and some large, fancy plants and big pots for the deck. When she got home and realized she'd forgotten to buy tools for hanging the hammock or potting soil for the plants, she left the whole business outside for when the spirit moved her. If it moved her.

The next day she just got in the car in the morning and drove; time to see the sights. Time to check out those little tucked-away antique stores she claimed she couldn't wait to visit yet had no real interest in. While she drove, she thought—mostly about Marcie and Drew. She was so proud of them both; so honored to have been the one to help them get to this stage in their young lives.

Finally, finally, finally that time of life she'd worked so hard toward was here—they were truly adults who could manage full, productive, happy lives.

Suddenly she realized she'd driven south for hours and was almost to the turnoff to Clear Lake. She pulled off the road. She could take the turnoff and just go home to Chico and forget this whole summer-on-the-mountain thing. Marcie and Ian wouldn't make fun of her, and Drew was in Los Angeles. The people at the office? They'd talk about workaholic Erin, but she was a partner—they'd talk quietly.

Then she remembered that day in the ladies' room at the courthouse when she'd overheard a conversation about her while she was in a stall. "She goes out with men, but usually once, and it never works out," one woman said. And the other had replied, "She is so uptight, the woman has no life!"

In all the years since she was old enough to date, she'd only dated four men more than twice and all four had had major complaints about her—she was not just uptight and self-protective, unable to let down her guard, but also overconfident, too serious, inflexible and, oh yes, bossy. She worked too hard and too much; she just couldn't relax. She couldn't count the number of times she had been told to *just let go...*

Three of those men had later hired her as their tax attorney and one came to her for his living trust and estate plan.

She made a wide U-turn and headed back to Virgin River.

After the garage sale was over, Aiden took what was left over to the Goodwill receiving depot as donation. When the cleaning, chores and yard work were finished, Aiden and Luke helped move Franci, Rosie and their suitcases into one of Luke's cabins.

In a couple of days Franci and Rosie would go to San Francisco to pick up Sean and bring him back to Virgin River. He had time for some leave, but by mid-July they had to be on their way to Montgomery. They had to find housing before Sean started Air Command and Staff College in August, a one-year program for senior officers who had the potential to be leaders. As in, generals.

The thought of Sean being a senior officer always made Aiden chuckle. He could almost see Luke as a general more than Sean. Sean had always been such a fuck-up. But he'd also been an honor graduate from the academy and a good stick—slang for a pilot with both good instincts and good hands.

After doing his family chores, Aiden was allowed his own time again. He dressed for a hike, but he took his car. He drove right up to Erin's cabin this time, hoping his garden hadn't dried up in his absence. There was no car there, as usual. And his garden seemed to be thriving.

But lo and behold, there was at long last a change. There were three pretty large plants sitting on the deck. Beside them sat three nice-looking ceramic pots. And that was all—no bag of potting soil. So someone had been around. He looked into the house through the French doors—no sign of life in there.

Also on the deck was an opened box displaying a macramé and wood something. He took a closer look. It was a hammock, the instructions lying out, but abandoned. There were no tools there for putting it up, but all that was needed was a screwdriver and small wrench to secure a couple of brackets. So he tended his garden and the next day he brought some potting soil and a couple of tools to put up the hammock. And why was he doing this? Because Erin was completely helpless and he had the time, that's why. Then he smiled a little, remembering the sight of that fantastic booty.

When Erin went fleeing back to Virgin River after her long drive, she stopped in town. She decided to just grab something she could reheat for dinner, so she went to Jack's bar. She recognized the only person there as the local midwife sitting at one of the tables, writing in some open folders. Erin had met Mel on her visit two and a half years before.

Mel looked over her shoulder and said, "Well!

Hello! I knew I'd run into you eventually!" She stood up from her table, pen still in hand, and came to Erin, giving her a friendly hug. "How's it going?"

"Great," Erin said, smiling. "Totally great."

"What can I get you?" Mel asked. "Come and sit with me and tell me all about the family."

"I just thought I'd stop off and grab something I can warm up later for dinner, but you…" Erin glanced at the table Mel had occupied. "You seem to be working."

"A little patient charting. I told Jack if he'd take David with him on errands, I'd do my charting over here and that way if anyone comes into the bar, I can fetch Preacher from the kitchen. The baby is asleep over at the clinic—Dr. Michaels is standing guard. Do you have time for something to drink?"

"I have nothing but time," Erin said with a laugh. "All summer."

"Wow. That must be an amazing feeling."

"Oh, amazing," she said. She glanced at Mel's drink and said, "Diet cola?"

"Gotcha covered," Mel said, going behind the bar. "So, Jack tells me Marcie and Ian are expecting… and what else did he say? Something about your younger brother…"

"Accepted into an orthopedic residency at UCLA Medical Center."

"Wow. I did some of my internship in my nurse-practitioner program there," she said. She brought Erin the cola. "He'll have enough broken bones and car wrecks to keep him busy. I saw the cabin—I hope you don't mind."

"Mind? I'm glad you did! What did you think?"

Mel leaned back. "Well, girl, I saw that place before and after. I don't know how you and Paul managed to get something that beautiful out of some pictures sent over e-mail."

"Collecting the pictures was the easy part," Erin said. "It's still small—just two rooms. Of course, I sent some design suggestions that Paul rejected for construction reasons—we had to modify the design in the kitchen and bathroom to accommodate new plumbing features. After that, it was furniture shopping, which I did well in advance so they could make the delivery date. He's really gifted, isn't he?"

"Paul built our house," Mel said. "He did that as a favor, but now that he's set up part of Haggerty Construction down here, he's the builder of choice. What I'm really curious about, Erin, is why you decided to do this at all. I don't know many people who can manage to take a whole summer off, and you planned it so carefully."

"It didn't really happen that neatly. Ian and Marcie were coming up here for the occasional weekend. Then Drew actually used the cabin as a getaway a couple of times. Both Drew and Ian have been in school and it was a great study retreat for both of them. I was the only one in the family not interested, at least not until the loo was moved indoors."

Mel laughed. "Understandable. I never did go for the idea of the outhouse. Still fairly common up in the hills, by the way."

"I thought I might like to borrow the place if it was spruced up a little. When Ian told me to go for it, I got a little carried away. He admitted he was thinking as far as a septic tank, while I added a whole room and had it rebuilt from the floor up, adding a nice big master bath and full kitchen. Not to mention a stone hearth and covered deck."

"The deck's the best part, I think. Watching a sunset from there must be pure magic. You and Paul make a good team."

"It's beautiful," Erin admitted.

"What made you decide to make a summer of it?" Mel asked.

She shrugged and looked into her cola. "Oh, I don't know. I've been accused of working too much, of not knowing how to relax."

To her surprise, Mel laughed softly. "I can relate."

"You can?" Erin said, eyes wide.

She nodded. "I was an E.R. nurse for years before midwifery, and then I was a midwife in a huge trauma center—we got the most complicated cases. A lot of our patients hadn't had prenatal care and were in serious trouble. My first delivery was a woman arrested on felony charges and handcuffed to the bed, surrounded by police. My older sister, Joey, said I was an adrenaline junkie."

"And then you came here," Erin said. Mel had actually shared her story with Erin on her only previous visit when she had come looking for Marcie to bring her home. Mel had told Erin her first husband had been killed in a violent crime and she'd fled L.A. in search of a major change.

"The joke was on me," Mel said. "I was looking for

peace and tranquillity and ended up being hijacked out to a marijuana grow op to deliver a woman in a life-threatening childbirth situation. I was almost killed by a grower who broke into the clinic looking for better drugs than his pot. And my own baby was born out at the cabin Jack and I lived in, by candlelight, because a bad storm knocked out the lights and phone. A tree blocked the road and we couldn't get to the hospital."

"Really?" Erin said, her eyebrows lifted high. "You didn't tell me any of that before."

"You came to get Marcie and she didn't want to be rescued," Mel said. "I didn't think it would help Marcie's cause much. Anyway, so much for me giving up adrenaline. I have to admit, though—most days are peaceful. It's just that when they're not, they're really not."

"Frankly, I could do with a little excitement," Erin grumbled. "I swear to God, if one more person sends me an e-mail about taking time to smell the roses…"

Mel just laughed at her. "Erin, don't be talked into feeling a certain way. If working is what's fun for you—then work!"

"You're not going to lecture me on balance?" she asked with a smile.

"Don't you have that? Family, friends, a getaway cottage in the mountains, an exciting job…?"

"Tax and estate law?" Erin asked, wide-eyed. "I think the fact that I find that exciting is one of the things that people think is most disturbing!"

"I wasn't going to mention that." Mel chuckled. "But if you find it exciting…"

Erin leaned toward her. "I've worked really hard,"

she said earnestly. "I did the things I set out to do. I have a very large client base. You can believe the partners never suggest I'm working too hard. The firm takes a lot of their pro bono cases off the backs of my rich clients who are in trouble with the IRS. My client base is so valuable to them, I had to threaten to resign to get a leave of absence from the firm. I hadn't taken more than a long weekend in ten years. Drew's in residency and engaged to be married soon to a lovely girl. Marcie and Ian are very happy, and expecting their first baby at the end of the summer. The pressure is off! I can now relax and enjoy life more and I can't think of one thing I want to do."

"Oh. My."

Erin leaned back. "It's true. Don't you dare tell anyone—but I haven't been here two weeks yet and I'm so bored I can't stand to wake up in the morning, facing another long, impossible, dull day! I've been putting in so many hours for so many years...."

"Law school then a busy practice..." Mel said. "That's been a long haul, I'm sure...."

"It started way before law school. I was busy as a kid, needed to help at home."

Mel frowned. "Marcie mentioned you girls lost your parents young...."

"Our mother died when I was eleven. Marcie was four years old. Drew was still in diapers."

Mel thought for a moment. "You must have done a lot of babysitting...."

Erin laughed. "A *lot?* That was all I did. I hurried home from school to take over from the babysitter we'd hired, start dinner, wash and fold some clothes, get their baths, settle them down for the night. The sitter usually left things a mess and I didn't want Dad coming home to that, he was already a wreck. Our dad tried, but he'd just lost his wife and it took him a good year to catch up with us."

"It hasn't just been ten years since you've taken a vacation, has it?" Mel asked softly.

"Dad died suddenly during my first semester of law school. I was still living at home, of course. Drew and Marcie were only thirteen and fifteen. It wasn't a problem for me to have complete custody of them, at least."

"At what? Twenty-two?"

"I was mature," Erin said dismissively.

"I'll bet," Mel agreed. "And now, having done a lifetime's work in a third of a lifetime, you're feeling a little put out to pasture? Like you don't have a purpose anymore?"

"Oh my God," she said. "I couldn't put it into words, but it's like I have to take the summer to figure out how to be alone, and happy and content alone, because what I am now is *alone*."

"And you're how old now? Thirty-five?"

"Thirty-six."

"Erin, my darling—you're thirty-six and you've been a mother for twenty-five years. You're going through empty-nest syndrome."

"What?"

"We make so many sacrifices to parent…we give up so much. Willingly, of course. It's what most of us want to do—to have a child and make that commitment. Sometimes it comes as a blow when they say, 'Okay, I'm all grown-up now. Back off and let me make my own decisions.'"

"But…but I talk to Marcie every day, and Drew at least a couple of times a week. We're still very close."

"Well, of course! They love you! But at long last they're on their own. They don't need you. You have all this time to make a new life…. Because your old life is over…"

"But I have women friends who load up a suitcase full of books or tapes or needlework and head off for a week of solitude and love it. Or go on these enormous walks through Ireland or hike the Grand Canyon and—"

"Erin, for one thing—they didn't start at age eleven. You've been dancing as fast as you can for twenty-five years, just trying to stay one step ahead." She leaned toward Erin and grabbed her hand. "You were just a kid when you had to start being a mother to your siblings. And there's a difference between getting away and feeling cast away. Besides, I bet you never had the luxury of finding great, fulfilling hobbies!"

And Erin thought, *I couldn't try out for cheerleading, not that I could walk and chew gum at the same time. But there was after-school practice, and after school was dedicated to the kids. I could be on student council, but I couldn't go to student-council camp. Well, Dad said I could, but the look on his face said it would be a huge burden and he'd worry about the kids without me there.*

But she'd never cared about that. Had she?

"Yeah, my dad depended on me," Erin said. "I was

going to do that up here. Find a great fulfilling hobby of some kind. So far I haven't thought of a thing."

"You're still trying to cope with the loss. The empty nest."

"Really?" she asked. "You think that's all it is? Empty nest?"

"*All?*" Mel asked. "Erin, that's a lot of loss. It's a little death. Some women just blow it off. When their kids go off to college or get married, they just close the vents in their children's rooms or turn those spaces into dens and sewing rooms. Other women really struggle and feel a lot of emotional pain. You were awfully young when you started mothering them."

"Huh," she said. She took a drink of her cola. "Well, what am I supposed to do for fun now?"

"Gosh, I don't know," Mel said. "There's bound to be a period of adjustment. You've probably been going through a period of grief already and maybe you're not quite done with that. Something will come to mind." The door to the bar opened and a man in rough-sewn work clothes wandered up to the bar. Mel looked over her shoulder. Then back at Erin. "Can you tend bar?"

Five

All the way home, Erin thought about what Mel had said. Of course she was right. The empty feelings had started when Ian and Marcie moved into their own home. She'd been so happy for them, but she also had that empty, lost feeling inside. And shortly after that, Marcie had told her she was pregnant. She had hosted a dinner to celebrate that event—Ian was absolutely lit from inside, he was so alive and excited, but her feelings were a mixture of excitement and emptiness.

It wasn't just the empty nest. She was also grieving that lost childhood, the lost young womanhood, and the fact that she was thirty-six and had never put any energy into a lasting relationship or children of her own. And how was she supposed to do that? Given a choice, there was no way she could have cast Marcie and Drew to the wind and told them to do their best while she worked on her personal life. Instead, she had helped nurse Marcie's disabled husband, Bobby, helped Drew study for the MCAT to get into med school and worked her ass off to build an impressive clientele that pumped money into her firm, into her bonuses, and helped pay for med school, which cost the earth.

Lost in her thoughts, she put the dinner she had brought home from Jack's in the refrigerator for later.

She took a low-fat yogurt and spoon out onto the deck, sat in her chaise looking out at the magnificent view and began to softly cry. She was thinking about the prom, of all things. She had picked out a prom dress one year, but she hadn't been asked. And why would she have been asked? She was never available for the social things. No one knew she was alive. *Fuck the prom,* she thought. *I didn't care about the fucking prom. Which is why I'm actually crying!*

"I should've gone on a goddamn cruise with a bunch of goddamn old people," she muttered, giving a sniff and a hiccup.

Suddenly, a head covered with dark hair and a full red beard peeked around the corner. "I didn't know you were home," Aiden remarked. "I didn't hear a car."

Erin's eyes grew round, she gasped, and then instinctively dug her heels into the chaise to push herself away from him. "What the hell are *you* doing here?"

He came around the cabin and stood in front of the deck. He was wearing his uniform of fatigue pants, T-shirt and boots and held a rake or something in his hand. "I thought you'd left. Given up and gone back to the city or something. But then I saw stuff, like the plants and pots, but no potting soil or fertilizer. I was trying to think of something to give you to say I regretted the head injury. I'm not taking responsibility for it, you understand," he said, putting up a hand. "But I was going to get you a plant or something, and then I noticed the garden. Uh, well, it was sort of a garden...."

Erin wiped impatiently at her cheeks, trying to be nonchalant about it. "It turns out gardening isn't my thing...."

"Yeah, I got that impression, but I thought maybe—" He bent at the waist and peered at her, frowning. "Are you crying?"

"Of *course* not!" she slammed back. "I have a little cold, or allergies, or something. My nose is runny, that's all."

"Oh. Sure. So I got to thinking, maybe you just needed a little help getting started. It's been a while, but when we were kids, my mom kept a garden and made us all help, so I..." He squinted at her. "Allergies, huh?"

It was then that she noticed the plants she'd bought were now potted and sitting in the corners of her deck. "You potted the plants?"

"And got your vegetable garden going. It's a little late, but with the right amount of fertilizer and water, you'll get some stuff. Tomatoes if there's enough sun. I put some flowers around the border. I planted sunflowers because they're fun—you can almost see them grow. You could use a border of flowers along the front of the cabin. They're on sale right now. I thought

I'd run over to the nursery sometime this week and get you some, if you don't mind. You can take it from there."

She put aside the yogurt and stood up. "And if I just pack up and leave?" she asked.

"You thinking of doing that?"

"It's possible I'll be needed at work," she lied.

"Well, I don't have anything better to do than check on your garden now and then. Maybe you'll be back in time to harvest a tomato or two."

She walked over to the edge of the deck to look into the backyard. There was a perfect square, the soil tilled and rich-looking, staked markers showing where things were planted. There was no mistaking tomato plants, much larger "starters" than she had begun with. The whole thing was bordered by a short metal-mesh fence and marigolds. She had read that much—marigolds would keep some of the bugs away.

"You put a fence around it?" she asked.

"It won't keep the deer away, but it might discourage the bunnies. For deer, you should pee around the edges." Then he grinned. "That's what I hear. There's an old woman who stops by the bar in town who has a garden about the size of a small farm—she swears by a human-pee border for deer."

"You hung up the hammock?"

"I probably should've asked," he said. "I saw it on the deck and I wondered if you just couldn't figure it out."

"I couldn't," she said. "I thought I needed parts."

"Nah, it's all there. Maybe you had another couple of trees in mind?"

"No. That's perfect."

"Listen, I don't mean to pry, but are you recently divorced or widowed or something?"

"No," she said, frowning, shaking her head. "Why would you ask that?"

"I don't know," he answered, also shaking his head. "Plants and pots, no potting soil…hammock, no screwdriver or wrench…vegetable plants and flowers, no hose or adult-size gardening tools. It's like the stuff the husband remembers to pick up."

She let a small laugh go. "Just never had time for any of this stuff before. And you're partly right—my sister and brother-in-law lived in my house for over a year. My younger brother—he's twenty-seven—was there till last year. I was always working—if I brought home a bookcase or patio furniture or a hammock, one of them took care of assembling it. And if they didn't, I knew who to call. Up here? Who do you call?"

"Well, maybe your friendly neighborhood vagrant," he answered with a big smile. "I'll get out of your hair." And he turned, leaned the hoe against the deck railing and walked away.

"Where are you going?" she asked.

He looked over his shoulder. "Home."

"Where's home?"

He stopped and turned. "My brother has some cabins along the Virgin River. I'm renting one while I think about what to do next. I'm unemployed, remember?"

"How could I forget? But I was informed by a very crabby nurse that you're actually not a vagrant, even if you look and smell like one. You're recently discharged from the navy. Can I drive you home? As a thank-you for the gardening help?"

"I like to walk," he said. "From home to here and back—a little over ten miles." This was all true, except his car was parked at the bottom of the hill at an outlook point. Just out of sight of the house.

"Would you like some water?"

"I have water," he said, bending over to pick up his backpack, which waited for him beside the garden. He also picked up the bow and quiver, machete and favored walking staff.

"Would you like a….a *beer?*" she tempted.

"You're being friendly, this is a whole new you." His white smile cut through the red beard.

"Well, you've done some nice things, and the E.R. nurse thinks you're relatively safe. Thank you for putting up the hammock."

"You're welcome. Thank you for offering a beer, but I might smell like a vagrant. Or a gardener."

Her smile was indulgent. "I'll bring the beer out to the deck," she said.

He chuckled to himself as he turned around and came back toward the cabin. But when he got to the deck in front of the pretty, open French doors, he didn't choose one of the chaise lounges. He was dirty and smelly; he'd dug around in the garden for a while. His hiking boots were muddy, his hands dirty, he was sweaty and smelly in general. Instead, he perched on the step, leaning back against a railing, and stacked his things on the ground in front of the deck.

She brought him a beer and, surprise of all surprises, one for herself. And she was smiling. She was looking real good in her fitted khaki capris, white T-shirt and sandals. She obviously got up and did her hair and makeup every morning whether she had somewhere to go or not, but then he'd already established she was a dish. Prissy and feminine.

He rubbed his index finger at his hairline in the middle of his forehead. "It'll grow back before you know it."

Her finger went there, as well. "Looks pretty awful, huh? Well, I can't do anything about it now, except be patient."

"It doesn't look bad at all." He took a long pull from his beer bottle. "Nice," he said. He held it away and examined the label. "Good beer."

"My brother-in-law left it."

"Your brother-in-law was here?"

"The hospital called my sister and brother-in-law and said they'd release me if I had a driver and wasn't going to be alone all night, otherwise they wanted me to stay overnight in the hospital." Erin shrugged. "Marcie knew I'd hate that. They drove up from Chico. Bailed me out."

His grin was huge. "I heard you in the E.R., Erin. You really know how to throw your weight around."

"I had a headache," she said, looking away.

He chuckled. "Any more head pain?"

"No, it's fine now."

"Why are you here? At this cabin?"

"Vacation," she said. "I haven't had a vacation in a

long time. Like years." She smiled slightly. *Twenty-five years,* she thought. Until Mel said it earlier, she hadn't really added it up.

"But why here?" he pushed. "Why not some spa in the islands? Or a resort somewhere exotic where there would be lots of singles to mix it up with?"

She shrugged. "Marcie, my little sister, age twenty-nine, is expecting her first baby, a boy. Our parents are gone, I'm the oldest, and this is the first baby, due the end of summer. I really don't want to be too far away, just in case she goes early, but I still wanted to get away."

"Ah," he said. "Now, I can relate to that. My brother's wife, Shelby, is expecting their first around the middle of July. Luke is the oldest. I could sit out this transition anywhere, but I don't want to be too far away." He smiled again. "Also a boy."

She tilted her head. "What did you do in the navy?"

"I was in the medical corps. Fourteen years."

"Why'd you get out?"

"The reason most people get out—the next assignment didn't look so good. It was a big boat for two years. I already did that once. Like I said, I want to be around for the next baby."

"But you're not married?"

"Divorced eight years ago. Short marriage, quick divorce, no children. You?"

She shook her head quickly. "Single." Never married, never engaged, never lived with anyone, never very involved. "This is embarrassing. I've forgotten your name."

"Don't be embarrassed. You had a head injury. It's Aiden."

"Well, Aiden, what do you suppose you'll do next? After the little nephew is born?"

He shrugged. "Same thing as before, I guess. Thing is, I'm really enjoying doing nothing. I hadn't been on leave in a while—that's vacation to you civilians. I'm in no rush. I could get used to this."

She didn't smile at that. "Doing nothing isn't as much fun as I thought it would be."

He lifted an eyebrow. "That so? What did you do for fun and relaxation in Chico?"

"Chico? How did you know I was from—"

"I dug through your purse for your keys…took you to the hospital…talked to the nurses to be sure you were all right… Plus, you just said your sister came up from Chico and I assumed…"

"Of course. Well, that's the thing—there wasn't a lot of free time in Chico, which is why I decided I had to actually leave town to get a break, but like I said—"

"You didn't want to get too far away. What's Chico like?"

"Nice town—not too big, not too small. Right on the other side of that immense mountain range. The hustle and bustle there isn't real intimidating, but we have everything, either in Chico or close by—colleges, hospitals, malls. Maybe a hundred thousand people? I haven't checked lately. Not a bad freeway drive to Sacramento or San Francisco. I think it's perfect, but I grew up there."

"Hospitals?" he said, lifting that brow again.

"Hospitals," she confirmed. "Thinking about that hospital job?"

He tilted his head. Almost a nod.

"I suppose the navy had you living all over the world.…"

"Yes and no. When you're aboard ship, you see a lot of water, but dock in some interesting places. I got off a ship about eight years ago and was stationed in San Diego. They must have forgotten about me. I was there the whole time except for a few temporary duty assignments in other places. Pretty unusual to be able to have one home base that long in the navy."

"And you don't want to live there?" she asked. "I love San Diego."

"I could live there," he said. "Or here—I could live here. But a guy like me, looking for hospital work, probably needs a bigger town than Virgin River."

"What's someone like you do in a hospital? Pass that bedpan around?" she asked.

"As it turns out, I'm pretty familiar with the bedpan. The question is, would a woman like you take a bedpan from a guy like me?"

"Maybe if you shaved…"

He scratched his beard. "You know, when the military keeps you shaved, spit and polished for a long time, something like this is fun. It's kind of like having a pet."

She laughed. "It looks like it might bark. You could always upgrade your job skills, you know. Take some training. Maybe be a paramedic. Or nurse. I bet male nurses are in high demand."

He smiled broadly. "Now, there's a thought." He tipped his beer bottle and drained it. "This has been real nice, Erin. Thanks for the beer." He put the bottle on the deck near her feet and stood, gathering up his stuff.

"What's the bow for?" she asked.

He slung it over one shoulder. "Mostly for looks, it turns out. On one of my first treks through these mountains I came face-to-face with a mountain lion who was not shy. Took him a long time to run off, and for a while there I thought I was going to be his lunch. I started carrying the bow and arrows when I hike back in here."

"What about that great big knife?" she asked.

"If a mountain lion gets close enough for me to use this," he said, hooking the machete to his belt, "I'm going to get scars. This is for weeds and shrubs blocking the trail, not for self-defense. Or homicide, as you originally assumed."

"Wouldn't a gun make more sense?"

"Probably," he said with a shrug. "I don't like guns so much. The boys—my brothers—they all hunt. I don't hunt."

"Hmm," she said, standing. "Sure I can't give you a lift?"

"No, you sit tight. I like to walk."

"You're sure?"

"Absolutely. Work on vacationing. I get the impression you're not that good at it yet."

"Yeah, that seems to be the case...."

"I put gardening tools in the shed and hooked up a

hose with a spray nozzle. There's also a sprinkler in the shed. If you think about it, give the tomatoes a drink."

"Wow. You really went to a lot of trouble."

"I didn't even think about it, as a matter of fact. Just seemed what needed to be done at the time. You're happy about it, though?"

"Sure. Of course. Really, thank you. Be careful, then."

"Always careful, Erin." He gave her a little salute and walked off.

So, the nurses hadn't told Ms. Erin Elizabeth Foley he was a doctor, Aiden thought. Interesting. And he hadn't learned what he had about her from digging through her purse and talking to the E.R. staff, but from reading her chart upside down as it sat open on the nurse's desk.

She had made a lot of assumptions about him, which was very unlawyerly of Ms. Foley. But it worked for him. He wasn't about to lie, but withholding was fair game. And not, as Noah had suggested, so that she'd feel really stupid. Rather, so she would be forced to know the man and not the credentials, if she was so inclined. Aiden was not self-deprecating—he knew very well what his assets were. He wasn't bad-looking, at least when he was cleaned up and shaved. He was intelligent and articulate, and absolutely had to be sensitive in his line of work, dealing with the most personal parts of a woman's anatomy for a living as he did.

And of course *he* thought he was fun, but that was so subjective. And yet, whenever he dated someone, ninety percent of the time he felt as though they weren't comfortable just being themselves around him. Now, *that* was a double-edged sword. Not only did some women try to impress him because he was a doctor, sometimes covering up their good old natural charm, but there was the flip side—hiding their psychopathic tendencies, like his awful ex, Annalee. Aiden just wanted to be a boy getting to know a girl. How hard was that?

He was probably overthinking, especially where Erin was concerned. She was an attorney, after all. And clearly a successful one—he could tell not only by her classy cabin and clothes, but by her confidence. Make that overconfidence. She would not be intimidated by a mere physician; she would not start acting as if there were bonus points involved in catching one. And it was very likely they weren't even going to be friends, much less anything more.

So why not just correct her misassumptions?

Because it would be fun, that's why. Let her get attracted to a guy who couldn't make in a year what she paid in taxes—fun. Uh-oh, he thought—he wanted her to get attracted to him? Well, she was hot. Gorgeous. That silky strawberry-blond hair, sweet complexion, incredible smile, beautiful long legs, tight butt… He had been struck by her physical assets the second he saw her, but then she had opened her mouth….

Today was better. She was just as hot, but when she

opened her mouth she was actually a human being. So, a little cat and mouse didn't really hurt anything. He wasn't lying; yes, he'd been at one with the bedpan and worse. Obstetrics could be real messy work.

He thought about these things as he walked down her mile-long driveway to the road. Probably another reason he was a little overly cautious where women were concerned—he'd had that wife. Hmm. He'd risked court martial when he crawled between her legs. He was fresh off a boat when he was completely seduced by a sexy young navy corpsman who worked in the hospital. She was the twenty-one-year-old daughter of Russian immigrants who wanted to get out of the navy and saw Aiden as her ticket. She was a sub-ordinate, enlisted personnel, and he was schtupping her. She was so young, but not only wasn't she exactly naive, she was the most gifted lover he'd ever experienced.

And they were quickly found out. In retrospect, she obviously leaked it. Aiden's commander suggested the quick fix of marriage and she would be discharged. Voilà, just what she was looking for. She dropped the placating behavior and turned on the shrew. It didn't take him long to understand—she wanted to leave the navy with a little pocket change. The price of his quickie divorce, handled by a friend of a friend, was ten grand. And a lesson hard learned.

Annalee certainly hadn't been in awe of him, the doctor. He had been exactly what she was looking for and she had used her many wiles to catch him, willing to do anything to please him, and please him she did.

Right up until she started screaming and throwing things.

And that brought to mind the fact that she was now looking for him. Fat chance, Annalee. Never gonna happen.

He got to his car, threw his stuff in the back and took off for home. As he drove into the cabin compound, he passed Rosie and her mom fishing in the river and gave them a toot of the horn and a wave. As he pulled up to his cabin, he saw Luke and Art having a heart-to-heart on Luke's porch, their facing chairs pulled close together. He gave another toot and wave. Then he went inside for a shower.

Luke had brought Art up from the river to the porch for a talk. He popped the top on a cola for him, told him to sit down and said, "Okay, I found where Netta lives and I talked to Ellen."

Art's eyes lit up and he got very excited. "Okay, Luke. Let's go there now."

"Not right now, Art," Luke said. "Ellen said you can visit on Sunday afternoon, and I'll be glad to take you. Today is Thursday, so you have to be patient. But right now I want to know—what kind of friend is Netta?"

Art looked a bit confused. "A good kind?" he said in the form of a question.

Luke was uncomfortable, and when he was, his neck got red and he scratched it absently. "Right. Good. What I mean is, when you visit with her, what will you want to do with her?"

Art straightened very proudly. "I want to date with her."

"Ah." Luke sighed. "Now we're getting somewhere. Have you dated with Netta before?"

"I don't think so. We talked and held hands sometimes. But Shirl used to make the girls stay on one side of the house and the boys on the other side, except for eating and TV."

"Well, I've got news for you—dating is mostly talking and holding hands. Also, eating and watching TV," Luke informed him. "But I have a couple of concerns, Art. Because you've been so excited about seeing Netta again, some things have come to mind. Like—do you know about sex?" His neck got redder.

"Yes," Art said confidently. "Yes, I do, Luke."

"Well, that's a relief." Luke let out a breath he'd been holding for a long time. "Thank God for that. Who taught you about sex?"

"My mother," he said. "Sex?" he asked. Then he made a check mark in the air with his finger. "Male!"

Luke dropped his head into his hand. "Aw, man," he groaned. He lifted his head wearily. He saw Aiden drive in after another one of his hikes. They all waved and then Luke said, "Listen, we're going to have to talk about some things before you visit with Netta. And I don't know where to start."

"Does she want me to visit with her? Ellen? And Netta?"

"Yes, Art. They're happy about it. Ellen said that Netta's asking about you. So it's all good. Except for the parts I haven't figured out yet."

"What parts? I don't know the answer to that."

Luke patted his knee. "Let's worry about one thing at a time, Art. One thing at a time." And then he heard an engine, like that of a big city bus, and looked up to see a big, flashy RV coming down the driveway to the cabins. "Oh, man, I have never been so happy to see my mother. That's Maureen and George, Art. They're visiting in a brand-new RV. That should take your mind off things for a while."

"What things?" Art asked.

"I rest my case," Luke answered, standing up and waving them in. Good God, when she said motor home, he had been picturing one of those little fifth wheels! He opened the door and yelled into the house, "Shelby! Baby, you don't want to miss this."

Rosie came running from the river, Franci behind her. Shelby came out on the porch and Aiden stepped out of his cabin wearing sweatpants and a T-shirt, rubbing a small towel over his hair and beard.

Aiden's quiet retreat time in Virgin River was officially over. His brother's place had become a madhouse.

Luke had a three-bedroom house and six one-room efficiency cabins. Art had one cabin as his own, Aiden rented one, Franci, Rosie and Sean would use another for a couple of weeks and two others were rented to tourists. Since Shelby and Luke did not provide restaurant services and the real attraction of the place was the great outdoors, the tenants weren't usually much in evidence. There was a couple in their sixties who were in Virgin River for bird-watching and a group of four college-age women who had planned a week of hiking.

With the gathering Riordans, it didn't take long for the compound to take on a carnival atmosphere. As Shelby's burden was still lowering and her walk was taking on that strain of a woman in late pregnancy, it was past time to put the nursery right. They already had a bassinet and small bureau in their bedroom for newborn needs, but Shelby's uncle Walt and his lady friend, Muriel St. Claire, wanted to be involved in the painting, papering and decorating of the baby's room. Of course, Maureen wouldn't be left out of that. And Vanessa, Walt's daughter and Shelby's cousin, couldn't stay away, either, and where Vanessa went these days, two small children followed.

Within a couple of days the place was teeming with Riordans and Booths. Right in the middle of all the action, Luke pulled Aiden aside. "I need your professional help, man."

"Shelby okay?" Aiden asked reflexively.

"Fine, she's just ready to explode. I need your help with Art. He's all steamed up about visiting Netta, who he says he wants 'to date with.' I had a talk with him, Aiden—he doesn't know anything about sex. Nada. Nothing."

Aiden just grinned. "Maybe he doesn't need to know anything."

"We can't take any chances. The last thing I need is Art getting some girl pregnant because he doesn't know anything."

"And you want me to…?"

"I don't know. Talk to him. Take him to Fortuna to see his girl and talk to the girl's caretaker or whoever that Ellen is she lives with. Make sure we're on top of this."

"You probably don't have the worries you think you do," Aiden said. "First of all, it's very likely Art is just excited to be with an old friend. He actually lived in the same house with the woman for a long time and they've bonded. Sexual intercourse probably never occurred to him, but even if it did, chances are he's infertile. It's not uncommon for Down syndrome men to be infertile. Not always impotent, however."

"She's not Down's, Aiden," Luke said. "Can you help? Because I can't get away from him long enough to go over to Fortuna and have a face-to-face with Ellen—Art always has me in his sights. Besides, look at Shelby. I should be close."

"I'll do this for you," Aiden said. "But stop worrying about Shelby. You're going to have plenty of time when she goes into labor. Maybe days." He smiled. "It's coming at you from all angles, isn't it?"

"All angles. My mother is here with a boyfriend! My buddy Art is in love and doesn't have a clue what that's doing to his head and he depends on me to keep him safe. And my wife is about to explode!"

Aiden grinned. "Calls for a beer."

"Don't be funny, Aiden. How can I drink a beer when my wife is this pregnant and my helper is about to commit sex without his knowledge. Have you seen him lately?"

"Whew. We might want to slip a little Xanax in that beer," Aiden said.

It was true that Art was very excited about seeing Netta. And he might even be in love. He was emotional and probably even hormonal about the whole thing, but as Aiden and Art chatted about the situation on the way to Fortuna, it was obvious that Netta was an important part of his past, his life, his experience, and he cared deeply about her. They liked the same television shows; they had worked together and helped each other and they both had lost their parents and were dependent on the state. Netta could read better than Art, but he wanted to teach her fishing. He also wanted to date her, but when Aiden explained that it would probably be best if they were just very good friends and spent time together regularly—watching TV, fishing and reading—Art accepted that so readily, it was probably what he thought dating was.

When Aiden arrived at the house where Netta lived, he introduced himself as Dr. Riordan, Luke's visiting brother. He thought it might encourage Ellen and her husband, Bo, to open up a little bit, but they seemed not to need any encouragement. They had raised their three children, were grandparents and had three special-needs adult women in their care—all of whom helped in their bakery part-time, their skills varying greatly.

Iced tea was served on the patio while Art and Netta enjoyed being reunited and fled to the backyard, still within view. It didn't take long to cut to the chase— Netta's brain damage was pretty extensive, the result of an early-childhood near-drowning accident. She'd come a long way; walking and talking had taken years to accomplish. She was a very tenderhearted, calm twenty-seven-year-old who had the mental capacity of a ten-year-old, just about equal to Art's. While both of them could identify a few words and most letters, neither could read very well.

The whole time Aiden visited with Ellen and Bo, Art and Netta were in the backyard, sitting on the edge of a sandbox for the grandkids, doing more staring at each other than talking.

"Your brother told me a little about how he came to be Art's guardian," Ellen said. "Of course, we got Netta when that group home was closed. It was a real difficult time for her—she lost her home, her job and her friends."

"Art, on the other hand, ran away when he was battered," Aiden said. "Luke found him digging through his trash. He had a big black eye."

"That's kind of unusual," Ellen said. "I mean, for Art to run away like that—it's enterprising. Wandering off or getting lost, that's not uncommon. Has he been happy with Luke?"

"Very content, as far as the family can tell. Luke was single when he ran across Art, but he's married now and expecting his first child soon. His wife, Shelby, and her whole family all love Art. But none of us has much experience with special needs or Down syndrome adults. Luke has some pretty obvious concerns—like when it comes to dating…"

"Sex?" Ellen asked. "Is that the concern?"

"Should it be?" Aiden asked.

"We'll have to join forces to keep an eye on what's happening with them," she said. "If their relationship starts to look too serious, it might be enough to distract them. For now, being alert chaperones will probably do the trick. All of our women are on long-term birth control just for safety...."

"Because you've noticed some need? Sexual acting out, that sort of thing?"

Ellen shook her head. "No, Dr. Riordan—libido can be all over the map with special-needs adults— some seem to have a very active libido, sometimes masturbating or flirting or even trying to inappropriately touch a member of the opposite sex with no regard to boundaries. Our women really haven't demonstrated any appreciable libido, but the birth control they're on helps with that and with PMS. We also have to keep them safe from pregnancy by a predator. We do everything we can to keep them safe, but we can't hide them from the world and the reality is, there are bad people out there who prey on the disadvantaged."

Aiden didn't often come up against things he was completely ignorant of—but this was one. His training prepared him to offer birth control for mentally challenged women who might have sex because they had no discretion, but this hadn't been a concern in his military practice. Predators? "Has there been an issue with sexual abuse?" he asked.

"No history of that as far as we know and no symptoms that we noticed, but it's a danger. Two of our women have Down's and their vulnerability shows on their faces. Plus, they're so trusting, so anxious to please. They so often will just do as they're told. But isn't Art...?"

"Infertile? My brother doesn't know if he's been tested. For that matter, Art doesn't seem to know if he's been tested. I haven't seen any of the signs of sex drive that you mentioned, and he's a very gentle soul."

"You probably would have had hints by now, if he had a high-functioning libido," Ellen said. "We belong to a support group for the parents and guardians of mentally challenged adults and one of our friends has a young man who masturbates quite a lot. It's sometimes difficult to distract him. I think what we have here with Art and Netta is a perfectly nice friendship."

"Maybe if we manage to arrange quality time for them, they'll be very happy."

"Mentally challenged adults fall in love all the time, Dr. Riordan," Ellen reminded him. "As a couple, they often end up living with one of their parents, or together in the same group home. It can be complicated in some cases, and I know people who would go to great lengths to discourage relationships like theirs. But doesn't everyone deserve to feel love and affection? No matter their disability? I see my primary job as keeping Netta safe and from getting in over her head. If what you say about Art is true, she's interested in a very sweet and kind man."

"Art is an angel," Aiden said. "And he's very functional. He's been with Luke a couple of years now and hasn't had a single problem. He loves working with

Luke, loves fishing in the river, never wanders off. It's been good for both of them."

After two hours of chatting, they came up with a plan. Twice a week, when possible, Art could visit. If Luke could just call in advance, there would probably be times he could drop Art at either the bakery or the house to see Netta while Luke ran errands. If either Ellen or Bo was available to take Netta to Virgin River, she could spend a few hours at the river, learning to fish and visit with Art. They would have phone numbers for each other. That was a good place to start. Just a little reassurance that they wouldn't lose each other in the system again might be an enormous comfort.

Art's behavior on the way back to Virgin River seemed to reinforce that idea. He clutched the piece of paper with Netta's phone number. Art had never spent any time on the phone, but just holding that number appeared to give him such confidence.

Aiden had a stop to make and Art was fine with that. Aiden drove straight up that road to Erin's cabin. "Where's this?" Art asked him.

"The person living here was trying to make a garden, so I helped," Aiden said. "I just want to check it. Maybe water it."

"Okay, Aiden."

Erin's car wasn't parked at the cabin, so Aiden took a six-pack of beer out of the back and sat down on the deck to write a note. *Chill this. My whole family is in town and it's a circus. See you soon. A.*

Then he went to look at the garden. Well, well— she'd been tending it. The soil was moist and the weeds were few. He went to the shed that was back against the trees, got out his tine cultivator and scrambled up the dirt a little bit. He bent to pull a few weeds, then dragged out the hose to spray it down. Art wandered around the backyard. "Don't go in the forest, please," Aiden yelled.

"I'm not," Art yelled back.

Eventually, Art ended up in the hammock, still strung between the trees. He was swinging himself a little wildly and Aiden hoped it wouldn't break loose. Art was not small!

"Hey," a woman's voice said. "I thought you'd given up on me." She was smiling and holding the six-pack in one hand. "I tried to keep it going."

"You did fine," Aiden said. He stepped over the short fence. "I thought I'd leave some beer and maybe next week…"

"Sure," Erin said. "Next week." She looked beyond Aiden. "Friend of yours?"

"Yeah, that's Art. Did I tell you my brother has some cabins on the river? Art's a helper of his. We were just out running some errands and I thought I'd swing by and check the garden. You haven't escaped back to the city yet?"

"Not yet. But I've discovered the best reason to work sixty hours a week is daytime TV."

"Only sixty." Aiden grinned. "Slacker."

She grinned back. "I guess the navy works you 24/7."

"Well, they do, but remember I told you my sister-in-law is very pregnant? Family is gathering. They tend to take up space and time."

"What kind of family?" she asked.

He shrugged. "My mother—in her sixties—arrived in an RV with her seventy-year-old boyfriend. That's hitting a nerve or two. One brother is due back from Iraq tomorrow, on leave, staying in the cabins with his family. My pregnant sister-in-law has a lot of family around here and they're always available, if you get my drift."

She had a kind of melancholy smile. "Sounds like fun, actually."

"I guess so." Art came up behind Aiden. "Oh, Art—this is Erin. Erin, this is Art."

"How do you do?" she said, nodding.

"Thank you," he answered, and they both laughed.

"I'm sorry, Erin, I have to get Art back. I'll see you later. The garden looks good."

"So do you," she said quietly.

Art perked right up. "Maureen says he looks…he looks…ghost…gast…"

"Ghastly," Aiden said by way of helping. "My mother put her hands on both sides of my face and said I looked ghastly. Horrible. Dangerous. So I guess you weren't alone in that early opinion." He turned and handed the long-handled tine to Art. "Would you mind putting this out in that shed?"

"Sure, Aiden." And he trudged across the yard.

"He's very sweet," Erin said.

"He is that. How are you doing?"

"Great," she said with a smile. "Totally great."

"Good. See you later."

"I'll chill the beer."

Six

"Are you going to date with her?" Art asked while Aiden was driving them back to Luke's.

"I think we'll just be friends," he said, though he had started hoping they'd be more. He wasn't sure when or how, but he'd figure that out after their next beer together.

"Luke says dating is talking and holding hands and watching TV."

Aiden thought, I don't remember Luke dating like that.

"Maybe dating with a girl is drinking beer, too," Art said.

Aiden chuckled. "You know, Art. Sometimes you catch more than you miss. Listen, would you do something for me, please?"

"Sure, Aiden. What?"

"Would you mind if we didn't tell anyone about the garden?"

"Why?"

"Well…" Aiden thought for a minute. "Well, at the end of summer when there are fresh tomatoes and some vegetables from the garden, I might get to have some. And I could surprise Luke and Shelby with them."

"Oh," Art said. "Okay, then."

By the time Aiden and Art got back to the cabins, Sean had just arrived and the carnival atmosphere had been cranked up a notch. There was nothing to compare to the air of celebration surrounding a returning soldier, or in this case, airman. The crowd wasn't limited to the Riordans and Booths; some folks from town had stopped by—Jack and Preacher, their wives and kids, other friends and neighbors. Luke had pulled out the large gas grill and two coolers were filled with ice, sodas, bottled water and beer. Walt Booth had brought wine; he uncorked the white and settled it against ice in the cooler and uncorked the red and put some bottles out on the picnic tables to breathe. Even the folks who rented the cabins were invited to join them.

After embracing his younger brother, Aiden set about helping Luke turn hot dogs and hamburgers on the grill. The women put out condiments, chips, potato salad and coleslaw. Preacher brought a couple of pies and Jack contributed a big tub of ice cream.

Sean could not be urged very far from Franci's side; he hadn't seen his wife in six months and his first night stateside in a San Francisco hotel was spent with his wife and little girl. His arm was securely attached to

Franci's waist or shoulders, pulling her closer whenever he could. His mother finally came to his rescue.

"Rosie, would you like to spend the night with Grandma tonight?"

"Do you still lib in dat RB?" Rosie asked, her eyes wide.

"Yes. There's an extra bed. And we can have popcorn and watch a movie if you like."

"But Daddy said you din't lib in dat RB right now. He said you libbed in sin. Where is dat?"

There was a slight hush just before laughter rocked the whole compound. When it finally let up, Maureen replied coolly to her granddaughter, "Ask your daddy, sweetheart. He's an expert."

Sean flushed scarlet, but when the laughter subsided he looked at his watch and announced, "Time to pack up Rosie for Grandma's, honey. Then we better get to bed so all these nice people can go home!"

Once the party had broken up and Aiden had helped Luke with cleanup, he retired to his cabin and turned on his laptop. He had seventeen e-mails, but he checked the one from his friend Jeff first. You didn't call her, you loser, and she won't stop calling me. No matter how many times I tell her that calling me won't get you to change your mind, she won't stop. Do a guy a favor, huh? Call Annalee. She says it's urgent. She won't tell me what's urgent, but she won't stop! Here's the number you probably threw away.

Aiden wrote back at once. She won't tell you what's urgent because nothing between us is urgent and talking to her at all is like inviting the plague into my life. Please—just tell her I'm dead.

Things in Virgin River had been pretty quiet, even if there was family en masse out at the Riordans' on the river. A couple of days after welcoming Sean home from Iraq, Jack Sheridan was in his usual place behind the bar when one of his favorite customers came in. Brie, his younger sister, was seldom seen around town during the day. She was a lawyer with an active practice that usually had her driving all over the mountains and valleys and as far as Eureka where she consulted with the D.A.

"Well, sweetheart," he said. "What brings you to my office?"

Brie jumped up on a stool. "I was hoping we could talk," she said.

"Sounds serious. Can I get you a drink to go with that expression?"

His sister didn't answer. "Jack, there's a pink elephant in the living room and it's a surrogate pregnancy." Jack's chin dropped and he stared down at the bar. "Are we going to talk about it or keep pretending it's not there?"

He lifted his chin. "What can I say?"

"Say something, Jack," Brie insisted. "Because Mel has been asking me to contact her old fertility doctor in L.A., to get familiar with all the legal ramifications so that I'll be ready to negotiate a contract. Meanwhile, she's got an appointment set up for later this summer to have her eggs harvested. Where do you stand on this?"

He looked away uncomfortably. "I don't want to," he finally said.

"Why? What's going on?"

Again he glanced away. Then he grabbed a glass and dish towel from under the bar and began to absently wipe out the water spots.

Brie closed a hand over his glass-and-towel action. "Put it down and talk to me. I'm all grown-up now and among other things, I'm your attorney."

"Did Mel ask you to talk to me?"

"No. In fact, we were on the phone a little while ago and she said she had a patient at Valley Hospital, so I thought it was a good time to come over here. Let's stop screwing around, Jack. It's obvious you and Mel aren't on the same page here—she's hounding me to get moving on this and you haven't even weighed in!"

"I'm worried about her," he said softly. "I was hoping this would go away."

"It's not going away, it's gaining momentum. Now, what's going on?"

Jack shook his head. "We don't need a baby. We're having enough trouble hanging on to two little ones with our schedules and obligations. Three might really tip the scales, but that's not it, Brie—if Mel hadn't had a hysterectomy and another one happened along, we'd manage. It's this idea she has that she has to beat the odds. Even a hysterectomy won't make her vulnerable. If she wants another one, by God she'll get one. Even if it costs thirty thousand dollars and involves a third party we've never met."

"Is it the money?" Brie asked him.

"God, no! I'd buy her the moon, you know that! What do we need money for? Our family is priority. It's just the whole idea. The way it happens."

"People do it all the time, Jack," Brie said softly. "It's a great solution for people who can't just have children the old-fashioned way. A growing number of people, by the way."

"I know this," he said. "I asked Preacher to look it up for me. He printed me off a lot of stuff from the Internet. Sometimes there's an infertile husband or wife and donors are used. I guess that's so people can grow their own rather than adopt. Whatever works, I say. This would be ours. Her eggs and my sperm would meet in a tube and then grow inside the body of some woman we've interviewed. Some woman we'll pay to be the incubator."

"Is that it, then? The idea that you don't know the woman and you pay her to do the job?"

"Partly," he said with a shrug. "That much is irregular, if you ask me. I mean, if we were a couple who met, fell in love and said to each other, 'By God, we gotta have at least five kids to be happy,' maybe I'd feel different. But we weren't that couple, Brie. We were a couple who thought we were using birth control in the first place. Mel kept saying two was one more than she'd counted on. A couple years ago Mel almost died in a uterine hemorrhage. John did all he could, but taking the uterus saved her life. And he told me to be prepared for her to struggle with the loss—but not Mel. She bounced right back, just grateful we have each other and a couple of healthy kids. Now, all of a sudden, she's hell-bent to have a third one, even though it's not something we ever talked about." He leaned his elbows on the bar. "Brie, she's ready for you to draw up a contract and has an appointment to get her eggs harvested and I haven't said I'd do it."

"Could it be she knows you will if it's important to her?"

"I'm afraid she's trying to push back time," he said. "I'm worried she's not really okay with being a thirty-six-year-old woman whose childbearing is over. It's like she's not okay with us, the way we are."

"No, Jack…"

"Do you know what I felt like when she got pregnant even though she wasn't supposed to? I felt like Atlas, that's what. I felt like a small god. Like an Olympian. Watching her get fat and moody, it was a *miracle* to me. My woman took me inside her body and created a life for us to share. Jerk off in a cup and watch it grow in someone I don't know?" He shook his head. "We don't need to do that, Brie. We just don't need to."

Brie's mouth actually hung open for a moment. Then she said, "Whoa."

He absently wiped the bar. "It's not the process that bugs me," he said. "Understand, it's not the process. I think the fact that this can happen at all—this surrogate thing—this is a gift from God. If Mel came to me—you know, when we met—without that uterus, and wanted a baby bad enough to do it the surrogate way, oh, hell, yes, I'd do anything for her. You know that, right? That I'd do anything for her? But I don't know if I'd be helping her much by going along with this. I'm not sure where this is coming from."

"Well, you better find out, Jack. Talk to her."

"Brie, she's not exactly talking to me. She's waiting for me to come around. When I bring the subject up, she just asks me to keep an open mind. She wants me to discuss my reservations with John Stone."

"Then talk to John. But don't let this thing fester between you. I'm dangerously close to getting in the middle of it, and I don't want to be there."

Out of sheer boredom, Erin decided to bake chocolate-chip cookies. She thought if she had them on hand and Aiden showed up, she could give him some to share with his friend Art. She could also freeze a bunch—Marcie and Ian were planning to come up for the next long weekend and Marcie *loved* chocolate-chip cookies.

June was growing old, she was on her fourth week in the cabin and she had stacked all the inner-growth books in a corner to be given away. On the deck beside her chaise where she relaxed between cookie batches was a tall glass of tea and a paperback with a pair of long, shapely female legs on the cover and a provocative title. Marcie was right about one thing—the damn book totally had her! Nothing like seduction to totally seduce her. She smiled to herself—she might just be learning this relaxation thing.

She had a huge bowl of cookie dough on the counter and when the timer went off, she went inside to scrape hot cookies off the cookie sheet onto the counter and make another batch. She inhaled deeply; the aroma was heavenly. Erin had a pretty healthy sweet tooth that she kept under control, but there was absolutely nothing quite as alluring as that fresh-cookie smell. After sliding a sheet of cookies into the oven, she dashed into the bathroom. Ah, how fantastic that she wasn't going to the loo out back! Besides, it was a spectacular bathroom for a cabin and she was proud of it.

Before she came out, she heard a noise and wondered if a hearty breeze was blowing things around in the kitchen. There was a bad smell. It almost hinted at a plumbing problem. Or perhaps that breeze had picked up a bit of garbage on its way through the French doors. When she came out of the bathroom she saw it was not a breeze.

It was a bear.

It was a very large bear—and he was eating her cookies and cookie dough, scooping it up with hands that sported long, dangerous claws.

She yelped in surprise and the bear lifted his head out of the bowl and it sounded like he belched. That's when Erin screamed.

She ran back into the bathroom and slammed the door, locking it. Then she dashed through the adjoining door to the bedroom and slammed that door. To be safe, she pushed the chest from the end of her bed up against the bedroom door. Then she closed the door that joined the bath to the bedroom and pushed her bureau in front of it. That was it—all the movable furniture she had. And it wasn't all that heavy.

Then she sat on the foot of her bed and said, "Fuck."

She hadn't even considered this possibility—a bear. Marcie had told her a story about a mountain lion trapping her in the outhouse. From that point on, Marcie had carried the iron skillet with her whenever she was outside. For that reason, Erin always had that big skillet with her. But while Marcie was just the type to plaster a threatening wild animal in the head with a skillet, Erin was more the type to squeal and run.

She remembered she had cookies in the oven. *Oh, this is rich,* she thought. *The cabin is going to burn down and me with it. Hopefully the bear dies first. Maybe I can get away before it's all one big ash.*

She did a mental inventory; there was only one phone—a cordless that was on its base in the kitchen. The computer was actually running—and it was out there, too. If her car keys were in the bedroom, she could climb out the window and make a dash for the SUV, but of course the keys were in their assigned place, on the hook by the door. Erin was very well organized and tidy—a place for everything and everything in its place.

There was a crash and she winced. She jumped off the end of the bed and started for the door to scream at the damn bear. This was a terrific lesson for Erin— for just a moment she was more concerned about the bear trashing the place than about it mauling her or burning the cabin down.

She forced herself to sit down. Then she flopped back on the bed. "I hate my life," she said out loud. "If I live through this I'm going home and back to work and I'm never doing anything like this again." There was another crash. Oh, that sounded like something very expensive. She lay there in misery for a long time. She could hear him moving around out there.

There was a little tapping at her bedroom window. She sat up and listened. Yes, a very light tapping. Would a nine-foot-tall black bear high on chocolate tap at the window? Wouldn't he just tear off the door and eat her? She crept quietly and carefully to the window and peered through the tiniest slit.

And saw green eyes and a red beard.

She opened the shutters and the window. "Aiden!"

"Hi," he said. "There's a bear in the kitchen."

"Run, Aiden! Run!"

"I'm going to come in, but you have to give me a hand. Help me take off the screen, then I'm going to throw my stuff inside and climb in. You might have to pull me—this window's kinda high."

"Why?" she asked, backing away a little.

He shrugged. "Well, first of all, there's smoke coming from the kitchen. And I was thinking about a beer."

"There's a bear in the kitchen!" she whispered furiously.

"Yeah. We better get him outta there." They pried off the screen and he threw his backpack and machete through the window. Then he leaped at the opening, got his arms locked on the bottom sill, pulled himself up and somersaulted right into the bedroom.

Erin got out of his way. The second he was sitting on the floor, she closed the window *and* the shutters. Then she crossed her arms over her chest. "Great. Now we're both held hostage in the bedroom."

"How long has he been out there?" Aiden asked, getting to his feet.

"I don't know. Half an hour?" There was another crash and again she winced. "He's obviously done eating and is busy tearing up the place. I swear to God, if he shits on my Aubusson carpet, I'll kill him with my bare hands!"

Aiden couldn't help but laugh as he dug around in his backpack. He pulled out what looked like a large can of hair spray or a small fire extinguisher. "Do you have anything in here that would make a loud noise, kind of like a metal spoon clanging inside an aluminum soup pot?"

"Huh?"

"They don't like that. This is repellent. A little clanging and some repellent and they usually just run off."

"Usually?"

"What are the options? I've been thinking about that beer all week."

"I know you have easier ways to get a beer." She sneered.

"You're right. Should I take my repellent, climb back out the window and leave you here to rot? You can sit in your bedroom until someone passes by and smells your decomposing body. *Or*—you can find me something that clangs!"

"I don't have anything in here that clangs!"

Aiden looked around, doing a three-sixty of the bedroom. His eyes stopped in the corner. He went over to a fancy potted tree; he opened the shutters and window, dumped a three-foot tree upside down out the window and banged the empty pot on the side of the house to get rid of the excess dirt.

"Hey!" she yelled. "That's *brass!*"

He walked toward the bedroom door with his arsenal in hand—brass pot and tall can of repellent. "Brass, brass, could save your ass…" He pushed the chest away from the door. "Erin, listen to me. Do *not* scream. It's a black bear and I didn't see a cub, so it should just run off. But don't scream and get it riled up. It could make him or her feel threatened."

"I already screamed at it," she informed him. "He didn't run off! Maybe he doesn't know he's a black bear!"

"Just stay in the bedroom. Quietly."

"What are you going to do?"

"I'm going to step into the next room and clang. If he comes at me I'm going to spray his eyes with this pepper spray. Then I'm going to have a beer."

"Oh God…"

"Yeah, praying works…" He opened the door, looking into the room. "Oh, good," he said quietly.

The bear was exiting the house through the opened French doors. On the one hand it was probably best to just let him go, but on the other—would he remember where to find the food? Aiden hated to think of Erin lounging in her hammock, dozing, while a bear rummaged around in her house. But Aiden didn't have a lot of experience with bears. He'd have to ask someone.

He let the bear lumber off. He wasn't a very big bear—six feet. Had to be a guy—in spring and summer the females came with at least one cub, unless she was a teenager and hadn't mated yet. Aiden followed slowly, cautiously. He got all the way to the deck in time to see the furry guy disappear into the woods. Then he put his pot and can of repellent on the table, picked up Erin's glass of tea and her book and closed the French doors. He looked curiously at the book, lifting one eyebrow.

Then he rescued the charred cookies and turned off the oven.

"Is it safe?" he heard from within the house.

"Well, unless you wanted a cookie. There were some casualties."

"The bear?"

"His work here was done," Aiden said. "He was alone and he's gone."

Erin walked into the great room. She looked around—the giant bowl she'd used to mix the cookie batter was in pieces on the floor, a chair was turned over, a cookie sheet was across the room on the floor. The three crashes were minor losses and the bear was gone.

"I'm getting the hell out of here," she muttered.

Aiden stooped to pick up the pieces of broken ceramic bowl. He dumped them in the trash. No mess there. The bear had cleaned it thoroughly. "You don't have to." He picked up her paperback. "I rescued your dirty book," he said with a smile.

"It's not dirty!"

"Oh? Too bad. It looks pretty good."

"It's just a…a…women's book…you know…"

He pulled a couple of beers out of the refrigerator. He took the tops off two bottles and handed her one. "I'd like to sit out on your deck with this," he said. "Especially since I walked ten miles to get here today and I know I'm not wearing your fragrance, but under the circumstances, maybe we'll just stay in. What do you say?"

"I'm getting the hell out of here!" But she took the beer; then she took a slug.

"It'll be okay, Erin," he said softly. "He's gone. I'll leave you the repellent. They don't have grizzlies around here. Black bears will usually run off unless you're between a mother and cub. Apparently they like chocolate-chip cookies. I don't suppose you tucked any away before Yogi came in?"

"No! And you can be damn sure I'm not making any more!"

He pulled out a chair from the kitchen table. She pulled out a chair and sat. He leaned toward her. "You don't have to go. If the doors are closed, I don't think they'll break in. Well, a raccoon might sneak in, but they'll often run if you just bang a pot."

"Do you have any idea what you're saying?" she asked.

"I'm saying—don't go, Erin. Just give it a few more days and you'll see—the wildlife won't bother you if you're unobtrusive. If you see a bear, bang a spoon inside a soup pot. Really, they don't like people."

She frowned. "Unobtrusive? What kind of a word is that for an EMT to use?" she asked.

He lifted a brow and grinned. "Big?" he asked hopefully.

"I don't know. I should pack and start driving...."

"Don't," he said. "We can have some fun, you and me...."

"I haven't seen you in days! I'm going—"

"The family was gathering and I had to help. To tell you the truth, they're already on my nerves. But I think they're all settled in now. Stay a few more days at least."

She leaned toward him. "Why?" she asked earnestly.

He shrugged. "You're the prettiest girl I've seen in Virgin River." He grinned. "I'll leave you the repellent, but you'll have to drive me to town. There's a bear hopped up on chocolate out there and I'll be unarmed." He leaned toward her. "Listen, take your phone and repellent into the bedroom and close those doors when you go to bed tonight. Put the dresser in front of the door if you want to. Make sure you don't have any food or garbage out where a bear could smell it or get to it, and see if you don't feel better about this in a day or two. You can always call the sheriff's department and tell them a bear got right in your house—they might put out an alert, just in case it's a troublemaker."

"My good sense says that staying would be taking a ridiculous chance."

"Really," he said. "Don't go. Not yet. Honest—I wouldn't suggest it if I thought there was any real danger."

She thought for a minute, then she shook her head and said, "If a bear eats me, you're going to feel terrible."

"I think if you leave I'll feel terrible."

Luke Riordan had always been an early riser, but it was definitely more pronounced now that he had a wife in the late stages of pregnancy. It was hard for Shelby to get comfortable, or stay comfortable, and sometimes she was up in the night rooting around for Tums or ice cream for the heartburn that inevitably settled in after she'd been lying down.

He had no complaints about the lack of sleep or the early hours. He wished she could have it easier, of course. It looked to him as if she was carrying way too heavy a load for her small frame, and he had concerns about her being able to give birth to his son. That kid was ready to ride a skateboard out of Shelby, and she still had at least a couple of weeks to go! Fortunately he was surrounded by experts. Mel said, "Yeah, I think I was pretty much that size or worse—amazing, isn't it?" Jack said, "I feel your pain, my brother." Aiden said, "She's sure getting there, isn't she?" No one was panicked, so he decided not to panic.

He woke early, wandered through the cabin area with a cup of coffee, checking out the grounds, which were usually peaceful at that hour of the morning. After just a couple of nights with the RV in the compound, George and his mother had taken it over to Noah's place so they could spend some quality time with George's family. Then they had reservations at an RV park in Fortuna where they could get a hookup, which meant their plumbing and electricity would be maintained by the park. Much more convenient. And since they had towed his mother's small sedan, they had no trouble getting around without dragging their entire house with them.

Sean, Franci and Rosie weren't up and about yet. Art wasn't a real early riser. Aiden had begged off dinner the night before, saying he was going over to the coast and would get something to eat over there. There was nothing mysterious about that. Why would a thirty-six-year-old bachelor feel like spending night after night with his brother and incredibly pregnant sister-in-law?

But as Luke walked past Aiden's SUV, he noticed the man had the backseat collapsed and there were a couple of new bikes in there. He peered into the window and saw they were trail bikes, a boy bike and a girl bike. Interesting. Couple of helmets there, as well. And there was a basket thingie—like something that attached to a bike. A picnic basket? Luke wondered. Well, how *precious*.

While Luke was standing there with his cup of coffee, the door to Aiden's cabin opened and he came out. Luke nearly stepped back in shock. Aiden was clean shaven. He didn't even look like the same man. With that beard gone and his black hair trimmed, Aiden didn't look *capable* of producing that big red bush on his face. "Whoa," Luke said.

"It got a little itchy," Aiden said.

Luke just grinned. "You lyin' sack of shit. You did it for a woman!"

"Get real," Aiden said.

"Who is she? You meet someone over on the coast?"

"Nah. I just got tired of looking like a vagrant, that's all. And Mom hated it."

Luke laughed heartily at that. "You are *so* full of shit," he said too loudly. "You have a boy bike and a girl bike and a fucking picnic basket in your car!"

Aiden stood still and glared at Luke. Aiden might not be the oldest, but he was very good at affecting a superior expression. "This camp isn't going to get five stars in the AAA brochure if you wake the guests at dawn with your asinine guffawing," he said.

"I would'a loaned you the Harley, Aiden, so you could take your woman on a manly ride," he said, grinning widely. "All you had to do was ask."

"Those manly rides crack heads and break femurs," the doctor replied.

"Yeah? Wait till one of those logging trucks tries to pass you while you're on one of those pussy things. You'll wish you had my Harley under you."

"You about done?" Aiden asked.

"Not even getting started," Luke said with a laugh. "Come on—who is she? What did you find over on the coast? And how long ago? When do you expect to be home? We have a curfew around here, you know."

Aiden walked around Luke, lifted the hatch and reached inside to pull out his nifty new basket.

He closed the hatch and went back into his cabin. "Don't wait up, asshole," he said over his shoulder. He slammed the cabin door. For someone who advocated quiet for the guests, he wasn't being particularly considerate.

Luke laughed again with delight—Aiden had a female somewhere. Big surprise—Riordan men didn't have dicks so much as divining rods. And they had always taken great pleasure in their brothers' conquests, provided they weren't total nutcases. Unfortunately, there had been some memorable ones.

Luke heard a sound and looked over his shoulder to see his wife come out on the front porch of the house, her belly preceding her. Her long hair was messy from sleep and she wore a pair of his boxers with the waistband rolled down under her belly and one of his T-shirts pulled over the top. How, he asked himself, can she look so pregnant and so sexy at the same time? He just shook his head and went to her. With one hand holding his mug, he slipped the other arm around her and pulled her against him. He kissed her forehead and his son kicked him.

"You get any sleep?" he asked her.

"Uh-huh. I feel pretty good. I feel huge, but good." She looked down. "I have ankles."

He looked down. "I see that. Nice." He backed up a step and sat on one on the chairs, pulling her onto his lap. "Come here. Sit on my lap and if you're sweet, you can have a little sip of my coffee."

"Mmm," she hummed, grabbing his mug. "What was all that noise? I heard you laughing."

"Aiden's got himself a summer girl," Luke said.

"A what?"

"A summer girl. He found himself a woman. He's got bikes in his car and—" Luke stopped as the door to the cabin opened and Aiden emerged with his basket. He balanced it on a hip and gave Shelby a wave. Then he got in his car and backed out of the cabin compound.

"What?" Shelby asked again, once Aiden's car was gone.

"Aiden's chasing tail," Luke said.

Shelby shook her head and sighed. "You are so delicate," she said, running her fingernails through the short hair at his temple. "Remind me, you are not allowed to train our son in the manly pursuits. I'll take care of that. You're crude, rude and socially unacceptable."

"What? Aiden's chasing a woman! How mysterious is that? I hope he gets lucky, that's all. But knowing Aiden…"

"Knowing Aiden, what?"

Luke shrugged. "He's kind of, I don't know, not exactly after it. You know?"

She laughed at Luke. "My dear husband, Aiden is totally hot!"

"Aiden?"

"Oh, yes. If I weren't married and seventeen months pregnant, I would so be after him!"

"Aiden?"

"Luke, you really have no idea."

"Baby, he's got bicycles in his car! I told him he

could have the Harley, but he's got bicycles! How hot is that?"

"He is completely and totally sexy."

Luke was quiet for a minute. "I don't want to hear this."

She laughed at him, kissed his neck, and his baby kicked.

"Bet he can't do that," Luke said, rubbing a hand over her big belly. "Bet he can't make one like this. This kid is going to come out half-grown."

Shelby just shook her head and moaned. "Oh, Luke, you are such a comfort to me. I don't know how I resisted you as long as I did."

Seven

Aiden drove up the road to Erin's mountaintop and was relieved to note her SUV was still there—she hadn't run. He got out of his own SUV, leaned against it in the opened door and hit the horn. He had to hit it again and again before she appeared, standing in the cabin door, a plush robe wrapped around her. Her feet were bare; she rubbed the top of one foot with the toes of the other. Her hair was mussed and he got a little turned on. She was without makeup; she'd been asleep and she woke up pretty and sexy. He counted that as a very good sign. "Oh, good," he said. "You actually got some sleep and the bear didn't eat you."

She squinted at him. "Aiden?" she asked. "Aiden?"

"I shaved and got a haircut. You can never tell when I might have an interview for a job or something."

"I meant to mention when you turned up with Art, I'm impressed you actually have a car. One that's under ten years old. Wow."

"Get dressed—I'm going to take you out and show you how to have fun." He wore shorts, tennis shoes without socks, a light jacket over a T-shirt, ready for a casual day.

"Huh? I was asleep!"

"It's time to get up, Erin," he said patiently. "Put on some shorts and tennis shoes. I have sunscreen…. You have that weak redhead's skin and we have to keep you from getting burned. I don't suppose you have a ball cap?"

"No," she said irritably.

"Well, I brought you a helmet, you'll be okay. I have bikes and a picnic lunch in the car."

"But I haven't had a shower! Or breakfast!"

"I can wait a little while, but let's not burn daylight. I'll buy you breakfast. Or grab one of those candy-ass yogurts for the road."

She crossed her arms over her chest. "What makes you think I want to go on a bike ride?"

"Total and absolute boredom, that's what," he said. He grinned at her. "Isn't that what drove you to bake for the bear? Come on, I *shaved!* How much effort do you want from me?"

"You could *ask,*" she instructed.

He slammed the car door and walked toward her. When he was right in front of her he said, "Don't stand on ceremony. You don't have anything better to do. Now how about you get dressed and let's head for the coast. I'll show you how to vacation. Then I'll bring you home and water your tomatoes." He grinned lasciviously.

She thought about this for a moment and decided to ignore the double entendre of his comment. Instead, she asked, "Bicycles?"

"Yup. With helmets and a picnic lunch."

"Well, all right. But after this, you have to ask in advance."

He lifted a brow. "Should I ask your secretary to put me on your calendar?" He grabbed her upper arms, turned her away from him and gave her a slap on the rump. "Move it—I don't want to wait all day for you!"

One of the realities of being a well-known, success-ful attorney—Erin couldn't remember anyone *ever* slapping her on the rump to get her going. *Ever.* Not even those few men she'd dated more than twice. She was conflicted—there was a part of her indignant that he'd take such liberties, part of her delighted.

It hadn't escaped her that under those smelly hiking clothes and the coarse red beard was an unbelievably handsome, good-smelling man. Almost knee-shak-ingly handsome. He had high cheekbones, glittering green eyes, pitch-black hair, a strong chin, expressive brows. And maybe if he hadn't had that bushy red beard before, she might have noticed he also had a fan-tastic physique—broad, muscled shoulders, a flat belly, a cute masculine butt, straight, powerful legs.

But he was a little arrogant, assuming that if he showed up, she would spend the day with him. Of course, he *had* saved her from the bear. Sort of. And he was right—she didn't have anything to do. Still, she didn't omit even a minute of her ritual grooming, though she knew the effects would be lost once she was biking—something she hadn't done in *years!* She was a little pouty in the car en route to the coast, but then when they were driving along a winding road on the high cliffs above the ocean, the beauty stunned her, dazzled her. "Ohhhh," she said, letting out her breath.

"'Bout time," he said. "What's not to like about a day riding along the ocean? You'll love it and you'll sleep like the dead tonight. Guaranteed."

Aiden parked his car at an outlook point and asked for her help getting the bikes out of the back. He had an open basket that he attached to the handlebars of his bike and put a plaid blanket in it. On the back he attached the picnic basket to the seat and fender. Their lunch, she presumed. He pulled a backpack over his shoulders; he was taking the whole load. Then he squirted sunscreen in her palm, and when she was done smearing it on her arms and legs, he fit the helmet onto her head. "I'll follow you," he said. "It's safer."

As he pulled back his hand to give her a whack on the butt, she skittered out of his way. He chuckled.

"Which way?" she asked.

"Any direction you like."

She looked north and south; south looked flatter. She mounted the bike and took off. And pedaled like mad, while behind her, traveling at a nice clip, Aiden was whistling.

Like every other aspect of her life, from her diet to her morning exercise program, Erin had a strict routine. She did some yoga and weights; she walked on the treadmill and StairMaster now and then. Forty-five minutes every morning. But endurance training like biking or running? She never had the interest or time. Within five minutes she was panting and sweating and behind her—that infernal whistling. But damn him, she kept going and refused to feel guilty that she wasn't any faster or stronger. After all, his days were probably spent working, and then working out right before a night of chasing women. *She* worked at least twelve-hour days in an office or courtroom. But she pushed herself on that bike for an hour, by which time she wanted to *die*.

When she was almost ready to throw in the towel, the air was pierced by a whistle and Aiden yelled, "Pull over!" She was so grateful she could have kissed him. He dismounted and was walking his bike down the beach on the hard-packed sand and she followed. Finally he stopped and pulled a couple of sports drinks out of the backpack, handing her one.

"What's the matter?" she asked a little breathlessly. "Tired?" She sank onto the sand with an *oomph,* making him laugh. She sucked down half her drink with a lot of glugs.

Aiden fell to his knees. "Little bit competitive, Erin?"

She wiped her mouth with the back of her hand. "Possibly." Then she smiled. "Okay, I admit it—I'm not in the best shape."

"Your shape looks pretty good to me."

"Well, now," she said. "I wondered if you were flirting with me. I mean, getting rid of my bear was one thing, but shaving?" She laughed. "I think when you shave and talk about my figure, that's definitely flirting. So, what is it you hope to get out of this flirting? Huh?"

"I don't know," he said. "What kind of law do you practice?"

"Estate and tax law." She lifted a brow. "How's your relationship with the IRS?"

"I've been in the navy. Not a lot to worry about hiding. And I'm a single man—my mother's in my will. She gets the life insurance."

"God forbid," Erin said.

"Is that what makes a girl so tough and competitive? Law school and a legal practice?"

"I think being a *girl* in law school and in legal practice is what makes me tough and competitive," she said with a smile. "Plus, there was a lot of pressure at the time. My parents died too young. I'm the oldest and had to look out for my younger brother and sister."

"The sister's pregnant, right?"

"Right. Due the end of summer. Ninety percent chance she'll have a C-section—the baby's breech. Marcie's hoping he turns, but right now she's scheduled for August 20, a couple of weeks before she's due."

"So that's when you leave?"

"A few days before that at the latest. Really, I'm not sure I can coexist with that bear.…"

"Damn bear," he muttered. "Just when you were baking for me…"

"I was baking for Marcie and Ian—they're coming up next weekend. And I was going to let you have some cookies for Art."

Aiden grinned at her. "Want to ride a little more before I feed you lunch?"

"Okay," she said tiredly, stretching out her back.

"This time let's go at a more leisurely pace. I promise, I'll let you win."

The second hour of riding was much more pleasant than the first; Aiden hung back so she wouldn't go too fast. Because she wasn't bent over the handlebars pedaling like mad, Erin was able to appreciate the ocean, the cool breeze, the vastness of a blue sky with so many powder-puff clouds. And all the while oblivious to the fact that Aiden was enjoying the shape of her butt and the length of her legs.

When Aiden whistled for her to stop the second time, Erin was almost disappointed. He rode down a length of hard-packed sand amidst a lot of huge, protruding rocks. The northern Pacific beach was very rocky. Aiden stood the bike on its kickstand and unfurled the blanket from the basket, spreading it on the sand. He detached the picnic basket from the rear of his bike, put it on the blanket and sat down.

"Not fancy," he said. "But besides chocolate-chip cookies, I don't really know what you like."

She sat on the other side of the basket. "At this point, I like everything. You've had me pumping a bike for a couple of hours." She helped herself first to a bottled water and took a long drink. Then she discovered a couple of sandwiches, apples and brownies. While they ate lunch, she asked him about his family and learned about the five military sons. He told her about growing up in the Midwest, the middle of the five boys. "We lived in a small three-bedroom house—three boys in one room and two in another. Our father was an electrician who had to take as much overtime as he could get to feed us all, which left our mother responsible for the raising and discipline, something she was very good at. We called her the Enforcer. She's an amazing woman. Very strong, and until recently, she was very narrow-minded."

"What happened recently?"

"She got herself a boyfriend. And she's living with him in an RV. They plan to drive around the country, visiting friends and children and seeing the sights."

"That actually sounds like fun," Erin said, biting into a ham sandwich.

"It does," he agreed. "Some of my brothers are disgruntled about it. I don't blame them—she was always so critical of the way we all seemed to be playing the field, dating a lot of different women... Until a couple of months ago, she was still twisting the ear of any son over thirty years old just at the suggestion he'd had sex with a woman he wasn't married to. Now my sixty-three-year-old mother is living with a guy."

"Just how many different women?" she asked cautiously. "I mean, when you say playing the field..."

He bit into his sandwich. "Not to worry, Erin. Of all of them, I was always the most careful. I haven't dated anyone in months. Well, that's not true—I've had dates—a couple of dinners out, met friends for drinks, that sort of thing. I haven't had sex with a woman in quite a while. And I always use protection."

Her cheeks actually glowed. "I didn't mean—"

"You should mean that, and you should ask, it's reasonable. Don't look now, but this is a date. The bear doesn't count, but this counts."

She looked down. When she raised her eyes, she said, "Is this when you ask me about my dating history?"

He shrugged. "Only if you feel like talking about it."

"I don't date much," she said. *At all. Ever.* "I've only been on a few dates the past year—all of them first dates."

"Hard to please?" he asked.

"I think so, yes."

"And you're busy," he said.

"Does that sound like an excuse? Because really, a lot of people depend on me and I take that very seriously."

"The little brother and sister?" he asked.

"Oh, they're all grown-up and doing great. But I have clients with serious tax issues. I also have clients with delicate family relationships who need help with their estate planning and trusts. There are other lawyers and paralegals and a legion of legal secretaries to help, but I'm the partner who manages that for the firm. I haven't taken a vacation in a long time." *At all. Ever.* "I had to plan this time off from the firm for a year."

"Why no vacations?" he asked.

"You know. The same reason as everything else. Busy. People depending on me."

"And you're here because it's close enough to get to your sister if she needs you?"

"Of course," she said. "It's my first nephew. The first baby in the family. And Marcie and I are very close. Plus, I thought it would be so relaxing up here. I hadn't accounted for the bear."

"Hopefully he doesn't bother you again," Aiden said, and lay down on his back on the blanket.

"Hopefully," she said, lying down also, on the other side of the picnic basket. "Aiden, did you grow up kind of poor?"

"Depends on your definition of poor. It's probably more accurate to say we grew up on a tight budget. My mother really knew how to stretch a dollar. We ate a lot of mac and cheese. We had a big summer garden and she canned. What she didn't grow she bought at the farmers' market. And the woman was a genius with soup. We ate so much soup that now I don't even *like* soup." She giggled. "Colin was the only one in the family to get all new clothes all the time because even though he was second born, he outsized Luke. The rest of us got new jeans when the hand-me-downs got handed down too much, but everything in our family was stretched as far as it would go. I got screwed—I was third. Stuff lasted just about long enough for me, but by the time it got to Sean or Patrick, it was too worn-out and had to be replaced. I guess that's why everyone enlisted—there was no hope of college being paid for. Although…"

"Although what?"

"There were some scholarships and financial aid. My brothers Sean and Patrick went to military academies— one air force, one navy. I had a partial scholarship…."

"And worked as an EMT," she filled in for him. "What's the most important thing you learn as an EMT?"

He thought for a second. "Load 'em and go, go, go!" She laughed and he turned on his side, facing her. "Really, getting someone to the hospital is what that job is all about. Although I did learn some good emergency procedures—resuscitation, how to stop bleeding, that kind of thing." He smiled. "What to do with a head wound. But an EMT is not usually as highly trained as a paramedic, depending on where you work." He flopped on his back. "How about you?" he asked.

"I don't know how to stop bleeding...." She yawned. "Did you grow up poor?"

"Nah, middle class. My dad had even saved a little for college. We had...I mean we *have* a four-bedroom house—everyone had a bedroom. I still live in that house. It's not a new house, but it's been fixed up regularly. Modernized and redecorated. It's a very nice house." She yawned again. "Big kitchen."

They fell silent for a while.

"Aiden?" she asked. "Did you go to the prom? In high school?"

"What?" he asked. "The prom?"

"Yeah. Did you go?"

"Hmm. Senior year. I had a girlfriend."

"I bet you've almost always had a girlfriend," she said softly, tiredly.

There was quiet again and both of them nodded off on the beach, side by side on the blanket, their bellies full, the sun shining down on them and the crashing of the waves all around them.

Too soon, Aiden was jostling her. "I hate to do this to you, Erin, but we have to pedal back. We can't sleep here all afternoon. We'll freeze to death next to the ocean at night and there are no lights on the bikes."

"Mmm," she said, sitting up sleepily. "But that was nice."

He slipped an arm around her waist, brought her up against him and kissed her forehead. "Told you you'd like it."

On the way home they stopped at a restaurant in Fortuna, a fish place, and ate out on the patio. By the time they got back to Erin's cabin, the summer sun was setting, which made it after eight. He walked her to her door and grabbed her jaw in one big hand, his other arm around her waist. "Close the doors like I told you, have the phone and repellent with you in the bedroom. You'll be fine." He pulled her closer and gently lowered his lips to hers. He moved over them leisurely, giving her lips a final lick before backing off. "Mmm, that's nice. Have a good sleep and I'll see you later."

He turned to go and she called, "Aiden?" He looked at her over his shoulder. "I had a good time," she said. "Thank you."

"We'll do it again," he said. "I'll always let you win." Then he winked.

While Erin slept, she dreamed of a handsome, sensitive, funny, testosterone-oozing man; she felt his lips on hers and his hands on her waist pulling her close, and she was swept away. It was like a fantasy come true, meeting this hairy, smelly homeless guy and clean him up and *poof*—he's a prince. And no question about it—he liked her. Things like this didn't happen to her. Thirty-six years old and, in the most unlikely place on the planet, she ran into the sexiest, most tempting man she'd ever met.

It was barely after sunrise when she heard the toot of the horn and when she sat up in bed, her entire body revolted. She flopped back down. She couldn't move.

She heard the knocking at the door and she tried rolling over. Agony everywhere. She lay there, still. Soon, he was right in her bedroom, standing over her. "That's what I thought. Stiff?"

"How in the world did you get in?" she asked.

"Well, the key was under the flowerpot and I think the bureau you pushed up against the door is empty. It slid like it was on glass. I'm pretty sure I'm smarter than a bear, but if I'm not… So, sore? Stiff?"

"Stiff doesn't touch it," she said. "That was very irresponsible of you. You have some medical training and should know better than to take me on an hours-long bike ride like that without making sure I'm up to it. Every muscle in my body is on fire. Even my neck hurts. Why does my neck hurt?"

"Leaning over the handlebars, straining your neck muscles forward in a desperate move to win a race. Want me to take off all my clothes and come in there, give you a nice rubdown?"

"If you touch me, I'll kill you. Go away—I can't move."

He sat down on the edge of her bed. "You took off like a shot on that bike because you're competitive, that's what. I'll put a bottle of over-the-counter anti-inflammatory medicine on the counter. Do yourself a favor—warm up your muscles in the shower and move around a little. The biggest mistake you can make is sitting around all day. I'll make you a pot of coffee before I go."

"Go?" she asked, half rising. Then she fell back onto the bed with a moan.

"I came over to make sure your muscles were all right. I have something I have to do today. I was going to take you for a hike through a redwood grove, but maybe it's for the best something came up. How about if I come back later? For dinner?"

"Can't," she said. "I'm terrified to cook up good smells because of that bear."

"Okay, fair enough. I'll bring groceries when I come and we'll make it together. It'll be fun." He stood up from the edge of the bed. "Listen, move around a little today or you'll lock up. I'll see you later."

"I thought we decided you were going to ask me," she said.

He grinned at her. "Stop telling me what to do. I'm going to write down my brother's phone number for you—you should call if you have a problem with the bear. Luke will come over and shoot him for you and he'd like that. Take the anti-inflammatory medicine every four hours whether you think you need it or not, and stretch your muscles gently." He leaned down and kissed her forehead. "Tomorrow we'll take it easy." He turned to go and looked over his shoulder. "Water my tomatoes," he said with a smile.

"Now they're your tomatoes? Not much of a gift…"

"I'll see you later."

And he was gone. Before long she heard the door close and the sound of his car leaving. Then she smelled coffee.

I'm going to have to start hiding that key better, she thought. But then she smiled. Maybe not. This was getting interesting.…

"Tomorrow?" she said to herself. "He's already planning tomorrow?"

Aiden did a lot of driving after leaving Erin—all the way to Redding and back. His headhunter wanted him to at least have lunch with a couple of OBs who had a practice there. The Redding docs were ready to expand and had been putting out feelers for the right physician.

When Aiden had started this ex-navy adventure, he wasn't sure what he wanted or where he wanted to settle, which allowed the headhunter to throw a really wide net. He thought he could be just as happy in a big city as a smaller one, as long as he was relatively close to Luke and Shelby, the only family that was no longer moving around.

The two doctors he met with in Redding, a man and a woman, impressed him on both personal and professional levels. They were looking for help because their practice was in high demand. In addition to OB-GYN they also offered a couple of hard-to-find subspecialties—fertility and perinatology or high-risk pregnancy, both of which interested Aiden. If things worked out, they could be offering him an associate's position that could lead to a partnership.

But now his thoughts were darting off in other directions; he was beginning to wonder what Chico had to offer. Or, failing Chico, perhaps Davis, Sacramento or even San Francisco, anything closer to Chico than Redding happened to be. Yes, the long-legged strawberry blonde was creeping under his skin, and when he thought about her it brought a nice warm rush to his blood flow and a tightening to his groin.

Yet another reason not to make a final decision right away—he'd like to see where this attraction to Erin was going. And for that he needed more time.

It surprised Aiden to realize that feeling this kind of optimism about a relationship with a woman was a rarity for him. He thought he'd been open to the possibility, but he suddenly realized he probably hadn't allowed himself to feel something like this in years. Oh, he'd experienced attraction and desire, but it hadn't seemed to blossom into anything strong enough to last. Now he wondered if that had been about not meeting the right woman, or more about him being reluctant to trust and unwilling to allow himself to be vulnerable. But he was tired of being alone, tired of keeping a safe distance. And something about Erin made him willing to take a chance.

A lot of his reluctance had undoubtedly been because of that one bad experience. But hell, it had been really, really bad. He'd like to think it was the recent attempt of the ex, Annalee, to reach him that had caused him to reexamine his extreme caution, but the truth was that even if Annalee's name hadn't come up at all, being careful where women were concerned had become a habit for Aiden. His experience with her, though long ago and short-lived, had been the darkest, craziest time in his adult life. Nothing had prepared him for the kind of insanity Annalee brought. From the day he met her, she was a series of lies and manipulations and even violent behavior. He had given her money to fly home to Georgia to visit her mother and five days later he'd been called by the credit-card company asking if his wife had his approval using his credit card to pay for her ten-thousand-dollar spa week in Acapulco. The only smart thing he'd ever done was not put her name on his accounts. Expensive new clothes appeared in her closet, yet he didn't know where she got the money; he wondered if she had shoplifted, but when he questioned her behavior or actions, it was either instant fireworks to include trashing their apartment or a complete collapse into a pathetic, vulnerable, needy child. It had been an unbelievable roller-coaster ride punctuated by wild, ravenous sex. He'd wondered if he was losing his mind.

The thing he could never quite reconcile was that there were periods of time Annalee seemed so *normal.* Cute, sweet, accommodating, precious. And God, was she beautiful. Not in a girl-next-door way, but in a classically gorgeous way—natural white-blond hair, dark eyes, slightly tanned skin, red lips and a body that could stop a train. She was only five foot two, tiny waist, round hips, large breasts.

After the first two weeks of marriage, he'd look at her and see the devil. He wasn't sure if she was mentally ill or the meanest, most conniving bitch on earth. He was still trying to figure her out long after he should have been divorcing her. But then he came home from the hospital early—on purpose—and found her in bed with a young sailor from the base. When Aiden yanked him out of the bed and slammed him up against the wall, the kid cried. He had no idea the girl was *married!* He'd met her in a bar at 10:00 a.m. He ran for his life.

It had been a wide-awake nightmare that lasted four months from the second he laid eyes on her till the divorce was over.

One of the residents in the hospital had just effected a divorce in a matter of days; Aiden got the lawyer's name and went to him at once. He took the papers to Annalee himself and after that she'd disappeared into thin air. He really thought he was done with her. And until hearing her name a couple of weeks ago, it had appeared to have been so.

Aiden had not met another woman in eight years who bore any resemblance to that she-devil who'd briefly messed up his life. And he knew beyond a doubt that Erin was nothing like that. In fact, he thought Erin was strangely like him. She'd obviously concentrated on her family obligations and her work, just like Aiden. She'd had some relationships, but nothing that tempted her into a long-term commitment, just like Aiden. She was serious and cautious, and she was very smart.

He was definitely wanting her. And it had been too long since he'd met a woman who made him feel that way.

Driving back to the Virgin River area from Redding, he began to plot his approach. He'd buy something nice for dinner and get her to tell him all about what made her decide on law school and then, for God's sake, *tax and estate* law. She didn't look nearly as nerdy as her specialty. Then he'd kiss her and fondle her for a while, gently, sweetly, and he'd leave her reluctantly. Next, he'd show up to take her for a walk through a redwood grove and sneak her behind the occasional wide and tall tree. And before very long, he was going to take her to bed. He knew it was probably just crazy man-thinking, but he believed that after he'd taken her to bed, he'd know if he should tell that headhunter to toss the net a little closer to the Chico area.

He stopped at a grocery store and while he had cell reception, called Luke. "Hey," he said. "I have plans tonight, but thought I'd check in. Everyone okay?"

"Fine here, but I wish you were going to come home. Mom and George are coming over for dinner and I thought we'd talk to them. About…you know… this idea of driving all over the country in an RV."

"Ah," Aiden said. "You thought we'd gang up on them."

"Well, I have my concerns. They're kind of old for this."

"They're both very healthy and alert. Neither one of them even needs glasses. You don't want me there—I think I'm on their side. Now, if Mom was heading out alone, that would be another story."

"He's seventy! She might as well be alone!" Luke said.

"Does this mean you're no longer concerned that your mother is having wild, sinful monkey sex with some guy in an RV?" Aiden asked. "Because any seventy-year-old guy who's capable of that can read a map and stop at a stop sign."

"Funny," Luke said. "Go. Have fun with your squeeze. Leave all the family issues to me. See if I care."

Aiden chuckled silently. A couple of years ago—before Shelby and the baby and Art and all these domestic tethers—Luke might not even have *noticed* where his mother was sleeping. Now he was up to his neck in *issues*. "When I get where I'm going, I'll give you a call and make sure you have a phone number so you can reach me if there's a brawl."

"Thanks for nothing," Luke said, hanging up on him.

Eight

Maureen and George had towed Maureen's sedan behind the RV so they could get around without driving the gas-guzzling motor coach everywhere. They were very comfortable at a small, friendly RV park just outside Fortuna. Most of the people they claimed as neighbors were passing through, visiting the redwoods, the coast, the mountains and the vineyards. They introduced themselves as George and Maureen and no one seemed the least bit interested in whether they were married. Most people did want a tour of their motor coach, however, as it was top-of-the-line and fancier than anyone else's.

They had a very nice routine. They drove into Virgin River almost every day—George liked to help Noah around the church and his fixer-upper house, and Maureen liked to spend time with her daughters-in-law, both of whom she found far more entertaining these days than her sons. They often went to Catholic mass on Friday nights, then out to dinner afterward. On Sunday mornings they liked to listen to Noah preach; George took such personal pride in the young pastor's skill. And watching the handsome young preacher stand before his congregation in jeans and a plaid shirt, his dog lying not far away, was something Maureen hadn't thought she'd ever see. "You Protestants," she said to George, laughing, "don't know anything about the beauty of ritual."

The real magic of Maureen's life happened in or around the RV with George. Things she didn't realize she'd been missing now fulfilled her—simple things like sitting on the sofa with her needlework while he sat not far away talking to the televised baseball games. George *loved* baseball and had a comment about every play! The difference between him being highly entertained or simply passing the time had everything to do with how much he talked to the TV. Baseball got lots of commentary; movies she selected for them got none until his eventual snore. She'd had no idea how much she missed the sound of a man's snore.

Maureen sat on their small patio, the canopy extended over her, enjoying a cool morning breeze, while inside, George washed up the breakfast dishes. She couldn't remember when she'd had someone to trade off kitchen chores with, and that brought her amazing happiness. And speak of the devil, he came out of the RV, the newspaper tucked under his arm and carrying two cups of coffee. He handed her the mug with one Stevia sweetener and a tiny bit of skim milk. Then he settled into the chair next to her with his black coffee and perused the headlines.

This was another thing she'd had no idea she'd longed for—a person to be quiet with. Someone to sit beside her, present, available but not invasive. For twelve years she'd been entirely alone and not lonely, and never realizing there was an alternative that could feed a need in her. Then George casually reached for her hand, holding it, and she was reminded of that other thing. She felt a zing of sweet affection balanced beautifully somewhere between passion and comfort.

Maureen had thought these feelings were so far behind her, she was surprised that a woman in her sixties could enjoy the same aspect of life that a bride in her twenties might. No, make that *more*, not the same. As a young woman she'd had inhibitions; she'd been self-conscious and difficult to arouse. Now, when her body was so much less appealing, she felt freer and more sure of herself. She gave a lot of credit to George, who helped her slowly build trust; George, who made her feel so beautiful and desirable. Maureen was the kind of woman who had pulled the sheet over her face during pelvic exams, even after birthing five children. Now, she showered with George sometimes. They laughed at how ridiculous they must look, their flesh so loose, the hair in private places all graying and thin. They laughed about how *well* those aging bodies seemed to work with a little unhurried coaxing.

She gave his hand a squeeze. "I've been thinking, George."

"Scary," he said.

"I've been awfully critical of my boys for avoiding love and commitment, for not settling down. I can't count the number of times I asked them what in the world their father and I did to put them off marriage and family. I didn't realize until recently, maybe they were aping *my* behavior. I thought I had no interest in a relationship. Or more honestly, that no man would have any interest in me. I had no idea what I was really doing was avoiding any possibility of that—the very thing my sons were doing until recently. For entirely different reasons, maybe. But the result was the same."

"Different reasons?"

"I always thought that a couple of them, Luke and Aiden for certain, shied away from serious relationships because of their terrible marriages. But how do I know? I just didn't want the complications in my life. I stayed completely away from social situations in which I might meet a man. Really, George—I had no idea I was avoiding it like I was. And I was so critical of women friends who were looking for love. I honestly thought they were acting like old fools."

He leaned toward her and kissed her cheek. "You've made this old fool very happy."

"Do you know what I find myself wondering lately? If Patrick and I would ever have achieved this kind of life. He died almost the moment the last of five sons was out the door. And you know what else I realized? Our marriage was strong and there was a lot of love between us, but it was all business. We worked so hard to keep the family going. Not only didn't we have a lot of leisure—we didn't talk much."

"I've been told I talk too much," George said.

"*Pah!* That's almost the best part of our relationship!"

He grinned. "I'm glad you said almost."

"You are very pushy," she said with a smile. "If you weren't, I never would have had lunch with you, much less moved into your motor home. If you'd bet me a year ago I'd be doing this, I would have put my life savings against it."

"We have a dinner date with your sons tonight," George reminded her. "Luke isn't very cagey—it's always obvious when he has something serious on his mind. They're going to give us a talking-to. Want to guess what it's about?"

"Living in sin?" she asked with a wink.

"Do you think so?" he wondered.

"It's just what I deserve. I would have been hell on wheels if any of them had informed me they were cohabiting with a woman without vows. George, why didn't I start minding my own business years ago? No wonder they couldn't stand to visit me for more than three days at a time."

"Easy does it, sweetheart. If they wanted to live with a woman without the benefit of marriage, I'm sure they did as they pleased, even if they moved her out when you made that rare visit. Didn't you say they usually came to you?"

"Usually."

"And Sean stayed with Francine and Rosie for weeks, once he learned they were a family, though they weren't married."

"They did. And didn't I just give them trouble about it for a while. Though Sean told me to get over it." Her mouth formed a slight smile. "I was proud of him for staking his claim like that. Mothers shouldn't be telling children over thirty how to live."

"There you have it. Now, do you want to make this easy on them? We can always get married."

"Yes, I think we should. But not for a year. This is a good idea—making sure we're right for each other. We're both too old to take ridiculous chances. Besides, I think God's too busy with other things to worry about this much."

He kissed her cheek. "As you wish. You can make sure I don't have an alter ego who's difficult and annoying."

She put a hand on his bristly cheek. "I'm the one with the alter ego—she's bossy and judgmental."

"She's been very well behaved lately," George replied sweetly.

Much later that day, they went to Luke's and had an extremely nice dinner with Luke, Shelby, Sean, Franci, Rosie and Art. After dinner, with the coffee and pie, Luke brought up the subject weighing on his mind. "So, Mom. George. We have some concerns about this plan you have to travel the world in an RV...."

George and Maureen looked at each other in sudden surprise.

"*You* have concerns, Luke," Shelby said. "It isn't necessarily unanimous."

"*I'm* a little concerned," Sean said.

"I'm not," Franci weighed in.

Suddenly George and Maureen, eyes still locked, burst into laughter. When they finally quieted, Luke asked, "Is that funny?"

George pulled a handkerchief out of his pocket and wiped his eyes. "Well," he said. "Sounds like a hung jury."

"Listen, I mean this in a very respectful way, but you're seventy, and that's a big rig you got there," Luke said, leaning forward earnestly.

"It is," George said. "I took a training course. It's not something you can jump in and parallel park, you know. And I wanted a house on wheels. Your mother and I—we're really not much for roughing it. And by God, we've earned some good times, I think."

"I'm going to take a similar course on driving it, in case George is ever indisposed...." Maureen said. Then she chuckled.

"What about this is so goddamn funny?" Luke asked with irritation.

"Oh, it's just that we thought you were going to hound us about not being married and living together," she said.

"No one at this table would have the b— " Shelby cleared her throat. "No one should hound you about anything," she said. "Especially a man who flew Blackhawks and rode motorcycles for over twenty years."

"Shelby, if you don't mind," Luke said.

"I do mind," she said, straightening and rubbing her hands over her huge middle. "I'm so happy about

Maureen and George and their wonderful plans. It sounds like fantastic fun! And there's no reason to worry. Now, if either of them were in the least infirm, we could talk about it, but…"

"I'll drive slowly and only make right turns," George put in. Then he grinned largely. He was clearly not taking the boys seriously.

Luke took a drink of his coffee and leaned toward them both. "You're worse than having a couple of teenagers. I just want you to be safe. I don't want to worry about you sliding off some mountain in that monster or ending up at the bottom of the Grand Canyon because your reflexes are a little rusty and you took a turn too wide."

Maureen tilted her head and smiled at her son. "Well, then, Luke, if you don't want to worry, don't. George and I are very cautious and plan ahead."

"Mom," Sean attempted.

Franci stood. "Stop. You flew jets that go over five hundred miles an hour and are just back from Iraq— you aren't allowed to take the temperature of anyone's life choices. The way I see it, if you and I decide to spend our retirement in an RV, I just hope to God it's as fancy as theirs. Now, this meeting is over. Who wants a drop of Courvoisier with their coffee?"

"I do," Shelby said hopefully.

"Who besides Shelby?" Franci asked.

Aiden carried through exactly as planned—he brought Chilean sea bass, mushrooms, rice pilaf, baby green beans and cheesecake to Erin's cabin for dinner and cooked with her. No bear. He found out that her undergrad degree was in accounting, so it was natural for her to pursue tax law. Law school? "I'd always been a good student and I saw potential. Once I started, I wondered if I hadn't taken on more than I should have, but it worked out. What did you want to do?" she asked him.

"Save the world," he said with a shrug. He thought maybe now would be the time to explain that he wasn't exactly who or what she assumed. "I was a crew member on an ambulance team in college, my part-time job, and the senior EMT delivered a baby. It was the most awesome thing I'd ever seen and I—" The timer on the stove went off and he jumped up to pull out the fish, distracting her.

Through dinner they talked about the most important people in their lives—to Erin it was her brother, sister and her brother-in-law. She told the story of how Marcie found Ian Buchanan in this very cabin, before it was, in her opinion, habitable. How Marcie fell in love with him and married him. When she mentioned that Drew graduated from medical school, he thought it was the right time to tell her.... But the phone rang and she dashed to it. She was only on a second before disconnecting and, with a big smile, said, "Remember I told you Marcie and Ian are coming up for the long week-end—Fourth of July. Would you like to meet them?"

"I would. Definitely," he said. "How is it you never married?" he asked her. "And don't tell me you didn't date, because any man with a pulse would ask you out."

She flipped the subject on him. "I dated—though

infrequently. But what about you? I can tell you've been a bar hound, out with a hundred women."

He was shocked. "What makes you think *that?*"

"You're confident, good-looking, and admit it— you're good with women. I'm a terrible pickup and you have me doing exactly what you want!"

He laughed at her; he almost said something about how he had to be good with women in his business. And the things he'd seen in his work as a gynecologist absolutely ensured he wasn't careless or frivolous about sex. "Nothing could be further from the truth! Honestly? The military keeps a guy busy and the only women I was meeting happened to be hospital staff. We had some fun, but it seemed like a bad idea to have too much fun, so it was just friends. You must have run into similar situations with colleagues? Lawyers you met on the job? Bottom line—no long-term relationships since my very miserable, very short marriage."

"Tell me about that," she said, leaning her chin in her hand.

And so he had, trying to keep the high drama of it all out of the story. Really, some of the things he went through with Annalee were not to be believed. He'd been a complete fool and he wasn't proud of it.

Before he left her that night, *very* reluctantly, he made good use of her lips. He pulled her tight against him so she knew he was completely turned on. He was more than a little grateful—he hadn't been that turned on in a while, and it was *fantastic*. All that night in his little cabin by the river he thought about Erin, dreamed about her.

The next day they went for a walk through a redwood grove, although poor Erin was still stiff and sore from her marathon bike ride down the beach. They held hands and talked about their families. Aiden learned about Erin's remodel by e-mail. "I'd done some remodeling around my dad's house the past several years, so I had an idea what I wanted. And the builder, a local guy, was easy to work with."

Aiden found himself telling her about how his brothers Luke and Sean met and married their wives, about his widowed mother who hadn't had a date in a dozen years, and George, about how Art came to live on Luke's property and his recent declaration that he had a girlfriend. And in between these stories, their arms were around each other and they kissed: deep, hot, passionate kisses that lasted a long time. "I love kissing you," he told her.

"I don't think this is kissing," she said. "I think this is making out. I haven't done this in a really long time."

He pressed her up against one of those majestic redwoods. With a finger, he stroked back some of that silky reddish-blond hair over her ear. "I should talk to you about something. About me, about what I do for a living."

"Doesn't matter," she said, shaking her head.

"It must matter, Erin. Aren't you a little concerned about getting involved with some sailor you've only known a few weeks? Kissed a few times?"

"Because of something as unimportant as income?" She shook her head again.

"What if there's more to me than meets the eye?" he asked her.

She smiled. "Lucky me. Here's what I want to know about you, Aiden. I have a good income—are you after it?"

"I'm not after that, no," he said suggestively.

"Are you likely to use me? Treat me abusively? If we were involved, cheat on me?"

"Never. And we *are* going to be involved."

"Want to know what I like best about you? That you aren't afraid to be yourself. When I met you, I'm pretty sure I was insulting—making cracks about your appearance, your *smell*…" She giggled. "Lord, did you stink! My brother-in-law, Ian, he said that until he got to know me a little better, he thought I was snooty. I'm not. But I know I can be judgmental. I was pretty hard on him, too."

"And stubborn," he said with a smile.

"And that. And the truth is—I'm always afraid to be myself. I'm always trying to measure up."

"There's no reason for that," he said. "You're perfect."

"I was fighting for my life in school, Aiden. My way of dealing with the pressure was to be perfect. Or maybe better than perfect. And then later, in my practice? My clients are my clients because they're incredibly successful and are closely scrutinized by the IRS."

"Understandable."

"I apologize if I offended you when we were first getting to know each other...."

He grinned. "And I apologize if I gave you a concussion."

"You chased away my bear. That zeros the debt. Can we go home soon?"

"Aren't you enjoying the redwoods?"

"I love the redwoods. But I'm hungry and it's a very busy weekend coming up. I'm having company and I want you to pick a time to come over and meet them."

"There's a town party for the Fourth," Aiden said. "Monday at Jack's. Well, behind Jack's. Preacher's going to fire up the barbecue and my whole family will be there. Will you and your family come?"

"Do we have to be invited? Because no one told me about it..."

He was shaking his head. "Everyone is invited. I think your sister and brother-in-law know a lot of the folks from town. They'd probably enjoy that."

"The point is," she said, "there will be lots of people around all weekend. Starting tomorrow evening for me, when Marcie arrives. So before all that starts, I want a little time alone with you."

He was quiet for a moment; his eyes shone intensely into hers. "Are you ready for that, Erin?" he asked solemnly. "To be alone with me?"

"We've been alone plenty of times," she said in a whisper.

"This time it's going to be different."

And she swayed toward him, offering her lips again. Her eyes drifted closed. In a breath she said, "Okay..."

* * *

All the way back to Virgin River the only thing Aiden could think about was Erin, her delicious mouth, the sweet scent of her skin and hair. While they made small talk about what they could have for dinner, he anticipated the satiny feel of her skin against his and he couldn't wait to get past this first time with her so they could have so many, many more times. They stopped at a Fortuna grocery and bought a roasted chicken, salad greens, shoestring fries for the oven and a bottle of wine. And as they drove and made more small talk—about the town party, the number of people who would want their undivided attention and how inconvenient that suddenly was—all Aiden could think about was how many different times, ways, places and positions he wanted to get her in. He was trying to remind himself that women didn't like to be rushed.

But, when they got to the cabin, he shoved the groceries into the refrigerator, grabbed her wrist and said, "Come on." She laughed as he dragged her to the bedroom. When he got her beside the bed, he pulled her against him so she'd know that he was as hard as a baseball bat…as if she hadn't gotten that message the previous few hours, especially when pressed up against a redwood. He covered her mouth in a searing, desperate, hungry kiss that made her moan. The moan came from so deep inside her that he was anxious to chase it, find it, please it and worship it. "God," he said. "Oh man, oh God…"

"Just how long has it been, Aiden?" she asked him softly.

"I can't even remember. But don't worry, I'll take good care of you."

"I'm not worried," she said.

He began pulling at her clothes while he kissed her. His hand was on the back of her head, his fingers splayed and threaded through her silky hair, his tongue in her mouth as he devoured her. He fell with her onto the bed, tugging her shirt off. Pretty soon she was helping him. They kicked off tennis shoes; shorts and shirts went flying and they were writhing together in just underwear. To his absolute delight, it was her hand that slipped under the waistband of his boxers, grasping him. And with that, he groaned and she gasped. That was always a good sign, he thought. A little gasp. He was pretty sure that meant he was of sufficient size to please her.

He struggled with her bra—it wasn't the easy kind. The clasp was in the back, so he rolled her a bit and worked it clumsily, but it finally gave way. She had to let go of him to let the straps slip off her shoulders and he heard a sound of disappointment come from himself. Then he heard his groan of pleasure when she put her hand back on him. Next, her panties. Where were the panties? His hands ran down her belly and hips. "Where are your panties?" he asked breathlessly.

"I think they went with the shorts," she whispered.

He chuckled against her mouth. "That was smart. Did I do that? Because that was *smart!*"

"I can't remember which one of us took off my shorts...."

"It's best when it happens like that," he said sagely. "I like it like that—working together as a team." Then he paused briefly to look down at her. She was nude and in the late-afternoon light, she was golden. He smiled; that strawberry-blond hair was the real deal. "Erin," he said almost reverently. "You're so beautiful. Magnificent. *Hot*." And then he dipped his mouth to her nipple, licked gently before he sucked, and made her almost cry out with pleasure.

He slipped his hand between her legs and gently probed. She was wet. She'd gotten wet *fast*. That was so fantastic. He massaged her a little bit and she squirmed against his hand, pushing against him, wriggling and whimpering. He loved those sounds. And she held on to him, stroking. Something had to give.

"Okay, baby," he whispered. "Stop for a minute." He pulled her hand away. "Don't get ahead of me here. I need a condom."

"Yes," she said. "Yes, please."

He pulled away from her, found his shorts on the floor and the condom in his pocket. He ditched the boxers, suited up and poised above her, kneeling between her legs. Then he dipped to her mouth and kissed her, deeply and lovingly. Against her open mouth he asked, "Feel ready?"

She nodded.

He gave her clitoris a few more strokes, felt her squirm beneath him, heard her murmurs and whimpers, and then slid in. "Ahhhhh…." came from him. "Ah, God! Oh, Erin!"

And he started to move. He grabbed her beautiful bottom so he could get the right friction, and he pumped. He pumped hard, he pumped slow. He went gentle and then fast. He lowered his lips to her nipple and sucked while he moved. He slipped his hand between their bodies and massaged her clitoris as he moved in and out. He covered her mouth with his and invaded with his tongue. He licked her ear and neck. Then he pulled out and went down on her, licking her there. He felt her nails bite into his shoulders and after a while he came back to her breast, then to her mouth. He was inside again, trying a slow and steady rhythm. He moved evenly, waiting for a hint from her. Finally he said, "Want to tell me what you like, honey?"

She shrugged. It was unmistakably a shrug. He was inside her, but he stilled and rose above her, looking into her eyes. He gave her a gentle little kiss. "You going to come for me, baby?"

"Go ahead," she said softly. "It's okay."

He felt a smile come to his lips. "A little tough getting there?"

"It's okay. You can go ahead. Really…I don't mind…"

He pushed her silky hair away from her face. "You don't have orgasms easily?" She shook her head. "Can you have them on your own?"

"That doesn't count," she said, glancing away from him.

He laughed sweetly. "They all count. I'm not in a hurry, honey. I'm sorry if I made you think that. Tell me what you like. Tell me what feels good."

She shrugged again. "I don't know. Exactly."

"Well…you have them on your own. Tell me what does it for you. Or show me. We'll get there."

"It's okay…you can—"

"Erin, baby, it *is* okay. I'm not *bored*. Let's try it together. Tell me. Show me."

She wrestled a hand free and held up two fingers. And she actually flushed. This sophisticated lawyer, who he knew wasn't afraid to take on the feds, blushed at the thought of telling her lover what would make her feel good.

"On the outside?" he asked.

She nodded.

"Oh, honey, that's easy." He brushed her hair back again. "I think you're worried about it. Now, listen, we have lots of time. I didn't mean to rush you. Just enjoy. And if my fingers aren't in exactly the right spot— move them. Take charge—it's all good." And then he slipped his hand between their bodies again, going after that erogenous nub, softly at first, then harder and faster.

He kissed, he suckled, he moved easily and rhyth-mically. He'd never been in a place like this before and he suddenly hated all the men of the world for making this sexy, hot woman think she had a problem because they were in a hurry. He stroked, he took a break to lick, he sucked and stroked. They were at it a long time and he made sure he took every second she needed. When he felt as if he was losing her or when he was getting too close and feared losing his erection, he changed his routine and pulled out for a while. He went to her breast, her neck, her sex. He tried to imagine what previous lovers had said to her, things that would make her feel inadequate because she didn't come for them. They would have told her to just relax, or to let go. Or, "Sorry."

While he was moving rhythmically inside her, his fingers on her clitoris, lips on her breasts and neck, he whispered, "You ever drive a standard transmission?"

"Huh?"

"You heard me. Ever drive a stick shift?"

"Uh-huh…"

"You know how impossible it feels when you're learning, trying to find that fit, that slot, that place where the gears don't strip? Trying to keep the engine from dying? But once you find it—you find it every time. Move my hand, baby. Let's find the gear.…"

"Ohhhh," she said, pushing his hand just a little bit lower. Her hips began moving against him. "Ohhhh."

He stroked her and pumped into her. "That's… nice…" And he moved some more.

"More," she whispered. "Harder."

"That's what I thought," he whispered back. He pounded into her, gritting his teeth to hang on.

"Ohhhh," she cried. "Oh, God. Oh, *God!*"

"Yeah?" he asked. "Yeah?"

What followed was a series of guttural grunts and groans and moans and cries, but the important thing was that he felt her tighten around him, heard her lose control, felt her nails dig into his butt, and just about nothing had ever been better. It was so good, he exploded like a maniac, just losing his mind while she lost hers. All these times he thought being with a woman who got off easy was such a big deal, because no question, a guy didn't need a whole lot. Shit. *This* was a big deal.

He kissed her eyes, her cheeks, her neck, her breasts, her eyes again. "Okay?" he asked.

"Oh, God," she said weakly. All the tension in her body seemed to melt into a heap of soft, useless muscle. Then, unbelievably, she laughed. Her green eyes twinkled into his green eyes.

"So, Miss Foley, what did you do on *your* summer vacation?"

Aiden held her for a little while, softly laughing in conspiratorial success. Then he excused himself to the bathroom, grabbing his shorts off the floor as he went. When she heard the door to the cabin open, she sat straight up in bed like a shot, her mouth open in shock. Was he *leaving* her? She heard the door to his SUV open and close and she thought, *My God, is he actually leaving?*

Then the cabin door closed and he was back, smiling. In his hand he had a box of condoms. She fell back against the pillows with an *oomph*.

"What?" he asked, shedding his shorts, leaving them again on the floor.

She stared straight up at the ceiling. "I thought you were going."

"Without my shirt and shoes?" he asked, dropping the box of condoms on the bedside table. He slipped in beside her, taking her in his arms. "We better talk about this. Have you actually been left, naked and post-coital, because you didn't orgasm quickly enough?"

She pulled back just enough to peer at him. "Okay,

medics are probably brilliant these days, but do they use terms like 'postcoital'?"

"I wouldn't think so. I'm not a medic. I'm a gynecologist. M.D., not novice. I was attempting to tell you earlier."

"Shouldn't you have told me a couple of weeks ago? Like, with that first beer?"

"Maybe," he said with a shrug. "If you'd asked me one straightforward question about my job or education or what I was actually looking for on the outside, I wouldn't have misled you, but I liked that you liked me even as a vagrant." He smiled widely. "But can we talk about this other thing?"

She took a breath. "I have never actually been abandoned naked and sweaty because I failed to…orgasm. But it has happened that there wasn't another date." Again the shrug, the glance away. "I guess a woman can be too much trouble."

"You're not too much trouble," he said, pulling her tighter against him. "This isn't as big a problem as you think. This can be worked out. Probably easily."

She lifted one blond brow. "Oh, yeah?"

"Have you talked to your doctor about it?"

"No. I mean, not before today." She smiled sheepishly.

"The first thing a doctor wants to know, if the patient is able to talk about it, is whether there's any history of early-childhood sexual abuse."

She gasped. "No!"

"Lucky you," he said. "It's a monster. Happens too

often. The next thing—can you get your own orgasm?"

"I believe I answered that already, counselor.…"

He chuckled. "You're the counselor, I'm the doc. Oh my God, a doctor and a lawyer in bed trying to figure out orgasms. What a riot."

"I fully intended to have sex with a medic, so don't blame me! Are you sure you're a gynecologist? Because I think that line's been used on me before…"

"Card-carrying," he said. "Are you angry?"

"Not angry. Actually, this usually happens the other way."

"The other way?" he asked, his brows knitting together.

"Where he tells me he's a gynecologist and really, he's a medic. Or rather, tells me he's a lawyer when really, he *needs* a lawyer." Then she smiled. "If you have any other serious secrets, can you please tell me now?"

"That's it—I have very little to hide. Back to us," Aiden said. "So basically, you know how to do it, you just haven't been with a guy willing to invest the time?"

She sighed. "As I understand it, men have a limited amount of time to invest.…"

His mouth took on an evil little grin. "Now, honey, if you want your woman to be happy, there are sacrifices that are worth the effort. Like pull out till she's ready. Like focus on her for a while and don't let her touch you if you're too hot. It's like I said, once you figure out what works, this can be done." He grinned again. "And done and done and done."

Her eyes lit up. "Are we going to do it again?"

"And again and again and again…"

"Are we going to eat?" she asked.

"Eventually," he said. "I have some things I think we should try. Fun things. Crazy things. Before the Fourth of July weekend keeps us from fucking our brains out."

"Ohhhhh… Would it be rude of me to call Marcie and ask her to come another time? Like next year? And exactly how much do you like your family? Because I think they're starting to rain on my parade…"

"No talking," he said, coming down on her mouth with his.

Nine

If there was one thing Erin never expected when a bushy-bearded maniac cut his way through her trees with a three-foot-long knife, it was a long afternoon and evening of the purest carnal pleasure she'd ever experienced. Aiden wanted to experiment, trying out a lot of different positions with her to see what made her feel best. She came apart explosively when she discovered that being on top, controlling his movements and the position of his hands and fingers, was special. *Very* special. She loved the naughty and deep way he laughed when she made discoveries like that.

Of course, there were some things that worked better for him than her—standing up in the shower being one. It was a bit scary. She was all slippery and afraid he was going to drop her, so it was not mutually successful. But it left him smiling. "That was selfish," she muttered to him.

"I'm a selfish bastard," he said, dropping to one

YOUR PARTICIPATION IS REQUESTED!

Dear Reader,

Since you are a lover of fiction — we would like to get to know you!

Inside you will find a short Reader's Survey. Sharing your answers with us will help our editorial staff understand who you are and what activities you enjoy.

To thank you for your participation, we would like to send you 2 books and 2 gifts — **ABSOLUTELY FREE!**

Enjoy your gifts with our appreciation,

Pam Powers

SEE INSIDE FOR READER'S SURVEY

YOUR READER'S SURVEY "THANK YOU" FREE GIFTS INCLUDE:
▶ 2 Romance books
▶ 2 lovely surprise gifts

▶ DETACH AND MAIL CARD TODAY! ▶

PLEASE FILL IN THE CIRCLES COMPLETELY TO RESPOND

1) What type of fiction books do you enjoy reading? (Check all that apply)
   ○ Suspense/Thrillers   ○ Action/Adventure   ○ Modern-day Romances
   ○ Historical Romance   ○ Humour   ○ Science fiction

2) What attracted you most to the last fiction book you purchased on impulse?
   ○ The Title   ○ The Cover   ○ The Author   ○ The Story

3) What is usually the greatest influencer when you <u>plan</u> to buy a book?
   ○ Advertising   ○ Referral   ○ Book Review

4) How often do you access the internet?
   ○ Daily ○ Weekly ○ Monthly ○ Rarely or never.

5) How many NEW paperback fiction novels have you purchased in the past 3 months?
   ○ 0 - 2   ○ 3 - 6   ○ 7 or more
   E4GP   E4GZ   E4HD

YES! I have completed the Reader's Survey. Please send me the 2 FREE books and 2 FREE gifts (gifts are worth about $10) for which I qualify. I understand that I am under no obligation to purchase any books, as explained on the back of this card.

194/394 MDL

FIRST NAME	LAST NAME

ADDRESS

APT.#	CITY

STATE/PROV.	ZIP/POSTAL CODE

The Reader Service — Here's How It Works:

Accepting your 2 free books and 2 free mystery gifts places you under no obligation to buy anything. You may keep the books and gifts a return the shipping statement marked "cancel." If you do not cancel, about a month later we'll send you 4 additional books and bill you ju $5.74 each in the U.S. or $6.24 each in Canada. That is a savings of at least 28% off the cover price. It's quite a bargain! Shipping a handling is just 50¢ per book in the U.S. and 75¢ per book in Canada.* You may cancel at any time, but if you choose to continue, eve month we'll send you 4 more books, which you may either purchase at the discount price or return to us and cancel your subscription.

*Terms and prices subject to change without notice. Prices do not include applicable taxes. Sales tax applicable in N.Y. Canadian resider will be charged applicable provincial taxes and GST. Offer not valid in Quebec. Books received may not be as shown. All orders subject to a proval. Credit or debit balances in a customer's account(s) may be offset by any other outstanding balance owed by or to the custom Please allow 4 to 6 weeks for delivery. Offer available while quantities last.

If offer card is missing write to: The Reader Service, P.O. Box 1867, Buffalo, NY 14240-1867 or visit: www.ReaderService.com

BUSINESS REPLY MAIL

FIRST-CLASS MAIL   PERMIT NO. 717   BUFFALO, NY

POSTAGE WILL BE PAID BY ADDRESSEE

THE READER SERVICE
PO BOX 1341
BUFFALO NY 14240-8571

NO POSTAGE
NECESSARY
IF MAILED
IN THE
UNITED STATES

knee in the shower. "Let's see if we can even the score." He pulled one of her legs over his shoulder while she leaned against the shower wall, and while a couple of fingers moved rhythmically inside her, he covered her clitoris with his mouth.

She gasped, then she moaned, then she almost collapsed on top of him. "Even," she rasped in a coarse whisper. And then, "I'm starving...."

He let go a sinister laugh. "Because it's almost ten o'clock and I've been working on you for hours. You're coming right along, too. Pun intended."

"Found the clutch," she said weakly.

"Every time," he agreed. He turned off the shower, wrapped a towel around her and himself. "I'll feed you. You need to keep up your strength."

Aiden heated the roasted chicken and fries in the oven while Erin tossed a salad. "Can I ask you something personal?" she began, her gaze concentrated on the salad. "I mean, I think it's personal..."

"Shoot," he said.

"What's it like being a gynecologist? I mean, being a man and a gynecologist."

He smiled and with a finger under her chin, lifted her gaze. "Ask me what you really want to ask me."

"A man, looking at the object of a man's desire all day long..."

"I don't get to do that," he said. "The object of my desire is right here." And he gave her a little kiss. "What I examine is medical—my concern is the female reproductive system. Which rocks, by the way. It's simple yet complex. And while ordinary exams might get a little boring, there just isn't anything to compare to helping new life into the world."

"Male doctors— I mean, it doesn't…"

He laughed at her. "My brothers ask me this all the time, but it usually takes a little more alcohol. No, male doctors no more get turned on by female anatomy than female doctors and nurses get turned on when caring for male patients. Now, you," he said, running a hand down her towel-covered back and slipping underneath to caress her butt, "seriously turn me on. And we need to eat a quick dinner."

"How long are you planning to stay?"

"Till you throw me out."

"Are you thinking of staying the night?"

He shrugged. "Unless you're uncomfortable sharing a bed through the night. It's up to you. But if you say yes, I'm not leaving before morning." He gave her another kiss. "Late morning."

"You're sure your family won't be looking for you?"

"I gave Luke the number in case Shelby goes into labor. She really needs to give me a break here and let me have a night alone with you before your family descends for the weekend." He grew serious. "If you'd prefer to spend the night alone, it's all right, Erin. Just tell me."

She shook her head; she wanted him to stay. "Have you ever been in love?" she asked him. "Maybe I should say, how many times have you been in love?"

It was his turn to shake his head. "I had some serious lust that I mistook for love as a young man."

"Not even your wife?"

"Especially not my wife…"

"But you married her!"

He took a deep breath. "I'm not proud of that. The fact is, I got off a ship after a really long dry spell and got thoroughly seduced by an enlisted navy medical secretary—I have no trouble believing she was far more sexually experienced than I was, and I admit, with a great deal of embarrassment, that I went into a trance. In the military, you just don't go boinking your subordinates, and I was facing serious trouble, so we got married and she was discharged, which turned out to be exactly what she wanted. I was set up from the beginning—I was a discharge chit and some pocket change. Three months later, we were divorced. It was a horrible experience."

"Was it a horrible experience for her, too?"

"I don't think so. I think she got exactly what she was after. And I think the experience goes a long way toward explaining why I found it difficult to have a trusting relationship after that. So. You? In love?"

She shook her head. "Never. Not even as a young woman. There were a couple of men I dated more than twice, but nothing much happened. We're still friends." Then she laughed. "Not really friends. They're clients."

He grinned largely. "Now, *that's* something that never happens to me," he said. "Former girlfriends never want to be my patients."

The timer buzzed and he pulled the chicken and fries out of the oven. She tossed and dressed the salad.

He carved the chicken; she pulled out plates. She had to retuck her towel around her several times. "Are we really going to eat dinner in towels? Naked, in towels?"

"You want to ditch the towels?" he asked with a smile.

"I've never done anything like this before," she admitted. "Nothing even close. In fact, I haven't done most of what we've done today."

He held out her chair for her. "Will you tell me something?"

"I'll try," she said.

"That first day—I caught you crying. Don't deny it—I caught you crying. Why?"

She laughed uncomfortably. "It's pretty silly."

"Try me."

"Oh—I was feeling kind of lonely, like maybe the dumbest thing I'd ever talked myself into was a whole summer alone on a mountaintop. I did something I don't usually allow myself to do—I was having a pity party. Somehow I started listing all the cheats of my life—including the fact that I never went to a prom."

"You asked me that—about the prom," he recalled. "What is it with girls and proms?"

"We never get over them," she said, shaking her head. "We say they're stupid and meaningless, but if we never got asked, or if we're stood up or have a disastrous time, the misery can last a lifetime. I haven't done that since, by the way. I'm completely over it." She lifted one eyebrow. "The loneliness. And the prom."

He carved off a slice of chicken breast and put it on her plate. "Eat. I'm going to take you back to bed and show you something more fun than prom."

Aiden found it difficult to get a good night's sleep while lying beside the sweet, beautiful, naked body of Erin. But he didn't begrudge the lack of sleep at all. In fact, he felt as though he could run ten miles. When the morning sun finally flooded her bedroom, he started nuzzling her neck again. "I think I just spent the best night of my life," he whispered to her.

"Mmm. Me, too. And I'm completely exhausted," she replied.

And he thought she might be just a little sore, too. "I'd be glad to make you breakfast," he said. "I'd be happy to roll you around in the sheets some more. But, honey, I bet you've had about enough. And you need sleep before your family arrives."

"I hope you like me a lot," she said through a yawn. "Because if you don't, I'll have to give this up. And I *like* this."

He laughed lightly. "I like you a lot," he confessed.

"Oh, good." She snuggled up to him.

"Are you hungry, honey?"

"No, I'm sleepy, Aiden. Every time you rolled over in your sleep, you had a new idea." She yawned hugely. "I'm very, very happy, but I'm tired. I need a little nap before company comes."

He kissed her on the cheek. "I'm going to set up your coffeepot and leave you. We'll see each other over the weekend, families all over the place. Then I want a date with you the second you're alone." He rolled over to scrape what was left of his box of condoms into the top draw of the nightstand and what did he find? "Whoa," he said, pulling out a not-very-mysteriously-shaped vibrator. "Toys. I didn't know we had toys!"

She yawned again. "Didn't I mention that? I told you—I didn't really date that much…"

He put the device away. "Gotta love a modern woman. We'll play with that another time." He rolled back to her and pressed his lips against hers. "Thank you, honey. I had a wonderful time."

He began to roll away from her when she said, "Aiden?" He turned back. "What is this? Is this a summer fling?"

He gave her another kiss. "At the very least."

"Hmm," she hummed, smiling and closing her eyes.

Aiden had worked up a pretty good appetite. He didn't want to bang around in Erin's kitchen looking for food, because she needed her sleep. He, on the other hand, felt as if he could bench-press three-fifty and eat a cow. He readied the coffeepot so she would only have to flip the on switch, and left the cabin.

He wasn't sure what he had in his place for food, and since he'd gone missing for a couple of days and it was 10:00 a.m., he ran through town and decided he'd get a bite to eat at Jack's. When he walked in, the place was nearly deserted. Mel sat up on a stool while Jack was behind the bar. They appeared to be having a cup of coffee together. When Mel turned toward him, her eyes lit up. "Hey, Doc! Haven't seen you in a while. How's it going?"

"Great," he said, sitting up beside her. To Jack he asked, "What are the chances Preacher's still making breakfast?"

"For you? I don't see a problem. Coffee?"

"Please," he said, giving the bar a couple of taps. "How's the Sheridan family?"

"Growing, always growing," Mel said. "If we can get David to stop peeing in the yard, we're going to really celebrate."

Jack leaned on the bar. "Tell her, Aiden—men love it when they figure out they can pee anywhere. Women hate it. Women hate the complexity of their sit-down lives. This is why I put the seat down—it's pity. I realize they have it rougher. Plus, we just have to shake…they have to wipe. Life just isn't fair sometimes, is it?"

Aiden couldn't help but laugh. "If you think I'm getting anywhere near this discussion, you're delusional."

"Fine, be a wimp," Jack said, pouring him a coffee. "I'll go back and talk Preacher into one more omelet."

"That would be appreciated."

Mel turned toward him. "You still logging on hiking miles?" she asked.

"More or less. And other stuff. Mostly kicking back—but I did have a quasi-interview with a couple of OBs who have a practice in Redding. Great practice, but I don't know about the location…"

"What are you looking for? As far as location?"

"Not sure," he said with a shrug, lifting his coffee

to his lips. He took a sip and lowered it to the bar. "Maybe more to the south…"

"Bigger city? Like maybe San Francisco? John Stone from Grace Valley was in an OB practice in Sausalito. Very successful, well-known and according to John, totally dysfunctional practice. Maybe you should talk to him about it, just so you can avoid the well-known dysfunctional shops."

"Good idea."

"Seriously, south of here? Like, where?"

He thought for a second, then felt himself smiling automatically. "Really, not sure, but I've just started kind of seeing a woman from Chico.…"

"Erin?" Mel asked immediately, with excitement in her voice. "Erin Foley?"

"You know Erin?"

"I do!" she said. "Oh, I love Erin. She's awesome, isn't she? How did you meet her? Because she's way out there on the mountain and hardly ever comes to town."

"I was hiking," he said. "I put in a lot of miles around these hills and valleys and came across her cabin." He decided to leave out the part about the concussion, but if he knew anything about Virgin River, plenty of people probably already knew.

Jack came out of the back and said, "You lucked out—no grumbling from the cook. He's working up an omelet and some sausage patties."

"Jack, Aiden has been seeing Erin Foley!" Mel said rather enthusiastically. "Isn't that great news?"

"I guess so," Jack said with a shrug. "Women get a

lot more excited about those kinds of hookups than men do. I'll tell you this, though. This place? A lot of guys, including me, come here thinking they're just going to have a quiet, peaceful life, do a little fishing, maybe in your case, hiking. But if you happen to run into a woman here—it's curtains, man. Quiet is out the friggin' window."

"Jack," Mel scolded with a little laugh.

"It's the truth, baby. I've seen it a dozen times, starting with me. I was way past getting married and having a family when this hot little mama came sashaying into town and I fell hard."

"Bet you fought it like a man, though, didn't you, buddy?" Aiden asked, taking a sip of his coffee.

"I fought it not at all, my brother. She did all the fighting, but I trapped her." He leaned toward his wife and gave her a small kiss. "Preacher will bring out your breakfast, Doc. I have to drive over to Eureka for supplies. We have a big town picnic on Monday."

"So I heard."

"You're coming, aren't you?"

"Me and every Riordan and Booth within a hundred miles."

Jack's lips split in a huge grin. "Now, that's what I like to hear." To his wife, he said, "I'll be gone about three hours, baby. Can you manage without me taking Davie along?"

"I'm keeping the babysitter all day. I'm going to catch up on some paperwork at the clinic and then I'm going home early. If there's nothing going on, that is."

"Perfect," he said. "Later, Doc." And he was gone.

Aiden focused on Mel. "So. I've known Erin a few weeks at most. How long have you known her?"

"I met her a couple of years ago, but hadn't seen her till she came back up here this summer. I know her sister, Marcie. Marcie came up here in search of her late husband's sergeant—her husband's best friend and the man he served under in Iraq. Well, actually, Ian wasn't just his sergeant and friend, but the man who saved Bobby's life. But sadly, Marcie's husband was catastrophically wounded—a quad with severe brain damage. He lived in a nursing home for a few years before a sweet, quiet death. And Ian was holed up in that cabin, almost as unresponsive as Marcie's husband. Do you know Marcie?"

"I haven't met her, no," Aiden said.

"Well, she's a spitfire. She was determined to find Ian and make sure he was all right, that he didn't have posttraumatic stress disorder or whatever. Ian had risked his life to save Bobby's and had been wounded in the process, then just disappeared. So Marcie felt she had to know what happened to him. But Erin was very concerned. She came up here to bring Marcie home." Mel laughed and shook her head. "Marcie wouldn't go and Erin was a little beside herself. She was used to calling the shots in the family, used to being the parent figure…"

"I guess things worked out," he said. "Marcie's the one having a baby, right?"

"That's right. I haven't seen Marcie since just before Christmas. She and Ian like to come up here for the lighting of the town tree."

"I hear they're due back for a visit—maybe they'll come into town."

"Oh, I hope so," Mel said. "She's an amazing young woman, but all that determination… I just can't imagine what it must have been like raising her."

Preacher brought out a steaming plate and placed it in front of Aiden. "Morning, Doc," he said. He reached under the bar for utensils rolled in a napkin. "That do it for you?"

"Perfect. I really appreciate it." Then to Mel he said, "Erin said her folks have passed away, so I guess you'll never know."

"Erin would be the one to ask. She raised her brother and sister."

The fork was midway to Aiden's mouth and stopped in midair. "She said she had a lot of responsibility…."

"Well, that's putting it mildly. Erin's mother died when she was eleven years old. Marcie was four and her little brother, Drew, was about two years old—still in diapers. As I understand it, their father was kind of oblivious—grief-stricken and all. When he wasn't grief-stricken and oblivious, he was working and Erin was needed to manage the house and kids. Erin rushed home from elementary school and then junior high to babysit, clean house, do laundry, start dinner and get babies settled into bed. Then, when the younger kids were just teens and Erin was in her first semester of law school, their father died. I think the youngest was thirteen. Really, she's been mothering since she was eleven."

The prom, he thought. "Eleven?" he asked. He put

a forkful of omelet in his mouth, though his horrendous appetite seemed to have dried up.

"Quite something, isn't it? And it's not as though she got them to the age of eighteen and could finally have a life of her own. Drew went to college and then medical school—Marcie said he'd never have made it without Erin. Oh—and Marcie? Well, she had a disabled husband and gives Erin all the credit for eking every available benefit out of the Marine Corps for his care. And she didn't just manage that—she was there at the nursing home along with Bobby's family and Marcie, helping hands-on. I know she doesn't look like your average nurse's aide, but Erin was as involved as anyone in the two families."

He took another bite, though he could barely swallow. Eleven? A full-time law student running herd on teenagers? A lawyer with a busy practice helping to care for a disabled marine in a nursing home? "Sounds like she had to work unbelievably hard her entire life...."

"To tell the truth, I think she missed a lot of her childhood," Mel said. She jumped off her stool and walked around the bar. She grabbed the coffeepot and refilled his cup. "Marcie and Ian just moved out of her father's house last summer. Drew went to L.A. to start his residency in orthopedics. I don't think Erin's had a life of her own before now." Then she smiled. "You just can't imagine how happy it makes me to think you've been seeing her. A good man to pass the time? That's perfect. So, don't tell me anything that will make me blush, but how do you pass the time?"

Aiden grinned at her and it was the best acting job

he'd ever pulled off. "Well, let's see—I chased a bear out of her kitchen."

"Get out!"

"I did. I think that's what made her decide I was man enough for other activities. She was baking cookies, left the doors open while she was in the bathroom and Yogi paid a visit. There's a bear out there somewhere with a bellyful of chocolate-chip cookies and cookie dough. Then I took her biking along the coast and almost killed her—apparently she hadn't indulged in any strenuous exercise that lasted longer than fifteen minutes. So, next, we had dinner together—lifting the fork worked out. A little sightseeing, a lot of getting to know each other...you know..."

"It's been a long time, but I think I remember. Jack took me to see the whales."

"I guess since we're all going to be around town for the Fourth, we'll meet each other's families," Aiden said. "I'm anxious to meet Marcie and Ian, but I don't know if I'm ready to introduce Erin to my family."

"Why ever not?" Mel asked in surprise. "You have a wonderful family!"

"Have you met my brothers? Do they ever shut up?"

"Oh, I see—you're going to be teased."

"Pretty much relentlessly," he said.

She patted his arm. "You're a big boy. You'll get through it. And if it's any comfort to you, I won't tease you. And if Jack starts, I'll step on his foot."

"Very nice of you, Mel," he said.

She looked at her watch. "I'm going to leave you. I want to get that paperwork finished so I can get home early today. When you're ready to settle up, Preacher's in the kitchen. Just poke your head in."

"Sure. Thanks."

"Good luck on the job search, Aiden. I wish you were staying close, but I understand your need to find a bigger town. We can't really support another OB around here."

"Mel? Do you think Erin missed things that she still thinks about sometimes? You know—things that the rest of us took for granted. Like football games and dances? Sports and other after-school stuff. The prom? Things like that?"

"Probably. She's been completely devoted to Marcie and Drew for twenty-five years. That wouldn't have left much free time. And I do know she never moved out of her parents' house. Most young people go away to college, get horrible first apartments with equally horrible first roommates. But Erin never left home because of the kids."

He was quiet for a moment before he said, "What an amazing woman."

"Isn't she? I'm so glad you two met." She walked briskly toward the door. "See you Monday at the picnic, Aiden."

"See you," he said. But he was thinking, she rushed home from school for child care and chores, and did that for twenty-five years? Aiden had grown up on the poor side, but he'd never missed a thing. He'd gone to the prom; he'd thought it was a totally useless waste of money not to get laid. It took quite a few years to recognize that girls didn't see it the same way. But the way Erin thought of it? That was way out of his experience.

He took his plate back to the kitchen and put it on the counter. "Hey, Preach. What do I owe you?"

Preacher looked at it and scowled. "Was something wrong with it?"

"It was perfect," Aiden said. He rubbed a hand on his stomach. "I ate some fish last night that was a little off, y'know? I didn't want to press my luck."

"Well, hey, I can't charge you if you can't eat it."

Aiden laughed. "How you guys make a living is beyond me. Pretend I ate it. What's the damage?"

"Eight," Preacher said.

"And coffee?" Aiden asked, pulling out his wallet.

"Eight twenty-five."

He put a ten on the worktable. He added a dollar. He added another dollar and pushed it toward Preacher. Nowhere he'd ever lived could you get a huge breakfast like that for eight dollars. Maybe the navy mess, but that stuff could be inedible. Preacher's food was fantastic. "Thanks," he said to the cook.

Preacher scooped up the bills. "And that, my friend, is how we make a living."

Ten

Jack had supplies to get, for bar and kitchen stock as well as the Fourth of July picnic on Monday. He'd convinced Preacher they should supply the ribs and beer and that got the big man leafing through his recipes for barbecue ribs.

But Jack had another mission. He had an appointment with Dr. John Stone.

Jack had a lot of respect for John. Although Jack had ended up delivering his own babies, John had been good backup. But more important, John had saved Mel's life when she'd suffered a postpartum hemorrhage. Of course, she'd lost her uterus, but John had tried to save it and understood that would be a hard loss for Mel. But her life, her life... What was there to think about? Jack couldn't live without her.

He only had to sit in the waiting room for ten minutes before John came out and shook his hand. "Jack, how you doing, man?"

"Good, good," Jack said. "It's been a while. You coming out to the picnic on the Fourth?"

"I don't know, Jack—I heard fireworks are out…"

Jack just laughed. "Listen, idiot, we don't like to send sparks over a lot of dry timber in the middle of fire season. You could come for the company.…"

"Might think about that. Come on back. I have the office. Dr. Hudson snuck out early. Her son bit someone on the playground."

"Ew," Jack said. "What do you do about biting?"

"There are many unproven theories," John said. "But no matter what you hear—don't bite back. I think that gets you a visit from Child Protective Services."

They entered the small office, and while John went to sit behind the desk, Jack sat in a chair facing it. "We're totally safe," Jack said. "Social services still has us on a wait list for the newborn baby that was left on the clinic's porch about four years ago."

They both laughed.

"So," Jack said. "You know why I'm here, right? To talk to you about how natural and everyday business this whole surrogate baby thing is for you…"

"Was," John said. "We don't do so much of that here. We tend to refer. We did have a woman who had a baby for her sister and we handled prenatal care and delivery. The clinic I worked with in Sausalito had a very busy fertility business—we could do everything but create life in test tubes. We could harvest eggs, collect and freeze sperm, inseminate, implant fertilized ova. The subjects…or parents and surrogate had their own lawyers to negotiate the terms and we had a consultant to keep us legal, but yeah, it was a pretty regular event."

"A good option for women who can't have babies on their own, I guess," Jack said.

"Really, it is," John answered. "We don't have many patients in the valley who are looking for help in that area. It's expensive, for one thing. Insurance won't cover it. But, Jack, if you've got all the stuff—the eggs, the sperm—and all you need is a womb… Think about it. Couples who couldn't have children with their own DNA twenty years ago are doing it now for not much more than the cost of adoption."

"Just a regular, standard, typical day at the office?" Jack asked with a big grin. "Tell me how that worked."

"Well," John said, leaning back. "We had our own surgi-center. We could harvest a woman's eggs there and use a very high-tech lab to freeze them and store them. We sent them the father's sperm…."

"*You* sent it?"

John chuckled. "We collected it and sent it. We had a very private, nice little bathroom stocked with reading material—the staff called it the masturba-torium."

Jack burst out laughing. "You are shitting me!"

"I am not lying."

"And if a guy wanted to stay in there all day…?"

"We could go a long way toward the respect of a man's privacy," John said with a little chuckle. "I mean, who knows if it's hard for him to get in the mood or if he's trying to beat his record, no pun intended. A little vial of sperm went lickety-split to the lab to join the eggs. The mother or, if the mother didn't have a viable womb, the surrogate, came to the clinic and we could either inseminate or implant. We had a very good success rate."

"And how many surrogates did this for a new house or a boat?"

"That wasn't my department. That's between the surrogate and the parents, and it's the legal department's job to make sure all the laws—strict laws—are followed, which is why we refer from the Grace Valley Clinic. I can recommend some very good clinics not too far from—"

Jack leaned forward and rested his elbows on his knees. He clasped his hands and hung his head. The small office fell silent. Finally he looked up at John. "This isn't the thing to do," he said quietly. "John, this isn't the thing to do."

John leaned toward Jack. "What are you doing here? You said you wanted to talk about it. Mel led me to believe—"

"I know. Mel led you to believe I was on board with this and wanted to know the particulars. Listen, John— that's not how it is. I told her I didn't like the idea. That we didn't need more children. I told her if she wanted to adopt a kid that otherwise wouldn't have a family, I could probably be talked into that, but…" He shook his head.

"What part of this bothers you? Because it's a reasonable alternative for a woman who can't physically give birth to her own offspring."

"What puts me off is my wife—all excited about

another baby, and she's not even having it! She wasn't this excited or upbeat when she got caught with our own. It's weird, John, and I'm worried about her. We were fine with what happened with the hysterectomy—disappointed, but fine with it. " Jack rubbed a hand across the back of his neck. "I don't know what it is, John. I'd do anything Mel asked me if it meant a lot to her, especially if we hadn't been able to have children of our own. I'd fill up your little cup in the masturbatorium. I'd probably want to pass on watching some woman I don't know give birth to my child, but for Mel I'd go through with the thing, but this isn't what we need. Something's wrong, John. And I don't know what it is."

John was leaning back in his chair. He picked up a pen and fiddled with it. He leaned farther back and frowned more as he listened to Jack talk. Finally he asked, "Has she had a hard time accepting her hysterectomy?"

"Like how?"

John shrugged. "Crying? Anger? Just plain complaining that her gut feels empty? Loss of libido? Anything?"

Jack shook his head. "Nothing at all. She breezed right through it. I hadn't heard a word about it until she came to the bar one afternoon and announced we were having another baby. And that we were going to do it in a very innovative thirty-thousand-dollar way with a stranger. It was like she took on a whole new, all-hyped-up personality. Not herself. Not at all."

"Oh, brother," John said, hanging his head. "Jack,

I'm sorry. I think I might have gotten caught up in the whole thing right along with Mel. Try to understand— it made me feel so good to provide this option to couples."

"Am I overreacting? Am I just some wimp who won't do what has to be done? Because I don't think I'm that kind of husband. Something about this and the way Mel is all worked up about it just doesn't feel right. I want her to be happy, but I want her to be normally happy."

"And it just doesn't seem like that's the case?"

He shook his head. "She's all over this thing. She's already asked Brie to look into the legalities so she can be in charge of the negotiating and the contract. It's a puzzle to me and I keep looking for the missing pieces...."

"Missing pieces?" John asked.

"You know—if we'd talked about a much larger family before the hysterectomy I could understand this—but I always thought she was okay with our two. She's a busy midwife and shuffling kids between the two of us is complicated sometimes. Or—maybe if she'd brought it up as a suggestion and wanted to talk about it, think about it, but that didn't happen, either. She'd made up her mind before she came to me with the idea. What don't I get here?"

"What she's feeling," John said.

"She's feeling like she wants a baby, right now, no matter how inconvenient it is—and she wants it to be ours."

"She might be covering up a feeling of loss with plans to have a baby with a surrogate," John suggested.

"That's what I told Brie—that Mel seems to be determined to beat this thing, to be in control of having a baby, even if she can't have it herself. Did you know that Mel and her late husband had a bunch of fertilized ova stored in some freezer in L.A.? They'd tried the whole in vitro thing, but in Mel's uterus. I keep asking myself—is it just because for someone like Mel, this is business as usual? Or is she trying to get beyond the whole hysterectomy by proving it won't stop her from having as many children as she wants? Like she's in denial about some things." He shook his head. "Not only haven't I ever been up against anything like this before in my life, I have no idea how to deal with it."

"You have to be honest with her, Jack. You have to tell her you don't want to."

Jack leaned back in his chair and stretched out one long leg till his booted foot hit the desk. "There's the problem. I told her. Several times. She's not listening to me at all. She pats my hand like a patient grandmother and tells me to keep an open mind and talk to John about it."

"Well, there you go," John said, standing up. "You talked to me."

"Not with an open mind," Jack said, also standing. "Now what?"

"Now you have to talk to your wife and tell her the truth—you're not going to do it because you don't think it needs to be done. Get the cards out on the table. All the facts—this wasn't an issue until recently. Make sure it isn't more about losing fertility, losing an organ, than about wanting more children. You have to tell her,

Jack—you're not a participant. Have a real honest talk. Maybe she is in denial. She might be running scared from the grief that's pretty normal in women who go through hysterectomies right in the midst of their childbearing years."

"Aw, Jesus," Jack said. "I've been through some serious grief with Mel. Her dead husband, you know. I can't say I look forward to something like that again. Maybe it would be easier to just visit the masturbatorium…"

"Some women," John said, interrupting, "go through a serious adjustment when they face the end of their childbearing years. It isn't just in the case of hysterectomies. Some women in menopause feel that with the absence of their periods. When they have to use lubricants, facing the end of all that womanly stuff of youth, they feel that they're just not as much of a woman. They feel like failures, like life is passing them by. I suggested a good lubricant to one of my patients and she said her husband rejected the idea, that if it wasn't natural he wasn't interested—he felt she wasn't in the mood if she didn't lubricate like when they were twenty. I told her to send him in to talk to me—that it *was* normal for a fifty-eight-year-old woman to be drier than a twenty-eight-year-old woman. Sometimes they feel old age staring them in the face.… They feel like grandmothers when they're way too young to feel that way. One woman cried in my office and said, "I'm way too young to be this old!" They worry that their femininity and youth are slipping away. It isn't logical, but it's real." He shrugged. "Sometimes it's just hormones and we have to make adjustments. Sometimes I prescribe antide-pressants for a while."

"I'm not doing my job if she feels that way.…"

John just laughed. "You can't control everything, Jack. Just take a media study—wrinkles and gray hair on men tend to make them look more worldly and powerful, but the world sees the same thing in women as the end. It's not so, but it can be an emotional battle for some women."

"That just doesn't seem like Mel," Jack said. "She's so levelheaded.…"

"If you've already told her you don't like this idea and yet she's made an appointment to have eggs harvested—is that levelheaded?"

"God," Jack said, dropping his gaze to the floor.

"Sometimes counseling helps. Sometimes just a husband's tender reinforcement that she's the woman you want no matter how her body changes… Listen, let me know if you need help. But for Mel's sake—face it down. Get to the bottom of this."

Jack was silent for a long moment. He took a deep breath. He stuck out his hand to shake John's and said, "Thanks. You were absolutely zero help."

John laughed. "I'm sorry I couldn't make it easier."

"Not as sorry as me."

"Good luck. But really, if it doesn't work out, call me. I'm willing to get in this with you two, but I'd like to be sure what we're dealing with, for her sake. Mel is really important to me, too."

"Now, *that* might help. I appreciate it."

* * *

Aiden was still feeling a bit melancholy by the time he got back to Luke's. He saw that Luke, Shelby and Art were sitting on the porch at the house, and Luke gave a wave. Aiden walked over. "How are you feeling?" he asked Shelby.

"Ready," she said with a smile.

"And how are you feeling?" Aiden asked Luke.

"Ready and so *not* ready," he said.

Aiden chuckled and looked at Art. "And good morning, Art. How are you feeling this morning?"

Art took a drink of his diet soda and said, "I want to get married with Netta."

Luke instantly lost all the color in his face and groaned. Shelby, however, just ran a hand over her big belly. "I don't think so, Art," she said. "You shouldn't get married now. We need your help around here—especially with the baby coming. Besides, it's hard to be married to someone who lives in Fortuna if you don't drive a car."

"Oh," he said. Then he turned to Luke. "Should I drive a car?"

"No!" Luke said harshly, clearly in a panic.

"We'll drive you wherever you need to go, Art," Shelby said more calmly. "Don't worry about that."

"Okay," he said. "You'll drive me to Netta's house?"

"Of course," she said, smiling. "I'd be happy to. In fact, I'll call Ellen and ask if Netta can come to the Fourth of July picnic in town. Would you like that?"

He smiled. "That would be good."

"Consider it done," Shelby said. "It will be fun to get to know her."

Aiden chuckled and sat down on the porch steps. "Art, why don't you go see if the fish are biting."

"I'm on my break," he said. Art was very careful of rules and routine. He liked following instructions, especially Luke's.

"It's okay," Luke said. "Go ahead if you feel like it."

"I feel like it," Art said with a smile. And he hefted himself up and lumbered off, stopping at the front of his cabin to grab his rod and reel.

When he was out of earshot, Aiden said, "Try not to worry so much, Luke. I think Art's pretty happy to be talking to Netta again. Ellen suggested we all just keep an eye on them and see how the renewed relationship is shaping up, make sure they're not headed for trouble or anything. But she also said there was no indication from Netta's behavior that she had a real active libido. Maybe this is something Netta mentioned to Art—Art's been talking to her on the phone, right?"

Luke nodded. "I have to punch in the numbers for him. They don't seem to talk that much, but they like being on the phone."

"Well, don't worry. Maybe you should ask to drop in to Ellen's support group a few times. Pick up some very important information—stuff that people just don't know. Things I didn't know, and I thought I was up on some of this stuff."

"Like what?" Luke asked.

"Well—here's something. I know I told you Netta's on birth control as a precaution, but not because she might accidentally have sex with some boyfriend like Art. It helps with PMS, for one thing. And to protect her from pregnancy in a worst-case scenario. Like sexual abuse—rape. There are predators out there who look for vulnerable women like Netta and her roommates."

"Oh, *God!*" Luke nearly roared, standing up fast as a shot. "You gotta be *kidding* me!"

"I had a similar reaction, but I managed not to stand up and shout about it. Made me think about things. It's a very dark, very tragic reality. Netta, by all accounts, is very eager to please—what's she going to do if a bunch of high school boys tell her to meet them after school? And—it's illegal to sterilize a mentally challenged woman… To get her an abortion would be a legal nightmare and impossible without her consent, which someone like Netta wouldn't be able to give. To let her give birth to a rapist's baby could be an even worse trauma. Her caretakers are taking the only precautions they can to keep her safe in a dangerous world. I'm sure there are a million more things to understand."

Luke's face was actually red. "Aiden, if I ever came face-to-face with a man who would sexually molest a mentally challenged woman, I don't know if I could keep from—"

Aiden stood, as well. "I understand completely. Listen, you've done a great job with Art and he's content, anyone can see that," Aiden said. "But I think you and Shelby would benefit from getting to know Ellen and Bo and maybe, down the road when there's time, you should try out that support group."

"Yeah," Luke said. "Yeah…"

"Try not to worry too much, Luke. Art's not going to marry Netta. And it's good he has a friend."

"I might have been a little tense lately—Mom being around, Art wanting to marry someone, Shelby ready to have a baby…"

"Ya think?" Shelby asked with a smile. "I'll call Ellen and offer to pick up Netta for the picnic, if Netta wants to come. It'll be fun."

"I should do it, baby," Luke said. "You're too pregnant."

"To drive a car?" Aiden and Shelby asked at the same time.

Aiden turned and went to his cabin, chuckling as he went. He flipped on his laptop, signed on to his e-mail account and found an e-mail from someone he didn't recognize. He opened it and read, Aiden—I have to talk to you. It's urgent. It's more than urgent. It's about our divorce. Call me at once. Here is my cell number. Annalee

He sat down and typed, No. Go away. Pretend I'm dead.

Within five minutes he heard a ping, alerting him of new mail. I'd love to, but that won't work. Call me at once!!!

Despite Erin's lack of sleep and her desire to spend the rest of her life in bed with Aiden, she was thrilled to see Marcie. Her sister looked absolutely beautiful—just as round as could be and happier than Erin had ever seen her. Her cheeks were flushed, her eyes bright and her laugh quick. Ian was bursting with both pride and a very special soft attentiveness toward his wife. Those two, who had been through so much, had reached a place of peace and contentment in their lives, in their marriage, and it gave Erin great satisfaction to have helped them along.

She didn't realize that she was looking a bit different to Marcie and Ian. She was calm and fulfilled, a lot more relaxed than was typical for her. It was something she could feel but didn't know would show on her face, in her lithe movements, in her twinkling eyes and secret smile. After their initial hugs of greeting, she poured them all iced fruit drinks and suggested they sit out on the deck to watch the sunset. Ian and Marcie went first, Erin following with a big aluminum soup pot and a metal spoon, which she casually put beside her chaise.

"Uh, Erin—what's that for?" Ian asked.

"Oh, I have that bear."

Ian and Marcie exchanged looks, then looked back at Erin. "What bear?"

"I told you about the bear," she said. "You know—the one in the house?"

"I think you might've forgotten to mention that...."

And then she tried to recall. Actually, she'd talked to them daily but had been leaving out anything in her summer at the cabin that had to do with Aiden, so she'd left out many things. But she was going to introduce him to her sister and brother-in-law, so she had better catch them up a bit. "Well, remember the vagrant who caused my concussion?" she began. By the end of her explanation and story, leaving out the more delicious details, they were both staring at her with wide eyes and open mouths. "What?" Erin asked.

"You fell in love," Marcie said softly.

"Don't be ridiculous," Erin returned with a flip of her hand. "I'm simply hiking and biking with someone and allowing him the privilege of chasing my bear out of the kitchen. By the way, I'm sorry about the cookies. I know how much you like them, but I was afraid to make more."

"You fell in love with a vagrant who turned out to be a doctor and you're like a completely different person," Marcie said. "Erin, you're all soft and cuddly."

"Oh, pooh—you're just very pregnant and sentimental."

"When do we meet him?" Ian wanted to know.

"Well—I have you guys in town for the weekend and he has tons of family at his brother's for the weekend and longer, but I guess we'll all be at the Fourth of July picnic at Jack's on Monday. Try not to embarrass me by making too much of this. All right?"

"All right," Marcie said, grinning from ear to ear.

Aiden had had total peace in the eight years since his divorce. He hadn't been able to find a woman to settle down with, but he'd been extremely pleased that he hadn't had to deal with that whackjob Annalee.

Well, apparently that was over—in true Annalee fashion. He should never have responded to her e-mail.

What followed were literally *hundreds* of e-mails. Call me immediately! I have to talk to you! You don't understand how urgent this is—and I'm not telling you anything until I talk to you and hear your voice!

He knew she was cutting and pasting, or maybe she'd set up her computer to keep sending every five seconds, but that didn't diminish the panic it threatened to fill him with. Just the thought of having her anywhere near his life at this time made him want to run as fast and as far as he could.

The only two people who could possibly understand his panic were his brothers Sean and Luke—the only two who had ever actually met her in the flesh. He had called them both—he'd said something like "I got in some trouble, got married to a nutcase a couple of months ago and now I'm working on a divorce, and I haven't told Mom." Luke, who had gone through his own horrific marriage/divorce crisis at roughly the same age, took some leave and flew to San Diego to make sure Aiden was all right. Aiden wasn't too all right and Luke called in Sean.

Try as he might to get her to leave him alone, Annalee kept coming around. When Luke met her, he asked, "Holy shit, Aiden! Is she human?" He saw how beautiful and sneaky Annalee was and couldn't believe she was real. Sean was the one who said, "Buy her off. You can make her go away with money." They even offered to pool their funds to finance her departure, but Aiden hadn't needed financial help. He'd been on a boat for two years; his money had been going in the bank.

Everyone in the family knew about her after it was all over, of course, just as they knew about how much trouble he'd been facing when he'd gotten mixed up with her. They also knew what it had cost him to get out of it. After all that had been resolved, his brief marriage to the little sex kitten had become a joke with his brothers—Aiden got off a big gray boat with a hard-on and the first willing woman he encountered was a sociopath with extraordinary skills in bed. Ha-ha.

Not so funny right now.

He turned off his computer. She might crash it with her e-mails. Tough. He'd just buy a new one. He knew from experience that even the slightest response could somehow set off the diabolical Annalee. In the past she had somehow managed to glean information about him and his family that he didn't intend for her to have. He was sticking to his guns—he was done with her!

On Saturday he went to Eureka, shopping. He couldn't find what he was looking for in the couple of dress shops he visited, so he ended up at a clothing-consignment store where he bought an emerald-green strapless chiffon dress. It was used, of course, but he was out of options. He wasn't entirely sure of Erin's size, but he thought he was at least close. There was no question about the color of her eyes—like his—that Irish green. He also bought a pair of silver slip-on heels. He had a scheme and that made him smile and forget all about Annalee.

That night the Riordans had a big family meal at Luke's and on Sunday everyone went to General Booth's house to gather with Shelby's side of the family. Everyone was there, including Tom Booth on leave after two years of West Point, with his newly engaged fiancée, Brenda, who was a college student in New York, not far from the academy Tom attended. They were only back in Virgin River for a couple of weeks of Tom's leave; Tom was headed for some airborne training with the army. In the academy, you didn't get summers off like civilian college. Active-duty military were always in training or on assignment.

And then came the Fourth, Monday. No one in Aiden's family seemed to notice how anxious he was to get to the picnic, or that he was the first to head in that direction. By noon he was there, craning his neck for Erin. He had a beer and it seemed like forever before she appeared with Marcie and Ian. Though he tried to be cool, he couldn't hide the light in his eyes. And to his satisfaction, the light in hers matched. He stood on the porch of the bar and looked way down the street to where they had parked and were walking toward him. He wanted to sprint toward her, pick her up, whirl her around and carry her off somewhere private. But that wasn't going to happen. The knowing eye contact was going to have to be enough for now.

He did greet her before doing anything else, however. He walked toward her at a controlled pace, took her hands in his and bussed her cheek. He met her sister and brother-in-law, fussed over the nice round belly Marcie sported, shook Ian's hand vigorously and congratulated him. And he conveyed, with his eyes, that he couldn't wait to get Erin alone.

The day was filled with new introductions and reunions. No one in the Riordan family had any idea who Erin was, so that was more than a little exciting to Sean and Luke. Maureen snuck up beside Aiden and said, "Oh my, she's lovely, Aiden. How amazing you met her here." Aiden saw Marcie embrace Jack and Mel like old friends; he overheard Ian explain that he was in his last semester of college. He would student teach at his old high school in the fall and, if things went according to plan, he would teach music there. He would direct the high school musical; when he was in high school there, he'd been the star, Marcie bragged. At around four o'clock, Ian Buchanan sang the "Star Spangled Banner" a cappella and almost brought Aiden to his knees with the beauty of his voice.

At a point after hamburgers, Ian handed Aiden a beer and said, "So. You and Erin?"

"I hope so."

"She's amazing."

"I couldn't agree more," Aiden said.

"We owe her just about everything. She's the reason everyone is okay—me, Marcie, Drew, absolutely everyone."

"Tell me why," Aiden said.

"She spent her whole life taking care of everything from the day her mother died a long time ago. I'm sure there was plenty she needed, but she worried about everyone else. There was a time I resented her for bossing Marcie and telling her what to do, but once I realized it was all out of love and total commitment, I got over it fast. I want Erin to have everything she ever wanted."

Aiden smiled at the man. He smiled in a way that would comfort him because that's what Aiden wanted, too. "Tell me about this baby that's coming."

Ian brightened at once. "His name will be Heath Bradley Buchanan and he's coming on the twentieth of August. It's scheduled. He's breech now. If he doesn't turn, he'll come by C-section. We're okay with that—as long as he's okay. He's right on target."

"You're so lucky," Aiden said.

"You have kids, Doc?" he asked.

Aiden shook his head. It was in his mind to say he'd just barely found the right girl, but instead, he said, "Still single."

"What a coincidence," Ian said. "Erin's single, too."

"I know," Aiden said with a laugh. "I love the way that worked out."

Shelby found an empty chair on the bar porch and grabbed it. She had finally wrestled free of Luke, who had been sticking to her like glue for the last couple of weeks. She had convinced him to go have a beer with his brothers and friends and let her relax in the shade for a while. With a glass of ice water, she rocked back and forth in one of the porch rockers and soon realized she had the best seat in the house.

From where she sat, she saw Art and Netta at the

picnic table farthest from the crowd. They sat opposite each other and ate their hamburgers and potato salad, apparently completely content, though it didn't appear they talked much at all. It was as though they each realized comfort in the mere presence of the other, and Shelby found herself thinking, *If that's not true love, I don't know what is.*

Brenda Carpenter's fourteen-year-old sister, Leslie, had a group of little kids gathered in a circle, holding hands and playing ring-around-the-rosy; she made sure she held the hand of the littlest one. Shelby made a mental note to get to know Leslie just a little better; the moms around here had tipped her—you had to get your babysitters before they discovered boys and were allowed to date. Fourteen- to sixteen-year-old girls were perfect. Leslie had control of both the Sheridan kids, both the Haggerty kids, Rosie Riordan and Christopher Middleton, and held one of Abby Michaels's twins on her hip. The moms occupied a picnic table not far away, enjoying a moment of peace without the kids climbing all over them.

Shelby's brother-in-law Aiden moved silently up behind Erin Foley, put his hands on her shoulders and when she turned her head to smile up at him, he pulled her backward behind the church where they were out of sight. She laughed to herself. Aiden was trying to play it cool around his brothers, but really, who did he think he was kidding?

She heard Mel shout from the backyard. "Jack!" And then Jack turned away from the grill he was manning with Preacher and young Rick Sudder in time to see little David had wandered away from the ring-around-the-rosy game to go pee on a tree. Jack approached his small son and towered above him, hands on his hips, glaring down at him. Finally, David turned, yanked up his pants and grinned up at his dad, who was shaking his head in frustration or disappointment or maybe even pride. Jack crouched for a stern talk and a finger shake that promised one more of those moments would get David a good talking-to.

Tom Booth sat on the ground, leaning up against a tree, Brenda sitting between his long legs and leaning back against him. Nearby, Ricky's fiancée, Liz, sat cross-legged on the ground visiting with them. The general and Muriel were sharing a picnic table and conversation with Maureen and George, Ellie and Noah. Kids and dogs ran everywhere; people sat in lawn chairs, on the ground, at tables, or just gathered in clumps to joke and laugh and catch up on the latest gossip. Preacher and Rick kept putting out food on the tables brought from inside; several coolers held iced beer, wine, sodas, water and juice. A donation jar was filling up—no one was ever charged for party food and drink, but tips were gratefully accepted.

Shelby felt the baby moving; the movements now were so powerful they could almost make her wince. She leaned her head back, closed her eyes and rocked. She might've even dozed for a moment or two. When she opened her eyes, Mel was standing in front of her, leaning against the porch railing, arms crossed over her chest. "Get plenty of rest now," Mel advised. "It won't be long before you have one peeing on a tree at the town picnic."

"I saw that," Shelby said with a chuckle.

"That's Jack's doing," she said. "You're going to want to watch out for Luke."

"I caught a break there," Shelby said. "He's real careful about things like that—he doesn't want Art dropping his drawers around the cabin guests."

"Speaking of Art—there's something new."

"Netta. Luke and Art ran into her when they were shopping and it turned out Art and Netta had been in the same group home before and consider themselves boyfriend and girlfriend. She's very sweet. I think it gave Luke quite a few new gray hairs…."

"Oh?" Mel asked, raising an eyebrow. "Why is that?"

"Luke does so well with Art, but he doesn't always understand Art's ways. He panicked—thought they'd have sex or something, get pregnant and move in with us. Look at them—how sweet is that? They're obviously very dear to each other, but they aren't going to rock Luke's boat to the degree he feared when he realized Art had a girlfriend." Shelby laughed and added, "You should've seen Luke's face when Art asked if he should get married. I thought we'd have to revive him."

"What did he say?"

"He pretty much choked and went white. I told Art no, he shouldn't, because it would be hard to be married to someone who lives in Fortuna since he doesn't drive a car and that settled it. For now. As I suspected, Art isn't real clear on what marriage really means. I think Art is perfectly happy with us."

"The baby will be exciting for him."

"Big brother Art," Shelby said. "Don't get Luke all stirred up, but I'm having contractions. Not serious ones, but I might be warming up."

"Good," Mel said. "Maybe you'll get your wish and the baby will come before Sean and Franci leave for his next assignment. Entirely possible—last time we checked you were headed in that direction."

"Believe me, if I could go a little early, I wouldn't be doing it for Franci and Sean."

"Getting a little uncomfortable, huh?" Mel asked.

Shelby nodded. Then her eyes clouded and a tear spilled down her cheek. "I know this is just silly and emotional and I know it is completely impossible, but I wish my mother could have been around for this...."

Mel reached out and smoothed back some of Shelby's hair, pushing it off her cheek. "I know, sweetheart. But I have a feeling she's watching over you. And you certainly don't lack for family!"

"Tell me about it. Some of them could just get lost for a while and I'd be fine." She sniffed.

"Family getting on your nerves?" Mel asked.

"Oh, don't get me wrong—they're fantastic to the last one. All seven hundred of them." Mel laughed at her. "Pregnant tears," Shelby said, wiping off her cheek. "I never get any warning...."

Mel just chuckled. "I remember," she said. "What's this little guy's name?"

"Brett Lucas Riordan," she answered. Then she

winced and said, "Ugh," as a large bulge protruded from the left side of her belly. "Do you think he knows that's not the way out?"

"My girl, you need to unload," Mel said, shaking her head.

"Soon," Shelby said. "And not a moment too soon!"

The day was drawing to a close, the sun beginning its downward slant, when someone came up behind Mel and covered her eyes with their hands. Mel instinctively whirled and faced a smiling Darla Prentiss. "Hey, there," Darla said.

"I thought you weren't going to make it today!"

"We had family stuff going on at my sister's house," Darla said. "But we still wanted to stop by and say hello. Mel, things are a little better. I wanted to thank you for being so sweet and kind."

"Oh, I didn't do anything that any friend wouldn't do. Did you get some counseling?"

"More than I bargained for. We saw a therapist recommended by the fertility clinic and then spent a little time with Pastor Noah Kincaid. A good friend of mine goes to your church and said he was a wonderful counselor. He helped us a lot. We might have to give your church a try sometime."

Mel smiled. "We love Noah. As I understand it, he was a counselor before he attended seminary. Very experienced. We're lucky to have him. And I'm so glad you're feeling a little better." She shook her head. "There's just no way I can express how sad it makes me that you and Phil haven't had better luck, nor how sorry I am for your loss."

"Time will heal," Darla said.

"Where is Phil?" she asked, looking around.

"Over there." Darla pointed. "Probably telling lies with Jack, Preacher and anyone who will listen."

Mel saw Phil standing in a clot of men including Noah and Luke, holding a beer, talking and laughing. "Is he doing all right?" Mel asked.

"I know he grieves as much as I do," Darla said. "But he's so wonderful—he puts all his attention on making sure I'm all right. I don't know if you can even understand this—probably the hardest part is that Phil should be a father. He'd be the best father in the world. He's strong and patient and kind and has more love in him than any man I've ever known. I'm so lucky to have him."

Mel smiled and gave Darla a hug. "Well, he's pretty darn lucky, too."

"Thanks for being there for us, Mel. You've been such a comfort."

Mel wasn't often moved to prayer—but in her heart she was saying, *God, can you cut these folks some slack here? They're so ready for a break!*

Eleven

The first thing Erin was going to remember to tell Aiden was that a few stolen kisses behind a tree or the church at the town picnic was not nearly enough. Ian and Marcie stayed over Monday night and left early on Tuesday morning; if they'd left after the picnic Erin would have asked Aiden to come to the cabin. But it was summer; people took vacation days and stretched out holiday weekends.

She had been so happy to see her sister and brother-in-law. She was completely okay with them leaving her to get back to her lover.

Once they were gone, she wondered why she hadn't formulated a plan with Aiden, finding out just how soon they could next be together. She wanted to call him, but something from way back in junior high about not calling boys you liked prevented her from doing so. She might have been far braver if it hadn't meant calling Luke's house to get a message to him.

It was a very long morning until Aiden called her at noon. "Have you looked outside your front door yet?"

"Why?" she asked. "And why aren't you *here?*"

"Just look," he said with a laugh. "And for once in your life, follow instructions."

And he hung up on her. Just hung up!

She opened the front door and found a large white dress box outside the door. She brought it in and opened it. Right on top of piles of green chiffon was a note. *Dress up for me and be ready at seven—I'm picking you up. A.*

She lifted the dress out of the box and actually winced. My God, it was obnoxious. All that fluffy emerald-green, flowing chiffon—she'd never buy something like that. Erin, five-nine and trim, was pretty much a little-black-dress woman. She strove for elegance and simplicity while this was entirely too froufrou for her. Did he just instinctively know she hadn't brought any kind of evening or cocktail dress along to the cabin? Was he taking her to the best excuse for a fancy restaurant he knew and didn't want her going in capris and flip-flops?

And as she examined the dress further, she realized that—ew—it wasn't new! It did have dry-cleaning tags, but good Lord, it was a used dress! And with it came a pair of silver slip-on sandals.

She just frowned her confusion. Would he be terribly insulted if she took a quick run over to Eureka and found something a bit more to her tastes? Something she considered appropriate? She couldn't even remember a time she might've bought a dress like this. It looked suspiciously like a bridesmaid's or prom dress, but even when she was seventeen…

Prom.

She started to laugh to herself. Oh, he wouldn't. Would he?

She had complained about missing the prom, and what appeared on her doorstep but a prom dress.

Perhaps it was premature and naive, but she trusted him. Completely and totally, she trusted Aiden. A woman of her age and experience didn't put her body in the hands of a man without believing in him very strongly. So she shrugged and took the secondhand dress off to the bedroom.

She still remembered the things she'd jealously listened to the girls in gym class say about the long day of primping, going to the beauty salon, having manicures and pedicures, about the series of picture taking at her house then at his parents' house—all things she'd never experienced. Well, she wouldn't be experiencing them now, either, though it did cross her mind to drive into Fortuna or Eureka to find a beauty shop that would give her one of those old-fashioned updos, all piled ringlets and curls.

Instead, she tended her vegetable garden (soup pot and metal spoon nearby), showered, painted her toenails and fingernails pale pink and whiled away the time. Seven couldn't get there fast enough.

When she tried on the dress, it was a bit too large and in a strapless, that wasn't a good thing—one wrong move and it would be around her ankles. She had to tighten it up with safety pins. And of course she hadn't brought a strapless bra to the mountains; she sagged a little bit, but he would just have to live with that. After all, he'd seen her naked and knew the thirty-six-year-old girls were starting to drop a bit.

She fussed over her hair, pinning it up and curling little dangling ends with her curling iron. By God, if she didn't look exactly like a thirty-six-year-old senior in high school! At last there was a knock at the door.

She opened it with a smile and there he stood— wearing a tux and holding a plastic box of flowers! "Oh my God, I guessed right!" she said with a laugh. "We're playing prom!"

He stepped inside and his free hand slipped around her waist to pull her close. He whispered against her lips, "When I'm done with you, you won't feel like there's anything you missed."

She pulled back just slightly. "Are you planning to be done with me soon?"

He shook his head. "It will be a very, very long time, honey. Very." Then he handed her a wrist corsage.

She opened it and sighed—an orchid. When she was in high school, the boys that put out for an orchid were *really* trying. She put it on her wrist and said, "This is fun, but I'm not sure I'm willing to be seen in public like this. Everyone will think we're dressed for a costume party."

"Well, if I remember right, first you go to dinner, then you go to the dance. Right?"

"I guess," she said, nodding.

He reached inside his jacket and pulled out four CDs—all late '80s and early '90s. Wilson Phillips, Billy Joel, Michael Bolton, the "new" Mariah Carey. "I picked only the slow ones. We have reservations at Jack's. We'll come back here to dance."

"Ohhh, Aiden. You are the sweetest man…"

"And we're going to do things we'd have gotten detention for. While we dance, I'm going to be all over you—kissing your neck, touching your breasts, begging…"

"You probably won't have to beg.…"

His lips were on her neck. "Of course, we have to do it in the backseat of the car.…"

"I might draw the line there," she told him.

"I bet I can talk you into it," he said with a laugh. "Let's go." And he put out his arm to escort her.

Erin hadn't been in Jack's bar often and therefore wasn't immediately aware that it was quite different on this Tuesday night. For one thing, it was lit by candlelight. Right by the window was a table set for two with fine china and a linen tablecloth. It was only seven-thirty, but the restaurant was empty. Jack stood in his usual place behind the bar, but he was wearing a white shirt. It took her a while to realize that this was a very special setup. In fact, Aiden was holding her chair out for her before it occurred to her, "Did you rent out the whole bar?"

"More or less," he said. "Jack said they weren't likely to be real busy and he gave me a deal."

Then Jack was beside their table, a clean dish towel

draped over one arm. "If you kids have some ID, I can serve you a drink. But…"

Aiden grinned up at Jack. "Want to give us a break, pal?"

He chuckled and asked, "Bottle of wine?"

"Raymond Reserve Merlot 2004," Aiden said.

"My pleasure," Jack said.

Erin leaned toward Aiden and whispered, "What is that?"

"The best you'll ever taste," he whispered back. "I bought a bottle and gave it to Jack earlier. Prizewinner."

"He doesn't carry it?"

"I doubt it—not much call for it around here. You'll love it."

Jack proved he wasn't a completely ignorant small-town barkeep. He brought the bottle to them, opened it and presented Aiden with the cork. Then he poured a small amount in the glass and passed it to Aiden to swirl, sniff, sip and accept. He poured for both of them and left the bottle. "I'll bring your soup and salads in a minute," Jack said. "Enjoy the wine."

"Try it," Aiden urged. Erin took a sip and let her eyes gently close. She smiled and nodded. Aiden reached across the table for her hand. "I know it won't be like it should have been for you, Erin. But we can have fun with it."

She gave his hand a squeeze. "When I was sixteen, I picked out a prom dress. I was determined I was going, but I was delusional—I didn't have a prayer of being asked. I didn't date, didn't even have a guy who walked me to classes, and on prom night my dad caught me crying about it. The next year on prom night he got a sitter and took me out to dinner. Dinner with my dad, that was what I did on prom night. This is so much better."

"There's only going to be one similarity between your prom-night dinner with your dad and tonight with me," he said.

"Oh? And what's that?"

"You'll be in bed early." Then he winked.

Jack brought them small bowls of clam chowder. Next came the salads and he asked how they'd like their filets cooked. Not long after that, peppercorn filets with a brown sauce, twice-baked potatoes and mixed vegetables, followed by the best cheesecake she'd ever tasted.

"I know you caught me sniveling about missing the prom," Erin said. "But I don't think I could stand it if you felt sorry for me. I'm not a Cinderella story. I had a lot of responsibility, but I was a happy kid. I was kind of a nerd, but—"

"You're not a nerd anymore," he scoffed. "You're so sexy and put together, you put models to shame."

"Fashion came much later, when I started interning at the law firm. I noticed that the most successful women attorneys *looked* like they should be successful. I've always been good at figuring things out. Things like that, anyway."

"I never felt sorry for you for a second, Erin. I don't know when I've met a woman I admire more."

After a moment of quiet, she said softly, "I don't think anyone has ever tried so hard to make me happy."

"Is that so? Well, I'm just getting started."

"You know what? I never liked surprises before I met you."

"I know," he said. "You like control. Finish your dinner, Erin. We have dancing to do."

"One question," she said. "When you found this dress, did you realize it was kind of…I don't know…"

"Used?"

"Um, that. And really not like me at all?"

"I did," he said. "They don't have prom dresses hanging around dress shops in July. But it was the color of your eyes and I thought it was the kind of dress a person would wear to a prom. When you saw me in this tux, did you realize it's probably the first and last time you will?"

"Not a tux man?"

"Honey, when I got out of that navy uniform, I felt nerves in my body relax that I didn't even know I had."

"That's a shame, because you clean up real nice." Then she grinned.

"Let's get going," he said, his eyes growing dark and impatient.

Once back at the cabin, Aiden put on the music, took her in his arms and danced her around the cabin a bit. His lips were on her neck, he held her close, and he whispered, "I'm sorry, baby. This isn't going to last long. I want to get you out of this dress."

"I'm really not that crazy about dancing, anyway," she said. "And I think the dress will probably look better on the floor than on me."

"Oh, I like your style." He lifted her in his arms and headed for her bedroom. Before he crossed the threshold, he stopped. "I have to tell you something. I probably haven't known you long enough for this, but I don't care. I've been looking for a long time, Erin. Of all the Riordan men, I was the only one who actually wanted to be married. They were all running from women, avoiding commitment, and I was looking for the right one. The one who would be as good for me as I could be for her—the one who would last. The one who wanted the same things I wanted. Someone I could respect and grow with."

"Hmm. You don't very often hear that kind of admission on prom night."

"Erin, I'm all done looking. I'm in love with you." And then his mouth came down hard on hers.

Given the fact that Aiden was trained to wake to the sound of a phone, any phone, he didn't worry about checking in with Luke or anyone else. He slept the sleep of the purely satisfied next to Erin, her soft, naked body flush against his. When he did roll over and wake, he noticed the bedside clock said 10:00 a.m. and he couldn't help but smile. He couldn't remember a time he'd slept that late, unless he'd been up all night in the delivery room or surgery. There was a pile of green chiffon on the floor next to the black and white of a discarded tux. He looked back at Erin and found she'd turned her head and her eyes were open.

She smiled at him. "How did that compare to your last prom?"

"I didn't get laid at my last prom."

"Not even in the backseat of your dad's car?"

"Not even."

"I'm really glad I was able to talk you out of that," she said. "Do we have to get up?"

"I'm sorry to say, we do. At least I do. I have to return the tux. Can I make you some breakfast?"

"Absolutely. Whatever you can find out there. I actually bought some real high-cholesterol man-food because Ian was coming for the weekend. There might be some eggs and sausage left."

"I'll see what I can find," he said.

"And I'll get a shower."

He liked this, waking up with her. He pulled on his boxers and started creating in the kitchen. By the time Erin came out in her terry robe, toweling her hair dry, he had coffee and toast ready, the eggs almost done. He kissed her seven or twenty more times between her first sip of coffee and the point at which he put her breakfast in front of her.

"I'm going to go home, change, get rid of the tux, check on the family and I'll bring dinner back. Informal dinner tonight," he said with a smile. "You don't have to wear your prom dress. How does that sound?"

"Perfect."

They cleaned up the breakfast dishes together and he kissed her ten or fifteen times before he could get out the door. Except for Luke's baby coming, he was going to spend every spare second with Erin. She had about six more weeks in her cabin until Marcie delivered, and during that time they could talk about their futures, their careers. He would unleash the head-hunter and get serious about finding work. In lieu of a practice that wanted him, he could always find hospital work in or near Chico.

Had he rushed her? he wondered. He'd ask. It would be perfectly understandable if she wanted a little more time to get to know him. In fact, though he'd confessed that he'd always been looking for a woman who could be the one, she hadn't exactly said the same thing.

When he pulled into Luke's compound, he knew immediately that something was different. Too many cars, for one thing. Too many people on Luke's porch, for another. He parked in front of his cabin and, wearing his tux shirt and pants, shirtsleeves rolled up, collar open, jacket slung over one shoulder, he walked toward Luke's house. Had he missed something by way of family plans? he wondered. In his concentration on Erin's prom night, had he forgotten some important gathering or event? His mother and George were there, Franci and Sean, too, and if he hadn't seen a very pregnant Shelby he would wonder if it was time. As everyone turned to watch his approach, he could see they were not wearing their happy faces.

Then he saw her. *Annalee*. She had been behind Luke, leaning against the porch railing. She stood straight and came around Luke. She was wearing that totally phony, contrived, I'm-so-young-and-vulnerable expression. She wore a black snug-fitting but classy sleeveless dress and black sandals—all so conservative on her tiny, completely perfect body, her white-blond hair pulled back in a clip, her huge, luminous blue eyes trained on him. Did any of them—his family—buy this shit? This wasn't *real!* He remembered that same little-girl look—she'd turned it on the hospital commander. Poor little Annalee. She could turn that whole image into a hot little dish in less than five seconds. Or a screaming, clawing banshee.

She walked toward the porch steps as he walked toward her.

"Aiden," she said in a soft, breathy voice.

"If you're not an apparition, I'm going to have to kill myself."

"You wouldn't answer my calls, messages or e-mails," she said. Oh, and there it came, the tears. By God, the woman should really act! She could cry on demand!

"I did answer. I said, we've been divorced for eight years—we don't have any business. Stop with the bloody tears, goddamn it! You flooded my in-box with hundreds of hostile e-mails! I'm afraid to turn the computer on—you probably crashed it!"

"Aiden, please," she said sweetly, pathetically. "There was nothing hostile—I was begging you to talk to me. I just meant to send a couple and only because I so need to talk to you."

"No! We're divorced! You have no business here!"

"But we're *not!* That's why I've been trying to reach you! The divorce—I don't know how it happened, but it didn't go through! We're still *married!*"

His mouth fell open and he felt the knife twist in his gut. She could still do it to him, totally surprise him. Totally scare him to death. He checked eyes with Sean and Luke and he saw that, thank God, they weren't buying her crap. Aiden briefly wondered, *Does everyone get one person in the universe who can throw them completely off balance like this?*

"That's ridiculous," he said.

"No, it's true. That lawyer we used? He's gone— *pfffttt*. Gone. Not a member of the California bar, never filed our divorce paperwork. I checked—it should be a matter of public record, but the only thing on record is our marriage."

The sudden suicidal urge he felt was real. He couldn't be married to this…this… "Then fine, I'll get a lawyer and make sure it's done right this time."

"But wait," she said, stepping toward him. "Can we at least talk about it?"

"No, Annalee, there's nothing to talk about. And you didn't have to come here for this. You could have told Jeff to tell me, or since you found my e-mail address you could have e-mailed me about the failure of the divorce. But you're here. There can only be one reason for you to be here. It's not about the problem with the divorce. You want something. Why don't you cut to the chase—what do you want *now?*"

"A chance," she said in a tiny voice. "Just a chance."

Again Aiden was stunned. Then he threw back his head and laughed. "A *chance?*"

"I'd like to try to work through this. I was only twenty-one years old and—"

"Did you bring back the ten grand you demanded from me to sign the original papers?" he asked. Then he stole a look at his mother out of the corner of his eye; oh, boy. She was not happy. He had no way of knowing who she was least happy with.

"Aiden, I was a kid, I was in trouble, I did a stupid thing and I've regretted it every day since. When I learned that the divorce hadn't gone through, that we're still married, I thought it was kind of a message. A gift from God. A chance for us to—"

He plunged his hands into his pockets and scowled at her, backing away. "Don't throw God's name around here, Annalee. You conned me. You used me, set me up, tricked me, almost had me court-martialed, almost cost me my residency, my *career,* and once I wrote you a check, you ran for your life. I don't even want to know what went wrong in your ever-complex scheming to bring you around here, but—"

"Aiden," Maureen said sharply. "Son."

"Mom, you shouldn't be hearing this. This isn't for you to hear. This was a horrible catastrophe and I'm not proud of it, but I swear to you, I was the victim. I was the—" And then he stopped. Sure, he was the victim in his mind, but he'd been a twenty-eight-year-old man, a doctor. He should have been so much smarter. He had thrown caution to the wind, went wild with this little tart and got caught breaking military rules. Stupid rules, he thought—you should be able to date whomever you liked, regardless of rank or commission—but that was not the case, so he was caught.

He couldn't prove she'd set him up.

"I was twenty-one," she repeated. "I thought I loved

you. We made some mistakes but I think we deserve—"

"No!" he said. "We are done! I'll get that divorce taken care of! You can leave!"

"Aiden," Maureen said again. "Sit down with the woman. You don't have to talk to her alone. One of your brothers or George can sit in. But, Aiden, you absolutely must—"

A very loud and long groan came out of Shelby. She bent over her stomach, holding it, groaning and then breathing deeply. Luke was immediately on one knee beside her, rubbing a hand along her back. It was quite a while before Shelby lifted her head, her eyes clouded with tears. "Sorry. As much as I wanted labor, I hate to leave before I find out how this comes out. But—I have to go to the hospital."

"Okay, baby," Luke said, helping her stand. "How long have you been having them?"

"Since what's-her-name got here. Call Mel to meet us there and grab my little duffel, will you?"

Luke was off to do her bidding. "Sean, we need you to keep tabs on Art. Aiden, if you can't come, we understand."

"I'm coming. Of course I'm coming. Annalee—I need you out of here. I'll take your phone number. I'll call you. I'll get this sorted out, but you are out of here. No way you stay on my family's property while I'm not here."

Annalee dropped her gaze and shuffled down the porch steps like a pitiful, rejected little girl, and Aiden took in his mother's pained expression. He noticed that

George put an arm around Maureen's shoulders and gave comfort.

Annalee walked to her car, opened the passenger door and took out a small, elegant clutch. She opened it, pulled out a business card and took it to Aiden. He studied it for a second. Annalee Riordan— Fashion Consultant. There was a cell number.

Okay, this was more proof in Aiden's mind that she was a liar and a con. Part of that divorce decree demanded that she resume the use of her maiden name— Kovacevic. And yet she was still using his name? How long had she *really* known the divorce hadn't worked? And had she had anything to do with that?

"We don't get cell reception in the mountains, Annalee," he said as calmly as possible. "My sister-in-law is in labor and I'm going to the hospital with them. There are some nice motels in Fortuna—go there. If you're anywhere near Virgin River, I'll get a restraining order. I'll call you when I'm free to talk."

She shook her head and tears poured out of her large blue eyes. "Why are you so cruel?" she asked him. "This isn't my fault. None of this is my fault."

"You're supposed to be using your maiden name," he said. "Not Riordan. You're just playing me again, Annalee, and you'd better move on. I mean it."

"Oh, Aiden…" She let her chin drop and she cried, placing trembling hands over her face.

He just stood in front of her, hands in his pockets. When she looked up, her tearstained face looking for all the world authentic, he said, "Save it. I don't buy it. Now, get out of here."

He heard his mother gasp in shock. Annalee lifted her chin and said, "All right, Aiden. I'll go. Please just take care of the divorce. You have my phone number and e-mail address if there's a problem."

"Fine. Go. Now." Then he watched as Annalee bravely turned, got in her late-model Lexus and backed away from Luke's house until she could turn around.

"I don't believe I've ever heard you speak to another human being like that in my life," Maureen said, clearly appalled. "Especially a woman. A woman in tears."

"Not just any woman," he said without looking at his mother. "Sean, I'm going to the hospital—Luke wants me to be there. It's not as though I can do anything— maybe he wants someone who can help him understand how and why things are happening. I'll take you, Mom, if you want to ride with me. Or if you don't think you can stand my company, George can take you."

"I don't think George wants to sit around a hospital, waiting for a baby to come, and I won't miss it. Besides, I'd like a chance to talk to you."

He shook his head a little bit. "I don't think there's any possible way I can satisfy your curiosity, but I'll tell you what I can." He turned to his brother. "Sean, please hear me on this—make sure Annalee isn't hanging around here. She's destructive. I wouldn't dare try to predict what she might do next."

"Aiden," Maureen began, "she's just a slight little woman who—"

"I won't let her hang around," Sean said.

"The thing you have to remember about her—no lie is too big a lie. Her stories have been so extraordinary, I think she believes them. I'm not even sure where she grew up—not in this country, that's for sure. Russia or maybe Bosnia—probably a place of grave unrest. The lying and manipulations—it might be something she learned in childhood, a survival thing. It's pathological…it's automatic for her. I'm not telling you that to make an excuse for her, but so you'll be on your guard. She's very convincing."

He felt his mother's hand on his shoulder. "What kind of lies, Aiden?" she asked him. "Do you think she'd lie about wanting another chance?"

He looked at his mother levelly, his expression angry. "Absolutely. She'd lie about anything, Mom," he tried to say gently. "She *has* lied about anything."

Annalee already had a little hotel room, though it was not in Fortuna. She was staying in Garberville for the time being, but not under the name Annalee Riordan. And she wasn't alone, but Aiden didn't need to know that. Annalee was with Mujo, her partner in every sense of the word.

Annalee drove around the countryside for a little while, then finally pulled into the little town of Virgin River. She sat in her car, refreshed her makeup and made sure her hair was just so before walking into the little bar at the center of town. It was a crapshoot— she had to choose between the bar, church or medical clinic. Since Luke's truck was not outside the clinic, she assumed they had not gone there to have the baby.

Baby. She wished she'd had a baby with Aiden. That was a major miscalculation of hers, not having a baby. That would have been a much better long-term arrangement. But at the time they'd married and divorced she'd been so young, the very idea of being tied down to an infant made her feel claustrophobic. Truthfully, it still made her cringe—she wasn't crazy about kids. But—she could have let him have the kid, then come back regularly to discuss taking over custody… That thought made her smile. An arrangement like that would be like an annuity.

She walked into the bar and, wearing her prettiest smile, jumped up on a stool in front of one of the best-looking bartenders she'd ever seen in her life. "Hi," she said cheerily.

"Hello, there. You must be lost."

"No," she said with a laugh, shaking her head. "Not in the least. But my timing is really off today. I was just visiting family and almost the second I arrived, my cousin-in-law was in labor, heading off to the hospital to have her baby, and the entire family was following. To tell the truth, I wanted to go along, but I'd barely met her, so it didn't seem like a good idea to horn in."

He lifted a handsome brow. "Shelby, by chance?"

"Exactly!" she said as if surprised. "My gosh, you must know everyone!"

"Pretty much," he said. "And sometimes it seems like all the women are pregnant, but that isn't really the case. I know she was due any second, and my wife was called out for a delivery."

"You're married to Mel, the doctor?"

"Midwife," he corrected. He put out his big hand. "Jack Sheridan," he said, introducing himself.

She put her much smaller hand in his. His palm was callused; she loved his hand. "Annalee," she said. "Annalee Riordan." Too bad the guy was just a poor country bartender. He was hot. She loved a big, rugged man. But she had to think about the future and she wasn't about to hook up with some low-income country boy. Well, she thought, smiling. Maybe for an afternoon or something. But she had bigger fish to fry. "I'm pleased to meet you."

"Can I get you something?" he asked. "Late breakfast? Early lunch? Cold drink?"

"Well, let's see." She looked at her watch. "I've been driving since about five this morning. Do you think it's too early for a bloody Mary?"

"Coming up," he said, turning away from her to fix her drink. When he put it back in front of her, he said, "Where'd you come from?"

"I just drove from San Francisco today," she said. "I was there on business and since I was on the right side of the country and most of the family seemed to be here, I thought I'd take a little extra time to visit. I actually live in New York." She slid her hand into the thin clutch and pulled out a fancy business card, sliding it across the bar to him. "There's a designer in San Francisco I wanted to visit, look at some of his new designs. I have some very important clients in New York who will probably be interested."

He looked at the card. "Aren't there a lot of fashion consultants in New York?"

"Exactly," she said, grinning widely. "That's just it—everyone in New York sees all the same things. They count on me to bring something new to the party on a regular basis."

He slipped the card into his pocket. "I guess it's pretty obvious—I wouldn't know the first thing about fashion. My wife used to have a lot of fun with it, before she settled here with me. I guess when she lived in L.A., she spent all her money on designer this, designer that."

"Woman after my own heart." She took a sip of her drink. "So…who's Aiden seeing? There wasn't much time to catch up. Like I said, the second I got there, everyone piled into cars and headed for the hospital."

"That would be Erin," Jack said. "Erin Foley. Nice woman. Up here for the summer."

"In town here?" she asked, sipping slowly.

"Nah. She's got a cabin about ten or fifteen miles out of town—out on the ridge. A view that would just knock you dead it's so beautiful."

"All the views around here are beautiful," she said. "I can't believe I've never seen this part of the country before. It's awesome. Just fantastic."

Jack lowered his chin and looked up at her from under hooded brows. "I hope you brought along some more practical clothes if you want to see more of it. I don't think you're going to enjoy yourself much, traipsing around the redwoods and rivers in your church clothes."

She straightened and a delighted look crossed her face. "Church clothes? I love it! You're absolutely right—I'm dressed for a business meeting, but I did throw some jeans in my suitcase. I just wanted, you know, to make a good impression on the family."

"You look kinda young to be such a high muckety-muck businesswoman," he said.

"I am, as a matter of fact. Twenty-five. But I graduated college at twenty—I was early getting out of high school. I studied and drew and designed every spare second and didn't really take time for my family. I haven't seen any of them since…I don't know when." She laughed lightly. "And as it turned out, I didn't see much of them today, either."

"I'm sure they'll all be around tomorrow. Or at least the next day," he said.

"So—tell me about this town. Tell me how you ended up being a bartender here," she said, leaning an elbow on the bar. "Been here all your life?"

Annalee knew how to get a man talking. She had perfected the smile and exactly the right technique of asking a guy questions about himself. Jack was a former military man who came to Virgin River for all the outdoor pastimes it offered; he was a fisherman, hunter, hiker, camper. He built the bar so he'd have something to do to pass the time when he wasn't enjoying nature. Then the midwife came to town and he married for the first time at forty, had a couple of kids.

She got a sense from him that he'd be really good in the sack and that he'd go a long way to protecting the woman of his current interest. It was somewhat tempting, now that she knew he was the owner of the bar, not some small-time barkeep. But it could screw up the rest of their plans, hers and Mujo's, so she acted as sweet and virginal as she could.

She had a little lunch, pushed the bloody Mary away after drinking only a third and left.

She drove to Garberville where she and Mujo had rooms. He was lying back on his bed, watching the news. "Well?" he said without looking at her.

"It isn't just Aiden visiting his brother. It's every goddamn Riordan you ever saw."

"Great," he grumbled.

"No, it is great," she said, sitting on the edge of the bed. "He was really angry to see me, but his mother was shocked at the way he treated me. He's going to have a time trying to keep me away from his family. And his woman."

Mujo sat up. "Woman?"

Annalee smiled. "I get the sense my *husband* is going to really need a divorce. Right away. And gee, I specialize is greasing wheels like that. I know exactly how to be very cooperative."

But clearly, Mujo wasn't pleased. He frowned. "We don't usually mix it up with a lot of people. Gets too complicated. It's a lot safer when you just go one-on-one. Like we planned."

"Trust me," she said.

He softly touched her hand, lacing his fingers in hers. Then he bent back her pinkie until she yelped. "Do *not* fuck this up. We're running low on money."

"Stop!" she said with a cry, pulling her hand away. "Relax. Be nice."

She used her disposable cell phone to get a number for Erin Foley and called. Her phone came across a caller ID as unknown—if they even had such a thing back here in the sticks. In a very professional, businesslike voice, she said, "This is the postal service. We have a package to deliver to Erin Foley. The address is smeared on the packing slip. Can you give me the address and some directions, please?"

And Erin said, "Sure."

"This is every man's nightmare," Aiden said to his mother as they drove to the hospital. "That his most embarrassing, shameful moments will have to be described to his mother. Is this what happens when you die and go to hell?"

"You'd better help me understand, because right now I can't help but think some darling young woman who was your wife is desperate and needs someone to lean on."

"Mother, she's acting exactly the way she did when I met her. Here's the stuff I'd rather you not know, so brace yourself. After med school, after my tour aboard ship, I was pulling GMO duty at the hospital until my residency started. I met her. She was the woman you met today—sweet, very young, beautiful. A walking dream. I'm not sure I actually fell in love with her, but that was tough to call. Except what I didn't know—she was enlisted while I was not only commissioned, I was in a position of authority. My boss found out—very interesting that he found out, since I'd been seeing her less than a week. She swore she never leaked it and I certainly didn't. To avoid coming up against charges of fraternization and possibly losing my residency bid, he suggested I marry her and that she accept a discharge, not honorable, not dishonorable. So that's what we did."

"Oh, Aiden, you must have been very involved with her," Maureen said.

He didn't blush; he was too angry to blush. "Very," he said. "We weren't married a week before it got strange. She had violent mood swings, and the sweet little girl would become a lunatic who screamed and threw things." He gave a hollow laugh. "I tried to get her help. I wanted her evaluated, but she wouldn't go along with that. She's not mentally ill, Mother—she knows exactly what she's doing. I can't prove it, but I'm convinced she saw me coming—young doctor, just off a boat and without female companionship for a long, long time…"

"But there are lots of women in the navy," Maureen naively pointed out.

"Mom, I couldn't date women who served on the ship—we were working together."

"Of course," she said quietly.

"Annalee, she told the most outrageous stories— she was everything from a spy for the resistance in Bosnia to a homeless teenager in L.A. She even once said she had cancer! I still don't know the truth about her. She wouldn't be around here unless she was after something. I need to get her out of our lives."

"But, Aiden, how can you be so sure?"

"Ask Luke," he said. "I called him, described how

crazy my life had gotten and he came out right away. I met him at the airport and brought him back to my apartment. Annalee wasn't home when we got there, so I shoved him in the second bedroom and told him to stay put and listen when she walked in the door. I confronted her about a huge credit-card bill and she started screaming and throwing things. He witnessed it. He understands what I'm talking about. He drove her to a hotel, gave her some money to hold her off and called Sean." He stole a glance at Maureen as he drove. "Luke and Sean got me through the worst of it. Mom, she wouldn't sign the divorce papers without a lot more money. I gave her ten thousand dollars to go away."

Maureen groaned. To her, ten thousand dollars was a fortune. And to Maureen, who couldn't lie if her life depended on it, this story must seem bit otherworldly.

"Now she tells me we're not divorced. Well, if that's true I'll get it taken care of right away. But here's the thing—don't listen to her, don't get sucked into her stories, her manipulation. I don't know what she's after, but five gets you ten it's got commas and decimal points. Money, Mother. Really, I don't know how far she'll go. She's a user and a liar."

Maureen was quiet for a moment. "I never knew all this. And you boys—you used to joke about your crazy wife. You *laughed* about it."

"After it seemed pretty apparent she was long gone, we laughed. What are you gonna do? I was an idiot— I fell right into it. But damn, I thought I was done paying for that lapse in judgment…"

"Aiden…" she said. "If you're really not divorced, what can you do?"

"Get a really good lawyer," he said.

When Aiden and Maureen got to the hospital, Mel was already there. Shelby was doing great but was only at four centimeters. It would likely be at least a few hours before it got interesting. Aiden visited her briefly, then begged off to run a couple of errands.

He returned the tux, then he called Erin. "Well, our evening is probably off. I got back to Luke's to find Shelby in labor. I just returned the tux and am on my way back to Valley Hospital to wait with my mother. I'm sorry."

"Good for her, too bad for us," she said.

"Yeah…"

"Are you all right?"

"Fine. I just hate missing the night with you. But Luke wants me to be at the hospital. He's been nervous about this."

"But everything is all right?"

"It's all good. She's going to have a nice delivery…"

"Aiden? What do I hear in your voice?"

He was going to tell her, but not now, not like this. "Disappointment, probably."

"Well, be tough. And no matter what time it is, please call me and tell me when the baby arrives. All right?"

"I will," he promised. "Erin…?"

"Hmm?"

"Erin, I— Listen, thank you for last night. It was really…special…"

She didn't say anything for a moment. "It was. It's always special with you. But something's—"

"I should probably get back, see how the mom and dad are doing. I'll give you a call when something happens. How's that?"

"Please," she said. "And whatever's bothering you? Try to let it go, will you? You're the one who takes everything in stride. I'm the one who stews."

He laughed slightly. "Let's not stew. I probably won't talk to you till morning. First babies tend to take their time."

"I just hope she goes real easy. Give her my best."

Twelve

Brett Lucas was born at three in the morning, seven pounds even. When he was placed on Shelby's chest, her arms went instantly around him, though he was covered with muck and blood, and she kissed his head over and over. Luke kissed them both while the pediatric nurse tried to dry the baby.

Luke was vaguely aware of his mother nearby, the clicking of pictures Aiden took, of Mel talking about the cord, the placenta, the need for a couple of stitches, but it all seemed to be happening far outside this little sphere he shared with his wife and son. He slipped a big arm under her shoulders to hold her closer and whispered, "You're the most amazing woman I've ever known and I don't know why you love me this much."

"I remember when I didn't think you'd ever come around," she said tiredly. "I knew you were perfect for me," she whispered back. "From the first day I saw you I knew…"

"I don't deserve you, I know that. Thank you, baby—thank you for my son."

"He has very black hair," she said.

Luke laughed softly. If you lined up the Riordan men, there was a resemblance, but at first glance they appeared more different than alike. Luke had sandy-brown hair and brown eyes; Colin dark brown hair; Aiden's hair was black and his eyes bright green—typical Black Irish, their mother always said; Sean had dark blond hair; Patrick was a redhead, that dark burnished red. "Black, like Uncle Aiden's. If I didn't know how much you love me, I'd wonder…."

"I'm going to have to talk to Franci and find out how she got a little girl out of a Riordan…" she mused aloud.

"Baby, you don't ever have to do this again, if you don't want to," Luke said.

"We'll talk about that another day…."

The nurse urged the baby away from them. "Come with me, Dad," she said. "We'll get him cleaned up, diapered, weighed and you can have him back."

Luke gave her another brief kiss. "I'll be right back, baby."

Before long Mel was standing beside Shelby, free of gloves and gown. "Cameron Michaels will be by to check him over first thing in the morning, but he looks beautiful and strong, Shelby. You do good work."

"He's perfect, isn't he?"

"Looks perfect to me. We'll get this bed put back

together for you. Is Luke staying the rest of the night with you?"

"I'm sure he will."

"I imagine there are lots of people who will want to see him right away, so try to get some rest," Mel said. Then she yawned. "As soon as we're all cleaned up here, I'm going to go home and see if I can get a little sleep before mine wake up for the day."

Little Brett was passed around a bit; pictures were taken with his grandmother, his uncle, his midwife and mostly his parents. It was a good hour before the room was finally quiet. There was a recliner Luke could use for sleep, but he was way too wired for that. He pulled it close to Shelby's bed and sat up, alternately gazing at her, then at his sleeping son.

And for Luke Riordan, everything in the world was better than perfect.

When Aiden drove his mother to the RV park that she currently called home she was very quiet in the car. "You must be exhausted," he said.

"Happily exhausted, and worried about you, Aiden. What are you going to do?"

He sighed. "First, I'm going to see what I can find out about this divorce that didn't happen. I have the papers. Then I'm going to try to explain to Erin why I'm going to be very busy for a while, trying to make sure I'm divorced. I suppose it'll mean seeing another lawyer, if what Annalee says is true." He glanced over at his mom. "She'd lie about anything, but she tends to lie about things that can't be proven—and this can be checked. She's right, marriage and divorce are both public records. How something like this could have happened is a complete mystery to me."

It had been a very long night, waiting for the baby to come, thinking far too much about all the complications he suddenly faced.

"Mom, I'm sorry. This whole thing, from the fast, short marriage to the panicked divorce—I must seem like someone you don't even know. Sometimes it seems like it happened to someone else. I'm sorry."

She squeezed his hand. "Aiden, you're one of the gentlest and most honest men I've ever known. I know you wouldn't have chosen a situation like that. I'm sorry you went through it."

I have no one to blame but myself, he thought. But he said, "Thank you, Mom."

He made sure she was safely inside her motor coach; George was at the door in his robe and slippers to greet her. At that moment Aiden couldn't have been happier that his mother had someone special in her life.

Aiden drove to Luke's and went first to his cabin; he pulled out the metal box that held all his important papers—his birth certificate, marriage license and divorce papers, his discharge papers. With a little tremor of nerves, he realized that the box hadn't been locked. It never occurred to him to lock it, especially in a place like Virgin River. He put the box in his SUV, locked the car doors and went to Luke's house to use his phone. He called Erin—it was after four in the morning. Rather than saying hello, she said, "The baby is here?"

"He has arrived—seven pounds and healthy. Shelby and Luke are very happy."

"Oh, thank goodness—I worried about her when you didn't call. Long labor for her?"

"Not too bad. Erin, can I come over? I know it's not even daylight yet...."

"Come," she said. "I need to feel your arms around me."

It made his chest swell proudly to hear that and he hoped that by the time he told her what he had to say, she still wanted him to hold her. "I'll be right there," he said.

When he walked out of Luke's house and down the porch steps, he saw movement among the cabins. The moon was high and bright and Sean stepped out of the darkness, out from between two cabins, one of Luke's rifles balanced over his shoulder. "What are you doing prowling around at this time of morning?" Aiden asked.

"A couple of hours ago I heard something out here," he said. "Could've been wildlife. I got up, thinking you might be back from the hospital." He shrugged and said, "When I couldn't find you or any animals, I decided it wouldn't hurt to stay alert."

Aiden actually laughed. "Who were you gonna shoot with that thing?"

"Anyone who shouldn't be lurking around here late at night. I think we need to consider locks. How's the little family? Luke and Shelby?"

"Good—seven-pound, healthy boy. Brought tears to Luke's eyes. I don't know when I've ever seen him on his knees thanking a woman before. I took Mom back to her house on wheels. George had waited up for her, I think. Sean," he said, pausing. "Did it ever occur to you that you might run into a scary little blonde out here?"

"I hoped," he answered. "If I said I mistook her for a deer, I'd be believed, wouldn't I?" Then he flashed Aiden a smile.

"Let's be careful there," Aiden said. "Not because I feel protective, but because I don't want any member of my family going to hell over her. She's just not worth it. Do you need me to take over watch so you can get some rest?"

"I slept a little before I heard noises. I'm all right. What about you? You want to go to bed?"

"Yeah, but not here. I want to go to Erin's. There's a good chance that after I tell her about my last twenty-four hours, I'll be right back."

"Go," Sean said. "She seems pretty reasonable. If you need someone to back up your story…"

"Thanks. See you a little later."

By the time he drove up the long driveway to Erin's cabin at the top of the ridge, it was nearly five in the morning. When he got out and stood beside his SUV, he saw a most amazing sight. There was a pink glow from the sun rising in the east; the moon was lowering in the west. The sun and the moon in the same sky had always seemed like magic to him. Their light seemed to meet over the road to Erin's cabin.

The cabin door opened and she stood there in her nightgown. "I heard the car," she explained.

"Come here, sweetheart. Look at this. Down the road that way, the sun is starting to rise. The other way the moon is saying goodbye."

"Hmm. I wonder if that's why they call this Moonlight Road. It's not marked, but that's the address." She stepped out beside him and his arm went around her shoulders. "Red sky at morning, sailor take warning," she said. "My dad always said the weather was going to be bad when the sun came up pink like that."

"Red sky at night, sailor's delight," he said.

"You know that saying?" she asked.

"I spent the last eight years in San Diego. I didn't have a boat, but I went sailing with friends sometimes. Water stuff—it's what we did there."

She turned to look up at him. "Don't you miss it?"

He shook his head. "My life has seemed pretty perfect here. But I guess all good things come to an end. I have something to tell you, and it's not nice stuff. I thought nothing could get better—not only was I completely relaxed for the first time in years, but I fell in love with the perfect woman. And—"

She gave him a moment to finish and then said, "And…?"

His arm tightened around her. "When I got back to Luke's after leaving you yesterday morning, my family was gathered. And in their midst was Annalee, my ex-wife, bearing the news that our divorce wasn't properly recorded and therefore, not legally filed."

Her eyes were wide as she looked up at him. "Are you kidding me?"

"I wish. I don't get it. Apparently, the lawyer didn't

follow through or something. But, Erin, we parted company after a very short, very embarrassing marriage eight years ago. If she's right, this is a technicality and I'll get it taken care of. It's a complication and I'm sorry. I have to get the situation resolved immediately. I'm going to have to find a good lawyer this time. Obviously the last one wasn't worth what I paid him."

"Want my help with that?"

"What I want is for you to look at the paperwork the lawyer gave me—he said it was done and that was all I'd need. Do you know anything about divorce papers?"

"A little," she said with a shrug. "They pass across my desk from time to time when I'm preparing living trusts, wills and estate planning. Not to mention taxes."

"This isn't the kind of thing you should be asking of the woman you love," he said.

"Let's not worry about that right now. Come on, come inside with me."

"Let me get my stuff," he said. He reached back into his car and pulled out the metal box. "My war chest," he said. "My few real important documents that I wouldn't trust to furniture movers—birth certificate, et cetera."

They went inside and Erin took the box from his hands and put it down on the kitchen table. "What's she like now?" Erin asked. "Eight years later? Does she want the divorce finalized so she can get on with her life? Maybe get married again or something?"

That was another story altogether—what she wanted. "It doesn't matter what she wants. I have only one thing to offer her and that's an official, documented, recorded divorce." He pulled Erin into his arms. "I'm just going to make this go away as fast as I can."

"Aiden, did you love her once?"

He shook his head. "Honey, it's impossible to explain what happened back then. It had a lot to do with being a young man barely off a long assignment on a ship, getting mixed up with someone I didn't know and should have been trying to avoid. Needless to say, we realized the mistake and made a mutual decision to end it quickly before it got worse."

She smiled patiently. "You don't really know me, either," she pointed out.

"Yes, I do. I know your family, what you do for a living, how helpless you are on a bike or in a bear scare." He tightened his arms.

"I'm good on a bike," she argued, but as she said that she leaned toward him, helpless in his arms, inviting his lips. "That's not a lot to base an opinion on."

"It's out of my hands, honey. I can't stop it. I've never felt this way about a woman before. I'd do anything to make you mine. Anything."

She leaned against him. "It's not really morning and you've been up all night. It might be easier to talk about this after a little sleep."

"Sleep?" he asked, his lips against hers. "I want to be inside you."

She felt her heart begin to race immediately. "I've always been so practical," she said. "This whole summer thing with you has changed me into a different kind of woman. I should wait until I completely understand this situation with your ex, but I can't. I can't and I don't care."

She took him by the hand and gently led him to her bedroom.

He slowly undressed her and got rid of his own clothes quickly. Erin fell beneath him, complete putty in his hands, in his arms. He kissed her with slow, deliberate, hot passion and began to unlock all the secrets of her body—secrets they'd found together so recently. He wound sweet pleasure around her and everywhere his fingers went, every time his tongue touched her, she would shudder in anticipation. This had never happened to her with anyone before and she had been thoroughly convinced it never would. But there was something about the way they came together that released the most amazing sensations and she couldn't summon caution. Now that she'd found it, she couldn't imagine ever living without this.

"Like that," he said softly, hoarsely. "Move like that, just a little. Gently. Slowly. Take your time...." And he rocked inside her, filling her, teasing her, the build of orgasm already so familiar to her, something she needed from him so desperately. And then he said, "Tell me when you're so close you want to cry."

"God," she whispered, feeling those inevitable tears of longing rise to her eyes, holding him so fiercely she wondered she didn't break him. "Please, Aiden," she whispered. "Now. Now. Now."

"Hang on just a little longer...."

"Now," she whispered. "Please, now…"

She heard his deep moan just as he pulled out just a bit. Then he said, "Come for me now, baby." And he drove himself into her, hard, fast, deep. Again and again and again, until she cried out, cried his name, came apart over and over and over. "Like that," he said. "Just like that. Lose control. Just like that…" And he joined her, letting it all go in a blast so powerful that it left him shaking.

He held her for a long time, keeping his weight from crushing her. Their lips met in a series of short, sweet kisses while they calmed. "You feel a little too good," he whispered. "I might've forgotten something.…"

"I realized that too late," she said.

"You're not on the pill, are you?"

"Why would I be?" she countered. "There hasn't been anyone."

"It's okay, honey. We can get ahead of it. That's something we should talk about anyway. Being together, staying together, maybe having children together."

"I thought that ship had sailed," she said. "I'm already thirty-six.…"

"Me, too. And there's still plenty of time."

She laughed in spite of herself. "That was really the lamest marriage proposal I've ever had. Also, the first. Can this possibly wait till morning? I mean, later morning?"

"As long as you tell me one thing," Aiden said. "Tell

me if you care about me half as much as I care about you."

She touched his cheek with her palm. "Probably twice as much," she whispered. "I love you. I think it's crazy, but I'm in love with you...."

He let out his breath as if he'd been holding it. "Then we can manage anything."

A few hours later, Aiden rolled over to an empty bed and the smell of coffee. He sat up, found his boxers on the floor and dragged them on. He ran a hand through his hair and followed the smell. He found Erin sitting on the leather sofa in the great room, a cup of coffee on a tray on the leather ottoman beside her, a sheaf of papers in her hand. She looked up as he entered. The expression on her face was troubled.

"Aiden, how could you not know this wasn't a final decree?" she asked.

He rubbed the back of his neck. "I don't know. The lawyer said it was all I needed, that it was done, she was blessedly gone and I was in residency, working a hundred and twenty hours a week. I was sleep deprived and..." He groaned. "Y'know, it never crossed my mind to have a second lawyer check my first lawyer's work. Besides, the check cleared..."

"Check?" she asked. "Payment to the lawyer?"

"No, to her. She wouldn't leave without a big, fat buy-off."

"There's nothing in here about a settlement," she said. "Jesus, who the hell handled this for you?"

"Obviously some idiot," he answered hotly. "Erin, she was fucking *crazy*, all right? I gave her money to go away! It was the best I could do at the time! Now I have to clean up the mess!"

"Don't get mad," she said, standing up and facing him. "You don't have a mess to clean up, Aiden. You have to start over."

"What?"

"This is an application for a dissolution of marriage, and it's eight years old. There's nothing about a settlement, so no record of a payment…"

"I have the goddamn canceled check!"

"Please," she said as calmly as possible. "I realize you have the canceled check, stored in a ziplock bag in your strongbox. A check made out to Annalee Somebody—not Riordan—and deposited in a third party's bank account. I'm afraid that isn't going to mean much. If she isn't incredibly cooperative—like a woman who wants out so she can get on with her life—you're going to need—"

"That isn't what she wants," he said. And in spite of himself, his face took on a dark flush. "But she can't be trusted, you have to understand that."

Erin swallowed. "And what *does* she want?"

He fidgeted uncomfortably, his lips pursed. "She said she wants to reconcile. It's nonnegotiable. I was done with her eight years ago and I'm more done now." He took a step toward her. "Erin, ask Luke about her. He saw her in action when she was totally out of her mind. Luke's the one who took her out of my apartment, put her in a hotel and gave her a fistful of bennies to keep her away long enough for me to find a lawyer. It might've taken me a while to be convinced she was completely crazy and dangerous, but Luke saw it in less than a half hour."

Erin let the pages fall against her thigh in utter frustration. "Why'd you marry her if she was so crazy?"

"I told you—it was a mistake!"

"You're raising your voice again," she calmly pointed out.

"It was a mistake," he said more calmly. "I was desperate for a little female company, met her at the officers' club, drank a little too much and ended up in bed with her. It wasn't until after that that I found out she was enlisted personnel assigned to my hospital. That kind of liaison is not allowed. Ever watch *60 Minutes?* Fraternization is considered a crime in the military—court martial is usually followed by dishonorable discharge—and all this was after I'd invested years in the navy. All this right before my residency— the navy's commitment to me—was just starting. I had to marry her to make it all look decent. Legal."

Erin was appalled. "After one slightly tipsy roll in the hay?" she asked, stunned.

He couldn't respond right away because he knew how it looked, how it sounded. In fact, he absolutely believed Annalee had taken all that into consideration when she picked him out, stalked him, blew his brains out with mind-bending sex that he'd been totally starving for, for a couple of years, and... He groaned. "It was more than once, but not much more. And before I could run for my life, it leaked, and it seemed everyone knew about our relationship. My boss gave me two choices—come up on charges for sexual harassment, fraternization and dishonorable discharge, which would make me look real goddamn desirable as a civilian woman's doctor. Or just make it legal so it looked like true love, not something nasty and sordid. I saw my life flash before my eyes."

"And your family? They know about this?" she asked.

"Sort of," he said. "My brothers know. Luke and Sean were involved. Colin and Paddy heard about it. It's not the kind of thing you explain in detail to your widowed mother."

"Oh, man," she said, shaking her head. "I wish I'd known this before you forgot that condom," she muttered.

He'd moved on her too fast, he realized that. But this was only the second time his life flashed before his eyes—the first was Annalee and hysterical fear, the second was now, when he'd finally found the woman he'd always wanted and she was so close to denying him. A few hours ago nothing mattered but them being together, maybe forever, and now she was regretting that absence of a condom—the little slip that could possibly begin to build them a family.

He grabbed her upper arms, feeling scared and desperate. "Listen, she's nuts, she's a liar and she probably just wants more money to go away. Finding out the divorce wasn't final was probably the best news she's had in years—she can cut a deal all over again and make me pay. Erin, I love you! This woman—Annalee—she's just a con artist! I'll get this fixed! I swear to God, I'll get this—"

"Aiden, Aiden," she said softly. "Please. You're hurting me."

He let go at once. "God, I'm sorry," he said, backing off. He crossed the room before he turned back to face her. "Listen, do you see?" he said. "I'm standing here in my underwear trying to make you believe that she's the crazy one. That I couldn't possibly have made this many stupid mistakes unless some huge con was in place—which cost me a lot of money and the respect of my colleagues. Come on, Erin, I'm smarter than that mess indicates. You have to give me the benefit of the doubt."

She took a deep breath. She put the stapled sheaf of papers on the leather ottoman and picked up her coffee cup. "We have an attorney in the firm named Ronald Preston. We call him Arnie Becker after that divorce shyster on the old series *L.A. Law.* He's completely within the law as far as anyone can tell, but the deals he manages to pull off are pretty amazing…and incredibly good for his clients. Here's me—giving you the benefit of the doubt. I wouldn't want someone like Ron handling my divorce unless I was divorcing a completely unscrupulous, greedy, horrible, dangerous person who was trying to get me before I got him. Ron's in Chico, but he has a fairly far-reaching clientele. And a full stable of assistants, secretaries and investigators."

After a moment of silence he said, "Thank you."

"Well, if you're being completely honest with me, you're welcome. If you're not telling me the whole truth, I'm sure I won't be able to go any further with you."

"I swear, Erin. It's all true. Especially the part about loving you."

* * *

Erin didn't want to obsess about how Aiden was handling the complications in his life, but it was impossible to blank out her mind. After giving him Ron Preston's name, phone number and directions to her law office in Chico, he said he'd call, but feared this whole effort would take up a lot of time he'd rather be spending with her. She told him the time would be well spent. She was sure she wouldn't ever be able to change her feelings about him, but she did think it would be in her best interest if he tidied up his personal life before they got any more serious.

The larger question was—if this didn't turn out well, could she ever forget him? For all the lack of romantic intrigue in her life, she'd never had her heart broken. Oh, there'd been disappointments. That seemed inevitable. But in the grand scheme of things, they were very small. There had been a man who suggested they weren't very compatible, that there wasn't true chemistry. She'd actually agreed, but was sorry they weren't going to give it more than a couple of dates to figure out. There was another whose ex-fiancée returned to the picture when they'd barely started dating. Yet another found her far too unavailable with her demanding legal practice and family responsibilities—he was looking for a woman who'd be there first for *him*.

These were not broken hearts but mere pinches. Minor letdowns. Besides, she'd known she'd been settling for less than her heart's desire with each one. They hadn't set her blood on fire, made her weak in the knees, caused her to lose control. She had long wondered if she was too fussy or just plain impossible to please.

Then came Aiden. He'd taught her how to have fun, how to enjoy the real companionship of two people who seemed perfectly suited. Then he'd taught her how to crave intimacy, something she'd pretty much been able to do without. Doing without it now, doing without *him,* would be very hard. She missed him so much in just a day.

He'd called twice. He'd been to an appointment with Ron in Chico; Ron had collected what Aiden described as a very large retainer for the job. Once back in Virgin River, Luke and Shelby were just bringing the new baby home, and his family had once again amassed. "Tomorrow," he said to her. "Nothing will keep me from you tomorrow."

A couple of days and she was aching for him. She'd never felt quite so vulnerable. Not quite a week since the Fourth of July and already she was hurting for him. He had definitely burrowed under her skin and—

She heard a car and for a second her heart leaped. She realized that if it was Aiden she would be hard-pressed to even ask him if he'd resolved anything. She'd probably throw herself at him and smother him with kisses.

It was not Aiden. It was a young woman in a very fancy car—a model Erin had actually looked at once. A classy and expensive pale blue Lexus—a fully loaded hybrid. That might be a hundred-thousand-dollar car. And the woman—very young, beautiful and tiny, but with enviable curves, stepped out and closed the door.

Erin stood in the cabin doorway. The woman smiled as she came closer. "You must be Erin," she said almost shyly.

"That's right," Erin said, and her gut began to twist because she had an ill feeling about who this might be.

"I hope you'll forgive this intrusion," she said. "This isn't something I ever thought I'd do. My name is Annalee Riordan and I've come here to ask you to give me back my husband."

That slight twist turned into a terrible clamp around her insides; she nearly doubled over with the pain. She called upon many years of practice at never letting anyone see her sweat. "I don't have your husband," she said.

"You're not the woman involved with Aiden?" she asked, looking very surprised. "Oh, I'm so sorry—you must think I'm an idiot. I thought it was you. I apologize. I'll go now." And she turned away.

"Why are you here? What is it you think I can do for you?"

She turned back and flipped her beautiful, thick blond hair over one shoulder. She shook her head dismally. "So, you are the one. Well, I'm not even sure. Tell him you're no longer interested in him, maybe? Tell him to give his marriage another chance? I mean, we made a lot of mistakes, me and Aiden—and I take responsibility for at least half the problems—but shouldn't we try to work it out, since there was some complication with the paperwork and we're not actually divorced? I took it as a sign. Maybe now, older and wiser, we can do better…"

Erin crossed her arms over her chest. "Please, don't take me for a fool. You were married three months before signing your divorce petition."

"Three *years*," she tossed back rather softly.

"The documents are dated," Erin pointed out matter-of-factly.

"Of course they are. So were the next documents and the next and the next. We went that route more than once. The first time was soon after we were married, probably three months. Those were probably the ones he showed you. In fact, we separated for quite a while—several months. There was always something, though…I'm not sure what it was… We always ended up back together for a while."

Ew, that caused a shiver to go up Erin's spine. Chemistry? That thing she was feeling with him now—that irresistible, insatiable hunger? "How long since you've actually lived together?"

"A long time," she admitted. "Four or five years, I think."

"There was a check," Erin said. "Also dated…"

"For ten thousand? Yes, that was the reason for the first separation. The abortion. It was a horrible fight. In the end he was very generous, since he didn't want a baby with me. I went home, saw a very good doctor, spent some time to think things over." She looked down. "I probably shouldn't have gone back to him. He was— He wasn't always easy to get along with, but I probably wasn't, either. He said I provoked him, and thinking back, maybe I did. I was so young when we got married. Young and not very smart."

She was very young-looking *now,* Erin thought—feeling every minute of her thirty-six years. "How young?"

"Eighteen."

Erin knew she was being taken for a ride here, but she didn't know how. "You seem to have done quite well for yourself, for a woman so young," she said, nodding toward the car.

"Thank you, yes," she said, smiling. "The car is a rental. It's important in my business to look successful when I'm meeting clients. I'm a fashion buyer and consultant. I was meeting a designer in San Francisco and the car is a business expense. I've only been doing it for a couple of years and it's gone so well for me."

Erin frowned. "Yet this whole time, longing for your ex-husband?"

"No," she said, shaking her head. "Oh, no, it isn't like that. It's true—I spent a lot of time wondering how I could have done things better. I regretted our mistakes, of course. I think anyone who goes through a divorce does—but I was moving on. And when I discovered something went wrong with the paperwork, I thought…" She shook her head as if it didn't really bear mentioning. "Well, I'll get out of your hair."

"Just how did you discover the oversight?" Erin asked.

She lifted her chin. "A man I was seeing for a couple of years asked me to marry him. I told him about my marriage and divorce, of course, as anyone would. He's the one who discovered it."

"When are you getting married?" Erin asked.

"That's looking doubtful now. The gentleman isn't happy about me meeting with Aiden. But I had to tell Aiden what we'd found out! I couldn't let him make the same mistake I almost made! What if he remarried and it wasn't legal?"

"This is all pretty far-fetched...."

"I imagine it seems so. Really, I'm sorry. I guess I'm a little out of my mind to even consider second chances. But I'd like you to know one thing—I might've been really young and not terribly experienced, but I loved him. I did. Even though our relationship was full of problems, I still—"

"You met his brothers, I understand," Erin said.

She laughed very suddenly. "Oh, yes. Only Sean and Luke. I never met Colin and Patrick, but I have no trouble picturing them. There were lots of photographs around our apartment, of course. The Riordan men would kill for each other. Quite the band of brothers there. Be careful—don't cross one of them." Then she laughed humorlessly. "God, what am I doing? I can see I'm just making a giant fool of myself. Again."

"Wait a second. You'll be needed to sign new documents...."

"Aiden can call me—he knows how to reach me if he wants me, which he seems to every now and then."

"What does *that* mean?"

"We haven't lived together in a few years, but he stays in touch."

"Is that so?"

She just made a face and shook her head. "Has Aiden

led you to believe we haven't seen or heard from each other in eight years? Has he really? Well, that wouldn't come as a surprise—he has a short attention span, my husband. I stayed in San Diego until a couple of years ago, when I finally tried to make a clean break. Please, be so careful. Aiden can make a woman believe anything. And I learned the hard way—it's dangerous to confront him, to fight with him. He has an ugly little temper."

"Aiden?" she asked, aghast.

"You haven't known him very long, have you, Erin?" Her expression was pained, sad. "Be very careful of him. Most of the time he's an angel, sexiest angel on earth, but he doesn't handle his anger well. He has a hair trigger."

Then she gave a wave of her hand and got in her car. She backed up, turned around and drove slowly away from the cabin, down the road.

Erin felt a very creepy chill run through her, but she wasn't sure where it came from. The perfect little beauty who claimed to want another chance with her soon-to-be ex-husband? Or Aiden, who she thought she knew so intimately but perhaps didn't really know that well. Aiden, who a couple of days ago grabbed her harshly in anger.

She'd prefer to think this young woman was lying. The problem was, she had no real way of disputing any of their claims. Either one's.

In the practice of tax and estate law, people could tell horrendous lies with all the innocence of a sweet baby. Money was at stake, sometimes huge amounts of money. Finger-pointing and swearing on a stack of bibles didn't cut any grass with the law—everything had to be documented and proven.

How did you prove your boyfriend wasn't calling his ex-wife? Maybe seeing her from time to time? Who did you believe when the stories were so disparate?

Erin called Ron Preston. "Did your new client, Aiden Riordan, happen to mention where his referral came from?"

"Yes, and thank you very much, Erin."

"Did he happen to mention why I gave the referral?"

"He met you at that vacation spot where you have the cabin?" he replied by way of a question.

"Hmm. Yes, that's correct. Met me, became a friend, dated me and now the ex-wife has appeared to state that she's not an ex-wife. He says they parted company after three months of marriage and haven't seen each other in eight years. She says they were together three *years,* filled out divorce papers more than once and have remained in touch." Physically in touch?

"Erin, I can't discuss this with you...."

"I understand that, Ron. The problem is, there is no way for me to check either story and I don't want to be..." She couldn't finish. Used? Abused? Lied to? Manipulated?

"I understand completely," Ron said. "You're emotionally involved, so I'm going to tell you something you already know. When I have a client whose story differs remarkably from the person they oppose in the process, I listen very carefully, check the facts, do everything I can to represent my client, but I don't necessarily believe them. That doesn't mean he or she is lying, it means that there are many assertions that are simply impossible to clarify. This is just about process, Erin. May the better man win."

"And if one of the by-products is that I'm emotionally *decimated* in the process?" she asked sarcastically.

"There's no law that says you have to believe everything you hear. Slow down. Don't leave yourself open."

She sighed deeply. "Thanks," she said. "Really, thanks. I needed to hear that. I hate it, but I needed to hear it."

"I suspect this will be resolved soon enough. Guard your flanks. And your fanny."

"Oh! That's crude!" she snapped at him.

"Do it anyway," he said. "Gotta run. Marriages are falling apart everywhere I look."

She hung up. That was why she hated him—because he was cold and went in for the kill. And that was why she had a grudging respect for him, because he *didn't* get emotionally involved. And where did that leave her? Aching for a man she was just a little afraid to believe in.

Thirteen

Mel Sheridan had a very busy week, beginning with being awake most of Wednesday night with Shelby Riordan. It was getting harder, she noticed, to pull those all-nighters and bounce right back. A lot of that could have to do with having two little kids, at least one of whom should be completely potty trained. Emma was two, David three, and when Mel had a sitter, a teenage girl was having more success than she was.

Of course Mel was busy. She had always been busy. The day after Shelby and Luke's baby arrived, she tried sleeping late, but that didn't work out. She went to the clinic and saw a few patients. There was a callout from a rancher who was having chest pains—she and Cameron left the clinic to attend to him. They transported him to the hospital and the whole emergency took a long time; Mel was late getting home. She was due a real deep sleep, but Emma didn't feel well. She and Jack were up during the night changing pajamas, diapers, sheets, and Jack said, "I hope to hell whatever this is doesn't go through the whole family."

It was the weekend before things seemed to calm down. Mel indulged herself a little with some catch-up—she got her house in order, called Leslie Carpenter to babysit so she could visit Shelby and the new baby, then took a long soak in the tub and joined the kids during nap time, resting up.

She needed a little quality time with her husband.

She fed her children, got them settled in bed early and Jack escaped from the bar, bringing their dinner. Since the kids were asleep, she went to some trouble; she put place mats and candles on the table. When Jack had dished up their dinner and they sat down together in a clean, quiet house, she said, "Lord, what a crazy week!"

"I agree. You feel okay? Because whatever had Emma all upside down and not feeling well, no one else seems to be sick."

"I feel fine," she said. "David's fine. I felt it was safe to go out to the Riordans' to see them because forty-eight hours had passed with no symptoms of any kind."

"And the Riordans are okay?"

"They're on a honeymoon with little Brett. He hasn't really found his voice yet. Any second he's going to let them know he has truly arrived."

Jack chuckled. Newborns had a tendency to be very quiet, just eat and sleep the first few days, and then *bam!* They let you know they're a member of the family, with needs.

"When I was delivering the baby I had a thought. I wondered if our surrogate would be open to the idea of me delivering our baby."

Jack's chin dropped. He put down his fork.

"Okay, that was pretty obvious," Mel said to him. "What's your problem?"

He lifted his gaze. "My first problem is that I don't want to spoil the only dinner we've had together in almost a week...."

"And your second problem?"

"I don't want to do the surrogate thing." There. He'd said it. Not exactly as he was committed to saying it—that it was off the table. He hadn't said he refused. God, he hoped she'd hear him this time.

But she slowly and carefully cut off a slice of meat—Preacher's outstanding pork roast in dark gravy—and lifted it in a leisurely fashion to her mouth. She chewed. She swallowed. "I understand that some men have a real resistance to the process, which is why I wanted you to discuss it with John Stone. He's familiar and comfortable with the whole thing. It's pretty routine."

"Not for me," he said. "I don't want to."

"For God's sake, Jack. Just have a conversation with John about—"

"I did," he said. "I had a long talk with John. I told him how I was feeling about it and he wasn't much help. Except to say that I needed to be a little more direct with you and give you the bottom line—I'm not doing it. I don't want a woman I don't know having a baby for us. Not under our circumstances."

Her expression was at first shocked, but then it melted into some kind of softness, like understanding. "Believe me, by the time the baby is ready to arrive, we'll know her very well."

He shook his head. "Listen, will you listen? I'm almost insanely happy that we accidentally had these two kids…you and the kids are my world. My whole world. Before you came into my life I had accepted that I wouldn't have kids. I didn't like that I had to accept being alone my whole life, but I had accepted it. Then you came along and rocked my world. If you'd come to me infertile and told me it meant everything to you to have one of our own—our DNA that will pee on a tree in the middle of a public picnic—I'd do this thing. Mel, I would if it were the only way."

"Don't look now, Jack. It is the only way."

"The only way to have a *third* child. But we already have a couple of kids. I'm satisfied with that."

"And I'm not!" she said sharply.

"Why not?" he asked. "Is it because your uterus was stolen during an emergency? We never talked about a lot of kids. The first one scared you to death and you complained about getting caught with the second one."

"Pregnant emotions," she said, waving him off, looking away.

"We never talked much about the hysterectomy, either. I don't know," he said. "I think we're dealing with something else here and you're not coming clean with me, which is totally unlike you, Melinda. You're so goddamn honest with me it stings sometimes. But not about this. You're trying to push me into something

I don't want. And I don't think you want a baby that bad. I think you want a uterus again."

She stared at him in utter disbelief. "That's perfectly ridiculous," she said. "If I had needed to talk about that, I would have."

"But we had a new baby, we had a forest fire, Doc died, we had Rick in Iraq and then home trying to adjust to a disability. Hardly small distractions. This is the first quiet spell we've had in a couple of years, Mel. If you need to talk about this now—"

She slammed her fork down on the table. "Are you out of your mind? Haven't you been listening?"

"No, I am not out of my mind and yes, I have heard every word. Mel. Having a third party have a baby for us is going to be painful, difficult, expensive and full of potential problems. I get that in some circumstances it's well worth it. We don't have those circumstances."

"I *do!* I *do* have those circumstances!"

He fixed his gaze on hers. Damn, she was some fireball. She was a fighter and when her mind was made up there was almost nothing that could pull her off the target. He just looked at her until he sensed she had simmered down a little bit. "Baby, something else is going on here. Talk to me about it. Please."

"I did talk to you! And I expected you to keep an open mind and research it a little bit! Jesus," she said, standing from the table. "When do I ask anything of you?"

She walked away from their dining room table and to her back he said, "Every day. Every night."

She turned back and stared at him.

"We do this together, Mel. It's not that easy sometimes. I keep the kids while you see patients, while you go out on calls. I cook and take them on errands and tend bar and do inventory with kids in backpacks and playpens. You take the kids to work with you and manage the house while I work early and late at the bar. We both have real long days and nights. We manage, but it's not easy. I do as much as you do and you're still tired."

"I haven't complained. And until now, neither have you. If you want me to, I can get a house cleaner and a nanny. I have some money saved."

"I think we get by all right. I like the time I spend with the kids. If we had another one, we'd manage and be happy about it. But I'm not going to the lengths you want me to for a third."

She got tears in her eyes. "Even if it means everything to me? Even if I want to so much it's all I think about? Day and night?"

He stood up from the table and went to her, standing in front of her. "That's what's weird about this. It came out of the blue. This isn't something you started talking about after Emma was born. When I asked you if you were doing okay with the hysterectomy, you blew it off. You were fine, you said. You didn't whimper and cry that you were so disappointed you couldn't have more children.... You said you had a lot of blessings to count and considered us damn lucky to get the two kids. Now, suddenly, this is a desperate move. It's out of character. I'm worried about you."

"This isn't anything to worry about," she insisted. "It's something to talk about doing!"

He shook his head. "I think the person who should talk to John is you," he said gently.

She stared at him openmouthed for a moment, then said, "Ach!" She turned and stomped off to the bedroom.

"Mel! You haven't eaten!"

"I've lost my appetite!" She disappeared around the corner.

"We still haven't talked about it!" he said to her departing form, voice raised. "We need to talk about *your* uterus, not someone else's!"

She poked her head back into the dining room. "There is nothing to talk about!" Then she escaped again.

He looked at the doorway to the bedroom. "Exactly," he said.

Erin thought about running home to Chico before she had to see Aiden again. She knew she was incomparably strong, but in this instance, she truly feared she might crumble. When she thought about all the heartbreaking things she had managed to survive with strength—her mother's death, her father's, Marcie's husband Bobby's catastrophic war injuries—it was amazing even to her she hadn't collapsed. Surely she could get through this without coming completely apart.

But she was so in love with him, and despite her practical nature she had been secretly hoping this was the real thing. Before this story even approached the ending, she was in the garden Aiden had laid for her, pulling weeds, dropping her tears on the freshly tilled dirt.

Then she heard his SUV grinding its way up her road; she knew at once it wasn't that smooth, expensive, quiet baby-blue Lexus. She stood up from the garden, mud on her knees, dirt under her nails, her soup pot and metal spoon nearby. She briefly wondered if she could bang it to scare him away.

Her front door was locked and he walked around the deck to the back. He stood at the edge of the garden and said, "I've seen the lawyer. Worst case, it takes a few months because she's uncooperative or unresponsive, but it'll get done. She doesn't have to agree to the divorce."

"Uncooperative? Unresponsive?" she asked.

"When she showed up at Luke's, she gave me a business card with a phone number on it, but it's a non-working number. There's no business number or address on the card. She's dropped out of sight. Typical, I'm afraid."

"Have you called her?"

He shook his head. "Why would I even try? I want nothing to do with her. And Preston advised me not to contact her—he tried to reach her. It's time for her lawyer to talk to my lawyer, if she has a lawyer."

She took a step toward him and damn it all, her voice trembled when she spoke. "She was here, Aiden."

His face got red—*instantly! "Here?"* he said, raising his voice. "How the *hell* would she know who you are or where you live?"

"Please don't yell at me," she said. "I have no idea how."

"God!" he barked. "Does this give you any indication of what kind of a person she is?"

Erin shook her head. "She's just a kid," she said. "A very beautiful kid. Just looking at her, I felt so middle-aged."

"Don't do that to yourself—you're perfect. Annalee used her looks to snag me—that incredible combination of blow-your-mind sex appeal combined with innocent youth. It's all an act. You should see how much older she can look when she's firing glassware across the room."

"She was only eighteen when she met you. How could she be so—"

"Twenty-one," he said. "I looked at her driver's license, for God's sake—I *married* her!"

"Oh, man," Erin said weakly, running a dirty hand through her hair. "Oh, man, this is so creeping me out."

"How do you think I got trapped in this mess to start with?" he asked her. "I know I was stupid, but I wasn't stupid in all these ways. I was deceived."

"What ways were you stupid?" she asked.

"I told you," he said impatiently. "Young, horny, picked up a girl in a bar… No matter what you might be tempted to believe right now, that was never a habit of mine. Listen, we have to work this out, Erin. I'm not going to let her fuck up our lives. We have to get this behind us."

"I have to ask you some things. I want answers—

calm answers. You lose your cool any more and I'm going to wonder what you're hiding."

He shook his head in frustration. "I know you're right, but try to understand—she's a pathological liar and she's cost me in the past. When she showed up at Luke's, my mother was horrified by the way I talked to her. She'd never heard me talk to another human being that way, much less a woman."

"Were you actually together three years, not three months?" Erin asked. The shocked look on his face told her he wasn't prepared for that question, or else he was a brilliant actor, better even than what he'd given Annalee credit for. "Have you been in touch all this time—you and your wife?" He couldn't seem able to close his mouth. "Did you give her that big check so she'd get an abortion?"

"Abortion?" he asked in shock. "Erin. No. No to all of that!"

"Is she going to say everything you tell me is a lie? And are you going to say everything she tells me is a lie?"

He didn't answer. He didn't even shake his head. He met her eyes steadily—green on green. He was done begging to be believed, she could see that.

"Answer this for me, Aiden. Please. When you found yourself married to this beautiful young woman, did you try to make it work? Did you hope you could make it work with her? The truth. Please."

"Even though I hated her? Even though I'd been trapped by my affair with her? Even though every day with her was sheer hell while she abused me, stole from me, deceived me, cheated on me and had sex with other men in my bed? You really want the true answer to that? Because I don't think it'll help my case with you. I don't think you'll respect me for it. The truth is—yes, I tried. And I didn't try for three years— it was three months. It was only three months because when I called my brothers and told them what had been going on since I hit land, Luke came right away. Then Sean, right behind him. They had her number in thirty seconds and wouldn't allow it to go on. But yes, if I could've transformed her into a wife, I would have. Not because I cared about her. Because I took an oath. Because in our family it takes a lot to get a man to take those vows and when we do… Ask Sean. Ask Luke. Don't take my word for it."

She felt a slight smile reach her lips; very slight. "She suggested your brothers would lie for you."

"I think that's probably the single truth she told you," he admitted with a nod. "Under most circumstances, they probably would. Lie for me, kill for me, risk their lives for me. I would for them. What she didn't mention because she doesn't understand—I'd never be in the kind of position that would require it. Neither would they. We tend to admit our mistakes and take our lumps."

"Aiden," she said. "This is so awful."

"I know," he said so softly she barely heard.

"Is there any way you can prove to me that she's lying and you're telling the truth?"

"I don't know," he said. Then something seemed to occur to him. "Did she tell you she wanted to reconcile?"

"Something like that, yes.…"

"She said that in front of my family." He frowned and shook his head. "I have no idea how this figures into her scheme, her plan. I assume it's more money—signing new documents will carry a price tag, just like the last time...."

"Well, that's easy. Don't pay her," Erin said.

"I *want* her to go away," he said.

"If what you say about her is true, she's probably counting on just that. Ron told you correctly—you don't have to have permission to divorce her. It might take a little longer without her cooperation, but Ron knows how to deal with that—he deals with it all the time. Just move forward."

"And us?" he asked. "Can we just move forward?"

Us? she thought. She wanted him so much; she wanted everything he said to be true. She wanted this insane, wild summer on a mountain to be the forever she thought was completely out of her reach. But she had to protect her flanks. And her heart. "I need something from you."

"Anything."

"I need you to give Ron Preston permission to share with me whatever information he finds about your case—about your last lawyer, Annalee, all the stuff that's in dispute. I know he'll have his paralegals researching in order to represent your interests and he can't talk to me about a client without the client's permission. Even though I'm a member of the firm."

"Done," he said.

"And I can't sleep with you until at least most of this is resolved."

"You don't trust me," he said, the pain in his voice obvious.

"Remember how you felt when you realized you'd been used, abused, deceived? I don't want to feel that way. What I want is for Ron to work his magic, get some facts and prove to me that I was right about you from the start. That's all I ask. And that's not a lot."

"Whatever you want," he said. Then he got a familiar glint in his eye and said, "You're not going to be able to make that stick, but as long as you tell me no, I'll listen and obey. It's just that you and me, together, is a little bigger than both of us." He straightened his spine and drew in a deep breath, putting his hands in his pockets. "One way or another, we'll get this done. I don't have any other shadows that can ruin this for us. It'll be terrible, not sleeping with you, holding you, loving you. But if that's what you need, I can do that. When this is over," he said, "I'm never letting you go."

"I don't want to learn you haven't been telling me the truth," she said.

"You won't," he said, shaking his head. "How long did you spend with her? An hour?"

"Ten minutes, tops," she said.

"And with me?"

Days! Days and nights! "You weren't completely honest," she reminded him.

"Aw, we were just having fun—I wasn't trying to manipulate you. What could I possibly gain by trying to convince you I'm a homeless vagrant?" He stepped toward her cautiously. "And there's one other thing—

you might not trust my brothers to sell me out, but my mother wouldn't lie for the pope. She's been foggy on the details of my marriage—I didn't tell her till it was over, and God knows I didn't tell her the worst of it until a couple of days ago, but she knows me. Take your chances on her, Erin. With my blessing."

She tilted her head and her eyes lit up. She smiled. This was true! She barely knew Maureen, but she knew what he said was correct. "That might help your case."

"I just want you to trust me again," he said.

She could have been seduced by him, she knew that. She was a woman who'd gone from being frustrated by her sex life to almost bored by it to a woman completely vulnerable to this man's touch. He was every man rolled into one—gentle and sweet, strong and powerful, generous and at times, demanding. Since he'd brought her libido to life, he was the one man who could finesse her into forgetting herself completely. He could make her lose control and all he'd have to do to set that train in motion was the merest touch, the smallest brush of his lips. There was a part of her that wished he would try. And there was no question that he knew it, too.

But he didn't. Instead, he bent to one knee and pulled out some errant weeds that she'd missed. Then he moved to the other end of the garden and pulled a few more. He picked up the handheld spading fork and began to break up clots. She just watched him for a few moments and then she knelt again to the same task at the other end of the garden.

"You have some blossoms here," he said in passing,

not looking at her. "In a month, you'll see tomatoes. Green ones, at least."

In a month, will I see my love life restored? she wanted to ask. In a month, will everything be all right?

They worked in companionable silence for a long time; every once in a while Aiden would say something like, "You might be able to pull up a small carrot in a couple of weeks," or "You'll have to be sure to come back up here in fall—the melons and pumpkins start late, but you wouldn't want to miss that." Finally he sat back on his heels and said, "Erin, why don't you shower while I finish up here and I'll take you to Luke's to see the new baby."

"I do want to see the baby. Is it a mistake for me to spend time with you? Should we just avoid each other until some of this mess gets resolved?"

He shook his head and smiled. "You'll be okay. I know you're disappointed and maybe a little worried about what's coming, but I think you know you're perfectly safe with me. I'm not going to try to trip you up—I want you to feel in control right now." Then he frowned and glanced away for a moment.

"What is it?" she asked.

He looked back at her, shaking his head. "I can't figure out how she knew who you were, where you were. I didn't have a conversation with her—I told her I didn't want her around my brother's property. No one in my family would have told her things without asking me first. I can't figure it out."

"She didn't say how she knew," Erin said. "And I didn't ask."

"It'll come out eventually," he said. "Go on, honey—clean up and I'll drive you over. Nothing like a new baby to take your mind off all sorts of dark things...."

Aiden Riordan opened the door to Luke's house, pushed Erin inside and announced, "Erin's here for a visit. I'll be outside with Luke and Art."

She found Shelby sitting on the sofa plucking baby clothes out of a laundry basket and folding them into neat little piles. She beamed at Erin. "Well, hello! What a nice surprise!"

Maureen Riordan was in the kitchen, busy taking cookies off a cookie sheet; Rosie was up on a chair, playing with a handful of dough like it was clay. Rosie had flour everywhere—on her hands, face, clothes. The house was filled with the wonderful smell of freshly baked sweets.

Maureen smiled and said, "Hi, Erin. How are you?"

"Fine, thanks," she said. She presented a gift bag to Shelby. "A little something for the baby."

"Brett's sleeping," Rosie said. *"Finally!"*

"Does he fuss a lot?" Erin asked Rosie.

She shook her head vigorously, her red curls bouncing. She reminded Erin so much of Marcie as a little girl. "No! He *screams!*" Rosie announced.

Shelby just laughed and put aside her laundry. "Well, he's a guy, what do you expect." Shelby reached for the gift bag. "Now, what's this? This is just too nice of you!"

"Really, it's nothing. I was shopping and got side-tracked by baby things—my sister is due next month and I was busying buying out the store for their little boy. I lost control," she said. "I have a big box to take back to Chico when it's time for the baby."

"And when's that?" Shelby asked.

"Third week in August."

"You must be so excited!" Shelby pulled a couple of little boy six-month-size onesies out of the gift bag along with a tiny pair of shoes. "Oh, Erin, how sweet! Thank you!" There was a little fussing in the next room and Shelby cocked her head. "Well, there's my call. I'll change him and bring him right back."

"My granddaughter and I are going to walk down to the river now that the cookies are all out," Maureen said. "We'll see you in a little while," she added.

Shelby was back in just a few moments with a tiny, tightly swaddled bundle with a bright pink face. He whimpered and squeaked in her arms, but she said, "Here. Try this out for a couple of minutes before I feed him."

"Oh…I don't… He's so tiny…. Are you sure?"

"Just like that," Shelby said, placing the baby in Erin's arms. "Hold him close and just move a little, back and forth. Or jiggle. They all love to be up against a warm body and in motion all the time." Shelby smiled. "You have to practice—you're going to be an auntie."

Erin felt clumsy at first, but very soon she loved the way he felt in her arms, against her chest. She loved his baby smell and his gassy little smile, the tiny fist he'd wrestled free from his swaddling and tried to cram in his mouth. She asked Shelby all about her delivery, about his sleeping and eating schedule, about how Luke and even Art were dealing with the baby. After a few minutes the baby's squirming and crying had Shelby reaching for him. "Here," she said. "I'll feed him."

Erin began to rise. "I'll just step out—"

"Don't be silly. Stay. Besides, I wanted us to talk." She rested the baby on her lap while she got ready and when she had the little one all hooked up, she looked back at Erin. "I don't know if this is appropriate, Erin, but I wanted to say something about that whole business with Aiden's ex-wife. How awful for you."

"Do you know her?"

"Never saw her before the day she showed up here," she said, shaking her head. "Luke had mentioned her a long while back—but she wasn't at all what I expected. Luke described her as a real hot number with about fifteen personalities. The woman I saw was pretty, but seemed very…unworldly? I did think she was a little on the sweet side to be the kind of successful businesswoman who could afford a fancy car. But I might've been a little distracted. I was in labor and didn't mention it to anyone. I wanted to see what was going to happen."

"And what did happen?"

"Not much. The labor got to be pretty obvious, Aiden told her he'd be in touch to finalize that divorce and ordered her off the property. I've known Aiden quite a while—I have to say, I've never seen him angry before. Even Maureen said she'd never seen him act like that—he was a stone. She was weeping and begging and he looked her right in the eye and said he wasn't buying it." She shook her head. "She must be a very bad person for Aiden to act like that. Of all the Riordan men, Aiden's the sweetest. Luke's the one with the shortest fuse, I think. But even Luke's very careful around women. Just look at the way they all treat their mother…"

After a moment Erin said, "Well, eight years is a long time. Maybe she's changed."

"If she has, then I guess there won't be any problem with Aiden wrapping up the divorce he thought he had eight years ago. If she's changed, she should be very cooperative and pleasant about it. Especially since he was clear—that's all he wants."

Uncooperative rang in Erin's brain. *Unresponsive*, the lawyer had told Aiden. A phone number that didn't work. That wasn't a woman willing to settle things up without causing trouble.

"She visited me," Erin heard herself say. "She was, as you say, harmless. Very pretty and innocent. She asked me to give her back her husband."

Shelby gasped. "What in the world did you say?"

"I told her I didn't have her husband. But the story she told me made Aiden look like a liar and an abuser. She said they'd been together a long time and in touch ever since."

Shelby shook her head confidently. "Well, since his mother or brothers didn't live with him in San Diego, only Aiden would know the truth to that, but an abuser? Not Aiden. I give Aiden credit for getting Luke and I through a rough patch. We'd broken up—Luke was so convinced I was much too young for him and that if we did have a commitment, in a couple of years I'd just regret it. I went to Maui to lick my wounds, and Aiden, who I'd never met before, flew to the islands to talk to me, to explain why Luke was so cautious. Because Luke was afraid of getting hurt. I love Aiden. Everyone in the family leans on him." She made a little face. "For the first time I wonder, does Aiden have anyone to lean on?"

Erin smiled in spite of herself. "He depends on his brothers a lot, and from what I understand, they're always there for him."

"I guess that's right. They're pretty tight." Then she laughed. "What's so funny is that they'll keep each other's back, but they scrap a lot over stupid, little things. Just like a bunch of little boys."

"You know what Aiden and I can't figure out? He said he never had a conversation with his...with Annalee. How did she know about me? About where to find me?"

"That's pretty weird. No one told her where Aiden was, only that he wasn't here."

"It creeps me out," Erin said.

"Well, Erin—he came home in the late morning, wearing a tux. I guess you would assume that had to do with a woman, not a night out at the pub with the guys."

"I guess," she said. "But still-—that just assumes a woman. Not me."

"She must have found a way to uncover what

woman," Shelby said. "But no one around here mentioned you." Shelby lifted the baby onto her shoulder and patted his back. "I hope this is over soon so you and Aiden can get back to enjoying summer."

"Me, too," she said. "Marcie's baby is coming August twentieth. I'll go home a little before that. That gives us a month, but I have a feeling it isn't going to be that simple."

It was not just a little visit. Erin stayed at Luke and Shelby's through dinner and with the leaves in their large dining table, the entire family settled down for a big meal prepared mostly by Maureen and Luke. Ten of them sat around a big, square table, laughing, poking fun and enjoying a summer meal of ribs, beans, coleslaw and potato salad. Erin wasn't exempt from the teasing. They ribbed her about her e-mail remodeling, insisting on a perfect, cushy, brand-new cabin before she would even consider a vacation in it. And Erin *enjoyed* that! She really hadn't felt so much a part of a group besides her own brother and sister before now.

It didn't take long for Erin to decide Aiden was either the smartest liar in the universe with the most cooperative lying family or he was a genuine guy that all these people could not be wrong about. In her heart she knew it was the latter.

When he drove her home later on she pulled him inside. "Are you absolutely sure?" he asked. "Because I don't want to come in if you have any doubts. I'd rather wait until you're convinced I'm telling you the truth. I'll wait till I can prove it."

"Aiden, that woman really threw me," she said, finding it impossible to say her name. "Since there was a time she really turned your world upside down, you have to understand…"

"Believe me," he said with a humorless laugh.

"You have the most wonderful family, but they're relentless in their teasing. I don't think they'd cover for you. Not for long, anyway."

"And that convinced you? Not me, but them?"

"It's not just your family, but the way you take care of your mother. I have a colleague at the firm who's in her sixties. She has always said, pick a husband by how he treats his mother, pick a wife by how her father treats her."

"Interesting," he said, thinking about that.

"The thing is, so much of my life has been about loss. Oh, don't think I'm whining—I'm pretty proud of my life, but there's been a lot of loss. My mother, my father, then my 'kids' grew up and left. And more subtle loss that I didn't realize had affected me—my childhood, my adolescence, those law-school years when so many men and women bonded to get through it and I hurried home to make sure things were taken care of—that Drew got to football, that Marcie made it to cheerleading, that homework was done… And in all those years, right up to this summer…" She ran her hands up and down his arms. "I never fell in love. Not till now." She shook her head. "I don't want to let go of it now." She blinked away a tear. "But if I'm wrong about you, it's going to really hurt."

"I won't let you down, Erin." He ran the knuckle of

his index finger along the line of her jaw and then under her chin, lifting it just slightly so that green eyes met. "Know what I'd like to say now? I'd like to promise you you'll never face pain, loss or hardship again in your life." He shook his head slightly. "You know no one can do that. I can make a couple of promises, though. As my wife, you'll never again face anything difficult alone. Even if something happens to me, both your family and mine will be there for you. The Riordans are pretty scrappy and argumentative, but they never fail to be there for each other, and their families."

"Wife?"

"Of course, wife. When I get these legal complications settled, which is already in motion, and when you're ready." He smiled softly. "You do have to say yes, of course."

It came out on a breath. "Yes. Of course, yes."

He kissed her, a kiss that started soft and sweet, deepened, hardened, grew hot and long and wet and left her gasping. He smiled, then chuckled at her near loss of control.

"You said…a couple of promises…"

He grinned and gave her a brief kiss. "Our children will almost certainly have green eyes."

Aiden felt the bed dip, smelled fresh coffee and opened one eye to see the love of his life holding a mug toward him. He smiled lazily and asked, "Are you sure it's time to wake up? Because I'm shot."

"Of course you are," she said. "Because you're a

sex maniac. I'm pretty tired, too. So tell me, Doctor—
is there going to come a time we sleep together and
actually get some sleep? Because at this rate we're
going to die young."

He laughed and wrestled himself to a sitting position, reaching for the mug. He took a sip. "My dad
used to say if you put a bean in a jar for every time
you have sex during the first year you're together, then
take a bean out for every time you have sex after that
first year, you'll never empty the jar."

She sipped her coffee. "Hmm, I don't know if that's
good news or bad...."

"Why are you up so early?"

"Aiden, it's not that early. It's eight o'clock. And
I'm up because I have a lot on my mind. Like—Sean
and Franci will be heading off to Alabama to his next
assignment in just a couple of days. Can we have them
to dinner here? Can you invite the whole family and
help me cook? Is it okay for Luke and Shelby to come
and bring the baby? Is he old enough?"

"Yes," he said, smiling. "Yes to all of that—except
you can invite them yourself. Come back to Luke's
with me later this morning. Next?"

"I have to go back to Chico before Marcie's baby
comes. What will we do, where will you be?"

He took a thoughtful sip. "I suppose I'll be wherever you want me to be...."

"Chico?"

He gave a shrug. "Would I be rushing you, crowd-
ing you, if I told my headhunter to look around Chico
to see if they need a good OB?"

She let out a relieved breath. "Would you? Because my family is there. Except Drew—but he grew up there. He could come back after he finishes his residency."

He put his cup on the beside table and reached for her. "Details, honey. Easy details, and we have plenty of time."

"But what if you don't like Chico?" she asked him, her brow furrowed.

"Will you be there? Because if that's where you want to be, I'll find plenty to like."

"You say that now, but…"

He shook his head and pulled her coffee mug from her hand, put it beside his and said, "Erin, there won't be that kind of standoff or dissent. I've been looking for the right woman for years and you're the one. Do you hear me? You're the one. You've lived in that town your whole life, built a career there. Do I look like the kind of fool who'd risk losing you over an impasse as silly as where we're going to live?"

"But what if there's no practice for you there?"

"God, you are dreaming up problems. If there isn't there will be one near. If there isn't one near, maybe I'll build one."

"Really?"

"Really… It's going to be fine. We have a million reasons to make this work."

"At least a jarful," she replied with a smile.

"Let's take a shower and have breakfast at Jack's on the way back to Luke's," he suggested. "We can talk all the way there, all through breakfast, all day if you want to. But first, a shower." He touched her nose. "No talking during the shower…"

"Are we going to put another bean in the jar…?"

"I wouldn't be surprised…."

An hour and a half later they walked into Jack's, holding hands. Rather than sitting up at the bar as usual, Aiden steered her toward a table because she had so much on her mind. She quizzed him about how he saw marriage, exactly. She wanted to discuss things like his religious commitments, because she'd fallen away from her church a long time ago. She wondered if he had strong feelings about how he wanted to be married. When she was young, she admitted, she'd had bride fantasies, but she had been a part of so many big weddings fraught with tension it no longer seemed important. And how about where he thought they'd live? Because she'd lived in her house all her life and wasn't sure if she'd find it a relief to have something new and different or the kind of change too difficult to make. The only subject that didn't come up was the most immediate one—Annalee. Erin, being a lawyer, knew that once you set the legal machine to work on an issue like that, there was little to do besides wait for it to work.

Through all of this they managed to order coffee and a couple of omelets, which Jack delivered on steaming plates in just minutes. "Here you go, you two. Say, Aiden—did you catch up with your cousin? Did you have a good visit?"

Aiden looked up in confusion. "Cousin?"

"Little blonde girl—Anna something… She said

she'd barely arrived at Luke's when everyone took off for the hospital."

Aiden pushed back from the table. "Shit." He shook his head. "Has she been around since?"

Jack shook his head. "Not that I know of. Something wrong?"

"Not my cousin, Jack. My ex-wife. She showed up unannounced, making waves, causing a few problems. It turns out our divorce papers from eight years ago weren't filed or recorded properly, so we have to do it all again, and she's not exactly cooperating. She even showed up out at Erin's place when I wasn't there. And I can't figure out how—"

"Crap," Jack said. "That was me. I bought into it. When she said she at least wanted to meet your girlfriend, I said Erin's name. God, I'm sorry, Erin."

But Erin had a very wide-eyed, startled look on her face. "I know how she found me. I was so rattled by her presence, by the things she said, I completely forgot. A woman called from the post office saying they had a delivery and needed directions." She swallowed. "There was never a delivery."

Fourteen

Aiden and Erin left Jack's and went on to Luke's, where they told Luke and Shelby, Sean and Franci what they had just learned about "Cousin" Annalee.

Annalee was obviously incredibly clever and yet her objective was still very unclear. "I know it's not really me she wants, regardless of what she says," Aiden said. "I'm fairly sure it's about money—money sure solved all our problems eight years ago. But how she intends to get it out of me is a real mystery."

Aiden explained that the business card declaring her a fashion consultant was a dead end. "No company affiliation, the cell-phone number isn't a working number. I can't get myself into the kind of devious mind-set that would tip me off on what to expect next."

"Maybe that's what she's counting on," Sean suggested. "That you'll get tired of looking over your shoulder and sleeping with one eye open and just pay her another ten grand to go away."

"I know someone who can get in that mind-set," Erin said. "Call Ron Preston and tell him about this latest. Believe me, he's handled some of the most notorious divorces on record. And the things people have been known to do to each other just blows the mind."

Aiden had planned to touch base with him after talking to his brothers anyway. He just wanted his family in the loop and alert.

Ron Preston recommended a temporary restraining order based on the fact that Annalee had visited and harassed Erin. It was impossible to serve such an order of restraint when the whereabouts of the suspect was unknown, however. "We'll put in a call to the local sheriff's department and the police departments of towns large enough to have more than a couple of officers and let them know that a TRO is forthcoming as soon as we can locate the suspect. In the meantime, keep your eyes and ears open, document everything that's at all suspicious and stay in touch. You'll be hearing from me."

Aiden made sure that in addition to Erin's number at the cabin, Ron Preston had Luke's house number. "There's almost always someone around Luke's to answer the phone."

If there was an upside to all this, it had removed the last microscopic shred of doubt from Erin's mind about who was lying. With that worry completely eliminated, she was the one to make the announcement to the Riordan clan. "When this is all resolved and Aiden is completely free of any legal complications, we plan to get married. We're not sure when or how, but that's what will happen."

Of course that was met with great happiness and an air of celebration that served as a relief from worries. The Riordan family got about the business of trying to plan out and enjoy their last couple of days with Sean, Franci and Rosie before they had to depart. Erin had felt completely welcome before they announced they'd get married, but now she was immediately pulled in as a member of the family. She felt embraced by them, protected and loved.

"I hate that you're leaving so soon after I've met you," Erin told Franci. "I'd love it if we had more time."

"We're going to have lots of time, don't you worry. Most of us on both sides of the family have military roots—we're used to traveling for holidays and vacations to spend time together. I suggest we plan ahead for some big family gatherings. We could find a beach spot for a summer vacation. Virgin River at Christmastime is fantastic and I know we can talk Luke and Shelby into reserving us cabins."

"I like that idea," Erin said. *And if we can ever get through this mess, I'm going to love this family,* she thought.

Luke and Sean managed to wrestle a couple of picnic tables into the back of Luke's truck to take out to Erin's cabin for a big family dinner. Aiden bought a new, large gas grill that could be stored in the shed when they weren't in residence but that he had no doubt would get plenty of use over the years. When clouds gathered in the afternoon, the men put the chaise lounges from the deck into the shed and placed two picnic tables there instead. Aiden grilled salmon under the cover of an umbrella and the entire family ate outside on the covered deck while a summer rain fell.

The next night they met at Luke's; dinner was a simple buffet because Sean and Franci were trying to pack the car and Maureen wanted to spend every last second with Rosie. Franci's mom from Eureka was there, as were Walt Booth and Muriel.

The next morning, when Sean's SUV was packed, the same crowd gathered for goodbyes. The brothers shook hands before embracing; Erin and Shelby hugged Franci close.

But the only one who Rosie cried over was Art. He got down on his knees to hug her and told her to be good in the car. She clung to him and tears came out of her eyes. "Will you bisit me?" she asked him.

Art looked to Luke. "Will I visit her?" he asked.

"Probably. And Rosie will visit you. They'll be back for visits, for sure."

So he said to her, "I'll visit you, Rosie. Be good in the car."

"I lub you," she said to him. "I *lub* you!"

And Art said, "That's because we're good friends. Thank you." And he held her tight for a moment. He added, "No fishing without Sean!"

That just about did in the farewell gathering. When Art finally stood to his full height, Sean stepped toward him with his hand out. "I'm going to miss you, Art. Be sure to watch over that new little guy—Brett Lucas."

"I will do that, Sean," he said, nodding.

Luke was not real good at sentiment. He walked over to the driver's door of the SUV and opened it for Sean. "Let's not drag this out—the women are all crying. I hate that part."

Sean laughed and gave Luke one last, brief hug. "Take care, bud. I'll be on the cell all the way. We'll keep you posted on our progress."

"Just drive like an old woman, that's all I ask. Now, get on the road!"

Maureen Riordan had said goodbye to her sons a hundred times; sometimes she'd even bid them farewell as they were going off to war. It was always a little hard, though they were grown men who had chosen their work, their lives, and she knew they were doing exactly as they'd planned. This time—kissing Rosie's cheek and knowing it would be a while before she could hug her tight added a new dimension to the melancholy of farewell.

But this time as Sean and his family piled in his car and pulled slowly out of Luke's compound, she leaned against George. His arm came around her and gave her a comforting squeeze. This was something she hadn't had in so long—a partner to take the sting of goodbye away when the farewells were finally done and everyone had to get back to their lives. This time when she got back to her life, there would be love, affection, a best friend and even adventure as they took to the open road.

She sniffed back her threatening tears and said,

"Well. They're off. I'll make more pancakes for anyone interested. And I brewed a fresh pot of coffee."

Through all the many goodbyes over the years, this one was the easiest and sweetest for Maureen because she had George. With George she had places to go, people to see, new experiences to explore.

George was the only one to really notice that her mood was neither happy nor sad, but serene. Comfortable and quietly blissful. He put an arm around her waist, nuzzled her neck and said, "You're looking especially beautiful, sweetheart."

"I'm feeling that way, too. Thanks mostly to you."

After Sean, Franci and Rosie left, roughly every twenty minutes Art said to Luke, "It's Tuesday."

And Luke would say, "I know that, but it's not one o'clock yet, Art. We leave right after one o'clock."

"I know that, Luke," he said. And then he'd study his watch for a moment.

The watch had helped Art in several ways—he felt more confident and he was always on time returning from the river or doing his chores. He could only tell the hour hand and occasionally he got the two hands mixed up, thinking it was two o'clock when it was twelve-ten, but not often. Luke had miscalculated when buying him a watch with hour and minute hands rather than a digital, but they were getting by.

On Tuesday and Sunday afternoons Luke or someone else from the household would take Art to Fortuna to spend a couple of hours visiting with Netta. The term *visiting* should be used loosely as the two didn't seem to talk all that much. On most of those visits Luke would go into the house with Art, say hello to Ellen and Bo and if they were present, the two other women who lived there. Once he was comfortable that all would be well, he'd ask Ellen if she minded him leaving to run an errand or two.

"Not a problem," Ellen would always say. "Art's a delight. Just be on time picking him up in two hours."

Luke always made it back a little early and waited until Art was ready to go. When he was leaving with Art, Ellen would always say, "See you at two o'clock next time. Not early."

"It's Tuesday," Art said for the umpteenth time.

"Tell me when it's one o'clock, Art."

At almost one, Luke went to give Shelby a kiss. "I'm headed to Fortuna, baby. Need anything while I'm out?"

"Just whatever you want for dinner," she said. "And if you go to Costco or Walmart, grab some diapers and baby wipes."

"How are you fixed if I don't do much shopping? Has the little pee pot got a few days' worth?"

"I'm good," she said, laughing. "If you don't go shopping, what will you do? Sit around Ellen's house and wait?"

"No, I should talk to Ellen and Bo about Art—get their take on this getting-married business. He's driving me to drink."

"You do that," she said. "Aren't you leaving a little early?"

"He's sitting in the truck, Shelby," Luke said a bit

tiredly. "When I invited Art to live here, I had no idea what I was getting myself into."

Shelby just laughed at him.

Their routine on visiting days was to leave Virgin River just after one and head into town. They'd have McDonald's—Art looked forward to that almost as much as fishing, visiting and shopping. All the way to Fortuna, Art kept saying, "Netta wants to be the bride."

"Not a good idea, bud," Luke said. "I think you guys are too young for that."

"But Netta wants to be the bride…"

By the time they finished lunch and got some gas in the truck, it was almost two and they could go to Netta's house. Art would almost always look at his watch before getting out of the truck and say, "Two o'clock!" It baffled Luke that if Art was so conscious of the day and time, why did he have to badger Luke all day long. But what really should bewilder Luke was the way Art could do that without making him want to jump off a cliff. In almost all other things Luke was impatient and could be easily driven over the edge.

Ellen opened the door and said hello, let them in. Art stood inside the front door until Ellen told Art where to find Netta. "Netta's in the backyard, Art. I think she's been watering flowers with the hose. Go find her." And then off he went, smiling. "Going shopping today, Luke?" she asked him.

"I wonder if we could talk about some things," he said. "If you have a little time."

"Sure. How about some tea or a soda?"

"Do you have a cola?"

"Coming right up. Let's sit in the living room. I'm sure Art and Netta will be fine and the girls are watching one of their favorite movies."

She poured herself a glass of iced tea, gave Luke a glass of ice and a can of cola and led the way. "How's the baby?" she asked, sitting in her favorite chair.

"Terrific. If you like getting peed, puked and pooped on and getting no sleep." Then he grinned and sat opposite her. "Turns out I happen to actually like it. He's really something."

She laughed. "How's Art doing with the baby?"

"He's very careful. He doesn't bother the baby unless he thinks something's wrong, like if there's too much crying. I think he has very sensitive ears. Noise seems to get to him. If there's a lot of crying, he'll point it out to us even though we're right in the middle of it, trying to quiet the baby. Shelby could be walking, jiggling, shooshing, and Art will say, 'The baby's crying, Shelby.'"

"It's probably disorder that bugs him," she said, laughing. "It's really the only thing Art has to go on. His routine is probably his greatest security. Besides you and your wife, of course. Haven't you noticed?"

Luke leaned back on the sofa. "Well, if his routine is his security, why does he start telling me first thing in the morning that it's Tuesday or Sunday? Fifty times, even after I tell him I know?"

"He probably doesn't want to forget. Or *you* to forget. It's very important to him."

"Hmm. But he goes off fishing sometimes—and it's not exactly on the schedule…"

"I bet it is. I bet something about it is routine—like he's finished his chores or had his breakfast or something. I mean, everyone's different, but most mentally challenged adults function best if they do things almost by habit. For example, the girls all know that after your shower you dry off, put on your bra first, then your panties, then dry your hair, then put on your clothes, then your shoes. One of my girls had her appendix out and we wanted to keep her in her pajamas and at least lying on the couch, if not in bed, for the day, and that just was *not* happening. I thought we were going to have a brawl. We settled for stay-at-home clothes—a sweatsuit—and kept repeating, 'no lifting' over and over until I was saying it in my sleep."

"That a fact?" Luke said. "That simple?"

She laughed. "Simple? Well, until it's not. Sometimes that stuff can get on my last nerve."

He leaned forward, elbows on his knees. "Listen, something worries me a lot. Art keeps talking about getting married. I happen to agree with you —who are we to deny anyone love and affection, regardless of their mental acuity? But Art and Netta? Married?" He shook his head. "I don't think that's a good idea. Someone would have to take care of them for life. Art's never going to be completely self-sufficient. He gets by just great, even stays in his own cabin next door, keeps it clean as a whistle, can fix some of his own meals if they're simple, but—"

Ellen was frowning. "Luke, are you sure about this? Netta hasn't mentioned wanting to get married."

"Art won't shut up about it, I'm telling you."

"I bet it's one of those real specific, literal things. Come on, let's go ask," she said, standing up.

"Just like that? Ask?"

"We might not get the answer, but we can ask. Leave your drink—we'll come back." She led the way through the house and out back.

Netta was still watering flowers and Art stood beside her, hands in his pockets, looking happy as a clam.

Ellen said, "Art? I have a question. Have you been talking about getting married?"

"I don't drive a car," he said with a shrug.

"I want to be the bride," Netta said right away, not looking at anyone.

"I know," Ellen said with a laugh. "I know, I know, I know. But do you want to get married?"

Netta looked at her and frowned in confusion.

"Netta, do you want to live here and work in the bakery?" And Netta said she did. "And Art? Do you want to live with Luke and Shelby?"

Art looked panicked for a second. He cast pleading eyes to Luke. "I have my own house, Luke. I help you."

"You absolutely do. You live with us, you help us and you fish in our river. You seem to catch a lot of fish—we appreciate that."

Art visibly relaxed.

"I want to be the bride," Netta said, showering the flowers with the hose. "I want to be in the wedding."

"You do such a great job in the bakery, Netta. Thank you for watering the plants. Your favorite show—all about weddings—will be on TV on Thursday. Do you two want some kind of snack right now?"

Both of them gave Ellen their complete attention and nodded.

"There are some apples in the basket on the patio table. Go ahead."

"Pizza would be better!" Netta said. "Pizza or chips!"

"Just fruit between meals," Ellen said. "We'll have pizza Friday night." Then she turned and walked back into the house while Luke stood there in something of a daze.

By the time Luke got back to the living room and to his cola, Ellen was sitting down in her chair. "Okay, you just totally blew my mind out there," Luke said.

"Phooey," she retorted. "You're the one who explained to me that Art's very literal."

"But you told Aiden that some special-needs adults actually fall in love and get married…"

"They do. They're as individual as the rest of us, in every way. But I don't think Art and Netta want to get married. Netta's really obsessed with the wedding show—she wants a wedding. Wants to be a bride, wear a white dress, have a party. She doesn't have a realistic concept of what comes after that. She knows what marriage is, sort of. She knows the people on the wedding show are getting married, knows that I'm married to Bo, but she doesn't really know what it means to be married. I thought it would make her so happy if I bought her a secondhand wedding dress to play around in—but she didn't want to take it off, so

I had to get rid of it." Ellen rolled her eyes and blew out her breath. "Boy, did I pay for that. She was furious with me for days. A little furious for weeks."

"I should know these things," Luke said. "For Art, I should know things like this."

"Listen, this is what I studied in college. This group home is what Bo and I do because we want to. Just three special-needs adults—only women. You do a great job with Art, but if you're committed to his quality of life, it wouldn't hurt for you to be just a little more involved in a support group of parents and guardians. You'd learn a lot and you could be involved in the community." She paused and smiled. "You'd hear about some challenges that make yours look like a walk in the park. But, Luke, even though Art is your only concern and he seems to be doing just fine, something might come up and you should have people on your side—people who can help you if you need advice."

"People like you…" It wasn't a question.

"I go to an afternoon support group every Thursday. We meet at a community resource center and all my girls go along—there's a nice, comfortable gathering and some activities for them while the rest of us chat. It's informal. We need the connection. We call it Happy Hour," she said with a smile. "There are small groups all over the place—some who meet for evenings, some for breakfast or lunch. There are seven in my group, which I chose because by that time of day Bo can handle the bakery and I can get away. When you get the baby under control and a little older, you, Shelby and Art should drop in. Art would enjoy himself, I think."

"I will," he said. "Listen, I know I'm not experienced. Art's so easy, I didn't think I needed to be...."

"I'm so glad that when something bothered you, you asked. You're doing great, Luke. Art's very lucky."

"Thanks," he said. But inside he was thinking it was really Art who had changed him, and he wasn't sure who to thank for that. "I'm lucky, I think. Good thing Art didn't need some expert, that's all."

"Oh, I think maybe you sell yourself short. Come join us when the baby's a little older."

"We will."

A good week had passed since Mel Sheridan had stormed away from her dinner, seriously miffed at her husband. That night she was angry and didn't eat, didn't curl up against him to sleep. But after that one night, she couched her pique in distant politeness that was completely alien to her personality. She was *angry*. And stubborn? She could not let go of it! In her mind there was no excuse for his lack of cooperation. A week later she was still holding back in a punishing way and she knew it, but she thought she was doing it in a way that didn't really cross the line into the category of horrible bitch.

What she'd been doing was avoiding the whole subject of the next baby, of the surrogacy. She went to the bar to see Jack, but far less often. When she did jump on the familiar bar stool to have quality time with him, their conversation was superficial. She fed the kids and got them in bed at night and fixed herself something easy—can of soup, fried-egg sandwich— leaving Jack to have dinner at the bar alone. She didn't snuggle against him and they hadn't made love. The absence of their usually rich, satisfying sex life for no reason other than her pissy mood was hard on both of them. But she'd be the last to admit it.

She knew exactly what she was doing and hated herself for it, but she did it anyway. She wasn't sure what would happen first—either she'd get over it or Jack would cave and go along with her plan.

"You haven't made up with Jack yet, have you?" Cameron Michaels said to her when they happened to meet in the clinic's kitchen for a coffee break.

"How can you tell?" she asked.

He laughed. "Right. Like it's not obvious you're pissed."

She poured them each a coffee. "Has Jack talked to you about this?"

He accepted the cup. "Mel, I'm not getting into this with Jack under any circumstances. Wasn't I clear about that? You're my partner, he's my friend, this is going to stay between the two of you. Period."

"But what's your opinion?" she asked.

He shook his head. "Nope. I'm not going there, either. Whatever you and Jack decide is good for your family, I'm happy for you."

"But would you do it if that's what Abby wanted?"

He just stared at her. "We really need to get your hearing checked. I'm not taking sides on this issue. It's too personal. Personal issues get a very big emo-

tional investment along with an unbelievable emotional memory."

"You're a wimp," she accused.

"Guilty."

"What if Jack *asks* you?" she wondered.

"I'll say the same thing to him."

"It's pretty hard to get a consensus when no one will
give me an opinion...."

He frowned. "A consensus on what?"

"Whether I'm crazy or not," she said with a shrug.

"Okay, I have an opinion about that," he said.
"You're not crazy. How's that?"

"Would you please tell Jack that?"

"No," he said firmly. "Besides, Jack knows you're
not crazy."

"I'm not so sure. He thinks this is about me not
grieving the loss of my uterus more than wanting
another child."

"Really?" Cameron asked. "That was quite a while
ago, wasn't it? Couple of years?"

"Exactly!" she said almost triumphantly. "Plenty of
time!"

"I'm a little lost. How could it be that?"

"It can't! But he thinks too many things happened,
taking my attention off my need to mourn, to adjust.
Like the surgery, the forest fire, Doc's death, Rick's
tour in Iraq and all the adjustments he and Jack were
making because he was injured...you know. But I'm
sure that's not—" She cocked her head and listened.
"I think that's my prenatal." She put down her coffee
cup. "Thanks for saying I'm not crazy."

He just gave a lame smile and a nod. But when she left the kitchen he said to himself, "Whoa. Interesting…"

Mel met her new patient in the foyer. She didn't know anything about her except her name, Marley Thurston, her age, eighteen, and that this would be her first prenatal. But there was a young man with her, solicitously pressing his hand on the small of her back.

"You must be Marley Thurston," Mel said, putting out her hand. "Mel Sheridan. How are you?"

"Fine," she said, taking the hand. "Nice to meet you. This is my boyfriend, Jake Conroy."

"How do you do. Can I get you to fill out a little paperwork for me before the exam?"

"Sure, but before I do that, can we talk about it? About the pregnancy? About stuff?"

"Of course. Follow me. The office is free—let's sit down in there." And she led the way. Once Mel was behind the desk and the kids were seated facing her, she started the discussion. "I sense you have some concerns? Some special needs?"

They looked at each other, then the young man actually looked down, leaving Marley to answer. "The pregnancy isn't planned," she said. "My girlfriend Liz Anderson she said if you can't help us, no one can." She shrugged. "That's why we came all the way from Eureka to see you."

Liz and Mel went way back; Liz and Rick were now engaged, soon to be married. Mel folded her hands on the desk. "That depends on what kind of help you need, of course. If I can't help, maybe I can direct you to the right place."

"The thing is…" Her voice caught and tears gathered in her eyes. She couldn't seem to go on.

"It wasn't… It was an accident," the young man said. "My fault. Totally my fault."

"Easy does it," Mel said. "These things do happen. Are you certain you're pregnant? We haven't done the exam yet."

She nodded. "Three months. Almost three months, I think. Mrs. Sheridan, we decided we can't be parents right now. We just finished our first year of college and you have no idea how hard it was. Not school—we're both good in school. But working and going to school and trying to keep up with bills. We both had to borrow tuition money. We're going to have to borrow lots more before…" She looked to her boyfriend for help.

"We've been together since high school and we want to get married, we really do, and we tried to think of a way…" Jake cleared his throat. "Our families aren't… Thing is, no one on either side ever got to college and they don't have any money to help. Marley said that if I really wanted her to, she'd quit school and we could live with her folks, in her bedroom, but—"

"But it wouldn't be good for the baby, either. Not good for us, not good for the baby, not good for our families. God," she said, pounding a fist on her knee. "We really screwed up. Really."

Mel took a deep breath. She didn't like where this was going. But before explaining that she didn't do terminations, she asked, "How is it you think I can help?"

"Well," Marley said, scooting forward. "We were thinking of an adoption. But we don't want the usual kind of adoption. We were wondering if it would be possible to have the kind of adoption where we know our baby is okay. I mean, it probably wouldn't be fair to be real involved in its life, we get that. But if we could know the parents first, maybe even pick the parents…"

"And get pictures," Jake said. "And then later, if he wants to know us, wants to know his brothers and sisters, if there are brothers and sisters…well, we'd be open to that because we don't want to give him up. I mean, we'd do about anything…"

"But we decided we have to think about him, too. We grew up pretty poor, both of us, and believe me… If he can just grow up in a good family, like maybe one where he's gonna have his own room, get to do things like sports and lessons, get a little help with college. You know, parents who will love him, protect him. That's the kind of thing we want for our kids." She reached over to Jake and grabbed his hand. "If we can't do an adoption that way, then we already decided, we're not going to do it. We can't live never knowing if he's okay. We can't just give him to some adoption agency and walk away and never even *know*."

"Is there any way?" Jake asked. "Any way at all?"

Mel smiled patiently, calmly, but inside, her heart *soared!* "Yes, Marley, Jake. Yes, it's usually called an open adoption. A lawyer handles the details, you meet prospective parents, get to know them a little and—"

They exchanged worried looks. "Lawyer?" Jake

said. "We don't have any money. I mean, I can pay for the doctor's appointment, but—"

Mel was shaking her head. "The expenses are usually covered by the adoptive parents. But it's important to realize that you have to make some commitments, also. You would have to promise to guard your health and the health of the baby—no alcohol, tobacco or drugs during your pregnancy, regular prenatal checkups, and once you've decided on an adoptive family and have a contract, you can't just change your minds while they absorb the costs, which are considerable. You have to be sure about this—and if you think you are, I can help."

"Oh, I want the baby to be healthy and I don't drink or smoke or anything," Marley said earnestly. "I just want him to be in a good family, and a safe home. How can I be sure of that?"

"Besides meeting the prospective parents, your lawyer would do a background check for you, make sure there are no problems like health issues, convictions, allegations of abuse, bankruptcy, all sorts of things."

"Would anybody out there like that want our baby?" Marley asked.

"Sweetheart, most adoptive parents wait a long time for a baby. Not very many young people are able to make hard choices like this."

"Even though we want to know about the baby after? Would anyone be willing to do it like that?"

"You sit down with your lawyer and plan to talk to only potential parents who can agree to those terms." She smiled. "They're not unreasonable or unusual terms. Of course, you do understand, an open adoption isn't the same as joint custody. You would have to sign off on parenthood, let the new parents raise the child in their way, as their own. It could mean never visiting your child, but yet always being up-to-date on how he's doing."

Jake scooted forward a little. "Like, would it be totally out of the question to watch him play ball if he was playing ball on a team? Or—"

"Or see a dance recital, if she was in a dance recital?"

"As long as you understand about things like custodial interference—the parents might not be freaked out by your presence at a single ball game or recital, but the child, depending on his age and the amount of knowledge he has about his biological parents, might be confused or upset by running into you everywhere he goes. I know you can create a scenario in your mind—this strange couple shows up at every Little League game, taking pictures of the same ten-year-old, cheering him on… He either realizes there's something off about that or you get arrested as potential kidnappers. Right? You have lots of time to think about issues like that and decide if you're still comfortable."

"We talked about that a lot," Marley said. "We don't want him upset or anything. We want him happy. Then, when he's, like, eighteen or something, if he wants to know us, if his parents don't mind too much, maybe we could…you know…be involved in his life a little. If that's not too crazy?"

God, Mel was thinking—what adoptive parent

could argue with kids as conscientious and caring as that? She would sign on for that deal. In fact, right now in her head, she already *had* signed on.

"I don't think that sounds crazy at all. But listen, before you get ahead of yourselves, let's do a history and physical, the exam, start a patient file. Oh, and if you're interested, my sister-in-law is an attorney. You could consult with her for free, then decide if you'd like her to handle the adoption for you. If it all works out, I could help you locate potential adoptive parents who are flexible about your terms."

Marley let out her breath. Then she leaned against Jake in relief and perhaps exhaustion. He held her close and said, "It's going to be all right, baby. Everything is going to be all right."

Mel walked over to the bar at that magic hour when there was hardly ever anyone there. She smiled as she walked in and hopped up on a stool, leaning toward Jack.

"Hey, baby," he said, leaning toward her for a kiss.

"I'd like to declare a truce," she said. "I'm sorry if you are."

He lifted a brow. "Does that mean if I'm not sorry, you're not sorry?"

She laughed. "All right, I'm sorry I wasn't very understanding of your feelings in the whole surrogacy argument. If you can't get into the idea, you can't. That's all there is to it. I've accepted that."

"I'm not sure what I'm supposed to be sorry about," he said. "Gimme a hint?"

"How about you're sorry you're so pigheaded?" she suggested.

"That would be a little like the pot calling the kettle black," he said. "But I could admit to being a little set in my ways. I love you, though. I'd do anything for you, as long as I knew it wasn't somehow the wrong thing to do. And I think you know that."

"I know that. Can I have a soda?"

"You bet…"

"And can we now talk about adoption?"

His movements were slowed slightly. He put the soda in front of her. "Why?"

"It was a compromise you said you'd be willing to make."

"That wasn't exactly what I said," he clarified. "I said if there was a child that wouldn't otherwise have a good, loving family, I'd be willing to consider that. Not quite the same thing."

"As I see it, adoption is exactly that. We're good parents, Jack. We have a secure future. We can give a child some things that their own parents might not be quite up to. And, as I've said, I'd like one more child. So?"

"What's involved, exactly?" he asked, pouring himself a cup of coffee.

"Not terribly much. I would put together an adoption package for our family, outlining our values, how we could benefit a child. There would be a standard background check, making sure that we aren't felons, abusers, bankrupt or suffering from illnesses that could make it difficult to parent, cut our lives short. That sort of thing."

"Money?"

"Of course money. The usual routine is to pay all the medical and legal expenses for the mother, plus our own legal expenses. Sometimes there's a bonus for the mother…a little something to help her get on with her life."

"But not like buying a baby?" he asked.

"That would be illegal," she said. "This is all pretty straightforward. Of course, Brie would be our lawyer as she is in everything—she's pretty straight and narrow."

"I hear adoption's kind of tough—that people wait forever to get a child. Were you thinking older child? Maybe a child of another race?"

"I'm open to that, but really I'm hoping for a newborn. That's what my heart wants—one more newborn. So? Would you do this with me?"

"On one condition—that we get a little counseling before we officially adopt."

"Before I start on our adoption package—or just before we sign the final adoption papers?"

"I'd like to do it soon, but I don't mind if you start the process."

"Why, exactly, do you want some counseling? This isn't about my uterus again, is it?"

He shook his head. "No. I've decided to stay away from that. I don't much like being frozen out."

"I said I was sorry.… So, why counseling?"

"To make sure we'd make good adoptive parents," he said.

"That's reasonable.…"

"And to explore why my wife would lie to me."

"What?"

"You've never lied to me before. Life has been pretty strange between us lately, but you've never lied before. You didn't just decide to give up your desire to hire a surrogate in favor of adopting a newborn. You have a baby lined up."

"Now, what in the world makes you think—"

He smirked and lifted a brow. "You're a midwife. Gimme a break here. Now, why wouldn't you tell me the truth? What's going on with you? I thought we could trust each other. Tell each other everything. When did all this change?"

She sighed. "Well, you've been very difficult lately," she said.

He touched her nose. "I believe this is the first time since the day we met that you haven't had your way with me. You, Mrs. Sheridan, have been very *spoiled.*"

"All right, I stipulate to being spoiled if you admit to being difficult...."

"Again with the pot and the kettle..."

"I have a new patient," she relented. "A lovely young woman. She and her boyfriend are good friends with Rick and Liz. Actually, Rick and Liz sent them to me. They asked for my help in setting up an adoption—one where they could give up their parenting rights to see their baby in a good home with loving parents, but adoptive parents who would be willing to share pictures, let them know that their child is doing fine. They understand they can't be involved—at least not until the child reaches maturity, understands about his adoption and decides whether or not to seek them out."

"We know it's a boy already?"

She shook her head. "Just using he/him. It could well be a girl."

"And they're doing this because…?"

"For all the right reasons—they've been together since high school, but they've barely finished their first year of college, and it's been a financially tough year. They know if they try to have the baby together, it will be a hardship on them and the baby. They want to get married eventually, have children—but they want better for this baby than they can reasonably give him. Or her. It was a very difficult and brave decision for them."

"And did you tell them you want their baby?"

"I did not. And even though I actually would love that, even I would recommend to them that they interview several potential parents."

"Uh-huh. But you can think of a hundred reasons why we're likely to stand out, can't you?"

"Well, I agree we're fair candidates, but—"

"But we come personally recommended by their good friends, have small children of our own, are financially stable, healthy, local and guaranteed to remain local, you're a medical professional who works with a pediatrician, we aren't felons or abusers, have an entire town to vouch for us… Need I go on?"

"There's more?" she asked.

"I bet there is," he answered.

"Are you going to go along with this?" she asked,

her eyes taking on that blue flash he knew only too well.

"Yes," he said. "But we're going to sit down with a counselor and make sure we're good potential adoptive parents, good for that baby. I think that's important. And if the counselor agrees, you can feel free to add it to your package."

She smiled happily. "Thank you, Jack. I promise, you'll never regret it."

Fifteen

Aiden and Erin had a busy couple of days after the departure of Sean and Franci. Not only did Aiden contact his headhunter and tell him he was ready to take appointments for serious interviews in the Chico area, they made a run down to San Francisco to shop for clothes. It was supposed to be a shopping trip for Aiden, who had been in uniform for a very long time and had only one civilian suit, maybe just a bit out of date for interviews. But of course, Erin, a self-confessed clotheshorse, managed to buy a few things for herself, as well.

"Why not start on the trousseau," he suggested. "Let's pick up some perverted and extremely fun nightwear."

What they started on instead was a ring. Aiden had it in his mind to have something original made for her, but on a pass through Tiffany's she saw a ring that just brought her to her knees. That was good enough for him.

She couldn't wait to tell her sister, whom she talked to at least once a day. She called her from San Francisco. Marcie shrieked with delight and demanded, "When am I going to see it?"

"I'll take a picture with my phone—stand by. I'll send it and call you back!"

A few minutes later, Erin got Marcie back on the line. "Oh my GOD!" Marcie said. "I want to see it in person! Does it weigh five pounds? Do I have to wait till you come home?" Marcie wanted to know. "Because the doctor says I'm done with long car trips."

"Aiden's hoping to interview in the Chico area. If anything comes up down there for him, I'll ride along with him. But, honey, do you realize how soon I'll be back for the baby? I'm coming before you have him, and you're having him in just a few weeks! How do you feel?"

"Enormous, but good. I'm ready, let me tell you."

"Soon, Marcie. Just be patient," Erin said. "Be sure to cook him long enough."

After spending a couple of nights in San Francisco, they sped back to Virgin River. They checked in with Luke to find everyone there was status quo and that Sean and family had arrived safely in Montgomery. Aiden and Erin spent the night in the cabin where more and more of Aiden's things, including his laptop, were appearing. He'd nearly moved in.

"I really didn't think life could ever get this perfect," she said. "If we have a home and good jobs in Chico, an ideal getaway on this mountain, what more could we want?"

"Besides my divorce? How about a kid or two?" he asked.

"What if I can't?" she asked him.

"What if I can't?" he parroted. "The fact is, we probably both can. You game?"

"Are you sure I'm not too old?" she asked.

"At thirty-six? I delivered a forty-two-year-old right before exiting the navy. It was her first. You're definitely not too old to have a baby. Do you feel like it's a little late in the game to commit twenty years plus to raising one?"

"I just thought it was one of those things that had passed me by, that would never happen. I know you have your heart set on it...."

"I'd like that, true. But parenting is definitely a team sport. We both have to be on that team, Erin. If you don't want it, I'm not going to push it."

"And that wouldn't change your mind about settling down with me?"

"At this point, nothing would change my mind about that. But how about we make an agreement right now—issues that really require two people to be of like minds, we either agree we both want it or we don't go there."

"What things besides having children?" she asked.

"I don't know. Moving," he said. "Major purchases. Expensive vacations. Sterilization." He shrugged and added, "Adoption?"

She went to him and sat on his lap. "I'd like to have a child of my own with a husband, but I'm worried about my eggs being too old or something. And I have some strong feelings about that."

"Which are?"

"You get what you get. If you decide to give it a go, you get what you get. I wouldn't terminate because a baby isn't perfect."

"I go along with that. See how easy it is to act on things you agree on? Is your period late, by the way?"

She laughed. "It's not time yet. That was something we acted on without agreeing first. Whoops."

"Really, I meant to have you check in with the local doctor or midwife about some emergency birth control, but we got distracted by all the insanity. We'll be okay, honey. No matter which way that flows, we'll be fine." He smiled. "Pun intended."

She fell asleep that night in Aiden's arms, thinking that she had never expected her life could ever be so calm, so sane, so reasonable.

But she woke up to someone hammering at the door.

Aiden rolled over with a groan and sat up on the edge of the bed, grabbing his boxers off the floor. "Find a robe, babe. I'll see who's lost their mind at—" he glanced at the clock "—five in the morning?"

She scurried to the bathroom where her robe hung on a hook, but before she could get it completely around her and securely tied, she heard the crash of the door as it banged open, Aiden's grunt and another loud thud. Then came the angry male voice that shouted, "Aiden Riordan, you're under arrest for battery and I'm going to read you your rights…."

By the time Erin got to the great room, still tying her robe, three sheriff's deputies stood just inside the door and the biggest one had Aiden slammed up against the wall, cuffing his hands behind his back. "Good God!" she shouted. "Hey! Where's your warrant?"

One of the deputies handed her a folded piece of paper and she flipped it open to read it.

"Battery? Who is it I battered?" Aiden asked as his hands were being secured behind his back.

"Your wife, Annalee Riordan, just like the warrant says," the deputy informed him. "You have the right to remain silent," he said, reciting Aiden's Miranda rights.

"When did this happen?" Aiden asked while the deputy continued.

"Last night," Erin read from the warrant. "But he was here, with me, all night. No one else was here. She wasn't here...we didn't go out..."

"Erin, call Ron Preston," Aiden said. "I'm probably going to need some local lawyer. Officer, ease up—I haven't even seen her in well over a week. She said I *beat* her?"

"That's the story."

"Pants, Officer. Shoes," he said. "Come on. I'm in my underwear!"

"That's how we know you're not armed," the deputy said.

"I don't even own a weapon!" he said hotly, turning around, straining against the arms that pushed him up against the wall.

"Settle down!"

Erin stepped forward, warrant in hand, her cheeks

inflamed with fury. "Slow down here—let me get him some clothes, and take it real easy on him—he's not resisting and will go with you willingly, so bear that in mind when you manhandle him. I'm an officer of the court and I've been with him the last seventy-two hours—most of it in San Francisco."

"Every minute?" another deputy asked.

"Except when he was trying on his new slacks or left the restaurant table for the men's room. This is bogus," she said. "This is a soon-to-be ex-wife making a lot of trouble. They've been separated for eight years. Dr. Riordan is trying to expedite the divorce so we can get married."

"*Dr.* Riordan?" one of the deputies asked.

"That's right," he confirmed, looking over his shoulder. "Are you sure she's really battered?"

"Oh, yeah. All banged up."

"Is she all right?" Aiden asked. "Was she badly beaten?"

"Treated and released," the deputy said. Then he sarcastically added, "Is there a beaten that's not so bad?"

"Slow down, gentlemen, and stop with the innuendo," Erin said firmly and authoritatively, even though she was both naked and shaking under her robe. "Obviously my fiancé knows nothing about this. Aiden hasn't been away from me for more than three minutes in the last three days. He'll go with you without any argument, but you're going to uncuff him right now and let him get into some clothes."

"I have no problem with clothes." The deputy

jerked up on the cuffed wrists, causing Aiden to wince. "You gonna behave?"

"I'll go with you," he said in a low growl. "Let's just take this a little easy, huh?"

Erin went into the bedroom and brought back a shirt, pants and shoes. "I'll get in touch with Ron and contact the D.A.—this is a bad, bad joke. I'll have you out in an hour."

"Maybe not, ma'am," one of the deputies said. "We won't have him processed in an hour."

"You might want to use your head and think before you book him. Is there evidence of any kind? Because the woman's a nutcase and he didn't hurt her. He'd never hurt anyone. Be very careful with this. And if you hurt this physician's hands, the county's going to be paying for a long, long time."

"Thanks for the advice," the meanest of the three deputies said. "We know what we're doing."

"You better hope so," Erin replied. "Because I never forget a face."

The second the deputies took Aiden away, Erin made a few phone calls, then rushed to the sheriff's department. A local attorney who turned out to be Jack Sheridan's sister and well acquainted with the D.A. met them there. Brie Valenzuela interviewed Aiden, Erin, then sat down with the D.A., and it was agreed there wasn't anything besides the woman's word on which to charge Aiden, and not only did Aiden have a perfectly good alibi for the time in question, the woman seemed to have dropped out of sight. There was no victim. No victim, no crime. But it was a very long day before Aiden was released without charges being filed.

They were both exhausted by the time they got back to Erin's cabin. Aiden wasn't just tired, he was demoralized. There was nothing like being taken away in the back of a police cruiser and thought to be the kind of animal who'd beat a small woman to take the starch out of a man's spine. He slumped onto Erin's sofa.

"We're going to figure this out," she said to him. "I'm going to fix you a drink. I have scotch or brandy.…"

"Pass," he said, grimacing at the choices.

She looked into the refrigerator. "I have two beers and a tablespoon or so of Merlot. Really good Merlot, but we drank almost all of it," she said.

"Gimme a beer," he said.

She got two out and popped off the caps, taking one to him and keeping one for herself. Sitting down beside him, she leaned back as he did and put her feet up on the ottoman. She took a deep drink of her beer and let out a tired sigh.

Aiden's hand came down on her knee. "Maybe you should go home, babe. I should go stay at Luke's and you should go home."

"No way," she said. "Not unless you come with me. A, you need an alibi and I'm going to make sure you have one every second, and B, I don't want to be away from you! If you feel you need to go to Luke's for some reason, I'll go stay there, too."

He shook his head. "I want you away from this. I hate that you're even involved."

"You'd be in worse shape if I wasn't."

"I'll make sure I always have someone around. Luke or someone."

"You'll have me around," she said. "I'm not going to give you a hard time about feeling real low right now. After the way that deputy treated you, I'm hardly surprised. But as soon as you catch your breath, I want you to come out fighting mad. Aiden, she's working you. I don't know why or how, but she's working you." She gathered up her hair in a hand on top of her head. "God, how could she beat herself to make it look like you'd done it? Throw herself down the stairs? How?"

"I have no idea. Nor do I know why."

The phone rang. Erin got up to answer it. Then she said, "Oh, Marcie, honey! I was just going to call you!" She threw an uh-oh look at Aiden. "No, no, of course nothing's wrong—did you leave messages? Oh, baby, I'm sorry—we barely walked in the door. I haven't even checked the voice mail. We were out all day—over on the coast. Didn't I mention we were going to do that? Honey, I'm sorry—but please don't ever worry. It's my job to worry about you, not the other way around." Then Erin laughed softly. "But, sweetheart, I'm not up here all alone anymore. I have Aiden, and we're almost never apart. Yes, you can relax—I'm in for the night and exhausted from a very full day. I'll be sure to call you tomorrow. I love you, too. Bye."

She went back to the couch and slumped beside Aiden.

"You haven't told her anything," he said.

She took a drink of her beer. "I told her you were previously married. I told her that on Fourth of July weekend."

"But none of this madness." It wasn't a question.

"She's hugely pregnant and her baby can't be born normally. I don't want her upset. If she goes into labor now, it's an emergency C-section. I don't want her to have the slightest worry."

"It might make sense to tell her the truth, in that case. And tell her we're on top of it."

"I did tell her the truth. There's nothing to worry about and we're almost never apart. I'll tell her all about Annalee the whackjob after the baby's born. And it will absolutely get her all hyper and wigged out, wanting every sordid detail. Marcie's always been the only one in the room who didn't close her eyes during the massacre scenes in bad horror films."

Aiden turned to her and lifted his eyebrows in question.

"She talked me into going with her to see *The Texas Chainsaw Massacre*. She never missed a thing. I was nearly crawling under the seat, hiding my eyes."

"She's a ghoul?" Aiden asked.

"She's too gutsy for her own good, not afraid of anything. She's braver than I've ever been. What the hell, it got her through some wicked stuff. I admire her. But I don't want her all zooped up on Annalee's craziness right now. Right now I want her growing my nephew to a healthy size and having a safe delivery."

He considered this. "Makes perfect sense, the way you say it."

"Because she's gutsy and I'm sensible." She turned toward him. "I love you. I'm in it with you. Trust me. Let me be in it with you."

He put his hand around the back of her neck, threading his fingers into her hair. "Of course I trust you. I just don't want you driven totally crazy right along with me."

"Too late. The woman's got me so nuts, she better be careful around me."

Five days after Aiden had been arrested, the phone rang at Erin's cabin. She answered and Annalee said, "Put Aiden on."

"Well, good morning, Annalee," Erin said. "Everything all right?"

"Put Aiden on. Quickly."

Aiden was sitting at the table with his laptop open, a cup of coffee beside him. When Erin extended the phone toward him, she said, "Guess who's turned up again?"

He took the phone at once. "This better be good," he said. He listened for a long time, then he finally said. "Of course, you realize that extortion is against the law." Again, he listened for a long time. "Would you like the phone number for my attorney so you can make that offer to him?" Again he listened. "Fine. I'll pass the offer along to my attorney…and, Annalee? You might want to get a really, really good one yourself." Then he disconnected.

Erin just stood, a frozen look on her face, waiting.

"Here's her offer. If I give her a hundred-thousand-dollar cash settlement off the books, she'll sign everything right away. Otherwise she plans to take me to court and sue me for desertion, abuse, battery, mental cruelty, imprisonment…" He laughed suddenly, sardonically. "Imprisonment? God, I couldn't get away from her fast enough!"

Erin took a step toward him. "Aiden, she can't prove any of those things!"

"But there was a report. Of course she can't prove anything—but what she can do, as she so cleverly pointed out to me, is circulate rumors, even using the press. She can make enough of a stink that no practice with one working brain among them would ever give me a chance as a woman's doctor. When I pointed out that blackmail was against the law, she said she hoped I had some recording device working. Then she said to make a decision within the week or she'd be beat-up again. And the police were probably tired of my lawyer girlfriend lying for me."

"Aiden! She can't get away with this!"

"But she can," he said. "I mean, she'll never prove anything—but can she make it real tough for me to carry on without a long history of innuendo and gossip that alleges I'm abusive toward women? Ruin my career? I think even if she goes to jail, she could still manage to create a lot of damaging suspicion about my character." He laughed suddenly. "Doesn't this all sound familiar? Except the price—the price has gone way up."

* * *

Mel was just hanging out in the reception area, a stack of lab results in one pile and charts in the other. Cameron was at the desk, working on the computer. They were in the process of trying to go paperless, filing all their patient charts on the hard drive. Mel had found them a perfect customized program, but it still required a lot of charting, filing, sifting, sorting and in-putting.

"The second we have an extra dime, we're getting at least a part-time secretary. I spend half my life on paperwork."

Cameron just grunted his reply. He was drowning in it as much she was.

Business was definitely picking up. They were now up to two appointment days a week, and with more people in the area getting insurance, they were both making a living, if a modest one.

The door opened and Darla Prentiss popped her head in. "Mel, hi! Got a minute for me?"

"Absolutely! How are you?"

"Fantastic."

Darla waved out the door and Mel heard the engine of a truck as it was turned off, the slamming of a door. Then Phil Prentiss was beside his wife. He pulled his ball cap off his head as he entered. His jeans, plaid shirt and boots were well-worn and a little dirty—he'd been working. Darla was dressed up, however—she wore her best creased pants and starched white blouse. She was clutching a large manila envelope protectively against her chest. "Mel," Phil said with a smile and nod. "Doc," he said to Cameron.

Cameron got up to shake the man's hand. "You two are looking good," he observed.

"You, too, Doc. Mel—may we talk to you a minute? A special request?" Phil asked.

"Right this way," Mel said, heading toward their office. "You know I'd do anything for you two."

Phil laughed; Darla joined him in laughter. "That's exactly what we're hoping."

When Phil and Darla were seated in front of her desk and Mel behind it, she couldn't help but grin at their youthful, secretive amusement with each other. She folded her hands on top of her desk. "Gonna let me in on the joke?" she asked.

Darla passed the envelope to her. "We're moving on, Mel. This is our adoption packet. We're still hoping God blesses us with a child, but I guess it's not going to be one we make on our own."

Almost in shock, Mel took the envelope. She was speechless.

"We got talking," Phil said. "It's pretty obvious there's another plan for us. There must be a need for a couple just like us to help out or we wouldn't find ourselves in this position. Truth is, if we'd had children we probably wouldn't consider adopting."

"You're going to stop trying?" Mel asked cautiously.

Darla nodded. "We're all done. If there's money to be spent now, we thought it might be better spent on a lawyer." She turned and smiled at her husband. "And on setting up a college fund. I imagine there are children out there who need us." She laughed a little. "There are probably kids looking for a place to grow up with fresh whole milk, garden vegetables and maybe a hayloft to jump out of."

"But what if you get pregnant again?" Mel asked.

"We've decided to go ahead and turn that off," Phil said, shaking his head. "First off, it isn't real likely. That doesn't appear to be a special talent of ours. And second, the kind of pregnancies we have are just too traumatic. We don't want to complicate a newly formed family life like that."

"I hate to sound like I'm just a crybaby—there isn't much in my life to complain about. But we don't want to try to get over another miscarriage. Besides, Phil and I always had faith that the right thing for us would present itself."

"You were never a crybaby," Mel said softly. "You always had the best attitudes of any couple I've ever known."

"We've been blessed in so many other ways," Phil said. "I mean, the farm is solid, the land is good to us, we found each other at an early age. I can't speak for Darla, but there hasn't been a day in my life that I didn't wake up and thank God for this woman. She's the best wife a man could ever have...."

Darla got a little bit of a girlish flush on her cheeks. "You know why he says that, don't you? If he's real sweet and romantic, sometimes I make two desserts."

He laughed low in his throat. "That's not all she

does for me if I'm sweet and romantic—but you don't want to hear about that!"

"Phil!" she scolded. Then she looked back to Mel, serious. "Mel, could you look through that envelope, please? Tell us if we've included the kinds of things a person who has to place a child would want to know? And if anything is missing, we'll add it."

"Sure," Mel said, almost numb. "Sure, let's see." She opened the envelope and pulled out some paperwork. There were several identical, copied résumés. "How did you know what to include?"

"We looked it all up online. Eventually I'm going to create a page for us so we can put this stuff up, too. So the next time someone is looking…" She shrugged. "We'll be there, ready to be found."

Mel scanned. It was all there. Personal information from ages to religious preferences to health reports. There was a description of their home life—large dairy farm, remodeled five-bedroom home, above-average income, savings and investments, clean legal history, long residency in the community, tons of community service. As Mel had known since the first time she met them—they were ideal. They'd spent a fortune trying to have a baby of their own.

"Are you at peace with this decision?" Mel asked, feeling a growing ache in the place where she'd once had a womb.

"We are, Mel. We have a real good life, a happy marriage. We've been trying too hard to make things happen our way when maybe that's just not the plan. And you know what else? If we're not meant to adopt, either, then a child won't come our way—we did the paperwork, but we're putting this in God's hands. If he sees fit to assist us in this, he'll send us the child we're meant to raise."

If God *sees fit?* Mel thought almost angrily. *God hasn't been much help so far!* But she covered her anger and said, "Well, how flexible are you? It doesn't say here just exactly what kind of child you want. That's usually part of the packet. Most couples have preconceived ideas—like a male child under six months old, Caucasian, that sort of thing."

They looked at each other and laughed again. "That would be us making out exactly what we'd have rather than us being open to what comes our way."

"Well, that could be a six-year-old biracial child. Or how about a child with disabilities?" she asked.

"There again, about the only thing we could be guaranteed with our own baby was its race. You think if our own baby had come with disabilities, we'd turn it back in?" She chuckled and shook her head at the absurdity. "I'll be honest, Mel—I've dreamed of holding a small baby close, of watching our child get teeth, learn to walk and talk, grow tall. But when you get down to it, about the only thing missing from our lives, our almost-perfect lives, is the laughter of children. I guess they come in all ages, shapes, colors and sizes."

"Here's something to kick around—a lot of young women who feel they have to place their child for adoption want to keep some kind of contact. They want to be informed regularly that their baby is doing well. They want pictures and stuff. And even if they relinquish custody for adoption, they might even want to turn up at a Little League game to see their child play ball," Mel said. She was so hoping to scare them off.

They exchanged curiously puzzled looks and she thought, Aha! They won't go for that!

"Now, doesn't that just make sense?" Darla said. "I have to admit, if I were forced to have someone else raise a child of mine, it would sure give me comfort to know they were growing up strong and good."

"That can be awfully complicated, you know," Mel said. "Having some biological parent looking things over all the time, maybe considering trying to interfere if she doesn't like the way things are going...."

Phil laughed. "Any more complicated than my cranky old dad watching that farm like he didn't retire twenty years ago? Threatening to take it back from me and my brother every other day?" He laughed and Darla joined him. "Mel, when you own a big herd and try to make your living off Mother Nature, you better be able to take complications in stride. No one more fickle than Mother Nature." He looked at Darla. "Didn't we surely learn that when trying to breed up our own family?"

Mel put the material back in the envelope. "Well, looks like it's all here to me, unless you change your minds and decide to be more specific about the kind of child you're looking for. Or—unless you want to try having your own just once more. You carried the last one pretty long—eighteen weeks."

Darla shook her head. "I'm afraid I'm just not up to it. I not only feel the loss so much, but I end up feeling like a failure. I know that's just silly, but…"

"I know the feeling," Mel said. "But how about a surrogate? Did you talk about that?"

"We did. It sounds like a pretty reasonable option for folks like us. But I'm thirty-five and Phil's thirty-eight. It's time for us to stop playing the conception lottery. Like I said, that money can start a college fund. You can bet there aren't any rich babies up for adoption. If we get a baby, it'll be a little one that no one could do that for. But we can. We've always had everything. Everything but children."

Phil sat back in his chair. "Gotta get me a kid to pester and hound the way my old man does me. Can't wait till I get to turn over the farm and then show up every day to tell him what he's doing wrong," he joked.

"Oh, Phil," Darla lightly scolded. "Your dad tries to help. He means well."

"What if a baby…or a young child, for that matter…never materializes for you?" she asked them.

"Well," Phil said. "If that happens, I guess we'll die with a lot of excess love in our hearts." He put his arm around his wife's shoulders. "There are worse things."

"Well, good luck with this," Mel said, handing them the envelope.

"Would you keep it, Mel? You have all the women patients in Virgin River. We're giving a packet like that to an agency in Eureka and another one to the biggest OB in the county. But maybe someone around here will turn up, right here where we live. If you come across anyone who needs us, would you mind just telling them? Maybe give out one of our résumés?"

"Sure," she said. "Sure, I can do that."

And she recalled—it happened just like this so many times that it was almost impossible to think of it as a coincidence. The first time was years ago, in L.A., when a young woman came into the hospital clinic, sobbing, saying she couldn't bring herself to terminate, but she was in no place to raise a child— the father didn't want her, wouldn't help, her parents were furious, et cetera, et cetera. Two hours later a woman in her thirties who had had a hysterectomy brought in an adoption résumé and asked if they knew of anyone looking for adoptive parents.... They came so close together they practically passed each other in the doorway. Mel had put them together and felt such a rush of warmth at having had a hand in making everyone's life a little richer.

She didn't feel that way at the moment. She stood up and put out a hand. "I'll let you know if I hear of any-one."

Darla took her hand first, then Phil did. "Thanks, Mel—you're just a treasure. We know it'll probably take a long time. We're patient. But giving that to you—that's the closest thing to having an angel in charge we can think of."

Hah! Mel thought. *If only you knew!* "Now, don't go giving me credit I don't deserve," she said, smiling. "I don't know of anyone at this point."

She walked them to the front door, bid them goodbye, then went back to the office. Well, she still had some measure of control here—once Marley and Jake chose her as the adoptive mother, all would be well. It wouldn't take them long, either. They'd met with Brie right away. Mel would be the prenatal practitioner of choice, and Marley might even be open to her delivering the baby. Worst case, she could direct Marley and Jake to John Stone, who would certainly let her in the room. They would be so relieved to have a close friend of Rick and Liz as the mother of their child.

She slipped the envelope into the bottom desk drawer. If she held her arms in just a certain way, she could almost feel the weight of the infant's head in the crook. If she just left that envelope in the drawer for a couple of weeks, a few at the most, her deal with Marley and Jake would be final. She'd even let them name the baby. That would convince them she was perfect!

It had happened this way so often, that the birth mother and the adoptive mother found each other by the merest chance, just when it needed to happen. Not only had it happened in Mel's practice, but she'd heard similar stories from so many nurses and doctors.

But it *had* happened again! The birth parents came to her for help and *she* was there for them! She was a good choice and totally prepared to raise their child and raise it as well as anyone could! As well as the Prentisses for sure!

She pulled the envelope out of the drawer and weighed it in her hand. She was so fond of Darla and Phil; they were the most wonderful people. It seemed like the biggest cheat in the universe that they hadn't been able to have a baby of their own. All they wanted to make their lives complete was a child to shower their wonderful love on.

She put the envelope back in the drawer. *It's my baby!* she thought vehemently. *I found it! I found it just when I was needing it!*

She pulled open the drawer and looked at the envelope sitting there. It had grown larger in size. Perfect health, good wholesome family life, lots of love, profound faith, wisdom and laughter and kindness beyond belief. They'd love a baby, but they weren't going to be narrow-minded—another child could need them. And they had no children.

I have two children, she thought. *Two healthy, happy, smart, beautiful children. Darla has never held a brand-new baby of her own close to her chest....*

But I need *one more. I need that one more! I need to feel that joy of motherhood one more time. I need that womanly purpose. And if I can't watch my own belly grow, I can watch Marley grow with the baby! With* my *baby!*

She closed the drawer. She slammed it closed. She put her head down on her desk. She felt pain in her throat and temples. Her stomach began to churn. *I'm coming down with something,* she thought.

It's not your baby, a voice said. *You want it to be your baby so much that you'll steal it from two of the most decent, deserving prospective parents on earth. And you will do that because...?*

"Because it's what I feel I need," she said aloud. Softly, but still aloud.

All she needed was a couple of weeks of silence, four at the outside, and it would be done. She would have successfully kept the Prentisses from knowing about the baby and the baby's birth parents from knowing about the Prentisses. And even if the birth parents found out about the Prentisses, they might *still* choose Mel and Jack. No harm done.

A few weeks for the birth parents to choose Mel and Jack, who did not need a baby to soak up all the extra love in their hearts. Darla and Phil would find a child eventually. Or die with a lot of excess love in their hearts. And Phil had said it himself—there are worse things.

This isn't who you are, Melinda, the voice said.

Then who the hell am I? she asked the voice. *I'm just a woman like every other woman, a woman like Darla, a woman who wants to fulfill herself. It's completely reasonable!*

Reasonable, she thought. To try to force your husband to procreate with the help of a stranger to the tune of probably fifty thousand dollars even though you've already built a solid little family? To lie to him, to trick him into an adoption that fell into your lap? To manipulate him with anger to go along with your needs? To promise to assist a couple you love and admire—then hide their request so you could have *more?* Oh—reasonable. For a total nutcase.

She put the envelope on top of her desk. She grabbed her purse and medical bag and went into the reception area where Cameron was still at the computer. "I apologize—I think I'm coming down with something," she said. "I need to go home. I'll leave the Hummer for you in case there's an emergency."

"I'll call Jack," he said, getting to his feet.

"No, don't. Let me take your car. I have a babysitter at home—I'll keep her and lie down for a few hours. I'm sorry...."

"What's wrong, Mel?" he asked, digging into his pocket for his keys. "Want me to drive you?"

"No. No, I just feel a bad headache coming on, a little nausea. I should just go home and lie down." She took the keys. "I'll be fine, just cover for me. Will you?"

"Well, sure. But..."

"I'll check in later, if that'll make you feel better. After I have a rest and some Advil or something. I'll get your car back to you before end of business...."

"I'm not worried about that," he said. "You're pale and weird. Let me drive—"

"I'll check in," she said, cutting him off and going out the door.

At about one o'clock Cameron walked across the street to the bar to grab a sandwich. He jumped up on a stool and said to Jack, "How's Mel?"

"Mel?" Jack asked. "You'd know that better than me."

"She didn't come by here? Before she went home? She didn't call you?"

"What?" Jack asked. "What are you talking about?"

"She left a couple of hours ago—went home sick. She looked pretty bad, actually. Pale as a ghost. She took my car and left me the Hummer. I hope she didn't have to pull over or anything."

Jack just frowned.

"It came on real sudden. The Prentisses came in, brought in their adoption packet for her—I found it on the desk. Just minutes after they left, she took off. She said she thought it was a headache coming on, but in all the time I've worked with Mel—"

"Excuse me," Jack said. He went to the swinging door that led to the kitchen, then came back through the bar on the way to the door. "Preacher will be right out to take care of you, Cam." And he was gone.

Jack got home as fast as he could with no idea what he'd find when he got there. Mel's moods had been weird, her personality off, her demeanor unpredictable. He'd tried to cope by just playing a little emotional balancing act, then going along as best he could. He'd never been through anything like this with his wife—she was the stable one while he was the one with issues, ranging from a little PTSD from combat to a temper if his buttons were pushed.

But never before had Mel confused him. She'd challenged him, scared him, saved him, but he always understood her. She was the straightest shooter he had known in his life.

When he walked in the house, fourteen-year-old Leslie jumped up from the couch, startled. "Jack!" she said.

"Mel home?" he asked.

"She said she didn't feel well.... She went to lie down for a while."

"Kids asleep?"

"Yeah. They should be down another hour. Everything okay?"

"Fine. Carry on. Do whatever fourteen-year-old babysitters do at nap time—talk on the phone, graze in the kitchen, nap, watch TV, whatever…"

"Sure, Jack," she said with a laugh.

He went to his bedroom, the bedroom he'd carefully soundproofed when he built the house to keep his wonderful, wild, noisy sex with Mel from being heard by kids or houseguests. She was lying facedown on the bed, sobbing.

He sat on the side of the bed and gently rolled her over. Her eyes were swollen, her face wet and splotched. "Jack," she said in a sob.

"What happened, baby?" he said, pulling her onto his lap.

"Phil and Darla came in with an adoption folder. They asked me to give it to anyone who might need them—to any birth mother looking for a good family for her child. Jack, I was going to hide it from Marley so she'd give the baby to us." She buried her face in his chest.

"But you didn't," he said, stroking her hair.

"But I was going to because I thought the one thing in the world that would make me feel right was a baby. It didn't really matter where it came from as long as it belonged to me. Belonged to us. Because that way I'd be a woman, a mother. I'd be whole again, like I was when we met…."

Major meltdown, he thought. Long time coming.

"You're even better than when we met," he said. "You're everything. If there's anything missing, I sure can't see it."

"Because you *can't* see it," she said. "But I feel it—there's a hole where the center of my life used to be. I remember—when I was married to Mark and we couldn't make a baby by ourselves, I felt like a cripple, but no one could see the limp but me. You can't know what it was like to drive to the clinic with a vial of sperm kept warm between your breasts, hoping this one would do it, make the baby…"

"Between your breasts…?"

"'Make it romantic,' the doctor would say. 'Try to forget this is all science and remember that the science is about you and your husband creating your child.…' We'd almost make love so I could collect the specimen, then jump into my clothes, into my car, rush it to the lab… But, Jack…I felt so unlike other women. So alien, so abnormal and strange. Do you know what the most commonly uttered prayer is? It's 'Oh, dear God, why can't I just be like everyone else?'"

"No one is like everyone else, baby," he said. "We're all so different. We all have such different things we need. Such different burdens to carry…"

"I didn't want to be obsessed with getting pregnant in my first marriage, but when I'd had a hard time for a year or two, it became everything to me. Everything changed when he died, of course—my losses just multiplied. Then I met you and without even meaning to, you filled that spot that had been wanting—filled it with life. Jack," she said. "Jack, I'm a midwife— giving life, delivering life, it just seems like the foundation. Jack, I miss it. I miss it so much and it's gone."

"It's only changed," he said. "You have children and you still carry your women through the process. You still bring babies into the world, but more important, women depend on you for their health. You get them through so much...."

"But I want it *back,* Jack. I'm not *done!* I want to be the woman you met, the woman you made pregnant without even trying."

"The woman I made cranky without trying," he said with a smile.

"I want to bleed again, can you beat that? I should be so happy to be free of periods—but I miss them."

"I miss them, too," he said.

"How can you?" she said with a sniff, sitting up straighter.

He shrugged. "So much of my life revolved around your periods—when you had them, when you didn't, *whether* you had them... You never had them after our first time in bed together, as it turned out. I was looking forward to arguing about whether it was all right to make love anyway, fantasizing you'd be shy about that while I didn't care...."

"You have always been way too horny for your own good," she said.

"Because it was you," he said. "Your body was always changing, going through phases. Moods."

"I still have moods...."

"But I miss it, too, Mel," he said. "I wanted to rub

your back because you cramped, wanted to hear you tell me you were too messy or cranky. I miss watching for the blood to come and knowing that—uh-oh— once again, it didn't come and you were going to get big and ripe and furious." He chuckled. "All that stuff changed suddenly for me, too. Scary sudden."

"But do you see? It made me a different kind of woman and there was no warning. It all changed too soon. It was supposed to change at forty-five or fifty, not thirty-five! I just figured out how to get pregnant after all that trouble and work and then *bam!* It was taken away from me again!"

He wiped the tears off her cheeks. "Replaced with children for you to raise and chase and yell at and swat and bring into the bed with us. Replaced with the wisdom that comes from survival and growth and balance. No more blood—no arguing about whether you can grit your teeth and let me love every last piece of you in spite of what time of the month it is. No more surprises—we can plan now. And once we're past this crisis, no more crazy mood swings…"

"You think this is just a crazy mood swing?" she asked.

"Nope," he said, shaking his head. "Nope—this is you admitting that losing a body part you found essential is very hard, but that you can admit it. That it's loss, just like it was loss for Rick to lose a leg. So guess what, Mel? We're not going to make any more babies. Luckily, we did that already. Now we can relax and enjoy them." He bit at her neck. "Now I can make love to you as much as you want. All the time, if you want.

We can get a sitter, lock the door and go at it like bunnies for days, if you want."

"That isn't making me feel better," she informed him.

"Multiple orgasms have *always* made you feel better," he whispered.

"Pah,"she scoffed.

He chuckled. "You sure fake it good, then. You've always been so mature about accepting what feels good.…"

"Jack, there's this place inside me, right here," she said, sliding his hand over her lower abdomen, "that feels empty, like something important is missing.…"

He pressed down with his big hand. "Because something that was there before, that you counted on, that you believed was an important part of who you are, is gone. Gone, Mel—because it was life or death. Those were the choices."

"I didn't realize how much I missed it, how much I'd like to have it back."

"I know, baby."

"What now?"

He shrugged. "If you feel like crying over it, I can hold you. Eventually, though, you're going to realize that you're ten times the woman you were when I met you and getting better every day, and that your womb never had that much to do with the you I fell in love with. Thank you just the same, though, for giving me children before you gave it up. And thank you for giving it up so we could be together…"

"That whole surrogate idea—what was so bad about that idea?" she wanted to know.

He shook his head. "Not sure. I just had this gut feeling you were trying to fill a hole in our lives that didn't exist. Compensating. Being somehow unrealistic about the life we have together, which is as close to perfect as anyone could have. You know, when people compensate, sometimes what they give up is far greater than what they get."

"I asked Phil Prentiss what he would do if they never got a baby and he said they'd die with a lot of excess love in their hearts.…"

"And let's not," Jack said. "Let's spend every drop. On the kids, on our families, on your patients, on the town. On people we don't know yet and the ones who have been our good friends forever. On each other. Let's spend our last drop as we're taking our last breaths."

Mel smiled at him, though a big tear ran down her cheek. "I have to give Phil and Darla's packet to that young couple.…"

"Of course you do," he said, wiping away the tear. "And it's going to double the size of your heart."

Sixteen

A few days after Aiden's arrest and release, his divorce lawyer called him at Erin's cabin. "I have news. You are not divorced. But then, you weren't exactly married."

Aiden frowned. "Excuse me?"

"Your wife has been the wife of many," Ron said. "She's a con—this must come as no surprise, eh?" he asked. "But you were her *second* spouse, while she was still married to her first spouse. Her first husband was and probably still is her partner and partner in crime—his was the name on the back of your check. She's used so many aliases, we're not sure we've tracked them all yet. The couple are Bosniak—Albijana Kovacevic and Mustafa Zubac. She isn't going to sue you, smear your reputation or do any of that. She can't afford to. They're wanted in five states."

Aiden couldn't speak. He could barely breathe.

"Aiden?" Ron asked. "Dr. Riordan?"

"Uh, back up. Are you sure about this?"

"I've e-mailed you some photos, but yes, we're sure. They have a scam they've been running all over the place. Pretty young Annalee or Busha or Cerilla or any one of her aliases, marries. Usually a fairly rich older gentleman. Not so rich it would stand out, but with enough in the bank to be a lucrative target—they don't invest much time. She's been a masseuse, waitress, dancer, child-care provider..."

"*Child* care?" he asked, flipping open his laptop and getting online.

"I know. Terrifying thought, isn't it? She treats them to her wild mood disorder and within a couple of months agrees to a divorce without a settlement if there's a cash incentive. It's pretty cost effective to give her fifty or a hundred grand to go away and the divorce is actually filed and recorded. Unfortunately for Albijana, some of her victims have had second thoughts after buying her off and reported the scam to the police."

"But before they marry her," Aiden said, "she treats them to a sample of her considerable sexual talents. This guy, her alleged partner—I've never seen him, nor did I know he existed—is her pimp."

"Pretty much," Ron said. "She's been married and divorced a number of times in a number of states. Yours was a fluke—your lawyer hadn't passed the bar after four tries, left a big stack of cases on his desk that were neither filed nor recorded, thus your marriage was recorded and not your divorce. That was a major screwup for them. It led to my staff finding that your marriage was not her first, that none of the subsequent marriages were legal. Bingo."

He looked at the laptop screen where he'd just opened up a photo. Erin, who was listening attentively and hearing little or nothing from Aiden's side of the conversation, looked over his shoulder. "God," Aiden said in a breath. The woman was Annalee; the man had a very sinister, mature look about him, but Aiden instantly knew that was only one of his looks. "That's her," he said. "And the guy? I caught her in bed with him—a young sailor who said he didn't know she was married, that he met her in a bar at ten o'clock in the morning. Jesus…he *cried*. I thought he was eighteen and scared to death— the only thing that kept me from beating him senseless."

"Mustafa Zubac, goes by the name Mujo."

"How'd you get the pictures?" Aiden asked.

"They've been arrested in the past several years. They just haven't been prosecuted for their pretty simple fraud. They get out on bond and make a run to another location."

"I knew she saw me coming," he muttered. "I couldn't prove it, but I always knew it—she caught me practically getting off a boat after a two-year assignment. A young doctor with money to burn. Jesus. But the navy? She went into the navy?"

"The history is sketchy, but I think what happened was she immigrated with her parents and hooked up with Mujo, a compatriot, after she'd enlisted. Albijana didn't have it easy in Bosnia—her neighborhood was in constant conflict, but Mujo had it even worse and was a member of the underworld at an early age, the only thing that kept him alive. Both of them learned how to lie, steal, cheat and scam, probably as a matter of survival when they were young. They're devastatingly good at it. And no one learns to live in the shadows like a couple of kids who grew up in a war zone."

"No kidding. Now what?"

"Well, here are your choices—when she calls to ask if the payoff and documents are ready, you can tell her you know the whole story and that there are warrants for arrests of herself and Mujo, and I'd be very surprised if you ever saw or heard from her again. Or, you can pretend you don't know and help flush her out for the police. The local police would love to take them into custody—the FBI would be happy to take them from there. It's entirely up to you."

"Much as I'd like to help, I'm going to pass," Aiden said. "I just don't want to create any more drama for my family or Erin. This has been as terrible as I want it to get."

"That's the option I would have taken," Ron said. "Don't be shocked if the local police ask for your cooperation, but it's entirely up to you—don't be pressured. In the meantime, we'll petition the court with the appropriate documentation to have your record of marriage to Annalee Kovacevic nullified and removed. We'll send you copies. That will take a couple of months, but we'll keep on it."

"I appreciate it, since I bought your colleague a big fat diamond and it doesn't look like she'll give it back."

He laughed heartily. "Congratulations! Have a date set yet?" he asked.

"Not till you deliver the all clear, Mr. Preston."

"We're on it. Hopefully it won't be long. Give us a heads-up when and if you hear from Albijana and deliver the bad news, will you?"

"When and if?"

"Well, I'm sure they'll be tagged as wanted immediately. If they sniff that out, they'll probably be on the move."

"Life could only be so kind," he said. "Thanks, Ron. I don't know how you did this, but thanks."

"I have a really good team—they're relentless at finding the facts. You'd be amazed at the things people try to hide, Dr. Riordan."

"Well, God bless you for it."

Ron Preston chuckled. "You won't be blessing me when you get the bill. Be sure to sit down when you open the envelope."

He refrained from saying, *Worth every penny*. Instead, he said, "Thanks. Talk to you later."

Erin and Aiden were not the only ones waiting impatiently for Annalee to contact them again. By the time Aiden had told the immediate members of his family about the dramatic turn of events, everyone was anticipating the outcome. They didn't have to wait long. At the end of the sixth day Aiden received an e-mail:

You've had plenty of time. Are the documents ready for me to sign? As we discussed? Annalee

Aiden was almost disappointed she hadn't called. It would be fun to hear the shock in her voice as he told her the scam hadn't worked. He e-mailed Ron Preston and asked for his recommended response. Ron e-mailed back that he should try the following:

They are not, Mrs. Zubac. Your marriage to Mustafa is the only legitimate marriage of record and it turns out I don't need a divorce after all. Get lost and don't bother me again.

Her e-mail and his response were forwarded to Ron, who, he assumed, would make sure the authorities got it, as well. After that, there was nothing for Aiden and Erin to do but attempt to get on with their lives. But Annalee had gotten the drop on him so many times, it was hard to relax. Nothing would be so welcome as word that she'd been apprehended.

He began to immediately regret not participating in that event.

"I'm worried about my sister," Marcie told Ian. "There's something wrong and she keeps denying it."

"How can you be so sure there's something wrong?" Ian asked.

"I can hear it in her voice. There's a tension, a nervous laugh that Erin *never* had, and she used to call me every day, sometimes twice a day, and now I almost always have to call her. Something's wrong."

"You're just being overly pregnant," Ian said. "What could be wrong?"

"She went to Virgin River, fell in love, got engaged and is starting a whole new life, all in about two months. What if something is wrong between her and Aiden?"

Ian cradled her little sprite of a face in his hand, looked deep into those mischievous green eyes and asked, "If there is, what can you do about it?"

"I can be there for her," she said. "If she'll just talk to me, maybe I can help. I do know more about relationships than she gives me credit for. Erin's kind of an oddball—she's pretty old to be having her first serious relationship."

Ian smiled and shook his head. "She'll be home in a couple more weeks. We're having a baby in three. This will keep. When she's home and the little guy is out, you two can talk about it day and night."

That was a very husband thing to say, Marcie thought. Were men wired to say things like *just relax?* But it wasn't good enough for her—she was sure she'd heard something in her sister's voice that indicated there was a problem. And even if Marcie couldn't make it go away, she was damn sure going to know what it was.

She was thirty-five weeks pregnant, had just had a doctor's appointment and everything was perfectly normal and on schedule. She'd be having her C-section at thirty-eight weeks—a couple of weeks before her due date. All was well. She could make a quick run up to Virgin River, spend one night with Erin, get the lay of the land and drive back in the morning. The doctor said no more trips, but not because a trip would throw her into labor or because anything was wrong—only because she was supposed to be near her doctor and hospital in case she went into labor early. If that happened, she could have her C-section early. It was very unlikely, he had said, but he wanted her to err on the side of caution.

Still, everything she read about first babies and labor said it usually lasted *forever*. Worst-case scenario—if she went into labor, she'd pull over and summon help, an ambulance or whatever.

After Ian left for work in the morning, she threw a few things into an overnight bag and wrote him a note.

> Took a run up to Virgin River to see Erin. I'll call and leave a message when I arrive safely—hope to be there by noon. I'll talk to you tonight. Be back first thing tomorrow. Do NOT worry, I feel great. And I love you.

She had cell reception most of the way and after three hours on the road, feeling great, she checked her cell and had not missed any calls. When she talked to Ian later, he was going to be very cranky about this, but she wasn't worried. He couldn't stay mad at her. Besides, he'd grown accustomed to the fact that she did as she pleased. She smiled to herself. That was how she'd captured him, after all—doing as she pleased.

By the time she neared the cabin, she wasn't feeling so great. Typical day for Marcie—late pregnancy was no picnic. For one thing she was small and her load was large; sometimes the pressure on her lower pelvis was wearing. She was probably a little dehydrated, though she'd had water with her the whole way. And hungry, though she'd had peanut butter crackers. She'd get a bite and maybe lie down for a while once she got to Erin's. She'd made fantastic time, she was proud of that—it wasn't quite noon.

Erin's SUV was not at the cabin and neither was Aiden's. They must be off on errands or something, but no problem for her. She'd eat something and rest. She opened the door and walked in; the blinds were all drawn and the place was a little dark. She closed the door behind her and went first to the new French doors, opening the blinds to the view. When she turned, she almost shrieked in surprise.

A blonde woman with a bruised and swollen face was pointing a small gun right at her. "Who are you?" the woman asked Marcie.

Marcie grabbed her chest in shock, then recovered herself. "I'm Marcie Buchanan and this is my cabin! Put that thing down before you hurt someone!"

The gun did not move. "Where are Erin and Aiden?" she asked.

"I don't have any idea! I just got here! What the hell are you doing here? What do you want?"

"I'm waiting for Aiden. I need a little money," she said.

Marcie opened her purse. "You can have whatever I've got. I must have fifty dollars, at least."

The woman laughed and it contorted her face. Her lip was swollen and split, her eyes were black and her face appeared a little lopsided. "Really?" she said. "Fifty *whole* dollars?" She laughed again. "Well, little girl, if we multiply that by about a thousand, we're talkin'."

"Ohhh," Marcie said, holding her middle. "I need water or something," she said. "I'm not feeling at all right...."

"Help yourself. Then sit down and take a load off. You might come in handy."

"I might be in labor," Marcie said. "Which would be a very bad thing."

"Not my problem." She shrugged.

"I need to use the phone...."

"Not happening, chickie. Get your water and sit."

"Oh, God," she moaned.

The woman smiled evilly. "Not at this address, babe," she said coldly.

Erin and Aiden spent a couple of hours in the morning riding their bikes along the Eel River in Fortuna, had an early lunch of seafood salad on the patio of a local restaurant and then went to Luke's to spend a little of the afternoon. Erin was caught up in holding the baby and helping with his bath, when Aiden said he was going with Luke to drop Art at Netta's house and run some errands. He promised to be back by five at the latest.

The baby was settled for his nap at around two when Shelby answered the phone and handed it to Erin. "Your brother-in-law?" she said by way of a question.

Erin grabbed it. "Ian? Is Marcie all right?"

"I don't know," he said. "She was worried about

you and left me a note—she decided to drive to Virgin River to see you."

"Worried about me? But why?"

"She heard something in your voice," he said. "I can't explain—but you know Marcie. She said she'd call when she got to Virgin River, but she hasn't. She should have been there by now, but there's no answer at the cabin."

"I'll go over there right now and wait for her. The minute I see her, I'll call."

"I'm on my way up there now and when I get there, if she's all right, I'm turning her over my knee."

"Ian, call the highway patrol," Erin said. "If she should be at the cabin by now and isn't, have them watch for her car on the off chance she's had car trouble along the way. Tell them the exact route she would've taken."

"Will do. Call me when you get to the cabin."

Erin hung up and turned a puzzled look at Shelby. She shook her head in confusion. "How weird. Apparently Marcie decided something is wrong with me. I told her everything is fine—but maybe I sounded a little stressed on the phone. Anyway, she decided she had to drive up here and see for herself. I'm going over to the cabin to wait for her."

"Want me to go with?" Shelby asked.

"Take advantage of the baby's nap and maybe get one of your own. I'll see you later. Just tell Aiden I went home."

When she pulled up to the cabin a little later, there sat Marcie's car. "Well, thank heavens," she said to herself. "The little scamp!" She walked in the door and spotted Marcie lying on the leather sofa. She stood right over her and said, "What the hell were you thinking?"

"Uh, Erin?" Marcie said. "We have ourselves a situation...." She tilted her head, indicating the other side of the room.

Erin turned to see a battered Annalee sitting in a chair on the far side of the room, well out of reach, with a small handgun resting leisurely in her lap. She gasped and jumped back in such surprise, she almost fell on top of her reclining sister. For a second she wasn't sure what had shocked her most—the fact that Annalee was there, the condition of her face or the gun.

She righted herself. "What the hell is this, Annalee? What can you possibly hope to gain with this little show?"

"Money," she said with a shrug. "Things have gone south on me, so I'll need some money."

"I didn't see your car anywhere...."

"Parked behind the cabin, out of sight," Annalee said. "Now, shall we just get down to business?"

"How much?" Erin said. "I'll write you a check."

"Right." Annalee laughed. "It'll have to be a little more liquid than that, I'm afraid. A cash transaction."

"And you're going to take hostages? Is that your plan?"

She laughed again and Erin actually winced at what that did to the appearance of her face. "Hell, no, that would only slow me down."

"Well, if you hold a gun on my pregnant sister while I go after cash, that would qualify as taking a hostage. I can't think of any other way you're likely to accomplish it. Aren't you in enough trouble?"

"Wait till you hear this," Marcie said. "It's actually pretty slick." Erin frowned at Marcie. "But it is."

"Lay it on me," Erin said.

"We're going to do it on the computer," Annalee said. "A transfer of funds or a bank draft, whichever you're capable of. Everyone banks online. I need fifty thousand transferred into my offshore bank and don't worry, I'll take it from there."

Erin just shook her head. "You're kidding."

"Not even slightly. You want to handle that for me, or do we wait for Aiden?"

Erin thought for a moment. "I can do it," she said. "It needs a phone call. Just to my investment account manager. She makes the transfer into my money management account, I can transfer it from there. Online."

"If you screw this up and tip anyone off, we're going to have trouble," Annalee said.

"I won't screw it up," Erin promised. "Then you'll go?"

"Absolutely. Why would I want to hang around here?"

"Where's your partner? That Mujo guy?"

"Well, that's the problem," Annalee said. "When we figured they'd be looking for us, he split. Left me high and dry. Not the first time, and he always comes around when things cool down, but for right now, I can't go anywhere without money. And as usual, he took what we had." She smiled. "I'll find him. I know just where to look."

"He did that to your face, didn't he?" Erin asked.

"Mujo has a bit of a temper, but then so do I. I guess I set him off."

"Annalee," Erin said, shaking her head. "Why in the world would you want him back? Can't you manage to get just about any man you want?"

"No one is like us," she said. "Me and Mujo. No one understands and no one is like us, that's all. That's how it is."

Erin shook her head. "What a life," she muttered. She walked slowly and carefully to the desk, precariously close to Annalee. She flipped open the laptop and logged on. Then she picked up the phone and placed a call. She cheerily greeted her account manager's assistant, explained she was making a large down payment on a lake house in northern California and asked that fifty thousand be transferred into the checking account of her trust. When that was done, she looked up at Annalee. "Now what?"

"The account number and transit number are right there, on that pad by the computer, all ready for you."

Erin took a deep breath and accomplished the rest. The whole operation took less than fifteen minutes, which was incredibly frightening. "Done," she said.

"I'm going to have to verify that," Annalee said. "Move away from the computer, please, and don't do anything stupid. I'd rather not shoot anyone today, but you must know what my freedom means to me."

"No problem. Verify away," she said, moving back

to sit beside Marcie. "Are you all right?" she asked her sister.

"Well, yes and no," Marcie said. "I'm doing okay, but I'm having some serious contractions. They're getting close and hard. The real deal. This means I'm supposed to call my doctor and meet him at the hospital. But at the moment…"

Erin jolted upright and shouted at Annalee. "Do you realize what's happening here? That my sister is in labor and has to be in a hospital for a C-section? There's no time to waste! There could be huge consequences if you delay us!"

Annalee looked up from the computer as if bored.

Marcie touched Erin's arm. "We've been over all that. Not her problem, she says."

"It's by God going to be her problem if she ignores it! Hurry up over there!"

"It's not recorded quite yet," Annalee said calmly. "Take it easy."

"Just check my transfer receipt," Erin demanded. "Banks usually take twenty-four hours to register a deposit."

"Well, you need to shop banks," Annalee said lightly. "Mine takes twenty-four to make the funds available, but they record almost immediately." She leaned back in the chair and idly played with her weapon. "It shouldn't be too long."

How could the woman be so calm in the face of her sister's labor, knowing the situation was so dangerous for Marcie? But then, if she was truly sociopathic, nothing would affect her. It was eerie, watching her calm.

It seemed to Erin to take forever, and as she sat beside Marcie she could feel her large abdomen harden and relax a few times.

"Have you timed them?"

"Five minutes or so. Nothing to worry about yet. Maybe she'll leave and we can carry on." She took a breath. "Ian's going to kill me."

"Once you're fine, he will. Can you concentrate on not having a baby? Something like self-hypnosis?"

"I don't know," Marcie said. "Up till today I've been concentrating on having him a little early...."

"Swell."

There was a little *ping!* across the room. Annalee said, "Well, now." She closed the laptop. "Nicely done."

"Hate to see you rob us and run, but we understand."

Annalee laughed. "You know, one of the things I admire most, especially from a woman under pressure, is a good sense of humor. But gee, that went so well, I think we should wait for Aiden and do it again. Double your pleasure?"

"As far as I know, Aiden isn't planning to come here," Erin said. "He's gone to Eureka with his brother and won't be back at his brother's house before dinnertime. I'm to go back over there later."

"Let's give him a little time to miss you," she said.

Erin leaned forward. "Don't take that chance, Annalee. If you wait till people start to worry about us, you might have waited too long. I gave you a nice little nest egg. Take off before you have a trail of cops on your behind." As if on cue, the phone rang. And rang and rang and rang. When it went to voice mail, Erin said, "Really. Don't press your luck. Or, if you need some more money, maybe I should just do it so you can leave..."

"Ordinarily I'd go for that idea, but typically there's a break point where people start to wonder what's up with the big withdrawals. In my experience, fifty thousand is on the high but safe side. Let's give darling Aiden a little time. Besides...I wouldn't mind seeing him just once more..."

"You do understand that if that was him trying to reach me, he'll come, but not without help. Law-enforcement help. Annalee, be smart. You can shoot us or even drag us both out of here at gunpoint, but you'll never get away. If you go now before anyone knows what's going on, you might even make it."

"It's so nice of you to be concerned, but I think everything will work out fine. We'll give him a little more time."

Marcie winced and a little groan escaped her. This was escalating.

"I have to go to the bathroom," Erin said.

"Hold it."

"I have to go now!"

"Wet yourself, see if I care. Can't you stay focused?"

"How long do you propose to wait for Aiden? Because I need to get my sister medical attention!"

Annalee glanced at her watch. "Maybe a little while longer. Don't worry—I'll be out of your hair before long. If things go well, I'll have enough money to *stay* out of your hair."

But Erin *was* worried. She wasn't sure who might come bursting in the door first—Ian or Aiden. Or maybe Aiden with law enforcement. If it got that complicated and messy, not only were people going to get shot or taken hostage for a getaway by a panicked Annalee, it might push Marcie too far into a danger zone for delivering the baby safely. As Erin understood Marcie's situation, the danger was to Marcie *and* the baby.

She could not face that. Would not.

She leaned close to Marcie and gently stroked her hair away from her face. "If I create a diversion, can you get out?" she whispered.

"No whispering!" Annalee shouted.

Marcie groaned; a deep and low growl came out of her. And then suddenly there was a small flood as her water broke and began to flow from her body, wetting the couch beneath both her and Erin and dripping onto the floor. "No," Marcie said weakly. "Don't think so, no."

"Jesus Christ, I thought you were faking about having to pee," Annalee said. "That's disgusting! Shame on you!"

Seventeen

Erin glanced at her watch. It was five o'clock. Ian should be arriving soon and Aiden would be back at Luke's to receive the news that Erin had gone to the cabin. Things were going to shortly start coming apart at the seams and there was one whacko woman in control of a gun.

And Marcie's water had broken. Although Erin didn't know much about childbirth, she knew this meant something significant. "What does it mean?" she asked her sister.

"I gotta have a doctor and an operating room pretty soon or we're toast. He's all upside down and backward, Erin. He can't come out."

Erin got sharply to her feet. She glared at Annalee. "All right, toots—this meeting is over. My sister's water broke and we're in motion now. Take off."

Annalee likewise got to her feet, waving the little gun. "Hey, sit down! I told you what we're doing here!"

"I heard," Erin said. "You're making a big mistake because it's just about time for a whole bunch of people to come running and find out why this very pregnant woman and I aren't answering the phone or checking in as promised. Go—you'll thank me someday."

"I'll shoot," she warned.

"I guess that's up to you," Erin said. "I'm getting towels!" She stalked purposefully toward the bathroom and was frankly a little surprised when no bullet hit her in the back. She kept going. She ran through the door that joined the bathroom to the bedroom, grabbed the can of bear repellent and tucked it under her arm. She picked up her handy soup pot and metal spoon and peeked out the other door into the great room.

No Annalee. Good. She'd followed Erin.

She pulled closed the bedroom door as she entered the great room, then dashed to pull the bathroom door closed, as well. Then she stood between the two doors and began to bang the spoon inside the pot and yell at the top of her lungs. She kept both doors in her peripheral vision and when she saw one of them begin to cautiously open just a crack, she dropped the pot and spoon and armed herself with the repellent.

Erin thought there was a fair chance she'd be shot, but she really didn't have any other choice. With luck, the gun was of a small caliber and the aim would be bad. Even if she was killed or incapacitated, she'd have done some serious damage to Annalee in the process and Marcie would be able to get to the phone.

She went to the door that was opened only a crack. She kicked it violently and sprayed as she rushed in. And sprayed and *sprayed*.

The gun went off before it dropped from Annalee's hands so she could cover her eyes, but Erin didn't feel shot. Annalee backed into the bedroom and Erin followed. As the mist from the pepper spray stung her eyes, she moved on toward a screaming, blinded Annalee. When she was close, she grabbed the canister by the neck and swung it as hard as she could, whacking Annalee in the head.

She heard a loud crack and Annalee went down like rock. Out cold.

Erin looked down at her. Totally unconscious if not dead, a trickle of blood running out of her nose, her mouth parted and her eyes open a sliver. "Ew," she said.

"Erin! Erin, are you all right?" her sister called desperately from the other room.

She ran back to Marcie. "I have to get you to the hospital."

Marcie shook her head and tears wet her cheeks. "Gimme the phone to call 911 and while I do that, make sure that woman's down for the count."

"I might've killed her," Erin said, fetching the phone. "She looks totally dead. Listen, I'll carry you to the car and we'll call ahead for help to meet us."

Marcie shook her head and got a terrified look on her face. It accompanied an expression of both pain and remorse. "I don't think we can make it. I feel like…I feel like there are boulders in my pelvis. I feel like…" She stopped talking to blink at the phone. And then she dropped the phone as pain gripped her and she howled.

Erin fell to her knees beside the couch. "Marcie! Baby! Tell me what to do!"

"I don't know," she groaned breathlessly. "I don't know.…"

Erin heard an engine and ran to the door, not sure who she wanted to see there most. When Aiden leaped out of his car, she yelled, "Aiden, hurry! It's Marcie!"

He backtracked briefly to get a bag out of the back that Erin had never even realized he kept there. She breathed a sigh of relief to recognize what was probably a doctor's emergency medical bag. "Why didn't you call me?" he asked as he jogged toward the door.

"Annalee," she said. "With a gun."

He stopped short. "Where is she now? Gone?"

"In a manner of speaking. I knocked her out," Erin said. "Or killed her. I hit her in the head with the bear repellent bottle. After I squirted her in the eyes. She's in the bedroom."

Aiden grinned suddenly, but proceeded quickly. He went immediately to Marcie, going down on one knee at the side of the couch. "Hey," he said. "Easy does it, I'm here. What's going on?"

Wide-eyed and terrified, Marcie breathlessly said, "He's not supposed to be born like this, Aiden. But I think he wants to be."

"Sometimes we have to work with what we've got, kiddo. How long ago did your water break?"

"Half hour? Forty minutes?" She groaned deep and

low as another contraction gripped her. "The doctor said he'll die! Aiden, he's going to *die!* Take him out the right way! I can handle it—just don't let him—"

"Easy, easy, he's not going to die. We're going to do everything right—just take some deep breaths and try to calm down. How many weeks here?"

"Thirty-five," she said.

"Good job." Aiden stood up and motioned Erin to stay with Marcie. "Time those contractions and absolutely *no* pushing. No matter what."

Aiden knew he had a lot to deal with even before he had a chance to take a closer look at the patient. For starters, he knew this was supposed to be a breech baby scheduled for a C-section; usually the breech baby didn't provide enough pressure to rupture membranes…unless that baby had dropped and was on its way out. The bloody fluids staining her pants and the sheer force of the contractions spelled out an emergency delivery was imminent. He opened his bag and withdrew a pair of latex gloves, then put them on. It was not, however, so he could examine his patient.

Gloves donned, he ran into the bedroom and pressed two fingers to Annalee's carotid artery. Steady pulse. He grabbed her by the ankles and dragged her unceremoniously through the small cabin and out onto the deck. He wasn't about to get any of her blood or body fluids on his hands; Annalee was high risk and he knew his hands would soon be plunging into Marcie's birth canal. He left Annalee on the deck, closed and locked the doors. He stripped off and tossed the latex gloves. He then locked the other cabin door and went again to Marcie's side.

"They're coming fast, Aiden," Erin said. "She's had two since you left."

"Thanks, honey. Marcie, I'm going to carry you to the bedroom, to the bed. Don't strain. Let me do the work. Erin—get two or three large trash bags and towels. Bring them to me along with my bag." Then he bent to lift Marcie. He smiled down into her eyes. "Trust me—we're going to get through this."

"Sure," she said in a weak breath. "Sure." Then she started to sob.

"It's going to be okay." He laid her gently on the bed. "We need to get your britches off, kiddo. Have to take a look." He was already tugging them down when Erin quickly reappeared. "Towels," he said to Erin. "Lots of towels. And get the phone, please."

When Marcie was stripped from the waist down, Aiden took a glance at her pelvic floor. He didn't see anything yet and was grateful. He really wanted to wash his hands, but the washing he could accomplish in as much time as he felt he had wasn't likely to do enough good anyway. He reached into his bag for new gloves. "Okay, sweetheart, bend and spread your knees for me. Let's see where we are."

Marcie obliged and Aiden was on one knee, his one hand on her belly, the other gently moving into her birth canal. What he thought was, *Holy fuck!* What he said was, "There we go, nice and easy. Pant for me, Marcie." Then he took his stethoscope from the bag and said, "Quiet for me, please…" He listened, and while it wasn't the best equipment to get a fetal heart rate, it sufficed—the baby was not yet in distress. "Good. It's all good." All the while thinking, Bad, this is all bad.

When Erin brought him what he requested, he placed a large bath towel on top of a spread-out trash bag and asked Marcie to lift a bit so he could slide it under her. "See what I did there?" he said to Erin. "I'm probably going to ask you to do that for me again in a little while—towel on top of the plastic."

"I don't care about the bedspread," she said.

"That's not the concern. There's lots of blood and fluid involved in a birth and it can get overwhelming—obscure the field of birth. Easier to keep it as clean as possible. Now dial 911, press the speaker button and put the phone over here on the bedside table for me. Then get me— Do you have rubbing alcohol?"

"No," she said, doing as he asked.

"Okay, bring the bottle of scotch. And I need string or twine or, failing that, shoelaces. And a bowl—medium-size bowl."

"Huh?" she asked, putting down the phone.

He looked at her, trying to keep his expression from being panicked or scary. "Please, honey. We move quickly now."

"Right," she said, dashing off.

The emergency operator answered and he said, "Aiden Riordan here, I'm a physician—obstetrician. I'm going to need emergency medical transport. Airlift, if that's an option. We'll need access to a neonatal intensive care unit."

"What's your situation, Doctor?" the operator asked.

"I have a woman in advanced labor with a breech presentation, thirty-five-week gravida one para zero, eight centimeters, membranes ruptured. I'm going to have to deliver. What's your ETA?"

"I'm showing your location at 400 Moonlight Road, Doctor. Is that correct?"

Erin was back and she nodded. "Correct," he said. "It's right on top of the mountain in a nice big clearing. What are you sending? Bus? Helicopter?"

"I'll let you know in a minute.... Please stay on the line...."

"Whatever," he muttered. "Marcie, I want you to take nice, slow, deep breaths. I'll breathe with you. Erin, get a basin or pan of lukewarm water and some washcloths. Where's that string? I need a couple of lengths about six inches long—there's a scissors in the bag. What are the chances you have a turkey baster?"

"Zero," she said. "Why?"

"I don't have everything I need in the bag—suction for one thing. But I can manage."

The phone came alive again. "We're sending helicopter medical transport from Redding, Dr. Riordan. ETA about thirty minutes."

"Be sure they're prepared to transport a preemie. Thirty minutes puts us over the line to get her to surgery."

"Can I put someone on the line to walk you through it, Doctor?" the emergency operator asked.

He chuckled in spite of himself. "Very kind of you,

thank you. I've got it. Can you send sheriff's department support? Humboldt County Sheriff's Department?"

"You're located in Trinity, Doctor...."

"No worries—just give 'em a call, will you, please. Let them know that a woman they've been looking for is here. Annalee Kovacevic. I'm sure they'll appreciate it."

"Can you spell that for me, Doctor?"

"I cannot, I'm busy at the moment..."

"Is that the woman delivering, Doctor?"

"Nope. Ms. Kovacevic is waiting on the patio, I believe. The patient is Marcie Buchanan and she's—" He stopped talking as Marcie let out a cry of pain followed by a loud grunt. Aiden checked her and he was seeing the backside of a rather small baby boy. Thank God she was early and the baby small. It improved their chances. "She's ready," he finished. And at that point, he was done with the emergency operator. He poured a little scotch in the bowl and dropped in his scissors and scalpel to sterilize the instruments. He'd perform an episiotomy if necessary; the scissors was to cut the cord, unless their transport made it first.

"Erin," he said. "Dampen a facecloth and stay at Marcie's head for now. Mop her brow, give moral support." Then to Marcie he said, "Listen to me now—we're going deliver the baby and—"

Marcie let out another passionate yell, bearing down in spite of herself.

"Stop, stop, stop," he said. "Get control and listen

to me. You have to work with me! I know it hurts, but everything depends on this! Marcie!" She cried out again and in desperation Aiden said, "Erin! Can you help? We need to work together!"

The contraction let up, and Erin, sitting up on the bed by her sister's head, wiped Marcie's brow and then turned her face so she could look in her eyes. "Marcie, look at me," she said. "Listen to me. Aiden needs your complete cooperation to deliver this baby. It's critical, Marcie. Hang on to my hands and listen to Aiden. Breathe deep and listen to Aiden."

"Will the baby be all right?" Marcie asked, a sob in her voice.

"He will be all right. We'll get through this," Aiden said. "Work with me. You've got to work with me. No pushing yet."

"I...have...to..."

"Gimme a second," Aiden said. "Pant, if that helps. Get control. Erin—coach her. Pant like a dog. Try that."

"It hurts," Marcie said. "God, it hurts."

"Yeah," Aiden said. "But you're there." And as he said that, he watched the buttocks of the baby, back up, thighs tucked underneath. "Marcie. Erin. You really have to listen to me. This is critical. When I say push, you push. When I say stop, you stop."

Erin gripped her sister's hand. She stared hard into Marcie's eyes. "We will...we can. Can't we, Marcie?"

Breathless, she said, "Yes. Yes. Please make it be all right."

"It's going to be all right," Aiden said. "Now, Marcie. Push now..."

The baby had to deliver himself all the way up to the umbilicus without any manipulation or interference—that was the safest way. It was actually hard to watch; to remain uninvolved.

"Good," he said. "Rest a second."

It wasn't going to take long; the baby was small and would come fast. The butt was out.

"Once more, Marcie—push when you're ready…"

She was *so* ready for that. She pushed and Aiden could see thighs and knees. "Stop pushing. Pant. Hold back." He ran two fingers up the baby's thigh to the underside of the knee, applied pressure, the knee bent and the right leg delivered. He did the same on the left side and both legs were out. He supported the baby around the hips; to grab the baby around the belly could cause internal damage to the organs. With his thumb on the sacrum, his hands around the hip bones, he slowly rotated the baby downward until the first shoulder appeared.

"Arrrgggghhhh…" Marcie growled.

"Don't push! Don't push! Don't push," he instructed.

The baby at this point was without oxygen and it was time to move quickly, but he had to be in charge and couldn't have the mother's natural urge to deliver trip them up. Aiden quickly moved two fingers up along the arm, applied pressure to the inside of the elbow to deliver the arm. He slowly rotated the baby in the other direction, repeated the maneuver to deliver the second arm.

This was the most dangerous part of the breech

delivery—delivering the head. It had to be done carefully. He supported the baby's underbelly with his left hand, buttocks up. "Marcie, do NOT push. Erin, I need you." He moved a hand to Marcie's pelvis. "In a second I'm going to ask you to press down right here." He slid two fingers of his right hand inside the birth canal, slipped them around the baby's neck in search of a cord. Luck was with him—no cord loops. He found the baby's maxilla and pressed down, tilting the baby's chin toward his chest.

"Erin, push down…Marcie, push the baby out. Now. Now. *Now.*"

And the baby slipped out. He was limp. Sluggish and worn-out and he'd been without oxygen, but not for a dangerous length of time. Aiden had a hand on his chest, flipped him over and stroked his back for a second. He was just about to turn him right side up and suck the mucus from him with his own mouth when there was a cough, sputter and lusty cry. Also, in the distant background, the sound of rotor blades.

"Nicely done, Marcie," he said. "Erin, lay a towel across Marcie. Let's clean this boy off, dry him and warm him. That's what he really needs right now."

Marcie was crying and reaching for him before there was a towel in place. "Oh, God, oh, God, oh, God," she cried.

Aiden covered the baby to keep him warm, but then he tied off the umbilicus. He could hear the chopper; he wasn't going to deal with the placenta. If the placenta delivered spontaneously, they'd take care of it.

Before the helicopter landed, the door to the cabin

was kicked open and Ian yelled, "Marcie! Marcie!" He stood in the bedroom door, a look of sheer fright on his face.

Aiden stood to his full height, stripped off his bloody gloves and smiled. He was splattered with blood and fluids. "Everything's fine, Ian. Your boy is here."

Ian fell to his knees in the doorway. His fists were pressed to his eyes for a moment. Then he looked up. "They're all right?"

Aiden walked over to him, lifted him up by the elbow. "They're in good shape, but they're going to the neonatal intensive care unit in Redding, to be on the safe side. The helicopter is landing. I'm sure you can hitch a ride."

He moved to the bed. Erin got out of the way and Ian took her place. He lifted a corner of the towel and ran a finger down the baby's belly. "God," he said in a breath.

Marcie looked into Ian's eyes. "Are you really mad?" she asked softly.

He nodded. "Yes," he said without a trace of anger. "God." He looked up at Aiden. "Is he going to be okay?"

"They'll check him over in Redding, but he looks good, cried right away, has good color, just big enough but not too big for that delivery.… I'd say you're in good shape there."

Erin was by Aiden's side and his arm went around her shoulders. Seconds later, paramedics with a litter were in the room, taking vitals, assessing the patients, asking for details of the birth from the doctor and whisking the new family away. As they were wheeling Marcie out, they heard one of the paramedics ask, "Ever been for a helicopter ride, Dad?"

"Yeah, once or twice, but never a real good one."

"You're gonna like this one—getting your family to safety…"

Seconds later, a deputy was in the doorway. "Thought you'd like to know we caught that woman you didn't beat up halfway down Highway 36 in her car, making a run for it. She went off the road—like she couldn't see where she was going. She's in custody."

"Thank you," he said.

Erin leaned against him. "The baby's okay, isn't he?" she asked.

"I think he looks great."

"Have you really done that before?"

"Sort of," he said with a shrug. "Sometimes in the case of twins, the second one is breech. If the mother goes into labor early and doesn't make a scheduled C-section to accommodate that breech presentation, we have to deliver. I've done that a few times. Little… what's his name?"

"Heath."

"Little Heath cooperated by being small. And you were a wonderful help." He kissed her forehead. "Thanks, baby. I couldn't have managed without you."

"Oh, God." A teary voice came from out of nowhere. "That's so…*beautiful!*"

Aiden looked around and then laughed when he realized the 911 operator was still on the line. "Got everything you need, my friend?" he asked.

She sniffed. "Yeah. If there's more the attending physician needs…?"

"No problem," Aiden said. "Soon as we hose out this room, we're on our way to the hospital. I'll check in there. Adios." He clicked off the speaker. Aiden looked at Erin. "You okay?"

"I was planning to be in the room with her when the baby was born, but I wasn't planning on seeing it. I really saw it. If I'm lucky enough to have a baby, I'd prefer not to do it that way," she said.

"I'd prefer you not to."

"Aiden, I gave Annalee fifty thousand dollars." His eyes got huge and his mouth dropped open. "She had it all worked out—a transfer of funds via computer to her offshore account. And she had a gun. I really thought she'd just leave after getting her money, but she didn't. I couldn't wait to see if she'd cooperate in time for Marcie to get help. Really, I waited too long as it was."

"So you crowned her?" he asked.

"Not exactly. After Marcie's water broke and I realized we were out of time, I sprayed her and then whacked her. I should've done it before I gave her the money."

"Of everything that went on here today, the money is the least of it. You might not be able to recover it, but believe me, where she's going, she isn't going to spend it."

* * *

Marcie and Ian's baby was small but perfect; Aiden and Erin spent a couple of nights in Redding to be sure things were looking good. Little Heath was cleared for discharge in just two days; Ian would take them home to Chico, and Aiden offered to tow Marcie's car for her.

Word of crazy Annalee and the emergency delivery were all over town, and when Aiden and Erin finally showed up at Jack's, drinks were on the house in exchange for details. In fact, the bar was busier than usual for a few days because the entire landscape of the town and its people was about to change as summer was drawing to a close. "Pretty exciting way to wrap up a summer vacation," Jack said to Aiden.

"Yeah," Aiden replied. "Remind me never to take another summer vacation like that!"

"What now, Doc?" Jack asked.

"We pack up, say our goodbyes and head for Chico. I'm sure we'll be back for the occasional long weekend, but I have two things I have to get taken care of right away. I need a job and a wife." He grinned. "I don't have the job picked out yet."

"Toldya," Jack said, giving the bar a wipe. "This place is hell on a man's plans for a quiet life of fishing…or hiking."

Aiden lifted his beer in a toast. "I'm okay with that."

There was packing up to do, farewells to celebrate. For a couple of nights, there were family gatherings of Riordans, plus larger crowds at Jack's to say goodbye to new friends and neighbors. George and Maureen were heading toward Montgomery to be on hand for the first day of Rosie's school; Luke had decided that once his family cleared out and Shelby got back to her nursing program, he was going to clear an area behind the cabins and install RV hookups for vacationers. Luke and Art promised to visit Erin's vegetable garden to water and weed, and then to harvest whatever they could.

Aiden had packed up and loaded his car and had Marcie's hooked up behind so he could tow it. He helped Erin load her belongings into her SUV. While she went back into the cabin to check locks and lights just one last time, he started her engine for her and leaned against her car, waiting. When she came out, he opened his arms and she walked right into them.

"Future summer vacations probably won't be as exciting as this one was," he said, tightening his arms around her.

"I can live with that," she said, giving him a kiss. "Are you at all concerned that Annalee could get out of jail and show up in your life again?"

"Not as long as you're in charge of the bear repellent," he said with a laugh.

"And you'd be smart to keep that in mind, mister," she threatened with a smile. "The days of giving me a concussion to win my attention are in the past."

"Very caveman of me, don't you think?" he asked.

"Oh, very," she said. She wrinkled her nose. "You did kind of have that cavemannish look and aroma.…"

He growled and nuzzled her neck. He kissed her,

then stroked her hair over one ear. "Let's hit the road—I'll follow you. Show me the way home, sweetheart."

Mel Sheridan went to the bar in the early afternoon, jumped up on the stool and leaned across the bar to kiss her husband. "Hey, baby," he said.

"It's today," she said, her voice soft.

"Want me with you?" he asked.

She shook her head and smiled. "No. I want to do this on my own." She glanced at her watch. "I just wanted to stop by for a minute first."

He slipped a big hand around the back of her neck and massaged a little bit. "We'll celebrate tonight, how's that? I'll sneak away a little early, bring something of Preacher's. Put out those candles again. How about that?"

"Sounds perfect. I'll drop by before I leave town." She gave him another quick kiss and jumped off the stool, heading back to the clinic.

Twenty minutes later she was standing in the reception area when the door opened. Darla and Phil came in. They looked a little bit concerned, or if not concerned, maybe perplexed. Mel smiled at them and said, "How are you two?"

"Good. Everything's good," Phil said, his arm casually draped around Darla's shoulders.

"Any news from any quarter on your adoption application?" Mel asked.

"Nothing yet, but we've been told it can take such a long time," Darla said. "We're prepared to be patient. Whatever is supposed to happen will happen. When you called, you said you wanted to talk to us about it? Did we miss something? Something we should add?"

She shook her head. "I have someone I'd like you to meet," Mel said. "Come with me." And then she led the way to the kitchen. When she got there, Marley and Jake stood up from the table. Marley was just barely beginning to show, her T-shirt pulled snug over her slightly rounding middle. "Marley and Jake, I'd like you to meet some very dear friends of mine, Darla and Phil Prentiss. They have a big farm in the valley and I've known them since I first got to Virgin River a few years ago." Then she turned to Darla and Phil. "Meet Marley and Jake. They've looked at your adoption packet, wanted to meet with you and talk. They're facing some very special challenges."

Marley's hands gently caressed the little tummy; Jake's left arm went around her waist while his right hand shot out over the table toward Phil. "How do you do," he said.

"I'm going to fix you some tea, Phil and Darla. Then I'm going to leave the four of you to talk. There aren't any patients scheduled so take all the time you want."

Darla's hand moved shakily to cover her mouth, and tears came to her eyes. "Don't cry, darlin'," Phil said. "If you get all mushy, these young people will think you're not tough enough to be a good parent." Then he chuckled and reached for Jake's hand. "It's an honor, son. Please, sit down. We're at your disposal— fire away."

Mel left them in the kitchen and went back to the

reception area. Cameron was at the desk. "You okay?" he asked.

"Fine. Yes. Do you want to get home early today?" she asked.

He shook his head. "I don't have to," he said.

"Then, would you mind taking care of our guests, if they need anything?"

"Not at all. Going home?"

"Yes," she said. "But first I'm going to walk across the street and hope the bar is empty. I think I want to feel my husband's arms around me."

"You do that." He smiled. "It's a good thing you're doing."

"There's a lot of love in that kitchen," she said. "I have a feeling they're going to be a great comfort to one another."

"Mel," he said, "you've been a great comfort to so many people. Please never forget that."

"Thanks, Cam. That's nice of you to say." And she thought, *We will have no wasted or excess love left over when we go. We will spend every last drop.*

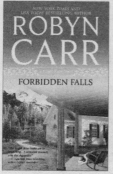
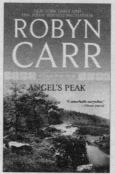

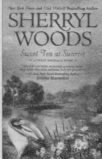

REQUEST YOUR FREE BOOKS!

2 FREE NOVELS
FROM THE ROMANCE COLLECTION
PLUS 2 FREE GIFTS!

YES! Please send me 2 FREE novels from the Romance Collection and my 2 FREE gifts (gifts are worth about $10). After receiving them, if I don't wish to receive any more books, I can return the shipping statement marked "cancel." If I don't cancel, I will receive 4 brand-new novels every month and be billed just $5.74 per book in the U.S. or $6.24 per book in Canada. That's a saving of at least 28% off the cover price. It's quite a bargain! Shipping and handling is just 50¢ per book in the U.S. and 75¢ per book in Canada.* I understand that accepting the 2 free books and gifts places me under no obligation to buy anything. I can always return a shipment and cancel at any time. Even if I never buy another book, the two free books and gifts are mine to keep forever.

194 MDN E4LY   394 MDN E4MC

Name _____ (PLEASE PRINT) _____

Address _____ Apt. # _____

City _____ State/Prov. _____ Zip/Postal Code _____

Signature (if under 18, a parent or guardian must sign)

Mail to The Reader Service.
IN U.S.A.: P.O. Box 1867, Buffalo, NY 14240-1867
IN CANADA: P.O. Box 609, Fort Erie, Ontario L2A 5X3

Not valid for current subscribers to the Romance Collection or the Romance/Suspense Collection.

Want to try two free books from another line?
Call 1-800-873-8635 or visit www.morefreebooks.com.

* Terms and prices subject to change without notice. Prices do not include applicable taxes. N.Y. residents add applicable sales tax. Canadian residents will be charged applicable provincial taxes and GST. Offer not valid in Quebec. This offer is limited to one order per household. All orders subject to approval. Credit or debit balances in a customer's account(s) may be offset by any other outstanding balance owed by or to the customer. Please allow 4 to 6 weeks for delivery. Offer available while quantities last.

ROBYN CARR

32646	SECOND CHANCE PASS	___ $6.99 U.S.	___ $6.99 CAN.
32695	DEEP IN THE VALLEY	___ $6.99 U.S.	___ $6.99 CAN.
32490	VIRGIN RIVER	___ $6.99 U.S.	___ $8.50 CAN.
32449	WHISPERING ROCK	___ $6.99 U.S.	___ $8.50 CAN.
32429	SHELTER MOUNTAIN	___ $6.99 U.S.	___ $8.50 CAN.
32174	RUNAWAY MISTRESS	___ $6.99 U.S.	___ $8.50 CAN.

(limited quantities available)

TOTAL AMOUNT	$ _____
POSTAGE & HANDLING	$ _____
($1.00 for 1 book, 50¢ for each additional)	
APPLICABLE TAXES*	$ _____
TOTAL PAYABLE	$ _____

(check or money order—please do not send cash)

To order, complete this form and send it, along with a check or money order for the total above, payable to MIRA Books, to: **In the U.S.:** 3010 Walden Avenue, P.O. Box 9077, Buffalo, NY 14269-9077; **In Canada:** P.O. Box 636, Fort Erie, Ontario, L2A 5X3.

Name: _____
Address: _____ City: _____
State/Prov.: _____ Zip/Postal Code: _____
Account Number (if applicable): _____

075 CSAS

*New York residents remit applicable sales taxes.
*Canadian residents remit applicable GST and provincial taxes.

MIRA®

www.MIRABooks.com

MRC0110BL